Too Strong to Die

by Erin Wade
© January, 2017

Too Strong to Die

By Erin Wade
Cover by Erin Wade
Edited by Carol Tietsworth
Copyright: January, 2017 Erin Wade
© 2017 Erin Wade

ISBN-10: 1544048521
ISBN-13: 9781544048529

www.erinwade.us

DEDICATION:
To the one that has always supported me in
everything, I have ever undertaken. You have
encouraged me and have always been my biggest fan.
You make me very happy. Erin
*****

Contents

Too Strong to Die

Chapter 1

By day he was—his real name didn't matter. By night he was Troy Hunter. Troy Hunter mattered. Troy Hunter was someone important.

It started out as a game, a fun way to pass the lonely nights. It had been easy, quite ingenious. He had wandered the shopping mall looking for a truly handsome man. He found a sales clerk in a large department store that was perfect.

Using a telephoto lens, he spent hours shooting photos of the handsome sales clerk. Most people had forsaken the 35mm camera for their simpler iPhones, but Troy Hunter knew the value of taking sharp, clear pictures from across the room.

A little shading, a few highlights in the hair and a deepening of the blue eyes and Troy had created a perfect photo of himself. Or, at least a perfect photo of Troy Hunter.

He set up his Facebook account under the name of Troy Hunter and established email service under the name of lonelyboy@gmail.com. He posted the handsome image of himself, created a fake biography, and began sending friend requests to women.

With few exceptions, the women readily accepted him as a friend. He concentrated on women in his state. He quickly amassed five-hundred friends. Then friends of friends began sending him friend requests.

Facebook was the perfect tool to mine for women. He established friendships by agreeing with the pathetic women who always posted slogans like, "It doesn't matter if YOU think I am fat, I know I am HOT!"

He always posted some comment like "I find you very attractive."

That would get the conversation going. Then she would update her frumpy photo with a new selfie. She would fix her hair, put on makeup and take a selfie shot so that her big breasts were clearly visible.

Troy would pull a cute puppy video from the news feed and post it on his timeline, commenting, "This is the cutest puppy ever."

Numerous women would flood his page with comments on the puppy. After a while, he would select a dozen of the most attractive, but needy women and begin to post comments singling them out.

Susie Johnson would post "I cooked a pot roast for dinner tonight. A photo of a pot roast surrounded by carrots and potatoes would accompany the post.

Troy would post, "Wow, Susie, that looks great. Your husband is a lucky man."

Soon Susie would move to the private messaging, and they would strike up a friendship. He juggled ten or twelve women at a time.

Troy's woman of the month was Tracy Slade, a single real estate agent in Burleson, Texas. He would concentrate on her entirely for now. Tracy had caught Troy's attention when she posted, "Nothing hurts more than love."

Her next post said, "When you put everything you have into a relationship and get nothing in return, it is time to move on."

Tracy changed her Facebook masthead photo every week. Each new photo was a little more daring than the last, with a little fewer clothes and a lot more makeup to cover the wrinkles. At first, Tracy's selfies had garnered comments like "nice," "pretty lady" or "looking good, mama." Now the only comments on her pathetic pleas for praise came from Troy.

Her Facebook page said she was thirty-two, but Troy suspected that was off by ten or twelve years. She was scaring the hell out of forty-five.

A former obscure pageant winner, she was still pretty. She obviously worked out and maintained a slim, toned body. Her dyed jet-black hair completed the package of a woman desperately trying to hold on to her youth and fading good looks.

Troy began complimenting her and bragging on her appearance. He sent her pictures of his little dog, a cute Poodle-Chihuahua mix named Charlie. He positioned his camera to take a photo of Charlie sitting between his legs. His tight jeans accentuated his muscular thighs and impressive package. He wasn't surprised when several private messages appeared in his message box. He smiled when he saw one of them was from Tracy.

"I thought it would be nice to have our discussions in a more private setting," Tracy messaged him. She sent him her personal email, and he emailed her providing his email address: lonelyboy@gmail.com.

Although he was online and incognito, Troy was still a little shy. He was never aggressive or suggestive. He always let the ladies take the lead. It was always the women who made the first sexual innuendos.

They had been emailing for three months, getting to know each other, when a heavy ice storm hit Texas on Sunday night. Troy emailed Tracy asking if she was being affected by the storm.

"I am iced in today," Tracy answered, "but this is Texas, the sun will be shining tomorrow. It has to clear up in time for the weekend. I am cooking Thanksgiving dinner for my family and some friends."

"I am an orphan," Troy typed. "It must be nice to have friends and family for the holidays. I envy you."

"You should join us," Tracy invited.

"I live out of state, remember," Troy emailed.

"I wish you lived here," Tracy replied. "I bet my nights wouldn't be so cold and lonely if you were here."

"I would like that," Troy typed.

"Have you given any thought to our meeting?" Tracy asked.

"Honestly, I try not to think about it," Troy answered. "Your friendship means a lot to me. It is enough that you take the time from your busy schedule to chat with me."

He sent her two more emails, but she didn't respond. He was frantic, afraid he had scared her or made her think twice about being so familiar with someone she had never met.

After an hour, he turned off his computer and went to bed.

~~~

Troy looked out the window at the melting ice. Tracy had been right; the sun was shining. He made coffee and dropped two pieces of raisin bread into the toaster. He had a big day ahead of him at the office. Things were beginning to shape up on his job.

He turned on his Ipad and checked his emails. He had three—sent after midnight—from Tracy. He drank his coffee as he read them.

"Sorry, I didn't answer your last emails. My electricity went off," Tracy wrote. The next email said, "How would you feel about filling out a compatibility questionnaire?"

The last email had the questionnaire attached to it. "If you want to fill it out, that is great. If you don't want to bother, that is okay, too."

He quickly typed, "I have to go to work right now, but I will definitely fill out the application tonight. I am applying to be your beau, right?" He typed in three smiling Emojis.

"Is that a position you would like?" Tracy typed back.

He didn't miss her double entendre. "I would like any position with you," Troy replied.

"Have a good day," Tracy emailed. "I look forward to receiving the application. I have three favorite positions, and I am certain you can fill all of them."

~~~

Chapter 2

Major Ricky Strong wondered what made men prey on women. In recent history, the Texas Rangers had not handled any cases of women preying on men. Oh, maybe to relieve them of their wallets and credit cards, but never to kill them just for the sheer thrill of killing.

Strong read the detailed report on the last body they had discovered in the Colorado River. Just like the three previous bodies they had fished from the lazy-moving waterway, the women had been strangled, and their hands had been severed to prevent fingerprint identification. The news media had deemed the killer the *Hacker* because the amputations had been made using a hacksaw. Ricky hated it when the news media glorified gruesome crimes by giving the perpetrators nicknames.

The latest body had extensive dental work, but no indication who the dentist might be, so there was no way to identify the dead woman from her dental work. She wasn't in the DNA database so for the fourth time this year; they hit a dead end.

Like the others, the body had deteriorated so badly the facial features were non-existent. The Rangers' forensic artist used digital software to create 3-D images of the four women. Except for small variances, the post-mortem reconstruction of all four women looked the same. The killer definitely had a type.

The only difference between the latest body and the other three was her missing breasts. The killer had removed both of Jane Doe 4's breasts. Ricky surmised it was because she had implants. The Rangers could use implants to identify the victim.

No doubt about it, their serial killer knew all the tricks of forensic identification. Ricky wondered if he was an employee in the law enforcement community. The lone identifying mark on the woman's body was a chain tattooed around her ankle.

"Major Strong, Deputy Director Rhodes, is on the phone for you," the receptionist announced over the intercom.

Deputy Director Rusty Rhodes rarely called Ricky directly. *I'm probably not going to like this*, she thought.

"Did you get the file I sent over this morning?" Rhodes wasted no time getting to the purpose of his call.

"Yes, sir." Ricky wondered why the Texas Rangers were handling this case.

"I want you on it," Rhodes barked.

"Why us?" Ricky asked.

"All of the women match the description of State Senator Christine Richmond's sister. She is bringing us hair and some fingernail clippings so we can get the woman's DNA. I told her to see you. Make certain the lab runs it against all four Janes. Do it while she waits. Better yet, take her to lunch while they run it."

"Isn't she that arrogant bitc…?"

"Yes, she's the one," Rhodes interrupted. "Handle her with kid gloves. She is chair of the Senate Finance Committee, and we need the approval of our budget requests. I need those additional funds for more officers and vehicles. I am counting on you Strong."

"She is still furious with us for arresting her when she chained herself to the front door of that abortion clinic," Ricky chuckled. "We should have left her there."

"Yeah," snorted Rhodes as he recalled the brunette beauty's drive to close all abortion clinics in Texas. "It always amazes me that the zealots think it is okay for them to break the laws when they protest about their causes but we should arrest everyone else."

"This will be my first interaction with her," Ricky said, "hopefully, I can start with a clean slate.

I just studied all the files on the murdered women," Ricky said, "If we can get a break on just one of them, I bet we will find they all have something in common other than a float down the Colorado."

"He is a serial killer," Rhodes agreed. "Oh, and Major, all the women fit the description of Senator Richmond. She and her sister were twins."

~~~

Ricky opened the spreadsheet on her desktop computer and studied the sparse details the agency had about the dead women. All four women were five-six, slender, had never given birth, and were natural brunettes. The lab had determined the women to be between thirty and thirty-five years old.

Ricky had never met Senator Christine Richmond but had seen her in television interviews, and her photo was constantly on the front page of the *Austin*

American-Statesman newspaper. No doubt about it, Christine Richmond was a beautiful woman. She was also very ambitious. It was no secret that the party was grooming her for governor and eventually president. *Yeah, I'll have to handle Senator Christine Richmond with kid gloves,* Ricky thought.

Speaking of the devil; Strong's door swung open and Senator Richmond—in all her glory—made her entrance. As usual, she was surrounded by her aides and flunkies.

"Oh," Richmond exclaimed, "pardon us, I thought this was Major Strong's office."

"It is," Ricky stood and smiled. "I am Major Strong."

"Oh, I see," the senator shrugged her shoulders indifferently. "I was expecting a ...," her sentence trailed off as if she knew she was about to say something politically incorrect.

"A man," Ricky finished the sentence for her.

"An older officer," Richmond smiled playfully, as she covered her faux pas. "You are very young to be a major."

"I suspect we are about the same age," Ricky bantered. "We both know age has nothing to do with ability."

"Still, I find experience more desirable," the senator smirked.

Ricky wasn't certain what they were discussing, now, but was sure Senator Richmond would get her way with any man. *That is why she prefers dealing with them, Ricky thought.*

"Please, have a seat," Ricky motioned to the chair across from her. She scanned the senator's entourage.

"There are additional chairs in the waiting room if you would like to wait for the senator there."

Christine nodded, and the group disappeared.

"I understand you have some items that will provide your sister's DNA," Ricky leaned across her desk.

Senator Richmond removed a baggie from her designer purse and handed the items to the ranger. "The hairbrush and toothbrush are hers. I assume the fingernail clippings are, too. I found them in her bathroom trash receptacle."

"I will take these to the forensic folks," Strong said. "It will probably take them a couple of hours to run all four matches. You and your, um, party might want to go to lunch. We should have the results by the time you get back." She had no desire to dine with a woman who had been disappointed she wasn't a man.

"I would like to accompany you to the lab," the senator said. "I will send my staff to lunch. Perhaps you and I can have lunch together afterward."

Ricky nodded. She holstered her .357 Sig then carefully covered it with her jacket. She didn't miss the body scan Senator Richmond did on her as she moved from behind her desk. She subconsciously smoothed her black skirt and walked to the door.

The senator dismissed her followers and walked to the lab with Ricky. Their heels made a pleasant clicking sound on the polished tile floor.

The forensic investigator assured them she would have the results in two hours or less.

"Where would you like to have lunch?" Ricky asked as they walked to her car.

"You choose, Major."

~~~

Ricky pulled her car onto the parking lot of the Roaring Fork Restaurant, a favorite of her coworkers.

"A booth," the major instructed the hostess. "A very private booth."

"A glass of Merlot," Christine informed the waitress.

"Coffee for me," Strong nodded. "I am on duty." She pulled a small spiral notebook from her pocket and flipped it open. "Do you mind if I ask you a few questions about your sister, while we dine?"

"I will do anything that will help you locate Kara."

"Was she in a relationship?" Ricky poised her pen to make notes.

"What do you mean?" Richmond asked.

"I mean, was she dating anyone?" Ricky frowned at having to explain the simple question.

"I don't think that is important," the senator said softly.

"If you want my help," Ricky held her gaze, "You need to let me decide what is important. Was she seeing anyone?"

"A man, you mean," the senator hedged.

"I mean, was she intimately involved with anyone of any gender?" Ricky glowered. "Lovers and spouses are always our first suspects."

"No boyfriends or girlfriends that I am aware of," Richmond mumbled.

"Why didn't you just say that in the first place?" Ricky grumbled wearily. She hoped Senator Richmond wasn't always going to be this difficult.

Christine shrugged. "What else do you want to know?"

17

"Has she broken up with anyone, an angry boyfriend or…?"

"No," Richmond blurted.

"Your sister is gay, isn't she?" Ricky said intuitively.

Richmond sat silently and sipped her wine.

Ricky nodded. "I'll take that as a yes. Did she have any problems at work, anyone who clashed with her or stalked her?"

"No. Look, Major, I don't want my sister's sexuality made the focal point of your investigation."

"I will do my best not to taint *your* reputation, Senator," Ricky smirked. She was finding the woman increasingly unlikeable.

"I was wrong to bring this problem to the Rangers." Christine shook her head as if clearing it of irrational thoughts.

Ricky inhaled deeply. "Does your sister have any distinguishing marks?" *Might as well draw her a picture*, Ricky thought. "You know, like tattoos, scars, birthmarks, or old broken bones. Anything we can look for on the bodies."

Christine leaned across the table increasing the privacy of the booth. Her perfect breasts strained against her blue silk blouse as if seeking freedom. The top button was unbuttoned, providing a clear view of the woman's endowments. Ricky slowly pulled her eyes away from the breasts' struggle to escape the senator's blouse.

The senator looked up into Ricky's blue eyes, "About three years ago, Kara had a breast augmentation."

Ricky's eyes uncontrollably darted from the senator's eyes to her breasts and back to her eyes.

"Mine are real," Richmond hissed through clenched teeth.

"I, I," Ricky stuttered, embarrassed that she had been caught ogling the senator. "Did she have a chain tattooed around her ankle?"

"Yes," tears filled Christine's eyes. "You have her, don't you?"

"Let's wait until forensics finishes with the DNA," Ricky said softly. "I don't like to jump to conclusions."

~~~

"I put the lab report on your desk," Becky informed her boss. Ricky nodded and led Christine into her office, closing the door behind them. She was sure the senator would not want an audience when she confirmed the latest victim was her sister.

The senator tossed her long, black hair back, away from her face and looked around the room. Major Ricky Strong had received several awards for Valor and Courage Under Fire. Annual marksmanship awards attested to her ability with a handgun. Her awards and certifications hung around a law degree issued to Erica Leigh Strong from the University of Texas.

Christine moved her gaze to the ranger who was studying the report. Ricky slowly raised her eyes and looked into the senator's eyes. Christine knew she didn't want to hear what Ricky Strong was about to tell her. She closed her eyes to stop the hot tears welling up behind long lashes.

"Jane Doe 4 is your sister," Ricky gently said. "I am very sorry. I wish I had different news for you."

Senator Richmond blinked back tears and put on a brave face. She said nothing, not trusting herself to speak.

Major Strong watched as the woman's face began to crumble. Creases moved across her forehead. Perfectly arched brows knitted together as tears rolled down high cheekbones to form rivulets in the dimples on either side of her perfectly shaped lips.

Fighting the urge to hold the senator and console her, Ricky rummaged in her desk drawer and produced a box of tissues. She shoved the box toward Christine. The senator nodded her thanks and took the tissues.

The noise outside her office told Ricky the senator's entourage had returned from lunch. She stood to open her door.

Christine caught the ranger's hand, "Please." Her pleading eyes said more than her words. Ricky nodded and left the room.

"We are still waiting for information," Ricky informed the senator's staff. "Senator Richmond would like you to return to your office. A Texas Ranger will escort her home later."

The staffers milled around for a few minutes, not certain what to do. The person who seemed to be in charge looked at a message that had just dinged into his phone. "She wants us to leave," he scowled as he led the exodus from the ranger's headquarters.

~~~

"I truly appreciate you're driving me home," Christine said as she wiped the tears from her eyes. "I don't want my staff to see me like this."

20

"Yeah, it would pretty much destroy your stone-maiden myth," Ricky teased.

"Stone Maiden, is that what they call me?"

"Don't be coy," Ricky raised an eyebrow. "You know it is. I am betting that's the way you keep people at arm's length."

"Well, aren't you Miss Observant?" Christine snarled. She stared out the window on her side of the car. She had no desire to engage in further conversation with Major Ricky Strong.

Ricky pulled her car close to the wrought iron gates that protected Senator Richmond from the rest of the world. Christine pushed a button on her iPhone, and the gates slowly swung open. They traveled up a long road that ended in a cul-de-sac in front of an impressive two-story Mediterranean house.

"Nice," Ricky whistled. "Do I need to walk you to your door, Senator?"

"I have imposed on you enough, Major," Christine said coldly. "You will let me know if you find any information on my sister's killer." She opened the car door and moved to swing her legs out of the car.

Ricky caught her arm. "I am truly sorry this happened to your sister," Ricky said honestly. "I will do everything I can to catch the bastard."

Christine Richmond's brown eyes darkened, "I know you will. Thank you." She slipped from the car and ran to her front door.

~~~

Christine quickly flipped through the newspaper. There were no stories about her sister's death. So far none of the television reporters had learned of Kara's murder. Major Strong was doing a good job of keeping Kara's demise under wraps. She wondered what the investigator had learned. It had been a week since the ranger had confirmed the Hacker's latest victim was Kara.

Ricky had accompanied her to inform her parents of Kara's death. She knew that the ranger had returned a few days later to question her mother without Christine being present. Knowing her mother, Christine was certain the major's visit hadn't been a pleasant one. Probably not a very productive one, either. Lady Gladys Richmond could be extremely difficult.

Christine fought the urge to call the ranger. Ricky Strong's amused smile and perceptive blue eyes flashed across her mind's eye. The attractive blonde woman fascinated the senator. She wondered why Ricky had chosen a career in law enforcement.

A knock on her office door pulled her thoughts away from Ricky Strong. "Come in," she called.

Major Strong nonchalantly walked into her office. "I was on this side of the river and thought I would check on you, Senator," Ricky smiled.

"I appreciate that," Christine returned the smile. "Please have a seat."

"I need a favor," Ricky said as she settled into the chair. "I am having trouble locating your sister's iPad and cell phone."

"Have you searched her apartment," Christine frowned. "I'm not certain she had an iPad. She was a successful graphic artist and worked with huge software programs. I only saw her work on her desktop."

"Yes, your mother allowed me to search her apartment," Ricky nodded. "I found nothing out of place. It was as if she rarely lived there. There was no computer."

"My Mother?" Christine tilted her head slightly. "My mother doesn't have a key to Kara's apartment."

"The one behind your parent's home?" Ricky frowned, perplexed.

"That isn't Kara's apartment," the senator scowled. "That's my parent's guesthouse."

A confused look crossed the ranger's face. "Your mother said…"

"My mother doesn't want you snooping around Kara's apartment. My sister lived a very different lifestyle from us. Mother doesn't want that revealed."

"I told you I would be discreet." Anger clouded Ricky's face as she stood. "Are you going to help me or not? If I must find out about Kara on my own, I will have no qualms about handing this over to the press."

The senator snatched her purse from the floor beside her desk, "Drive me. I will take you to her apartment."

Kara Richmond lived in a penthouse in the Austin Heritage Apartments. "Wow, she must have been one heck of a graphic artist," Ricky exclaimed as they rode the private elevator that opened into the suite.

"I own this building," Christine informed her. "Kara was an excellent tenant. Always paid her rent on time."

"You were twins?" Ricky said candidly.

"Yes," Christine frowned.

"Did you ever feel she was in trouble or may be involved in something dangerous?"

"No," the senator answered honestly. "As you know, I didn't approve of Kara's lifestyle, but I never felt she was in danger."

"Aren't twins supposed to have some sixth sense about one another or something like that?" Ricky asked.

"We weren't clairvoyant if that is what you mean," Christine wrinkled her nose distastefully. "Once she declared her affinity for women, I publicly distanced myself as far from her as possible."

"Yes," Ricky mumbled. "What others think of you is always more important than having a loving relationship with your sister or anyone else."

"I don't need you judging me, Major Strong," Christine declared vehemently. "I just need you to do your job and find my sister's killer."

Before Ricky could stop her, the senator stormed out of the room, slamming the door behind her. Alone in the dead woman's apartment, Ricky pulled on gloves and began a methodical search of each room.

Photos of Christine and Kara were all over the apartment; on the walls, atop the fireplace, and on Kara's desk. It was obvious the two women had been very close at one time. On the coffee table was a scrapbook of Senator Christine Richmond's accomplishments. Obviously, Kara adored her sister.

There were photos of Kara with other women. A wedding book was also on the coffee table. Ricky turned each page, feeling like an intruder. Kara and a beautiful brown-haired woman held each other in their arms, smiling as they posed for the camera. Each of them wore an elegant white wedding dress.

Photos of a wedding party filled the second page. A single picture filled the third page; Kara and the woman kissing. Ricky recognized the other woman as a local television weather girl named Blaize Canyon. Ricky wasn't sure if that was her real name or a made-up one.

Ricky perused the entire album. She was upset that Christine had not told her Kara was married. Where was Kara's wife? Why hadn't she filed a missing person's report?

Senator Richmond and her parents were conspicuously absent from the wedding photos.

Ricky turned on Kara's computer and prayed it wasn't password protected. The Gods were good to her; the computer opened to the desktop. She clicked on Kara's email and smiled as more than two-thousand emails flooded the inbox.

This is going to take some time, she thought. She called the CSI team and gave them directions to Kara's apartment.

~~~

"This isn't the crime scene," Ricky told team leader Lane Mason as his forensic investigators fanned out to examine each room of the penthouse. "I want the computer delivered to my home."

Lane frowned, "My people can comb through it for you, Major."

"I know, Lane and I appreciate the offer," Ricky smiled, "but I know this case inside out, and I might be able to spot things your folks won't recognize."

"You know our computer geeks are supposed to go through the computers?" Lane insisted.

"Please," Ricky grinned mischievously, "I promise not to hurt it."

"We will back it up first, then turn it over to you," Lane wheedled. "If you will take me out to dinner tonight."

"Really, Lane," Ricky feigned disgust, "are you resorting to blackmail?"

Lane laughed. His brown eyes danced as he watched Ricky leave the room. "Roscoe's at seven. Don't stand me up," he called after her.

Ricky nodded and waved a hand in the air.

Ricky searched the lobby for Senator Richmond. The woman was nowhere in sight. She walked to the concierge's desk and asked if the dark-haired beauty had requested a cab.

"You mean Senator Richmond?" the young woman replied. "She has been gone for two hours."

"Why does that not surprise me?" Ricky scowled.

Chapter 3

Lane emptied the pitcher of beer into his glass. Ricky sipped her Dr. Pepper. "My people took that computer to your place this afternoon," Lane said. "Since you insist on going through it yourself, I have my people working on the other things we found in the apartment."

"Did you find anything of interest?" Ricky asked.

"You know your dead girl was a lesbian?" Lane snorted.

Ricky nodded. "I need to keep that under the radar for now."

"What you may not know was that she recently entertained a man in her apartment."

"Are you sure?" Ricky frowned.

"Um, hum, we found semen on her sheets and male pubic hair in the bathroom. Speaking of bathrooms, I need to check this one out. Be right back."

Ricky mulled over the newest information about Kara's paramours. She didn't see Senator Richmond until the woman was standing at her table.

"Major Strong, your receptionist told me you would be here," Richmond declared as she surveyed the bar and grill with obvious distaste.

"My receptionist is not at work now," Ricky scowled. "It is after five."

"I called her at home," Christine confessed.

"Seriously?" Ricky intentionally drawled the word.

"I want to discuss my sister with you."

"Unlike you, Senator," Ricky glowered, "Some of us have a private life. Right now I am enjoying mine."

"Drinking beer?" Christine huffed indignantly.

"On a date," Ricky stood and walked to meet Lane.

"Dance with me," Ricky said under her breath as she pulled Lane onto the dance floor. Christine watched as they danced a graceful two-step around the dance floor.

"Who's the looker?" Lane asked as he swung Ricky around so he could get a good look at the beautiful brunette at their table.

"No one important," Ricky exhaled slowly. "Is she still there?"

"Doesn't look like she is leaving anytime soon," Lane chuckled. "Want me to kiss you?"

"Yeah," Ricky grinned wickedly.

The senator watched the handsome man as he kissed Ricky. As the kiss ended, Christine stomped from the establishment. Obviously, she had misread Major Ricky Strong.

~~~

Ricky showered and pulled on an old T-shirt. It was soft and light, one of those T-shirts that felt like home. She pulled a bottle of water from her refrigerator and settled on her sofa. She had left Lane at the restaurant with some of his admirers.

She turned on Fox News and watched half-heartedly as Megan Kelly tried to decide whether she was a Republican or a Democrat. *Maybe Kelly was the best news commentator in the business*, she thought. *One can't tell what party she supports. That is the way news people should be, unbiased, simply reporting the news and keeping their personal politics to themselves.*

The trumpeting of her phone made her jump. A quick check of the number showed her the Austin police were calling her. "Strong," she barked.

"Major Strong," a woman's voice spoke hurriedly, "I am so sorry to bother you, but Senator Richmond insisted I call you."

"Of course she did," Ricky said sarcastically.

"The ambulance took her to Seton Medical Center," the woman continued.

Ricky sprinted to her bedroom, placing the call on speakerphone so she could talk as she dressed.

"What happened? Is she okay?"

"I don't know ma'am. I was just told to call you."

"I'm on my way there now," Ricky said breathlessly. "Thanks for calling me."

~~~

By the time the ranger reached the hospital, she had gotten the report from the police detailing the attack on Senator Richmond.

A nurse's aid led Ricky to the room where Senator Richmond was resting peacefully. "The doctor will be here soon to let you know how she is."

"Thanks," Ricky silently moved to Christine's bedside. The senator looked pale and had a black eye. There were several stitches above her right eye. Ricky looked for any other signs of injuries.

A blonde doctor opened the door and motioned for Ricky to step into the hallway.

"Ricky," the doctor looked into her eyes, "she insisted we call you. Otherwise, I wouldn't..."

"It's okay, Cassie" Ricky squeezed the doctor's arm. "I am working on a case involving her. Is she okay?"

"She has a slight concussion and a few bruises, but otherwise she is okay physically."

"Physically?" Ricky whispered, "Mentally? Please don't tell me someone molested her?"

"No, she is a fighter. Evidently, the attacker snatched her right off the parking lot of that restaurant by the University. Roscoe's, I believe is the name."

"Dammit," Ricky cursed. "Dammit. It is all my fault."

"I don't see how you can blame yourself," Cassie frowned. "She shouldn't have been in that part of town— alone—that late at night."

Ricky shook her head. "May I sit with her?"

"Sure, call me if you need anything."

Ricky silently pulled her chair closer to Christine's bed. She watched the woman's face as she slept. Senator Richmond was truly a gorgeous woman, even with a black eye and stitches. Ricky couldn't pull her eyes away from the senator's full red lips. The lips— relaxed in sleep—looked soft and sweet. Ricky leaned over and gently kissed the sleeping woman.

Nice going, Strong, she chastised herself. *The woman gets mugged in a parking lot, and you take advantage of her while she is out cold.* She missed the slight smile that played on the senator's lips.

The sun was beginning to push the darkness away when Christine Richmond opened her eyes. She lay still for a long time assessing her situation. She was pleased to see the ranger sleeping in the chair beside her bed. She turned her head slowly to get a better look at the blonde woman. She allowed herself to recall the soft, sweetness of Ricky's kiss. A kiss she would never acknowledge.

Ricky's long lashes fluttered, then lids raised to reveal sleepy, blue eyes. The deepest blue eyes Christine had ever seen.

"Hey," Ricky said softly, "how do you feel?"

"Like the tackling dummy for the UT football team," Christine tried to smile, but the pain was excruciating.

"Do you feel like talking?" Ricky leaned forward to look into Christine's eyes.

"Yes," Christine suppressed the natural urge to nod her head.

"Do you remember what happened?"

"Since you couldn't tear yourself away from your boyfriend long enough to talk to me, I walked back to my car. A white van had parked beside my vehicle, but I didn't pay it any mind. As I was opening my car door, the van door suddenly slid open, and a man grabbed me." Christine shuddered as she recalled the strength of the man.

"He wrapped his arms around me from behind and pinned my arms to my side. When I started screaming, he cursed in Spanish as he pulled me toward the van opening. Fortunately, I had worn high heels, and I stomped on his instep with all my might. He howled and let me go. I ran toward the club, but he tackled me. I hit the asphalt hard. That's the last thing I remember. I did manage to scratch his arms, so I have his DNA under my fingernails."

Ricky smiled appreciatively. "You did good, Senator. CSI has already processed you. We should have a DNA match sometime today."

"How did I get here?" Christine looked around the hospital room.

Ricky pieced together the events of the attack and completed the senator's story. "Two off-duty police officers witnessed the attack and yelled at the man as they ran across the parking lot. The attacker tossed you to the ground and got away in the van. The officers got the licenses plate number, but the attacker had stolen the van earlier in the day.

A doctor wearing street clothes entered the room. "How do you feel this morning, Senator?"

"Good," Christine smiled weakly. "I'll be better when you release me."

"Um, I suspect you will not follow the doctor's orders," she smiled. "So I am forced to keep you for a couple of days for observation."

"What? No!" Christine tried to sit up, but the pain in her head pushed her back against the pillow.

"I demand to see my daughter," Lady Gladys Richmond pushed aside the doctor and charged into the hospital room.

"Mother!" Christine briefly closed her eyes against the verbal onslaught from her mother.

"What is going on, here? Why wasn't I notified sooner?" The stout woman glared at Ricky. "What are you doing here?"

Ricky caught the woman by her arm and forcibly pulled her into the hallway. "Christine has a concussion and needs to rest quietly. She doesn't need you or anyone else upsetting her.

"If you will lower your voice, I will tell you what happened."

The woman glared at Ricky and opened her mouth to complain, but the look in the ranger's eyes warned her against any further outbursts. She stood silently seething.

Ricky related the events of the previous evening.

"What are you doing about it?" Lady Richmond demanded.

"We are searching for the suspect." Ricky's voice was a low growl. "If you hadn't misled me about Kara's apartment, this might not have happened.

"I need you to understand something, Mrs. Richmond. One of your daughters is dead, and the other has been attacked by a stalker, possibly the same man. Christine's life is in danger."

"You promised no one would learn about Kara's, awful lifestyle." Lady Richmond slapped a newspaper across Ricky's chest. "What the hell is this?"

Speechless, Ricky unfolded the paper. The wedding photos of Kara and Blaize Canyon spread across the entire front page. The headline read, *Senator Christine Richmond's twin sister married to a woman.* "What the..?"

"That is exactly why I wasn't forthcoming with you. But I see my daughter was fool enough to trust you. I suggest you get some control over your minions and let me worry about my daughter."

Fury swept over Ricky as she read the front-page story. The photos accompanying the article were the same ones her team had removed from Kara's apartment. Heads were going to roll over this.

Ricky's hatred for the mainstream media deepened as she realized the entire article was more about Kara being a lesbian than the fact that she had been cruelly murdered and dumped into the Colorado River. The article was specifically written to embarrass Senator Christine Richmond.

Ricky could hear the cawing voice of Lady Richmond as she harped on her daughter. Ricky thought about charging back into the room and forcefully removing the squawking woman, but decided that would probably create more problems than it would solve.

During Lady Richmond's tirade, the doctor escaped the room and continued her rounds. Ricky walked to the nurse's desk and located Cassie. "Can you get the old crow out of Senator Richmond's room?" she begged.

"Just watch me," Cassie grinned. Within minutes of entering the room Dr. Cassie Warren was escorting Lady Richmond to the elevator. "Yes, ma'am, we will call you as soon as she can have visitors."

Ricky called her sergeant and arranged for two officers to guard the senator around the clock. She quietly entered Christine's room. The senator's eyes were closed.

"Is she gone?" Christine asked.

"Yes," Ricky chuckled as brown eyes fluttered open.

"She gave me a splitting headache. Please ask the doctor if she can give me something to ease it."

~~~

"That should stop your headache quickly," the nurse patted the senator's arm. "You should be able to sleep now."

As the nurse left the room, Christine caught Ricky's hand. "Please stay with me?"

Ricky nodded and pulled her chair back beside Christine's bed as the woman fell asleep.

A dozen text messages later, Major Strong had ascertained that none of her team had even spoken to the press, much less given them photos of Kara Richmond and her wife. Assured that Christine was peacefully sleeping, Ricky walked into the hallway.

"There is only one other person who could have released those photos," Ricky whispered into her cell phone. "Pick up Blaize Canyon. I want her in my office by four this afternoon."

Ricky slipped back into Christine's room and resumed her vigilance beside the senator's bed.

~~~

Blaize Canyon was one of those women who had spent her life chasing after fame. Unfortunately, her beauty was fading faster than she could run to catch the elusive television or film job that would catapult her into the bright lights of stardom.

She thought she had found her gold mine when she convinced Kara Richmond to marry her. Too late, she discovered Kara's proclivity for women had cost her the family inheritance. Lady and Armand Richmond had disowned Kara when she announced she was gay.

A letter arrived the day after their wedding, disinheriting her.

Blaize looked up as Ricky entered the room. "Miss Canyon?" Ricky raised a quizzical eyebrow.

"Yes."

"I am Major Ricky Strong. I appreciate your willingness to talk to me."

"I didn't have much choice in the matter," Blaize frowned. "You did send your troopers to pick me up."

"I am concerned for your safety," Ricky smiled and took her seat behind her desk.

"Why?"

"Kara Richmond has been brutally murdered. I believe she was your wife." Ricky watched as the woman fidgeted in her chair.

"I am sure you know her bitch of a sister." Blaize snarled. "The great Senator Richmond made it her personal crusade to make gay marriage illegal in Texas. So, no, I am not legally married to Kara."

"Did you know she was missing?" Ricky queried.

"No, I was out of town, auditioning for a news job in Houston." Blaize tried to look distraught. "I just learned of her death yesterday when I returned home and found your people crawling all over our apartment."

"You did live together?" Ricky asked.

"Yes."

"When was the last time you saw her?"

Blaize pulled her cell phone from her purse and looked at her messages. "About two weeks ago. She sent me a text message telling me she was going to Amarillo to do a magazine layout for a clothing manufacturer."

"So you were in the apartment alone while she was gone?" Ricky grimaced. She could already see the DNA evidence they had found becoming useless.

Blaize nodded, yes.

"Who was the man sleeping with you while Kara was away?"

"I didn't…"

"Don't lie to me," Ricky slammed her fist on her desk.

"William Roberts," Blaize whimpered. "He is the newsroom director at the station where I work."

"Did you provide the photos to the newspapers?" Ricky pushed for answers.

"Yes. I thought the story might get me enough publicity to make the Houston station notice me. It worked. They are doing an exclusive interview with me tomorrow."

Ricky nodded. "Thank you for your time, Miss Canyon. Oh, and I am sorry for your loss."

"What loss? Oh, yeah," Blaize feigned pain, "I'm not sure I will ever get over that."

##

Ricky leaned her head back on her chair. Christine had led the fight against gay marriage in Texas. Thanks to her the "don't ask, don't tell" policies were still the guiding rules for all law enforcement organizations in Texas. She was anti-abortion, and she was the most infuriating woman Ricky had ever met. *And the most beautiful*, Ricky's thoughts betrayed her. The sooner she cut all contact with Senator Christine Richmond, the better off she would be.

The thought of the senator's soft, full lips made her inhale.

Ricky's ringtone pulled her from her reverie. "Major Strong," Christine said curtly. "I am being released at eight in the morning. I will expect you to be here and take me to my home."

"Look Senator," Ricky said testily, "I am not your taxi service."

"It is your fault I am in the hospital," Christine insisted. "The least you can do is take me home."

"How do you figure it is my fault?" 'Ricky demanded.

"If you hadn't been kissing everyone in that dancehall, I wouldn't have been on that parking lot alone," Christine accused her.

"I didn't take you to the club," Ricky defended. "You were stalking me. Nevertheless, I will have someone pick you up and take you home in the morning."

"I want you to take me home," Christine said in a reasonable voice. "Please."

"Oh," Ricky laughed, "the great Senator Richmond knows the magic word. I will see you in the morning."

~~~

Ricky poured her second cup of coffee and walked outside. She sat on the porch swing, stretched her five-foot-ten frame across the seat and watched the first rays of sunlight wash over the place she called home, a two-thousand-acre ranch southeast of Austin.

The ranch was her idea of heaven. Her great-great-grandparents had settled it in the 1800's. Unlike much of the dry land in Texas, her ranch bordered the Colorado River which provided water year around for her cattle and horses.

Few people were aware of where Ricky lived. She maintained a modest apartment in downtown Austin. She only went to the ranch on weekends and for vacations. Her ranch foreman Tex Strong had grown up with her on the ranch, and she considered him more a brother than a cousin and often called him Bro. His father had helped her dad make the ranch profitable. She and Tex continued the arrangement their parents had made years ago. They split the profits from the ranch operations. In recent years, the discovery of vast reserves of gas and oil had made them both extremely wealthy. Of course, one would never know it to look at them. They continued to live their lives as usual.

She watched Tex as he hooked the hay baler to the tractor. Tall and muscular, the Texan was stronger than a bull and as loyal as any human could ever be. Handsome and well educated, he had always been a favorite with the women.

"Mi amore, there you are," a beautiful Italian woman walked from the house. "I was afraid you were gone."

"Martina," Ricky placed her coffee cup on the porch railing and stood to embrace the dark-haired beauty.

"You are troubled, Cara," Martina studied the ranger's face. "A bad case?"

"Very bad," Ricky nodded. "Almost as bad as yours, maybe worse. At least in your case, we knew who the bad guys were. I have no idea who the perp is in this case."

"Let me refill your coffee, and you can tell me about it." She quickly returned with two cups of coffee and sat beside Ricky on the swing.

Ricky told her the story as she knew it. "I have a feeling I am not even close to the killer. Thanks to Blaize Canyon, he may know we are on his trail."

"Is Senator Richmond safe?" Martina asked.

"I am not certain," Ricky frowned. "I don't think the attack on Christine is connected to our serial killer. I need to find one tiny thread to pull so I can start to unravel this case."

"You may need to put your senator in protective custody," Martina suggested.

"God help us if that becomes necessary," Ricky laughed at the thought of trying to make Christine Richmond drop out of sight. "That would be like trying to hide the Colorado River," Ricky added.

"Do you ever regret leaving your old life?" Ricky asked seriously.

"No, never," Martina smiled. "Every time I look at Tex and our son; I thank the Lord for my new life. I thank the Lord for you. You saved my life."

"I had ulterior motives," Ricky teased. "You are very hot you know."

Martina feigned shock, then hugged the ranger. "If I were into women, Cara, you would be my lover."

"The first time I saw that look in Tex's eyes, I knew he wouldn't rest until you were his," Ricky grinned. "You drove him nuts, making him wait two years. He was so nervous about proposing to you. He had a million reasons why you would say no. It never occurred to him that you might love him, too."

"He is wonderful," Martina exhaled slowly. "I am a lucky woman. He loves me in spite of what I was. It took me two years to get my head on straight after my encounter with your FBI agent."

"Tex loves you for what you are; a strong, beautiful, wonderful woman." Ricky leaned down and kissed her on the cheek. "He is a very lucky man."

~~~

Chapter 4

Troy opened his Facebook page. It was time to troll for a new girlfriend. He smiled when he saw the new photo posted by Brenda Davis, a shapely brunette who had just gone through an emotional divorce from a cheating husband. *There are worse things than a cheating husband*, Troy thought as he posted a response to Brenda's newly updated masthead.

"Beautiful lady. Your X must be a moron."

"My sentiments exactly," Brenda posted back.

"I will take you in, mama," some Mexican guy posted. "One night with me and you will forget all about him."

A private message appeared in Troy's Facebook private message box. *Got her*, he grinned.

He spent the next hour communicating with Brenda before she sent him her personal email: brenda@doglover.com. He quickly typed in doglover.com and stepped into Brenda's real world. A pet grooming salon in Roundrock, Texas. The website advertised the address, phone number and hours of operation.

A quick search on whois.com provided him her home address. He was always amazed at the people who refused to spend the few extra bucks it cost to buy website privacy.

He emailed Brenda and wished her a glorious day.

After an hour of reading about what a cheating son-of-a-bitch her ex-husband was, Troy informed Brenda he had to go to PetSmart before it closed. "Charlie is out of dog food."

"Send me a pix of Charlie," she typed back.

Troy knew human nature. The longer people had to wait for something, the more desperately they wanted it.

"I will take one and send it to you when I return," he promised.

~~~

Armand Richmond tried to stay out of his daughters' lives. The death of Kara shook his world. He knew no good would come of her so-called marriage to that small-town weather girl, but he hadn't expected her to die.

He pinched the bridge of his nose as he glanced at the newspaper, again. *God, did they have to run the photo of them kissing?*

He said a silent prayer, thanking the powers that be, for Christine. Chris was the level-headed one, the one he could always count on to make him proud. The one he had groomed to take over his manufacturing empire.

He briefly wondered where his son was. A lazy, good-for-nothing, Randall Richmond had been his father's biggest disappointment.

During college Randall had fully embraced the drug scene, preferring a hazy fantasy land to the realities of day-to-day life. It had required donating a wing to the UT library, but Armand managed to buy

Randall a Bachelor of Science Degree in Communications.

Richmond Ship Builders International was one of the largest ship manufacturing conglomerates in the world. Although it was a rough and dangerous business, Armand was confident Chris could handle the rigorous demands of the corporate world. She had easily made a name for herself in the good old boy's club, of the Texas State Senate. Both his adversaries and his friends had the utmost respect for her.

Chris had laid the groundwork to lead the right-to-work supporters to a state-wide victory and defeat the unions' aggressive move to require employers to hire only union employees. Texas had long struggled to attract and keep large manufacturing plants in the state. Consequently, Texas had the fourth best economy in the world. Both the unions and the federal government fought to take over anything that was flourishing. They had Texas in their crosshairs.

It was getting more difficult every year because the unions kept driving up wages and insisting on more benefits while employees were less productive, working fewer hours each week.

Texas was a right-to-work state highly coveted by unions because it was one of the few states with a robust economy and millions of workers. Chris had introduced a bill to make it illegal for any company to require any organization's membership as a prerequisite for employment. Armand was positive the law would put the unions in Texas out of business. Most workers did not like paying the high union dues, and companies didn't like dealing with the demanding, gouging union bosses.

Automation had saved his company. Although he preferred human employees, the unions were making it impossible to afford them. No wonder companies were fleeing the United States in droves. Other countries offered workers a tenth of the wages demanded by U.S. employees.

Workers in union companies were grumbling louder and louder about the exorbitant amounts of money demanded by union leaders to pay union management's salaries and support the bloated union hierarchy that was only a campaign machine for the left-wing liberals that had highjacked the Democratic party.

Armand did worry about Chris dealing with the Teamsters Union. They were the most ruthless union in the U.S. and would stop at nothing to accomplish their goals.

He wondered if Kara's death and the attack on Chris had been because of his latest agreement with a vote by his employees to oust the Teamsters from his docks.

Armand picked up the letter he had just received from his son. He reread it before tossing it into the wastepaper basket. He was disappointed to learn Randall Richmond was still alive.

~~~

"I appreciate you're picking me up," Christine said as she fastened her seatbelt.

"Did I have a choice?" Ricky smiled good-naturedly.

"You always have a choice, Major Strong." Christine looked at Ricky's profile. Although the ranger always wore makeup, it was subtle. She looked like the all-American girl next door. Her golden hair fell in waves on her shoulders. Her smooth tanned face was one any starlet would envy. Ricky moistened her pink lips with the tip of her tongue. "Please stop that?" she frowned.

"Stop what?"

"Staring at me," Ricky said.

"Why would I stare at you, Major?" Christine was enjoying tormenting the beautiful woman chauffeuring her.

"Oh, for the pure joy of it," Ricky's blue eyes twinkled mischievously as she glanced at the senator. She was pleased to see the blush that was creeping up the senator's neck.

Christine laughed, "Take me to lunch, Major."

"Do I have a choice?" Ricky grinned.

"Of course, you do. It is Saturday. I assume even Texas Rangers get a day off," Christine smiled.

"Then would you like to go to lunch with me, Senator Richmond?" Ricky laughed.

"I would love to," Christine nodded. "Would you run me by my home so I can shower and change clothes?"

"I'll drop you off then run to my office to pick up a report I need?"

"Give me an hour," Christine nodded.

~~~

Ricky checked her watch. Thirty more minutes before she picked up Christine. She had dropped off the senator and driven to her office to pick up a report from forensics. She decided to buy a newspaper.

Senator Christine Richmond's Twin a Lesbian. The headlines shrieked. The witless writer had gone

46

into great detail about how twins usually shared the same traits. He detailed how Christine had single-handedly rallied enough votes in the state senate and house to block gay marriage in Texas. He ended his stupid drivel with a quote from Shakespeare, "The lady doth protest too much, methinks."

Ricky tamped down the urge to find the fool and choke him. She pitched the paper in the nearest trash bin and wondered if Christine had seen it.

##

Ricky nodded to the two rangers standing guard outside Christine's door. Clyde Barrel and Roger Crate were the perfect models of a Texas Ranger. Both were over six-three, and each weighed around two-hundred and thirty pounds. She was glad to see the protection unit had followed Christine from the hospital. She rang the doorbell.

When Christine opened the door, Ricky couldn't stop the smile that spread across her face. Senator Richmond was stunning in a pair of light-colored blue jeans that clung to the woman's perfect curves. The low-cut, magenta-colored sweater was just low enough to get attention, but not flaunt the senator's perfect body. It allowed about an inch of her midriff to show between the sweater and jeans.

"Do you approve, Major?" Christine teased. She was surprised at her own brazenness. Ricky's stolen kiss had let the senator know how much power she had over the ranger. Power was something Christine Richmond knew how to wield.

"Most definitely," Ricky nodded.

"The senator will return around six," Ricky instructed the rangers. "Until then you fellows can kill time any way you wish."

"You planning on a long lunch?" Christine smiled as she settled into the passenger's seat.

"I thought we might have lunch at the Oasis on Lake Travis if that meets with your approval."

"It certainly does," Christine nodded. "I don't usually have time to go there, but I love it."

As they drove, Ricky filled in Christine on the progress they had made in the case. They discussed Blaize Canyon and her lack of ethics.

"We have arrested the man who attacked you," Ricky smiled, proud of how quickly her team had apprehended Manuel Juarez. "He won't talk, but I haven't personally interviewed him yet."

"Are you a successful interviewer?" Christine watched Ricky's face as she talked.

"I can be very persuasive," the ranger nodded.

The hostess led them to a shaded table on the top floor of the restaurant. The Oasis was one of Austin's unique and outstanding restaurants. Built into the side of a cliff overhanging Lake Travis, every table provided diners with a gorgeous view of the lake and was known as the Sunset Capital of Texas.

The beauty of sunsets on the lake—viewed from the Oasis—was world renowned.

"Two Oasis Daydreamers," Ricky ordered. "Oh, wait, are you on medication?"

"No," Christine smiled. "Whatever you just ordered, sounds good."

"This is a side of you that I have never seen before," Ricky smiled.

"What is that supposed to mean?" Christine frowned.

"You are usually very cantankerous," Ricky explained. "I have never seen you so laid back. Are you certain you aren't on drugs?"

They sat silently while the waiter placed huge hurricane glasses filled with Bacardi Razz Rum, Bacardi O Rum and strawberry piña colada mix in front of them.

"It is a beautiful drink," Christine beamed. "And delicious, too." She took another sip of the rum-based concoction through her straw.

By the time the two finished their second Oasis Daydreamer, they were laughing and exchanging stories like old friends. The ranger discovered a different side to Senator Christine Richmond. She was warm and funny. Ricky loved the way Christine leaned into her.

"We get to keep the glasses," Christine giggled as she lined up the four hurricane glasses along the side of their table. "Four more and we will have service for eight."

"Maybe we should order lunch—or dinner—Ricky suggested as she checked her watch. "The food here is excellent."

"You order for me," Christine placed her hand on Ricky's forearm and squeezed it firmly.

Ricky ordered and shyly smiled at Christine.

"Bring me another one of these," Christine held up her empty hurricane glass.

"How did you get the name, Ricky?" Christine pulled her chair closer to the ranger.

"My dad called me that when I was a baby, and it stuck. How about you? What do your close friends call you?"

Ricky was aware that the woman had pulled her chair right next to hers, leaned against her and was hugging Ricky's bicep between her breasts. She knew the senator was drunk.

Give me strength, Ricky prayed.

"My friends call me Chris," the senator murmured. "You may call me Chris."

"Um, Chris. That is not as formal as Christine, but I like Christine. It suits you."

The sun slowly deserted the sky amidst glorious magentas, golds, purples, and blues. "You are right," Christine hugged Ricky's arm tighter. "The sunsets here are breathtaking."

Ricky looked down at the face of the woman leaning on her shoulder. "This is the most beautiful one I have ever witnessed," she murmured.

~~~

Senator Christine Richmond awoke to the sound of silence except for the jackhammer inside her head. She lay perfectly still and tried to recall the previous night. She vaguely remembered being half carried to the car by...*Oh, God, Ricky Strong.*

She moved slightly, and the cool sheets felt good against her body. She deeply inhaled as she realized she was naked from the top of her head to the bottom of her toes. She wanted to be furious but didn't have the energy.

She finally found the strength to reach the shower. She wondered why Ricky had stripped her naked. The ranger could have left on her underwear.

The hot water peppered her body, and for the first time, she wondered if Ricky was still in her home. She lathered her long black hair and fantasized that the woman was downstairs making coffee and cooking breakfast. *God, I could use a good cup of coffee and something greasy,* she thought.

She dressed and gingerly made her way downstairs, holding tightly to the stair railing. Her disappointment at finding the kitchen cold and empty was palatable.

Eight hurricane glasses had been washed and turned upside down to dry on a kitchen towel. A neatly printed note leaned against one of them. *You got your serving for eight. I hope your head survived the collection process. Your clothes are in the washing machine. Call me, if you feel like breakfast. I know a great greasy spoon place that is guaranteed to cure a hangover.*

The idea of breakfast with Ricky pleased her much more than cooking. She located her purse, and cell phone then called the ranger.

"Good morning, Senator," Ricky's low, sensuous voice made Christine's heart jump.

"You sound so much better than I feel," Christine whined.

"Um, you insisted on collecting the last two hurricane glasses by yourself," Ricky chuckled.

"How soon can you get here?" Christine asked. "I am starving and dying for a cup of coffee." The senator jumped when her doorbell sounded.

"That would be me," Ricky laughed.

Christine smiled. She liked the ranger's instant response. She was surprised at how happy it made her that she would open the door and find Ricky Strong standing there. She hesitated, savoring the moment the beautiful blonde would enter her world.

Ricky's smile was a thousand watts as she scanned the senator. "You look great," she beamed.

"I'm escorting her to breakfast," Ricky informed the guards. "Why don't you fellows get some breakfast? We'll be back in a couple of hours."

Christine admired the lithe body of Major Strong as she followed the woman to her car. Ricky was gorgeous in anyone's world. Her wavy blonde hair pulled back into a ponytail, and her tight jeans moved with her toned body. *She looks eighteen*, Christine thought.

Breakfast was everything Ricky had promised, greasy and great. The strong black coffee slowly chased away the nagging headache Christine had been suffering.

"I started going through your sister's emails last night," Ricky said as the waitress refilled their coffee cups. "I was surprised to see that you two communicated often. I thought you were estranged."

"No," Christine grimaced. "I loved her. I just had to appear to keep my distance. As the champion of traditional marriage, I couldn't afford to be seen cavorting with my openly gay sister. People would love to tie me to that lifestyle."

"Why?" Ricky felt a cold knot settle in her stomach. She was positive Christine had not seen the newspaper yet or the field day TV news was having with her conservative reputation.

"Because I am such a...bitch," Christine chuckled. "Gays hate me, women who want to murder their unborn babies hate me, illegals hate me, and the unions hate me."

"You may be the only person in the world who likes me, Ricky." The coy look in her eyes told the ranger that it was important to the senator that she like her.

"I like you, very much," Ricky smiled.

"Why?" Chris asked.

"You are pro second amendment," Ricky nodded. "You are exceptionally supportive of all law enforcement. You are an avid supporter of free speech, and you are pro-right-to-work. You are anti-abortion. You believe in enforcing our borders to keep out illegals. You and I are more alike than different."

"Is that all you like about me?" Christine pretended to pout.

Ricky reached across the table and took Christine's hands in hers. "I love everything about you, Christine Richmond. I love the way your hair curls around your beautiful face and falls in soft waves on your shoulders. I like the sparkling intelligence I see in your incredible brown eyes. I can't get your lips out of my mind. I desperately want to kiss them. You are the woman of my dreams.

"I believe I have made it painfully clear how I feel about you, at the risk of embarrassing myself."

Christine closed her eyes. "I am afraid I have the same feelings about you, but I would never act on them."

"Fair enough," Ricky frowned. "I just needed to understand the game rules. Good friends it is."

Christine sipped her coffee. "Did you find anything interesting in Kara's emails, anything that will help find her killer?"

"Not yet. Your sister was a very popular woman. I did find one thing I didn't know about you."

"You mean something that isn't in the Texas Ranger's profile on me?" Christine grinned. "I find that difficult to believe."

"I didn't know that you are a widow," Ricky said softly. "I never knew you were married."

"That was a long time ago," Christine exhaled slowly. "I don't like to discuss it."

"It may have some bearing on the man who tried to abduct you," Ricky informed her. "It turns out Manuel Juarez is the muscle for the Teamsters Union. Since your husband, Phillip Howell was killed in an altercation on the docks with a gang of Teamsters there may be some connection. The authorities never charged anyone with his murder.

"If it isn't too painful, I would like to hear all the information you have about the Teamsters."

"It isn't painful," Christine shrugged. "It just makes me angry in more ways than one.

"Phillip Howell wasn't my pick for a husband." Christine bowed her head for several minutes as if trying to decide how much of her story she wanted to share. "My father chose him for me. He was twenty-five years my senior and the owner of a successful ship building company in Portsmouth, VA.

"Father saw our relationship as a marriage made in heaven, a joining of two kingdoms. I saw it as marrying my father. Phillip saw it as marrying the woman of his dreams. I suffered his idea of a honeymoon and the first six months of our marriage long enough for him to name me the sole beneficiary in his will, even though I told him I didn't want it.

"I told him not to leave his wealth to me, that I didn't love him and wanted out. I found I couldn't tolerate him touching me or kissing me." A shudder of revulsion shook Christine's petite frame.

"The day before Phillip died, Father and I had a horrendous argument. I told him that I was divorcing Phillip and had contacted an attorney to remove me from his will. I told him there was nothing he could do to stop me.

"Strangely enough, Daddy said he understood and that he was wrong to push me into a loveless marriage."

"What happened on the docks?" Ricky asked.

"The Teamsters were striking," Christine shook her head, loathe to recall the incident, "Father brought in a team of strike breakers. Honestly, they were only thugs who specialized in union busting.

"They showed up on the docks ready to go to work or fight. When the Teamsters blocked their way, a terrible brawl broke out. For some unknown reason, Phillip thought he could stop the fighting. Someone knifed him, and he bled out on the docks before anyone even knew of his injury."

Christine bowed her head. "I didn't love him, but I didn't want him to die. It was horrible.

As his wife and still in his will, I inherited Phillip's company and everything he owned. Daddy happily combined my inheritance from Phillip with his ship manufacturing company and became the largest ship builder in the U.S."

Ricky reached across the table and covered Christine's hand with her own. "I am sorry," she softly said.

"Well," Christine tossed back her hair—as beautiful women do—and smiled weakly, "it seems Kara's emails are full of family secrets."

Ricky found herself wondering what it would be like to kiss those full, red lips and have them kiss back.

They talked and shared their family histories until the lunch crowd entered and waitresses changed shifts.

"We should go," Ricky said as she called for the check. "I want to continue going through Kara's emails. Do you know anything about her Facebook accounts?"

"If you mean user names and passwords, try looking under a file titled *Yellow Brick Road*. My sister was a brilliant graphic artist, but not much on computer security. She kept a list of all her accounts along with their access information on an Excel spreadsheet on her computer."

"Take me with you to your place," Christine smiled. "Maybe I can help you go through the emails."

"No, you need to rest. Doctor's orders," Ricky smiled sadly. "I am not certain it is good for us to spend too much time together. I could get used to having you around."

Christine nodded knowingly. "How about you, any ex-husbands or lovers you want to talk about?"

"No," Ricky chuckled.

"You know what they say, Major," Christine teased, "confession is good for the soul."

"My soul is fine," Ricky grinned.

"I find it difficult to believe that a woman as gorgeous as you, has no ex-lovers," Christine insisted.

"I didn't say that," Ricky chortled. "I said I have no one I want to talk about."

"Oh," Christine raised perfectly arched brows and wondered how many lovers the beautiful woman had entertained.

"I am going to keep two rangers assigned to you at all times," Ricky told Christine as they pulled to a stop in front of the senator's home. "I want to make certain no one makes another attempt on your life."

"Could you come in for a few minutes?" Christine asked shyly. "I am not quite ready to be alone."

Ricky nodded and followed the senator into her home. As soon as they were inside the door, Christine turned to face the ranger and looked up into her eyes. Christine ran the tip of her tongue along her lips, moistening them. She pressed her lips together then moistened them again, making certain Ricky was watching. "Thank you for the best two days of my life," she said huskily.

"A woman can only be so strong," Ricky mumbled as she closed the distance between their lips.

Ricky's kiss was gentle and sweet, tentatively seeking a response. Christine slipped her arms around the ranger's neck and pressed the full length of her body into Ricky's softness. Her tongue teased Ricky's lips requesting entry. Ricky gave her an open invitation and caressed her tongue with her own.

~~~

Later as they lay in each other's arms, Christine kissed the little hollow at the base of Ricky's throat. "You are the first woman I have ever been with," she said huskily. "No one has ever made love to me like that. It was…breathtaking."

"I won't lie to you and say you are my first," Ricky stroked her lover's silky back, "but I can truthfully say no one has ever made me feel the way you do. You are truly special, Senator Richmond." She grinned as she captured Christine's lips. "You are without a doubt the best kisser I have ever met."

"Why, thank you, Major," Christine kissed her again.

"I know why men love us," Christine sighed as she snuggled further into Ricky's softness. "We are so soft and silky. The touch of a woman is electrifying and gratifying and just…pleasing to all the senses."

Christine snuggled further into Ricky's side and inhaled the soft fragrance of her. "May I ask you a question?" she said softly.

"Um hum," Ricky murmured.

"Why did you strip me naked and wash my clothes last night?"

Ricky raised on one elbow and gazed into the brunette's deep brown eyes. "Because you vomited all over yourself and my car on the way home," she grinned.

"I did not," Christine huffed.

"Yes, you did. You threw up in your own lap, then proceeded to cover my console, dash, floorboard and door. I cleaned it up on the way home last night. It took me two hours to get the smell out of my car."

"Good," Christine giggled, "I was afraid you took off my clothes and didn't find me desirable."

"No chance of that." Ricky pulled Christine into her side. They both slept the sleep of contented lovers.

The doorbell jerked them from a deep sleep. Christine could tell by the continuous ringing that someone was leaning on the button. She looked out the front window to see her mother's Mercedes parked next to Ricky's Lexus.

"Oh, God," she whispered loudly, "my mother is here."

The look of absolute terror on Christine's face told Ricky she did not want her mother to find the ranger in her bedroom.

Ricky hastily threw on her clothes. "Let your mother in." She pulled Christine to her for one last kiss. Grabbing her leather boots and holster, she sprinted down the stairs to the back door.

"Mother," Christine greeted her glaring parent as Lady pushed her way into the house. "What are you doing here so early?"

"I am here to check on my daughter," Lady Richmond screeched. "The one released from the hospital with a concussion, who never bothered to inform her mother."

Ricky made a loud commotion opening and closing the back door. She spoke loudly as she made her way from the kitchen to the family room. "It looks like everything is okay here, Senator. I am leaving my men with you. There will be two guards at…, oh, Lady Richmond; I didn't know you were here."

Lady narrowed her eyes and glared at the ranger. "Why wasn't I notified of my daughter's release?" she demanded.

"I notified your husband," Ricky moved to stand beside Christine. "I assumed he would pass the information along to you."

"He did, this morning," Lady growled.

"The good news is we have the attacker in custody," Ricky smiled. "I am certain the senator is safe, but until we settle this, I will have two men with her at all times."

"I suppose we have you to thank for this," Lady slammed yesterday's newspaper down on the kitchen island. "You have destroyed my daughter's career!"

Wordlessly Christine read the paper. The color drained from her face as she followed the writer's reasoning that since Kara and Christine were twins, they were probably both gay.

"Have you seen this?" Christine demanded.

"Yes, but I…" Ricky stopped talking. The look of betrayal in Christine's eyes was heartbreaking.

"Chris, I had nothing to do with this," Ricky moved toward the brunette.

"You need to leave, Major Strong." Christine's voice was cold and controlled as she backed away from Ricky. "And in the future please address me as Senator Richmond."

~~~

Chapter 5

A storm of emotions swirled through Ricky's head as she scrolled thru Kara Richmond's emails. After four hours of prowling through the dead woman's life, Ricky still had no leads.

She kept pushing the memories of last night from her mind. It was difficult to think with the vision of Christine leaning above her lowering her lips to kiss her passionately.

Making love to Christine Richmond had been like riding a tornado, wild and unrestrained. More than once Ricky had begged for a moment to catch her breath. Christine's wanton abandonment had surprised the ranger at first, but she quickly allowed herself to be sucked into the vortex of the brunette's passionate demands.

I can't believe she could clutch me to her like that then dismiss me so easily, Ricky agonized over the cold look in Christine's eyes as she held open the front door for her to leave.

Suddenly an email caught the ranger's attention. "I am glad you got off the Facebook page, some of those guys are scary. You should be careful about communicating with them. They could be psychopaths."

The email was from lonelyboy@gmail.com.

Ricky wondered at what point Facebook had turned into a lonely hearts' club.

Ricky followed the thread of conversation between Lonely Boy and Kara, wondering why an avowed lesbian would pick up a guy on Facebook.

After several weeks of emailing back and forth, Lonely Boy asked if Kara was her real name. Kara was smart enough to give him a phony last name. "My real name is Troy Hunter," he volunteered. Troy asked her why she was on Facebook. She explained that she loved her sister and that her sister wanted her to date guys.

Troy seemed to have the instincts of a shark. "Men aren't all they are cracked up to be," he emailed.

"I have a confession to make," his next message read. "I think I may be bi-sexual. I mean, if the right person came along, it wouldn't matter to me if it were a man or a woman."

"I think I am the same way," Kara had emailed back. "Falling in love with a guy would certainly solve my issues with my sister."

"Why is she so important?" Troy asked.

"She is a big muckety-muck in politics. If it ever came out that I am gay, it would hurt her career."

"Not in today's climate," Troy replied. "Gays are open, and no one pays them any attention."

"In Texas, they do," Kara replied.

"Let's talk about happy things," Troy's message read. "I have attached a photo of Charlie; he is my baby."

The attached photo was a precious little dog that looked like a Shih Tzu. Troy spent the rest of the conversation talking about Charlie.

Ricky backtracked to see if she could figure out from what Facebook group or page Kara had connected with lonelyboy@gmail.com. She located the filename Christine had given her and, found Kara's Facebook login information. She ran a search on Spokeo.com to make certain who owned the gmail address, lonelyboy@gmail.com. She discovered it did indeed belong to Troy Hunter. A quick search of Facebook friends produced three Troy Hunters. The last one Ricky checked had the lonelyboy@gmail.com address.

Her heart skipped a beat as she scrolled back through Kara's posts and things posted to her. Troy Hunter started out by making nice comments on her posts, like: "You are right, Kara." Then he would post something and say, "Kara you will like this." Troy's communications with Kara shifted to her emails. Kara had stupidly given him her email address: kara@disignbykara.com.

Ricky went to Kara's website. The information under Contact Us provided Kara's cell phone number and the address of her apartment. An easy trail for a serial killer to follow.

Their emails had stopped the day before Kara died.

Ricky wondered why an avowed lesbian was Facebooking with a total stranger. She was surprised that Kara was so flirty and was lured to her death by a man on Facebook.

Following a hunch, she called Blaize Canyon. After the pleasantries, she asked the question burning in her mind.

"Blaize, did you ever use Kara's computer to communicate with others?"

"What do you mean?" Blaize asked cautiously.

"Did you ever exchange information using her Facebook page or email people on her email account?"

After a long silence, Blaize answered. "Yes."

"Anyone important?" Ricky asked.

"One fellow I liked," Blaize said. "His handle was Lonely Boy. I felt sorry for him."

"Was Kara aware of your interaction on her accounts?"

"Yes, but she didn't mind," Blaize explained. "She knew I was just having a bit of fun. No harm was done."

Unless you count Kara's death, Ricky thought as she disconnected the call.

##

Ricky clicked on Troy Hunter's photo and went to his timeline. The photo on his masthead showed an extremely handsome man in his early thirties. She read his personal information. She noted where it said he had gone to high school and college and made a note of where he worked. He was divorced. She was certain all the information was bogus, but it was a place to start.

Opening her own laptop, Ricky set up a Facebook page. She selected a photo of an attractive brunette from a stock photo website, established a Gmail account and like magic Alessa Morris was born. She pulled some photos from her mobile phone of Martina's new puppy and posted them on the site. She sent friend requests to several people. Some accepted immediately. She did not send a friend request to Troy

Hunter. She wanted to appear to have an entrenched presence on Facebook before contacting him. She was certain he was her guy. She thought about serving Facebook with a subpoena to obtain legitimate information on Troy Hunter but recalled the public fit they had thrown last year after receiving such a request. In the end, Facebook had provided the information, but by then the perp had abandoned the site and disappeared.

She decided that her best bet was to try to entice Troy to strike up a friendship with her.

Using Kara's Facebook connection, she scrolled through Troy's timeline. She located six women who looked very much like Kara Richmond. She emailed the photos to herself so she could run them through facial recognition tomorrow.

Ricky looked at the time on her laptop. It was three in the morning. She knew she had avoided going to bed to keep her mind from filling with thoughts of the night before and of Christine. *God, I wish she had never entered my life,* she thought.

~~~

Ricky had overslept and hurriedly showered and dressed. She was backing out of her drive when her cell phone rang.

"Major Strong," Ricky recognized the dispatcher's voice.

"What's up, Lilly?" she answered.

"Big fight going on in the warehouse district. I am sending you the address. Your team is already there."

Ricky swung her state issued truck around and headed for the central freight district of Austin. She wondered how her team had managed to beat her to the scene.

There was a major brawl going on when she pulled into the area. With lights flashing, she turned on her siren full blast and continuously honked her horn. She sounded like the cavalry had arrived. Brawlers and TV news reporters scattered in every direction as she drove her vehicle into the crowd.

She could see two of her men backed into a corner behind a dumpster. "What happened? Where is the rest of the team? What are you two doing here? You are supposed to be guarding senator..." She gasped as Christine walked from behind the dumpster.

"Your officers saved my life, Major Strong," the prissy woman declared.

"Good job fellows," Ricky smiled a crooked smile then walked back to her truck as the Austin Police arrived. She spoke briefly to the officer in charge explaining her men were on a security detail with the senator.

"Wasn't very smart of her to hold her anti-union kickoff campaign in the heart of the warehouse district," the policeman noted. "She is lucky she wasn't hurt."

"Yeah," Ricky nodded as she stepped into her patrol vehicle.

"Major Strong, Major Strong," Christine couldn't move fast enough to stop Ricky from leaving.

~~~

Troy logged onto his email. He had several emails from Brenda. The first three were normal, "Hey, just checking on you," or "Hope you had a good day. By the eighth email, she was getting needy. "Please answer me. I miss talking to you."

He checked his Facebook account to see if Brenda had returned to trolling. She had. *Typical*, he thought.

Her first post of the morning said, "I don't let very many people into my life so if you're a part of it, just know that I value you and you mean a lot to me."

That night she posted, "Stop expecting loyalty from people who can't even give you honesty!"

Troy hugged himself as he imagined the woman was now heartbroken because he hadn't emailed her.

"The next morning, she posted, "No matter how broken you are, there is someone out there who will love you enough to put you back together again."

Or take you apart, Troy thought.

He wondered if women were truly stupid enough to believe someone would come along to pick up the pieces of their pathetic, needy little lives and make everything right for them.

That night she had posted more sickening, slobbering sayings, "Time passes, and you begin to see people for who they really are, and not who they pretend to be."

He snorted as he read the last post. These women rarely saw what men were. In their desperation to get a man; they willingly overlooked any shortcomings.

Troy fired off an email to Brenda along with the photo of Charlie lying between his legs. Within minutes, he received a reply.

"I was afraid something happened to you," Brenda wrote.

"I had an accident and was in the hospital for the past three days. Slight concussion. I am fine now. I was worried sick about Charlie. A nice policeman was kind enough to take my door key to my neighbor so she could feed Charlie." Troy knew he had put two thoughts in Brenda's mind. One; that he liked and trusted the police and two; he had a female neighbor who was willing to care for his dog.

"I am happy you are okay," she wrote.

"I missed communicating with you something awful," he typed. "I never realized how important your friendship was to me until I couldn't reach you. I just didn't have access to a computer in the hospital."

"I missed you, too," she wrote. "Have you ever thought about us meeting? Maybe somewhere between our respective towns. Halfway?"

"I would like that," Troy answered. "I have to wait until my doctor releases me to drive." He didn't want to seem too eager.

He spent the next two hours reading her whining emails about how no one knew her true worth or appreciated her.

"Sometimes I feel that I have no reason to live," she whined.

She is right, Troy thought. *There is no reason for her to live.*

~~~

Chapter 6

Ricky spread out the six photos she had pulled from Troy Hunter's timeline and compared them to the renderings from the 3-D imaging software. Three were almost a perfect match. She ran all six through facial recognition then ran a cross check against the Missing Persons' reports. By day's end, she had identified six women.

Two had run off with their boyfriends. One had taken a job in Las Vegas to get away from her overbearing parents, and the other three were in the Ranger's morgue.

Ricky contacted the relatives of the three she suspected were her Jane Does'. Parents and estranged husbands were bringing in items that the lab could use to make positive DNA identification.

She opened her laptop and logged into her Alessa Morris Facebook page. She tried to think of something sappy and insecure to say. She wrote, "I know I am a puzzle, but I am worth the time to put the pieces together."

She read the post, shrugged her shoulders and pushed enter. She would have to search other Facebook pages for more sad material. As much as she was hurting over Christine, she found it difficult to have a public pity party.

~~~

Scott Winslow turned off the television and exhaled loudly. Every local and some national stations were carrying the story about Senator Christine Richmond.

He was sorry she had lost her sister. No one should lose a loved one in that manner. He prayed the authorities would stop the monster that was preying on Texas women.

The mainstream media had a field day over the weekend trying to taint the senator's name by implying she might be gay because her twin sister was gay.

Her press conference in the warehouse district this morning had pushed that story to the bottom of the news list. The shot of the senator emerging from behind a dumpster flanked by two Texas Rangers had spread over the newswires like wildfire. She had taken on the union and won. The union thugs' attempt to get their hands on her showed what a bunch of gangsters they were.

Scott shuddered. He hated to think what could have happened if that Texas Ranger hadn't driven a truck into their midst. He smiled to himself as he recalled how the thugs had scattered like mice scurrying from a lion. They didn't stick around long enough to realize the cavalry was a lone woman in a pickup truck.

He tidied his desk and pulled the Bible from his bottom drawer. Senator Richmond was a devout Catholic. She would be in his office in three, two, one!

"Scott," Christine burst through his door, her minions right behind her. "Thank you for taking the time to see me."

He always made time for her. He loved her. Of course, she didn't know it yet, but one day soon he would work up the nerve to ask her out.

"It is always a pleasure to see you, Senator," he walked around his desk and clasped her soft hand between his.

"That was quite a show you put on this morning," he waited for her to sit, then moved to his chair behind the desk. "You could have easily been hurt, you know."

Senator Richmond waved away his concern and launched into the reason for her meeting. "The governor wants me to spearhead the wall our new president is building," she grimaced. "I wholeheartedly agree with the building of the wall, but I don't understand why I was selected to lead the publicity for it."

"Of course, you understand," Scott snorted. "Your mother is Latino. We need a Latino face on the project."

Christine bowed her head and considered his statement. "I don't want to be involved just because I am half Latino. I have never used my ethnicity to advance my political career. I don't want to start now. I am proud to be an American, and I don't want to use my Mexican heritage for political gain.

"I am spearheading the non-union movement. I think it would look better if someone else led the charge to build the wall."

Scott walked around his desk and sat down on the edge of it so he could look directly into her eyes. "The party is considering backing you for governor next term. With your looks and political acumen, you will probably be the first woman president, but you must pay your dues. You can't close the door when the party comes calling. Right now, they are calling for you to throw your influence behind building the wall.

"You were re-elected by a landslide. Texans love you; they will support anything you advocate."

"I need to give careful thought to this," Christine frowned. "I have a lot on my plate with the union business and my sister's funeral."

Scott nodded. "Let me take you to dinner. We can discuss it more."

"I can't," she said. "My mother is expecting me for dinner tonight. I must go."

"Of course," Scott smiled. It irritated him that she had dismissed him so easily.

~~~

Christine cupped her mother's elbow as her father supported his wife on the other side. Lady Richmond held up well until Blaize Canyon rushed forward to place a rose on Kara's casket. Lady seemed to crumble at the sight of the woman she blamed for her daughter's death. Armand lowered his wife into her chair and put a protective arm around her.

Christine fought back the tears. She surveyed the mourners to see if her brother Randall was in the audience of those attending the funeral. He wasn't.

The senator looked around trying to find something to concentrate on so she could get her mind off the horrible scene before her. A large oak tree, about fifty feet away caught her attention. A lone woman, in a black dress, stood beneath the tree.

When the service ended, the woman moved from the shadow of the tree. Sunlight danced off her blonde hair. Christine caught her breath as she realized that Ricky had paid her respects to Kara.

"Dad, can you get Mom to the car? I need to speak with someone."

Christine stood beside Ricky's car. The ranger was surprised to see her there. "Shouldn't you be with your mother?" Ricky said softly.

Ricky had no time to react. Christine threw herself into the blonde's arms and wept uncontrollably. "I am very sorry for your loss," Ricky said sincerely. She tightened her arms around Christine and held her close, whispering words of consolation into the grieving woman's ear. Christine felt good in her arms. Ricky wished she could hold her for the rest of her life.

"Would you like to get a cup of coffee?" Ricky whispered.

Christine nodded her head against the ranger's shoulder and pulled back slightly. "Please, just hold me a little while longer."

Ricky held her for a long time, stroking her long black hair and kissing the top of her head. As the mourners left the cemetery, the family car pulled alongside Ricky and Christine.

"Will you take her home?" Lady Richmond seemed to realize her daughter needed the reassurance of the ranger.

"Yes," Ricky nodded.

Christine felt safe for the first time in days. She never wanted to leave the soft warmness of Ricky's arms. She could tell by the way Ricky held her that she had missed her, too.

The tears eventually turned into unflattering hiccups, and like magic, Ricky produced a tissue. She gently blotted Christine's eyes, careful not to disturb her mascara. *God bless the person who invented waterproof mascara*, she inanely thought. Christine turned her face up to the ranger allowing her to blot the tears. It took all the strength Ricky had to refrain from kissing the gorgeous brunette in her arms. More than anything she wanted to ease the pain Christine was suffering, not add to it.

~~~

Christine slid into the passenger's seat, and Ricky closed the door. She waited until Ricky settled in her seat before speaking. "I owe you an apology," she said.

"That's not..." Ricky stopped as Christine held up her hand.

"I learned that Blaize was the one who provided the photos and information to the news media," Christine said softly. "I was wrong to accuse you. I am sorry."

Ricky nodded then started her car.

They discussed mundane things over coffee, avoiding the elephant in the room.

"That was a nice turnout for Kara," Ricky noted. "She certainly had a lot of friends."

"I was disappointed that our brother didn't attend her funeral," Christine said sadly.

"I didn't know you had a brother," Ricky frowned. "Where is he?"

"No one knows," Christine shrugged. "He may be dead. He was heavily into drugs and Daddy disowned him, cutting off all support until he cleaned himself up."

"I'm sorry," Ricky grimaced. "I didn't know."

Christine shrugged. "How could you? My family never speaks his name. He has been dead to my parents for years."

"But not to you?" Ricky said softly.

"I remember Randall as a little boy and a teenager," Christine smiled slightly. "He was funny and sweet. I don't know what happened. If he is alive, I hoped he would see the news coverage and attend the funeral."

"Are you making any progress in catching Kara's killer?"

The ranger shook her head, no. She didn't want to tell Christine the approach she was taking. It was dangerous, and civilians didn't need to be involved.

"Looks like you are getting a lot of publicity from your press conference Monday," Ricky smiled.

"Thank you for that, by the way," Christine grimaced. "I don't know how those hoodlums knew I was holding a press conference concerning the union."

"Well, you did send out an announcement to the news media inviting them to attend your press conference in the warehouse district," Ricky pointed out. "I am betting they didn't think you were handing out free kittens."

Christine laughed for the first time in a week. Ricky laughed with her. "Take me home, please," Christine said hoarsely. "I need to be with you." Her dark eyes were almost black. Ricky recognized wanton desire when she saw it.

Ricky pulled her car into the circular drive. She didn't put it in park. She did not intend to get out of the vehicle. Christine looked at her questioningly. "Aren't you coming in?"

"No," Ricky murmured. "I don't think that is a good idea."

"I want you to," Christine begged. "I need you with me tonight."

"You are upset and very vulnerable," Ricky noted. "I don't want to wake up next to you in the morning when you regret the night before."

"I won't," Christine sighed.

Ricky leaned across the woman and pushed the door open for her. "Goodnight, Senator Richmond," she said.

~~~

Troy Hunter had accepted Ricky's friend request as Alessa Morris days ago and occasionally communicated with her.

Ricky made another pot of coffee. She had been on her Alessa Morris Facebook page for over four hours. Most of that time was spent on Troy Hunter's timeline watching him entrap a beautiful brunette named Rosie Raye. When an obvious hooker named X-citement tried to engage Troy online, Rosie posted for him to "check messages."

Both Rosie and Troy disappeared from Facebook after that. Ricky tried everything to reach Rosie, but Rosie hadn't accepted her friend request. Ricky knew Rosie was now emailing Troy. Too late, she realized she should have befriended Rosie days ago, but she was afraid that might scare off Troy. She berated herself for not doing it anyway.

Ricky left her computer on and took a shower. She pulled on her favorite old sleeping shirt and a pair of running shorts. Her email was dinging when she walked back into the kitchen.

"Thank God, Rosie accepted my friend request," she thought.

She tried to think of a way to warn Rosie about Troy without tipping her hand to the serial killer. Finally, she private messaged Rosie to be careful picking up men on the internet.

She received a scathing message from Rosie telling her to mind her own business. Ricky emailed Rosie's Facebook photo to her office computer so she could run racial recognition on it.

She also received an email from Senator Christine Richmond, thanking her for her kindness and restraint during a very difficult time.

Ricky sadly shook her head and went to bed. She knew that an intimate relationship with Christine Richmond would only end in disaster and would ultimately destroy both their careers.

~~~

"Major, we have another floater in the Colorado," Becky breathed excitedly into Ricky's phone. "The team is bringing her in now. I wanted to give you a head's up."

Ricky rubbed her neck. It hurt from bending over the computer most of the previous night. It was not the way she wanted to begin her day. She had an awful feeling she already knew who the victim was. At least they had recovered the body quickly. Hopefully, they would be able to extract DNA that would identify the woman.

The ranger watched as the facial recognition software worked its magic. It flashed a match and, as she had expected, pulled up the name Rosie Garland. The woman had been smart enough to use an alias online, but not smart enough to avoid a tryst with a serial killer.

Ricky called Becky into her office and gave her the information on their latest victim. "Send Lee Phillips and Tim Tanksley to her home. We need to confiscate her laptop. Tell them to take a grief counselor. They need to break the news to whoever lives with her."

They had come up empty handed with the three facial matches Ricky had pulled from Troy's Facebook page. Relatives had brought in items containing DNA, but none had matched the DNA of the women in the morgue.

Ricky turned on her laptop and started looking for lovelorn posts she could steal. The thoughts of Senator Richmond that were running through her mind were hot and steamy, not very appropriate for posting on Facebook.

She found a whiny one and posted on the Alessa Morris page. *If another girl steals your man, there's no better revenge than letting her keep him. Real men can't be stolen.*

You are right, Troy Hunter posted.

She didn't acknowledge his post. She didn't want to appear too eager. She would post some more tonight.

"Major," Becky's voice came through the intercom. "The Deputy Director is on the line."

Ricky was certain he was calling to find out where they were on the Hacker case. She wondered how much longer they could keep the serial killer's activities from the press.

"We have already identified the latest victim," Ricky told him as she answered the phone.

"That is good to know," her boss chuckled. "Since I am pulling you off the case."

"What? No, boss! I am very close," Ricky tried to control the anger in her voice. She wanted to catch the bastard Hacker herself.

"Not my doing," Rhodes huffed, "Governor's orders."

"Governor?" Ricky couldn't keep the disbelief from her voice. "How did the Governor get involved?"

"Scott Winslow," Rhodes said. "He has requested a full-time security team with Senator Richmond at all times. It seems he wants only our best and brightest guarding his next Governor. He specifically requested you."

"Of all the low down, sorry…"

"Ricky," the Director cut her off, "Your permanent assignment is Senator Christine Richmond until further notice."

"I have had a security team on her around the clock since we discovered her sister's body," Ricky explained. "Why do I have to…?"

"Because the Governor asked for you," Rhodes growled. "It won't be forever. Senator Richmond and her task force are making a tour of the Texas/Mexico border. The President requested her as the face of the project to build the wall between our two countries."

"He couldn't have picked a better politician for that job," Ricky agreed. "When can I expect to leave on this little vacation?"

"Senator Richmond is expecting you at her home at six this evening so she can brief you on what to expect. Be there on time."

"Yes, sir," Ricky hung up the phone. She knew what to expect. Christine Richmond would torment her until she couldn't think straight. It was bad enough she couldn't get the gorgeous brunette out of her thoughts; now she had to be in her presence twenty-four/seven. "My life will be a living hell," Ricky said out loud.

~~~

"Mia Cara," Martina called out as she opened the back door to Ricky's home.

"In here," Ricky answered.

"What is the meaning of this?" Martina demanded as she surveyed the weapons her friend had laid out on the bed.

"I am on a special assignment thanks to our Governor," Ricky exhaled loudly. "I think I will need all the firepower I can conceal."

"Where are you going, Cara, Iran?"

"Not quite that bad," Ricky laughed. "I will be touring the Mexican border with a group of politicians. "It is time to build the wall. I have a feeling things will get very dicey."

"Who is going with you?" Martina asked.

"Crate and Barrel," Ricky smiled a tight little smile. "They are my best guys when it comes to backup."

"I don't mean that, Cara," Martina frowned. "Who are you guarding? It must be someone important. The Rangers don't send you out just for the fun of it."

"Senator Richmond," Ricky shrugged.

"The one you kept from being strung up last week?" Martina smirked. "Be careful, Cara. She looks dangerous."

"I'm not afraid of danger," Ricky chuckled.

"I didn't mean physical danger," Martina grimaced, "I meant danger to the heart."

"Where are Tex and Brady?" Ricky wanted to change the direction of the conversation.

"Picking up the wranglers who are helping with the branding next month. Tex wants to work with them for a while before sending them out to round up our cattle. Of course, Brady had to go with his dad."

"Of course," Ricky smiled as she began cleaning her guns and loading the magazines.

"What does that fit?" Martina gestured toward the magazine Ricky had just loaded with thirty-three rounds.

"My Glock 19," Ricky frowned. "I love my Sig, but I want to have plenty of firepower if things get bad. This baby can create quite a firestorm."

Martina left the room and returned quickly. "Take this," she handed Ricky a soft leather holster encasing a Beretta Nano 9mm."

"An ankle holster," Ricky grinned. "I didn't think of that."

"It saved my life on several occasions when the mob was after me," Martina frowned. "Wear it, Cara. It may save your life, too."

Ricky checked the gun. "It only has eight bullets."

"If you are a good shot, one bullet is all you need," Martina smirked.

Ricky nodded and hugged the woman she considered her best friend.

~~~

Chapter 7

Ricky rang the doorbell. She could hear the click of Christine's heels on the marble floors.

"Ricky, please come in. Give me a second to change, and I will make dinner. There is wine chilling." Christine called over her shoulder as she walked up the stairs. "You will find a corkscrew on the island, please open it and pour us each a glass. I'll just be a minute."

Ricky opened the wine and poured a glass for Christine. The oven was preheating, and a covered casserole dish sat on the cabinet. She was tempted to lift the cover to see what the senator was cooking.

"Oh, that is much better," Christine charmingly smiled as she entered the kitchen. "I hope you like lasagna."

"I love lasagna," Ricky nodded as she handed Christine her wine.

Christine looked at the empty glass behind her. "Aren't you drinking?"

"I never drink while on duty," Ricky half-smiled.

"Aren't you off duty?" Christine tilted her head as if she didn't understand.

"I was told to report here at six for a briefing," Ricky frowned. "Did I misunderstand?"

Christine inhaled slowly. In her mind, she counted to ten. Ricky Strong could be infuriatingly stubborn.

"Yes, okay. I will brief you while the lasagna cooks then you can consider yourself off duty and make the salad."

Ricky smiled slightly. She rather enjoyed antagonizing the senator.

Christine went over the travel schedule and discussed her security concerns. "The drug cartel will do everything possible to keep the wall from being erected."

"What kind of support will we have from the border patrol?" Ricky asked.

"We have a team assigned to accompany us wherever we go," Christine frowned. "There will be the usual news media waiting for me to make a mistake, but they won't be on our bus. Why? Are you concerned?"

"Of course, I am concerned," Ricky huffed. "Something could happen to you and..."

Christine held her gaze for several seconds before Ricky looked away.

"I will be meeting with the governors from the border states of Mexico," Christine talked as she slid the lasagna into the oven. "We will travel along the border and check the condition of any existing wall then meet in El Paso for a combined Mexico and U.S. official meeting.

"The Mexican government has pledged its cooperation in building the wall, but I am not naive enough to believe they mean that. Drug money from the U.S. makes up a large part of the country's economy."

"So, who put the target on your back?" Ricky frowned.

"It is dirty work," Christine nodded, "but that is what elected officials are supposed to do. Take care of our state and American citizens."

"You could die," Ricky flatly stated.

"I trust you won't let that happen, Major," Christine grinned mischievously.

"I assume every bureaucrat who stands to profit from the wall will be tagging along," Ricky scoffed.

"Unfortunately, yes," Christine nodded.

"How will we travel?" the ranger inquired.

"We will fly into McAllen where the border patrol will pick us up. We will visit the headquarters of the Rio Grande Valley Sector of the Border Patrol and spend the night in Edinburg. You and I and two drivers will be in a motor coach. My staff will travel in a second motor coach."

"The luxurious homes on wheels, built by Thor?" Ricky grinned. "The ones that are built to withstand mortar fire. The million-dollar armored buses that are built like a tank?"

Christine nodded. "When you put it like that, it sounds like a waste of taxpayer's money."

"No, it is money well spent," Ricky smiled. "It is probably the only way the border patrol can keep you safe. I am certain we will encounter snipers and other assassins that want to send a grisly message to the President. When do we leave?"

"A couple of weeks. Plans are still being finalized," Christine downed the last of her wine.

"Who requested my presence on this little suicide tour?"

"I did," the senator smiled. "Is there anything else you want to know?"

"No, I'm good for now," Ricky shrugged.

Christine walked to the island and refilled her wine glass. She filled the other one and carried it to Ricky. "Then consider yourself off duty, Major. The salad ingredients are in the crisper at the bottom of the refrigerator."

They dined and opened the second bottle of wine. Ricky asked Christine if she had ever visited any of the border towns.

"No," Christine frowned. "Frankly, they have always scared me."

"They should," the ranger nodded. "El Paso is just across the border from Juarez, which is considered the most dangerous city in Mexico and one of the most violent in the world.

"We broke up a human trafficking ring there a couple of years ago, but another popped up almost overnight in its place. We have undercover agents there now.

"This is serious business, Senator."

Christine cringed when Ricky continued to use her official title.

"Do you have any idea what you would bring on the white slavery market?"

"Not as much as a blonde Texas Ranger," Christine smirked.

"Please don't take this lightly," Ricky said softly. "This is extremely dangerous. I wish you wouldn't do it."

"I have to," Christine cried. "If I want to be Governor, I have to prove I am strong enough to handle the tough jobs."

"Oh, so that's what this is all about?" Ricky scowled. "You want to be Governor."

"Let's talk about something else," Christine frowned. "What do you do for fun?"

"I love to ride horses," Ricky grinned as she thought about her stallion. "I love dancing, bowling, boating, the theater and hanging out with people I care about." She wanted to tell Christine about her ranch and horses. She wanted to talk about Tex, Martina, and Brady. Tell her that they were the most important people in her life, but she couldn't.

Martina was in the witness protection program. Ricky had spirited her away when mobsters managed to locate her. Now Ricky was the only person in the world who knew who Martina was and where she lived.

Ricky still looked for the leak in the program that had resulted in Martina almost dying. *I will find it*, she promised herself.

Christine watched the ranger's eyes. She could tell the woman was no longer with her. She wondered who or what had pulled the blonde away from her.

"What about you, Senator, what do you do for fun?"

"I...I...I don't know," Christine realized she didn't do anything fun for fun's sake. "The most fun I have had in my life was the day we spent at the Oasis and had breakfast together the next day then we..." her voice trailed off as she realized that the best time of her life had been with Ricky Strong.

"Tomorrow is Saturday," Ricky grinned. "My day off. I will pick you up at nine for breakfast, and we will go from there. Okay?"

Christine nodded.

Ricky rinsed their plates and placed them in the dishwasher as Christine cleared away the remnants of their meal.

"I better go, if I am to be back here in the morning," Ricky smiled as she moved toward the door. "Thank you for a fantastic dinner.

Christine caught her hand, "Or you could spend the night with me."

Ricky felt her insides turn upside down. "Or I could spend the night with you," she whispered as her lips took control of the ones she had been dying to kiss all evening.

Christine Richmond was everything a woman should be: soft, loving, responsive, demanding and oh, so good to hold.

Still holding her hand, Christine led the blonde upstairs into her bedroom. It was cool and dark. Ricky slowly eased her onto the bed and began to caress her as Christine writhe against her.

Christine nibbled at Ricky's lips and whispered in her ear. Ricky tentatively ran her tongue along the woman's full bottom lip, then engaged her tongue in a dual of passion as their lips moved seductively against each other's.

The way Christine kissed seemed to suck the soul out of Ricky. She knew she was lost. Her hands slowly moved under Christine's blouse, thrilling at the feel of warm, silky flesh.

Christine moaned. She couldn't get enough of the blonde beauty exploring her body. Ricky's fingers trailed a stream of fire from her stomach to her breasts, then slowly circled her nipple. "Please," Christine whispered. "Please love me, Ricky."

If Ricky's hands started a stream of fire, her lips caused a volcanic eruption that sent hot lava spreading throughout Christine's body. Ricky nipped and kissed and sucked as her hands discovered new and wondrous ways to send heat waves throughout her lover's body.

By the time the ranger had removed their clothes, Christine was pleading for more. Please, baby, please, suck me and fuc..." Ricky's demanding lips on hers turned Christine's pleas into ecstatic moans as the blonde's hands worked their magic.

The ranger's weight on Christine as she arched to meet the blonde's movements, sent a wave of pure pleasure rolling over Christine. "Yes, oh yes, Ricky. Please, please, I am yours. Anything you want. Please, baby."

##

The early morning sun cast a ray across Ricky's eyes. She lay still, relishing the soft, warm body in her arms. She had been with a few women in her life, but never a woman like Christine Richmond.

Ricky held her breath afraid she would wake her lover. All she wanted to do was hold the woman in her arms forever. She marveled at how perfectly Christine's body molded into her own.

Christine smiled as she awoke to find Ricky wrapped around her. She lay on her side, her back against Ricky's firm breasts. Ricky's arm was under her neck. Her other arm was draped over her waist, wrapping Christine in a warm, soft cocoon. Their legs were tangled, making as much contact as possible. It was as if they couldn't get close enough.

Ricky's soft, warm breath was on her ear. "Are you awaking?"

"Umm," Christine hummed as she pushed her firm buttocks into her lover's abdomen. Ricky held her tighter as she slowly moved against her. Christine gasped at the pure pleasure of the feelings elicited by the blonde's body undulating against hers.

"I could wake up like this, every morning for the rest of my life," Christine murmured. "Every morning."

"My thoughts exactly," Ricky whispered in her ear.

~~~

Ricky awoke, suddenly aware that Christine was no longer in her arms. She slowly slid her hand to the brunette's side of the bed and found it coldly empty.

She turned over on her back, dreading what the senator might have in store for her: a note that said "that was nice, now please leave" or cold, dark eyes that regretted falling into bed with the ranger.

Soft, warm lips kissed hers, as Christine sat down beside her. She was still damp from her shower and smelled heavenly. "Are you going to sleep all day?"

Ricky slowly opened her eyes and smiled as the gorgeous woman leaned over to kiss her again. "What time is it?"

"After two," Christine grinned happily. "I think I wore you out, Ranger."

"Maybe," Ricky laughed, "but I rejuvenate quickly."

"I am starving," Christine kissed her again.

"If you want to leave this house," Ricky smiled, "you need to stop kissing me. Let me get a quick shower, and I will take you to a late lunch."

"I don't know," Christine kissed her again. "Kissing you is very nice."

Faster than lightning Ricky grabbed her lover and flipped Christine onto her back. Christine gasped for air. "My, you are very strong, Major. Strong enough to have your way with little ole' me."

"This is me being strong enough to get into the shower," Ricky laughed as she slid from the bed.

They laughed and talked over lunch, finding it difficult to keep their hands off each other in public. "I want to kiss you," Christine smiled shyly.

"Do you like paddle boats?" Ricky asked.

"I don't know," Christine frowned. "I have never been in one."

"You are a Texas state senator, and you have never ridden in an Austin White Swan paddle boat?" Ricky squealed, feigning indignant righteousness.

Christine laughed. "I love…" She stopped short of finishing her sentence. The two gazed into each other's eyes for several seconds.

Ricky paid the lunch check and led Christine to the car. Half an hour later, she was holding the brunette's hand on the seat of a White Swan paddle boat, letting the current of the Colorado River carry them across Lady Bird Lake.

"I love the Colorado River," Ricky said. She put her lips lightly against Christine's ear and whispered, "And I love you."

Christine moved closer to Ricky, wishing the ranger could put her arm around her, but she knew that wasn't the thing to do in public.

"This is lovely," Christine said softly, "but can we go home and be alone together?"

Ricky squeezed her hand and started pedaling the boat back to its dock.

~~~

"Ahh," Christine fell back on the bed gasping for breath. "I have never experienced anything like this," she gulped air. "I think I love you, Ricky Strong."

"I love you too, Senator Richmond."

"How long am I going to have to pay for that?" Christine laughed. She rested her head against Ricky's shoulder and trailed her fingers between the ranger's breasts.

"We need to talk about how we are going to handle us," Ricky exhaled.

"I know," Christine sighed. "I don't know what to do."

"I could lose my job if it ever came out that I was sleeping with the haughty Senator Christine Richmond," Ricky teased.

"Haughty," Christine snorted. "Well, my constituents would certainly stop voting for me if they ever found out I was between the sheets with the arrogant Major Ricky Strong."

"Arrogant," Ricky squealed. "I'll show you arrogant."

"Umm," Christine hummed, "and I'll show you haughty."

Later Christine laid on her back. Ricky propped her head on her elbow and looked down into her dark brown eyes. "We still need to talk," she smiled.

"Yes," Christine's breathing slowed as she caught her breath, "but first, could you just show me *arrogant* one more time?"

Sunday was a repeat of Saturday as they explored wondrous ways to please each other. It was late afternoon when Ricky's stomach protested being empty. "Apparently, I am hungry," she laughed.

"Do you eat leftovers?" Christine smiled.

"I love leftovers, especially leftover lasagna," Ricky grinned. "I'll make a fresh salad. You do the French bread."

They discussed the upcoming trip and how to prepare for it. "It can be a war zone along the border," Ricky informed Christine.

"Surely, they won't attack a State Senator," Christine's look of disbelief made Ricky chuckle.

"Do you think murdering drug cartels care about titles? They kill border patrolmen. Nothing is sacred to them.

"Do you know how to handle a gun?"

"Somewhat," Christine frowned. "My father taught me when I was younger, but I haven't fired one in years."

Ricky noticed it was getting late. As much as she wanted to stay with Christine, she also wanted to contact Troy Hunter before they left town. "I need to go to my place," she grimaced. "I need clean clothes, and I have to prepare for work tomorrow."

"Take me with you," Christine pleaded.

"What would Crate and Barrel think if I moved them to my apartment to guard you for the night?"

"Dismiss them," Christine insisted.

"No, I don't feel comfortable doing that," Ricky scowled. "Aren't you exhausted?"

"Don't tell me I have worn out the great Ricky Strong," Christine laughed.

"Now you are just bating me," Ricky grinned.

"When will I see you again?" Christine coyly asked.

"I will pick you up from work tomorrow," Ricky replied. "Can you get away early?"

"Yes," Christine nodded enthusiastically. She wrapped her arms around the ranger's waist and looked up into her blue eyes. "Bring clothes to spend the night."

Ricky pulled her tightly against her and slowly kissed her soft lips. "I will."

~~~

Ricky wrote her report in detail. She gave explicit instructions to check on Alessa's Facebook for a Troy Hunter using the email lonelyboy@gmail.com. She wanted her successor to be able to arrest the Hacker if something happened to her on the border tour. She had a bad feeling about the entire trip.

~~~

Chapter 8

Ricky opened her Alessa Morris Facebook page and posted. *They give you the false sense that they can't live without you, but leave you, in the end, feeling like you can't live without them!*

Within seconds, Troy Hunter posted on her timeline. *Where have you been? I have missed you.*

"I didn't think anyone knew I existed," Ricky typed.

"How was your day?" Troy posted. "Mine was pretty lonely."

"Lonely Boy, I can cure lonely, honey," X-citement posted.

Ricky frowned. She had seen posts from X-citement before.

She scrolled back through Troy's timeline and noticed that X-citement always made an appearance whenever Troy was trying to move a mark from Facebook to private email. She knew X-citement was an alias Facebook page for Troy.

She private messaged Troy and provided him with an email address for her alias. He quickly began emailing her. He was extremely smooth. He told her funny antidotes and stories about his dog, Charlie.

"Gotta' go," Troy emailed. "My sister is at the door. She is taking me out for my birthday."

"Happy Birthday," Ricky emailed back, then signed off Facebook.

Ricky's mind immediately jumped from Troy Hunter to Christine Richmond. She missed the senator. *The woman is addictive*, she thought.

~~~

Ricky put things into motion to find out who owned the email, lonelyboy@gmail.com and the Facebook page for Troy Hunter. When the ranger showed the judge the evidence she had compiled, the justice hadn't hesitated to sign the subpoenas, compelling Google and Facebook to produce the information she needed. Ricky hoped to get the address and phone number for Troy Hunter.

Of course, Google did nothing to verify any of the information provided to obtain a Gmail account and Facebook was just almost as bad, so she could easily hit another dead-end.

At two-thirty, her cell phone rang, and Christine's beautiful face filled the screen. Ricky had taken the brunette's photo while she slept. "Ricky Strong," she answered. She wasn't quite ready to let Christine know her face was on her mobile phone.

"Major Strong, Senator Richmond, here," Christine matched her formality. "I have waited long enough for you to call me."

Ricky chuckled into the phone, "And I have waited long enough to see you. Can you leave your office in thirty minutes?"

"Can't you get here any faster than that?" Christine sighed. "You know; turn on those flashing lights and sirens?"

"Thirty minutes, Senator. I will pick you up in the parking garage on the same level as your office. I will wait for you by the elevators."

The ranger called Crate and Barrel to inform them she would be taking over Senator Richmond's security until midnight. Even though she planned to stay overnight, she felt safer with the other two rangers also watching Christine's house.

~~~

Ricky watched Senator Richmond as she stepped from the elevator. She wore her usual high heels and fitted business suit. The ranger was sure she had met prettier women, but she couldn't recall even one right now. She leaned over and pushed open the car door for Christine.

Crate and Barrel waved goodbye and walked toward their car. Ricky quickly checked for onlookers, then kissed the brunette who eagerly returned the kiss. "Hi," Ricky said softly. "I've missed you."

"To where are we going?" Christine asked as she buckled her seat belt.

"Shooting range. I think we need to get in some practice before we take on the Mexican drug cartel," Ricky frowned.

"Would you run me by home first so I can change?" Christine smiled seductively.

Ricky caught her breath. "I would love to."

~~~

Ricky rolled over and checked the time on her cell phone. Christine pulled her back against her. "Do we still have time to visit the gun range?" the brunette asked.

"Um, hum, if we get up now," Ricky kissed her again, a slow, searching kiss. One that lingered long after their lips parted.

Christine caught her lover's face between her hands and pulled her lips back to hers. "I love you, Ricky," she whispered.

Ricky didn't need to respond. Christine knew from the way the other woman held her that she was loved.

While Christine dressed, Ricky looked over the Kimber Micro .380 pistol her lover kept for protection.

"This is a sweet gun," Ricky whistled her appreciation of the small concealed carry weapon. It is very accurate with little recoil. I like an all metal gun. They are hard to find nowadays. Someone paid a pretty price for this."

"Daddy bought it for me," Christine smiled. "What do you use?"

"Sig, state issued," Ricky said. "For accuracy, it probably has about twenty feet on your .380, and when it hits, it kills."

"Then teach me to shoot a Sig," Christine shrugged agreeably. "I have placed myself in your hands, Major Strong, in more ways than one."

"You say the sexiest things," Ricky smiled as she pulled Christine into her arms and nibbled at her lips. "You are the most desirable woman I have ever met. I adore you."

"That is as it should be," Christine sealed the kiss.

~~~

The gun range was beginning to get crowded when they arrived. Off-duty rangers were practicing in preparation for their annual qualification tests. Ricky had reserved the two practice lanes furthest away from the others. She wanted Christine to be comfortable shooting the gun.

A couple of the men pulled Ricky aside and asked for an introduction to the "looker" with her. She simply shook her head and mumbled something about how that woman was way out of their league.

"What do they want?" Christine glanced around the bay. She could smell the testosterone in the shooting range.

"To date you," Ricky grinned. "I told them you were way out of their league."

"You are sweet," Christine touched her hand briefly sending a shockwave throughout the ranger's body. They put on their electronic ear protectors, and Christine was surprised to learn they could easily talk with each other while blocking the deafening blasts from the guns.

"Teach me to shoot your gun," Christine said.

"Lock your elbows," Ricky instructed. "My gun has a lot more kick than your .380."

"Damn!" Christine cursed as the Sig kicked up. "I didn't even hit the target. What good is it, if I can't hit anything with it?"

Ricky placed a calming hand on her shoulder. "You will be hitting targets by the time we leave here tonight. I promise."

Ricky took a stance behind the smaller woman and wrapped her arms around her. "Lock your elbows to steady the gun."

Ricky showed Christine how to sight-in the Sig. "This is a little different from your Kimber. Your Kimber is a single action gun. The Sig is double action. The first shot is the hardest. Squeeze off the first shot then just barely let off the trigger. You will feel a slight click. Don't let the trigger all the way out. Now it is ready to fire without much pressure on the trigger."

Christine pushed her back into the ranger and spread her legs slightly for a better stance. She loved the warmth of being backed into Ricky's arms. She pulled harder on the trigger, trying to make the gun fire smoothly. It recoiled, but not as much as before. Ricky's arms tightened around her. By the time, they shot a hundred rounds thru the Sig, Christine was hitting the target with every shot.

"You do everything well," Ricky smiled at the senator as she took her gun.

"You fire your gun, I want to shoot several rounds through the Kimber," Christine nodded.

Ricky watched in awe as Christine placed six rounds right in the center of the target's head.

"Do you carry?" she grinned. "You have a license to carry, don't you?"

The senator nodded, yes, reloaded her magazine, shoved it back into the Kimber and repeated her previous performance.

You've got to love a woman who reloads her own magazine, Ricky thought.

~~~

The women spent the next week practicing at the gun range and going over the schedule for Christine's border visit. The schedule changed daily as the senator's office worked to coordinate everything with the border patrol and the Mexican officials.

Ricky gave up all pretense of living at her apartment and moved her clothes to Christine's.

"I love waking every morning in your arms," Christine turned to face her lover and kissed the little valley between her breasts.

"Umm," a half-awake Ricky pulled her tighter against her. "I can't even find the words to describe how wonderful it is to begin each day with you in my arms."

"I have to be in my office early this morning," Christine said. "The governor is calling to give me instructions."

"I have to spend some time with R&D this morning," Ricky frowned.

"R&D, as in research and development?" Christine raised her perfect brows.

"Yes, something about being able to track me at all times. "They probably want to put an ankle bracelet on me like they use on convicts who are under house arrest."

~~~

The governor's instructions had been brief and to the point: make the Mexican authorities understand the U.S. will build the wall with or without their cooperation. Make certain they understand that The National Guard will be staged along the southern border of the United States, if necessary.

Christine finished briefing her staff and checked the time. She wondered if Ricky was in her office. She called the ranger.

"Hello, beautiful." Ricky's happiness at receiving the call was evident in her voice. "Are you calling to take me to lunch?"

"I am," Christine chuckled. "Should I pick up you?"

"Better let me pick up you, so you don't have to drag Crate and Barrel all over town. See you in twenty."

They finished lunch, and Ricky's phone rang. "Yes, sir, I am with her. Yes, sir. We can be there in thirty minutes. You, too, sir."

"Other than me," Christine's brown eyes danced, "what was that all about?"

The ranger deeply inhaled. "I need you to do something for me. It is important."

Christine nodded. She could tell by the seriousness of Ricky's voice that she needed to listen closely.

"We are going to our R&D lab. When we get there, they are going to chip us."

"Do what?" Christine was incredulous. She had spearheaded the fight against the federal government's plan to chip all American citizens. Strangely the government only wanted to chip Americans, not immigrants or illegals.

"No way in hell is anyone chipping me," the senator scowled. "Are you crazy?"

"Honey, will you just listen for a minute?" Ricky pleaded. "This is a matter of life and death."

Christine held her tongue but continued to fume.

"You have no idea how dangerous your little border tour is going to be," Ricky continued. "I know you think this will be a walk in the park because you believe in it so strongly, but I am telling you, this little Mexican holiday can turn deadly in a heartbeat.

"If we get separated, or anything happens, I want to be able to find you. If we are kidnapped, I want my team to find us. The chips will make that possible. Once we are back home, we will remove them."

Christine glared at Ricky.

"I hate it when you go all *"bitchy Senator Richmond"* on me," Ricky mumbled. "Do you honestly think I would ask you to do something that is detrimental to you?"

"Of course, not," Christine grumbled. "It is just that chips give the government total control."

"Look, I completely agree with you," Ricky sheepishly grinned. "But these are extenuating circumstances, and the chip could save our lives."

"Okay, let's get it over with." Christine squeezed the ranger's hand.

~~~

"That didn't hurt a bit, did it?" Ricky pulled Christine's hand onto her leg as she pulled the car into the Austin traffic.

Christine rubbed the tiny spot on her shoulder where the chip was implanted. "No worse than getting a flu shot," she grimaced.

"Are you ready to leave on Monday?" Ricky asked.

"Not really," Christine sighed. "I have a thousand things to do before I can leave."

"Me too," Ricky nodded. "I am taking the day off tomorrow to get my guns and ammunition ready. I also have something to do to follow up in Kara's case."

"Do you have any solid leads?" Christine asked.

"I am close," Ricky nodded. "I want to set a trap before I leave town."

"I do need to pick up dry cleaning and make certain I have something to wear," Christine nodded.

"I have seen your closet, Senator," Ricky teased. "If you never shop again, you would never run out of clothes.

"I think I had better move back home tomorrow and spend the weekend getting things in order. I will meet you at the airport Monday morning."

"Tonight, will be our last night together?" Christine said, obviously hurt that her lover would leave her alone.

"We both have plenty to do before we leave," Ricky frowned. "As much as I hate to admit it, you do distract me."

~~~

Although they had often spoken on the phone, Christine was seriously missing Ricky. She had used all her womanly wiles to entice the ranger to return to her bed Saturday night.

"I need today and tomorrow to finish my business before I leave town," Ricky argued. "Believe me; I would much rather be with you."

Christine reluctantly agreed to meet at the airport on Monday.

Sunday night was insufferable. She hadn't been in the ranger's arms in three days. Friday morning didn't count. The senator paced the floor. She couldn't sleep. She knew it was crazy, but sleep simply wouldn't come without Ricky sleeping beside her. She knew she couldn't go another night without Ricky

Strong. She wondered when the beautiful blonde had become so necessary to her happiness.

A call to Ricky's cell went directly to voicemail. Either she was talking on her phone or had turned it off. She knew Ricky never turned off her phone. *Probably in the shower, Christine thought.* She left a message.

Christine poured a glass of wine. *Maybe that will relax me enough to go to sleep.* She finished the wine and decided to go to Ricky's apartment. Crate and Barrel were sitting in the car across the street. Christine wondered if she could slip out the back. She called a taxi and gave them the address of the neighbor behind her.

Black jeans and sweater made her look like a cat burglar as she slipped out the back door of her home and slithered along the fence and through the shrubs.

Damn, I forgot about the wrought-iron fence around this place; she thought as she confronted the tall fence. *But there is a gate hidden in the shrubbery that leads into the neighbor's back yard.* She followed the fence, stepping on a feral cat that ripped her pant leg to shreds before howling and scampering away through the bushes. *Ricky Strong better be worth this,* she gasped.

She cringed as the metal gate screeched on hinges that hadn't been oiled in years. The gate opened into thick shrubbery like the green growth on her property. She prayed the neighbors had no watchdog.

Christine breathed a sigh of relief when she spotted the cab at the curb in front of her neighbor's house. She slipped in and gave him the address for Ricky's apartment.

~~~

She pushed the call button for Ricky's intercom and waited for Ricky to buzz open the door leading to the elevator. She wondered why the ranger didn't answer. A couple entered the lobby and opened the door to the elevators.

"Okay, I will be right up," Christine loudly said as if talking to someone on the intercom. She followed the couple onto the elevator. She was thankful Ricky lived in the large apartment at the top of the building.

She hugged herself as she stepped off the elevator into the hallway that would lead her to the woman she loved. She rang Ricky's doorbell several times and was perturbed when no one answered. She knocked on the door, "Ricky, it is me," she called.

Christine jumped when her cell phone rang Ricky's ringtone. "Ricky, where are you?"

"Where are you?" Ricky countered. She knew the answer was not going to be good.

"At your apartment."

"I'm not there," Ricky slowly exhaled.

"I am aware of that," Christine said angrily.

"Christine, I am working on something," Ricky explained. "I don't know what time I will be there. Where are Crate and Barrel? Did you give them the slip?"

"Goodbye, Major Strong," Christine fought to keep the emotion from her voice. "I will see you at the airport in the morning."

"Honey!" Ricky knew the brunette was angry.

"Mia Cara," Martina passed Ricky the roast, "your senator?"

Ricky nodded.

"Senator?" Tex looked around the table. "What senator?"

"Mom, I ate all my green beans," three-year-old Brady grinned impishly at his mother.

"Broccoli," Martina raised a perfect eyebrow at her son.

"Don't like," Brady pouted.

"Daddy is eating broccoli," Tex made a big deal out of putting a fork of broccoli spears into his mouth. "Umm, this is good," he smiled at his wife.

Brady reluctantly forked a piece of the green weed on his plate and began to chew it. He didn't know what his mother had done to it, but it was cheesy and good. He nodded and ate the rest of the vegetable. "Now may I be excused?"

"Yes, Mia Amore," his mother smiled.

"Okay, tell me what is going on?" Tex frowned. "And why I am always the last to know?"

Ricky explained her upcoming assignment and finished with, "The senator can be extremely difficult, to say the least." She began to clear the table. Martina joined her.

"I am taking Ricky to the airport early in the morning," Martina leaned down and kissed her husband lightly. "You and Brady will be on your own while I am gone."

Tex moaned as if mortally wounded and kissed his wife's fingertips. "Do you want me to go with you or I can take Ricky?"

"No, you have the man coming in the morning to look at the white stallion," Martina smiled. "We will be fine."

Chapter 9

Christine watched through the plate-glass windows of the airport as Ricky's car pulled to the curb. The ranger emerged from the driver's side. Christine smiled and started to move toward the door, but a dark-haired beauty stepped from the passenger's side of the car. The Texas breeze whipped her long black hair around her perfect face. The long skirt she wore whipped around her shapely legs. She tossed her hair back out of her eyes and smiled at Ricky.

The senator's eyes narrowed as she watched the woman meet Ricky at the back of the car. She put her arms around the ranger and hugged her tightly. Ricky bent down and kissed the woman on the cheek, then hugged her again. Ricky shook her head, 'no' then kissed the woman on the forehead. The trunk of the Lexus popped up, and Christine could no longer see them.

"The lying piece of..." Christine mumbled. She could think of no names bad enough to call her two-timing girlfriend. "That is who she has been with the last three nights."

Fury burned through Christine like a Texas wildfire. *How could I be such a fool?* She thought. She watched as Ricky hoisted a large duffle bag onto her shoulder, handed the woman her car fob and hugged her one more time.

The woman seemed reluctant to let the ranger go, catching her hand and pulling her down for a kiss on the cheek and a whispered goodbye.

Christine hurriedly took her place in the long security line.

Ricky's eyes lit up the moment she saw Christine. *God, I have missed her*, she thought.

"Good morning," the ranger greeted the senator. "Come with me; we can check in over there." Ricky motioned toward a checkpoint that had no line. She took Christine's carry-on bag and moved away from the crowd

At the checkpoint, Ricky showed the TSA agent her Texas Ranger's ID and badge. "This is Senator Christine Richmond. She is with me." Ricky showed the agent another form, then slipped it back into her pocket.

Christine couldn't keep from commenting. "That was easy," she noted.

"It is nice to avoid those long lines," Ricky smiled. "Where is your entourage?"

"They arrived early." Christine didn't want to admit she had detached herself from the group to greet Ricky alone.

"I am glad to see my team stayed with you," Ricky nodded behind her. For the first time, Christine realized that Crate and Barrel were walking behind them. Both carried bags identical to Ricky's.

"They are like ghosts," the senator frowned. "I didn't know they were with me."

"Good," Ricky laughed, "That is how they are supposed to work. Out of sight, out of mind and ever present."

They silently walked to their gate. Ricky was certain half of Christine's legislative staff was milling around the waiting area.

"How many people are with you?" she whispered.

"Twenty-eight," Christine said curtly then moved away from the ranger to talk with her assistant.

Ricky realized she was getting the cold shoulder but didn't know why. *I guess she is still mad at me about last night,* she thought. She walked to Crate and Barrel.

"Did you fellows bring plenty of firepower?"

"Just like you told us, boss," Crate nodded. "We got chipped, too."

"They will remove the chip as soon as we return, right?" Barrel asked. "I don't like anyone knowing my every move, not even Daisy and Becky."

"I have a bad feeling about this whole deal," Ricky spoke softly. "I want to make certain we can locate each other at all times, especially the senator."

"You don't look half bad in glasses, boss," Crate grinned. "How do I look?"

"Like a college professor," Ricky laughed. "Wear them at all times. Tiny, twin cameras with sound and video are built into each side where the earpiece meets the frame. They look like screws. Daisy and Becky can talk to us through a device built into the earpiece behind our ears. Pretty ingenious, huh?"

"Hey, Becky," Crate said softly, then grinned ridiculously when the woman responded.

Office romance, Ricky thought.

The ticket agent announced that the plane was ready for boarding and called Christine's group first. Ricky tried to get beside the senator, but the woman was the first to board. By the time, Ricky boarded, Christine was seated in a window seat. Her assistant was next to her. Ricky placed their carry-on bags in the overhead bin and took the seat behind the senator. *It's going to be a long flight,* she thought. *I will apologize to her first chance I get. Oh, well, I can use the sleep.*

Christine was furious when she realized the ranger was sleeping like a baby. *That ravishing beauty probably wore her out last night*; she thought as visions of Martina brushing Ricky's cheek with her lips replayed in the senator's mind.

By the time the plane landed, and the entourage began unloading Christine had worked herself into a rage. Her staff knew that look and spoke to her only when necessary. Unfortunately, Ricky wasn't that knowledgeable about Christine's moods. She pulled their bags from the overhead bin and tried to make her way through the crowded aisle to catch up with the senator.

As they left the plane, Christine was engulfed by representatives of the border patrol and whisked to a waiting vehicle. Ricky caught up with them as the driver was closing the limo door. "I am part of Senator Richmond's security detail," she explained as she pulled back her jacket exposing her badge and gun. She opened the door and squeezed into the car.

Ricky frowned as Christine gave her a *go-to-hell look* then continued talking to the director of the border patrol.

The rest of the day included formalities; a tour of the headquarters facility, a dinner in Christine's honor and a briefing with the senator's retinue.

Ricky knew some of the border patrolmen assigned to escort them on their tour. They were former Texas Rangers who opted for the excitement of catching illegals and drug smugglers. After the briefing, several of the men and one woman circled the blonde and exchanged greetings.

Agent Leah Davis caught Ricky's arm and pulled her away from the group. "Do you have time for a drink and catch-up conversation?" she asked.

"Umm, as much as I would like to," Ricky smiled, "I have to stay with Senator Richmond at all times. She is my assignment."

"Bring her, too," Leah grinned. "She looks like she could use some loosening up."

Ricky's eyes followed Christine as she moved around the room. "I think she needs rest right now. It has been a long day. But we can visit during this tour."

"Sounds good, Major," Leah agreed. "I hope you rest well. We do have a big day ahead of us tomorrow."

"Is that your woman in this port?" Christine hissed as Ricky touched her arm.

"What? No! I don't...What is wrong with you, Christine?"

"You need to call me Senator Richmond!" She yanked her arm from the blonde and stomped away.

"Oh, here we go, again," Ricky growled. She walked to Leah. "I think I will have that drink with you after all," she smiled. "Just give me a moment to talk with my team."

The ranger instructed Crate and Barrel to stand guard over Senator Richmond. "I am going for a drink with Agent Davis. I'll relieve you at nine."

~~~

Christine slammed the door to her room and overcame the urge to throw a lamp at the mirror. Her rage had grown as she had watched Ricky and the female agent enter the hotel bar together. She couldn't believe she had fallen for a two-timing womanizer. She had never been attracted to a woman. *Why in the world did I fall head over heels for Major Ricky Strong?* She thought.

She knew why. Take away the womanizing and Ricky was strong and soft at the same time; kind and easy to be around. She was thoughtful and understanding, dedicated to her job and determined to right the wrongs of the world. Add that she was drop dead gorgeous and you had a perfect package.

Then why would she cheat on me? Christine asked herself. *She knows I love her. Haven't I proven that?*

Her heart skipped a beat as she heard the door to Ricky's room open. "I'll watch her for the rest of the night. You get some sleep," the ranger instructed Crate and Barrel.

Christine held her breath hoping Ricky would knock on the door separating their rooms, but she didn't. Water started running, and Ricky softly hummed as she prepared to take a shower.

Probably washing that floozy's perfume off before confronting me, the senator thought. *At least she didn't spend the night with the woman.*

After several minutes, Christine heard Ricky's electric toothbrush. She thought of how minty Ricky always tasted when they retired for the night. A wave of longing and desire swept over her. She waited for Ricky to knock on their shared door. Instead, she heard the ranger arrange a wake-up call for tomorrow morning, then silence. A quick check under the door showed the light was off in Ricky's room

She is going to sleep, Christine thought furiously. *I am dying, and she is sleeping.* She fought the urge to stomp her foot and scream.

~~~

"So, twenty-five international bridges and legal border crossing," Ricky was looking at a map with Agent Davis. "Is she visiting all of them?"

"She requested that we take her the entire distance," Leah shrugged.

"That is over 1,200 miles," Ricky said incredulously. "That will take over a week. I understood we would be here no more than four days."

"She changed her mind last night and asked the Director to make the arrangements," Leah frowned. "I don't know if his secretary has done that yet. Maybe you can talk some sense into the senator.

"We had planned to leave from here and travel toward El Paso. If we go down to Matamoros, we will end up doubling back to here. That will add at least two more days to your trip."

"She can be stubborn sometimes," Ricky grimaced. "In fact, she is the most..."

The look in Leah's eyes stopped Ricky midsentence. "She is behind me, isn't she?"

Leah nodded and mumbled something about finding breakfast and scurried away. Ricky dreaded turning around. She never knew who she would be confronting: wonderful, amiable Christine or bitchy Senator Richmond.

"Are you going to turn around or do I have to talk to your back for the rest of the trip?" Christine sharply said.

Bitchy Senator Richmond it is, Ricky thought as she turned to face the brunette.

"Good morning, Senator Richmond," Ricky said coolly. "We were just going to the hotel restaurant for breakfast. May I escort you?"

Christine nodded, and Ricky led the way.

Crate and Barrel joined them at a table for six. Leah carried her tray to the table and sat down next to Barrel.

"Agent Leah Davis, have you met Senator Christine Richmond?" Ricky made the introductions. "You know Crate and Barrel from your days as a Ranger."

"You were a Texas Ranger?" Christine practically glared at the woman. "I suppose you served under, Major Strong."

"Yes," Leah nodded. "She taught me a lot."

"Umm," Christine smiled disingenuously. "She has taught me a great deal, too."

"How are the twins and Raymond?" Barrel asked.

"They are wonderful," Leah's eyes lit up as she discussed her sons and husband. "Four-year-old boys are a handful."

Christine looked down at her hands. *I guess I was wrong about her and Ricky*, she thought. "Agent Davis, please advise your director that I will stay with his initial plans for our trip. It isn't necessary to go to Matamoros."

A broad smile covered Leah's face, "I am glad. I was dreading the extended time away from my family."

The others finished breakfast and headed to their rooms leaving Christine and Ricky alone at the table.

"Christine, I don't know what is wrong," Ricky said, "but you need to know, I don't sleep around. You are the first woman I have been with in over five years."

"Then who...?"

"Major Strong," a big black man slapped Ricky on the back, "I heard you'd be here. To what do we owe the pleasure?"

"My team and I are escorting Senator Christine Richmond," Ricky motioned toward Christine. "Senator, this is Jeremiah Jones, best running back in the NFL, now one of the best border agents in Texas."

"Senator, my pleasure," Jeremiah nodded.

For the first time since the airport, Christine smiled a sincere smile, "Agent Jones, it is nice to meet you." Her extended hand was gently engulfed in a big bear paw.

"We better get moving," Jones said. "The others will be here soon. We'll meet in the lobby in fifteen minutes. Senator, it is a joy to have you with us." He turned to Ricky and grinned, "You always get the good assignments."

Christine put the last of her toiletries into her travel bag as Ricky opened the door between their rooms. "We need to get on the bus," Ricky informed her.

Christine nodded and picked up her purse as Ricky took her luggage. The ranger's hands were full when the senator caught her by the lapels and pulled her down for a searing kiss. "You are incredibly sexy in those glasses." She wheeled around and left.

It took Ricky a moment to recover from the burning desire that shot through her body and pooled in her stomach. *I don't know how long I can ride this rollercoaster*, she thought.

"We will visit McAllen, Rio Grande City, and Roma today. We will spend the night in Laredo," Jeremiah went over the schedule with everyone gathered in the lobby.

Ricky looked around to see if any unfamiliar faces were with them. She knew everyone, but she still didn't like discussing Christine's schedule so openly.

As they entered the bus, Ricky took Christine's luggage to her bedroom. She left her own luggage sitting by the entryway. "Where do you want me?" she asked Christine's assistant.

The assistant consulted a notebook filled with schedules. "The bedroom next to the senator. Your other two men, ah, Crate and Barrel," she snickered, "are in the bedroom across from yours. Two twin beds."

Ricky was happy to find that Christine hadn't changed any of the security arrangements they had previously discussed. She carried her luggage to her bedroom and pulled out her laptop. *Time to play with Troy Hunter*, she thought. She hoped she could hold the man's interest during her border tour. Nothing would please her more than handcuffing the serial killer.

"Becky or Daisy," Ricky said softly, "I am turning off these glasses until we reach our first stop."

"Okay, boss," Daisy whispered back. She continued to watch Ricky's movements with the chip monitor.

Ricky turned on her laptop and quickly opened her alias' email. There were half a dozen messages from Troy, but none last night or today. He sounded desperate. Ricky hoped he hadn't deserted her for another mark.

She decided to have a pity party on Facebook. She opened Alessa's Facebook page and posted:

I've always dreamed of going to a tropical island for a couple of weeks. We would stay in a romantic bungalow. Windows open, there would be lace curtains blowing in a light breeze along with warmth coming from the sunshine shining thru the lace. Although this would be heaven on earth, I'd be in heaven just being with the man God intended me to go thru life's journey with.............But I have no man to do this with... I have been hurt; I guess I am not beautiful, everyone hurts me.

That should be sappy and whiny enough to get his attention, Ricky thought. Within five minutes, Troy sent her an email. "I won't hurt you, pretty lady," it promised. "Where have you been?"

"My job took me out of town," Ricky posted. "Are you okay? I missed you."

She spent the next hour emailing with Troy. He sent her new photos of Charlie and told her a couple of sweet jokes. "I wish I could take you out to dinner," he emailed.

"That would be nice," Ricky emailed back with several smiling emoticons.

"Let's plan on that when you have time," Troy typed.

"I would like that," Ricky responded. "I am ready to move into a new relationship, and I have grown very fond of you through these emails."

They said their goodbyes with promises to email tomorrow.

A firm knock sounded at her door as Ricky turned off her laptop. "Come in."

Christine peeked around the edge of the door. "We are close to our first stop," she smiled. "Will you be with me at all times?"

"That is the plan," Ricky shrugged. She couldn't stop her eyes from roving over the senator's perfect body. "You know; you should button that blouse as high as it will go. We are in an area where you don't want to show off your assets unless you are selling them." She checked out Christine's expensive high heels. "You will die tonight if you wear those shoes all day.

"You would be better off to wear slacks or a pantsuit, something with a high neck, and comfortable shoes. It is going to be a strenuous trip."

"Believe it or not, Major," Christine smirked, "I have been dressing myself for the past thirty years with no repercussions."

"You never know when we will be forced to make a run for it," Ricky said adamantly. She was uneasy that Christine still wasn't taking the dangers of the trip seriously.

The bus slowed to a jerking stop. Ricky steadied Christine as the brunette lurched forward. She released her as soon as the bus rolled to a complete stop. "I'll be right behind you," the ranger said as she put on her glasses and pulled on a jacket to cover her gun.

Television news crews followed every move Christine made. Texans adored their senator and she always drove up ratings when she appeared on talk shows, or footage of her appeared on the news shows. Reporters were having a field day with the trip.

The visit to McAllen was brief. The downtown area was over five miles from the border but had suffered tremendously under the rampaging drug cartels. Christine listened as the locals related story after story of their daughters raped and their sons murdered by the marauding drug dealers.

Their next stop was Rio Grande City, forty miles west of McAllen. The town had not flourished as much as McAllen and many old; historic buildings were crumbling. Rio Grande City residents had their horror stories to share about the drug cartels.

A small, dirty blonde-haired child followed Christine everywhere she went. The girl was obsessed with the beautiful Texas senator. As they were boarding the bus to go to the next town, the child held her arms up to Christine, begging to be picked up.

To Ricky's surprise, the senator went down on one knee, swept the child up in her arms and hugged it. The little girl tentatively touched Christine's earrings and smiled brilliantly. "Do you like these?" Christine smiled as she pulled the jewelry from her ears. "Give them to your mother."

The little girl hugged Christine tightly, then wiggled to be put down. She ran to her mother sharing the earrings the senator had given her.

"And I thought she was a cold-hearted bitch," Daisy said through Ricky's earpiece. "I think I am becoming a fan of Senator Christine Richmond."

"Me, too," Ricky sighed.

~~~

"Listen up folks," Jeremiah quieted the crowd. "We have about a ninety-minute drive to Laredo. We will have dinner and spend the night in a decent hotel.

"Keep in mind that Laredo is the third most dangerous town in Texas. While it is a thriving metropolis, it has the most dangerous underbelly you can imagine. Drugs, prostitution, thieves, and kidnappers are all waiting to score and consider unsuspecting visitors a prime target. Stay together. Stay in the hotel and do not roam the streets.

"After Laredo, the trip will become even more difficult. We will leave the Texas highway system and begin driving on the unpaved road that runs along the wall. Senator Richmond wants to see the condition of the current wall from here to El Paso. So, fasten your seatbelts. It will get rough. Any questions?"

During the question and answer period, Ricky's mind wandered to the dark-haired senator. Although Christine was civil, she was still very cool. Ricky wondered what she had done to upset the volatile woman. *Life with her will never be boring*, the ranger thought. She inwardly shrugged as she realized she no longer saw a life without Christine Richmond in it. She wondered if the senator felt the same way.

##

Chapter 10

Ricky pulled out one of the two dresses she had packed for the trip. She liked formal political dinners almost as much as she liked getting a root canal. She decided on the emerald green dress with the high neck and low back. She styled her blonde hair to fall around her shoulders and down her back. She wasn't vain, but she knew she was a head-turner. She finished applying her makeup just as Christine knocked on the door between their rooms.

"Come in. It's unlocked," Ricky called as she slipped into her heels.

"I just want to see…," Christine sharply inhaled as she saw the blonde. "You are beautiful," she whispered. "Just beautiful."

Ricky openly appraised the brunette. "Thank you. So are you. I will have to fight the men off you tonight."

"You're the only one I want *on* me tonight," Christine said salaciously.

"It's not nice to tease the help," Ricky scowled as she picked up her evening bag and slipped on her glasses. "Time to go."

"Not that I mind. I think they are very sexy," Christine smiled slightly, "but why are you wearing glasses?"

"I forgot my contacts," Ricky lied.

122

"I didn't know you wore contacts," Christine frowned.

"There is a lot about me that you don't know, Senator," Ricky said honestly.

##

"Wow, ladies," Crate grinned as the two women entered the ballroom. "You are gorgeous."

"Yeah," Barrel agreed. "You do know you are walking into a room full of hot-blooded Latinos, don't you?"

"What is that supposed to mean?" Christine demanded.

"It means don't get all huffy if they put their hands on your ass," Ricky grinned. "Of course, they will make it seem accidental or just part of steering you in the right direction."

Christine glared at her nemesis. "I trust you will be watching my backside, Major."

"Oh, you can count on it, Senator," Ricky grinned lasciviously.

Christine couldn't stop the flush of heat that ran up her body. "God, sometimes I hate you," she whispered.

"At least I arouse some emotion in you," Ricky shot back. "Incoming receiving line. Watch your backside."

Both women smiled and graciously responded to the introductions of the local officials. They were seated side-by-side at the table with Mayor Ramos, his wife and grown son Roberto. Ricky listened, entranced as Christine chatted with their host in perfect Spanish.

After dinner, various local dignitaries welcomed the senator and her friends. Wild applause greeted Christine as she stepped up to the podium. Ricky knew that Laredo was ninety-six percent Hispanic making it one of the least ethnically diverse cities in the United States. She was surprised the senator delivered her address in English instead of Spanish.

The senator spoke about the wall and the president's hope that it would decrease the poverty in their area by making jobs available only to American citizens. "We no longer want American citizens competing with illegals for American jobs," she said.

She talked about the additional jobs they would create in the border patrol and support jobs that would be available for American citizens. "I stress American Citizens," Christine emphasized.

"Legal immigrants will always be welcome in the United States. We welcome those who wish to become U.S. citizens and obey U.S. laws. We welcome those who wish to find a better way of life and to help our economy flourish. What we cannot continue to do is support illegals who only come to America to get on our welfare rolls. Every nation's economy has a breaking point, and the U.S. economy is badly bent right now."

Christine switched to fluent Spanish, "I spoke to you in English tonight because that is the language of the United States. Anyone who wants to be successful and thrive in the U.S. must take the time to learn English. Just as one desiring to do well in Mexico must learn to speak Spanish."

Ricky was extremely proud of the Texas senator as she laid out her vision for Texas and all Americans.

She understood why Senator Christine Richmond had such a loyal following. The woman was impressive and truly cared. No one applauded louder than Major Ricky Strong when Christine completed her speech and sat down.

"I am extremely proud to be seated next to you Senator Christine Richmond," Ricky said. The pride showed in the way her eyes sparkled.

Christine realized that Ricky had said, "Senator Christine Richmond," for the first time with something akin to reverence. She wished women could publicly dance together. She desperately wanted to hold the blonde woman in her arms.

"Senator," Roberto Ramos bowed from the waist, "please allow me the honor of this dance?"

Ricky's eyes narrowed as she watched the man pull Christine into his arms and move her around the dance floor.

"Your son is very handsome," Ricky said to Mrs. Ramos.

"Yes, we are very proud of him," the woman nodded.

"He appears to be very successful," Ricky smiled.

Certain the blonde couldn't speak Spanish; Mayor Ramos spoke sharply to his wife in Spanish, "Tell her he is a wealthy industrialist. I must check on the shipment to El Paso later tonight." He smiled pleasantly at Ricky then spoke in English. "Please excuse me a moment, I must speak to the caterer."

"My son is a wealthy industrialist," Mrs. Ramos smiled proudly. "He owns many warehouses.

"I read that Laredo is the oldest crossing point along the U.S.-Mexico border," Ricky smiled genuinely. "It is our nation's largest inland port of entry, and most of Laredo's economy is based on international trade with Mexico. I think that owning warehouses would be a very lucrative business."

Ricky didn't take her eyes off the couple on the dance floor. She almost laughed when Roberto's hands slid past Christine's waist to cup her hips. She fully expected the woman to slap him.

"Can you direct me to the ladies' room?" she asked Mrs. Ramos.

As she walked to the ladies' room, she spoke just loud enough for her earpiece to register her voice. "Crate, cut in on Senator Richmond. When the dance ends, both of you walk around the room with her while she networks. Stay close to her."

"Americans don't like whiskey," a waitress held a tray out to Ricky.

"They do if it is distilled correctly," Ricky answered the code words for her contact.

"Roberto is the white slave runner," the girl whispered. "A load of girls is bound for El Paso tonight. Watch out for your senator." She smiled then moved away to serve another guest.

Ricky visited the ladies' room in case anyone was watching her. She ascertained she was alone, then notified her team of Roberto's profession. When she returned to the hotel ballroom, Christine was laughing at a story Roberto was relating.

"Ah, how did we get two such beautiful ladies with us tonight?" Roberto slimed.

"Just our luck," Ricky said sarcastically. "Senator, we need to go. We leave very early in the morning."

"But Major Strong...," Christine started to toy with the blonde, but the look in Ricky's eyes stopped her. "Of course, you are right. Time flies when one is having fun."

"Perhaps I could accompany you to Del Rio," Roberto offered.

"You are welcome to do so," Ricky said, "But you must provide your own transportation. We are maxed out."

"I am certain the senator can find a space for me," Roberto smiled at Christine.

"That isn't up to the senator," Ricky frowned. "That is a decision that is mine alone."

Roberto begrudgingly nodded then took Christine's hand, bowed and kissed it. "Until we meet again, Senator Richmond. I hope it will be soon."

~~~

The silence during the limo ride back to the hotel spoke volumes about the mood of the women. Ricky recalled how concerned and caring Christine was about her constituents. She saw another side of Christine Richmond she had never seen before, and she loved her even more.

Christine was trying to reconcile the Ricky Strong she knew and the woman she saw kissing the dark-haired beauty at the airport. Ricky had chosen to spend their last three nights in Austin with another woman.

Christine pulled off her heels as soon as the elevator door closed. "You were right my feet are killing me. I am going to wear my house shoes all day tomorrow."

Ricky laughed at the vision of the impeccably dressed senator meeting dignitaries in her house shoes.

"I was very impressed with you tonight, Senator," Ricky said as she waited for the brunette to open her door.

"Thank you," Christine smiled appreciatively. She limped into her bedroom and collapsed onto the sofa.

Ricky went to her room. Christine was bitterly disappointed. As tired as she was, she wanted to be with the ranger.

"Would you mind removing your pantyhose?" Ricky innocently asked as she returned to Christine's room.

"Why don't *you* remove them?" Christine smiled sensuously.

"I, um, I am going to massage your feet," the ranger said holding up a tube of foot cream. "This stuff is incredible."

"Oh," Christine blushed. She chastely eased off her pantyhose and returned to her seat on the sofa, mortified that she had misread the ranger's intentions.

Ricky pulled the brunette's feet into her lap, forcing Christine to lie back against the arm of the sofa. She began to massage the cream into the left foot.

"Oh, my gosh, that feels so good," Christine moaned softly as the ranger's strong hands rubbed the soothing cream into her aching foot. "What is that? It is wonderful and cooling."

Ricky squeezed more of the cream into the palm of her hand then handed the tube to the senator.

"You are right about many things," Christine said softly.

"Umm, yes," Ricky smiled cockily, "I did see Roberto rubbing your…"

"I don't want to hear it," Christine said abruptly. "Thank you for sending Crate to save me."

"Roberto Ramos is the kingpin in the human trafficking ring we are trying to bring down." Ricky ran her thumbs back and forth over the balls of Christine's feet.

The senator closed her eyes and marveled at the feel of the ranger's hands stroking her aching feet. "I love your hands on me," she murmured as she drifted into a relaxed sleep.

"So, do I, Senator," Ricky smiled. "So, do I."

~~~

"Our destination today is Del Rio," Jeremiah informed the group. "It is a good three-to-four-hour ride. In two hours, we will make a brief stop at Eagle Pass for a luncheon honoring Senator Richmond.

"There will be a meeting with local politicians in Del Rio and another dinner tonight. We will stay in Del Rio's nicest hotel tonight and breakfast there in the morning. I think you will like it."

They boarded the bus that had become their traveling home. Christine went over the plans for the day with her staff and Ricky went to her bedroom to check in with Becky.

Ricky sent an email to Troy Hunter just to keep him interested. If his attention were on her, no other poor woman would die.

Eagle Pass was struggling between being a quaint Mexican town and a thriving city. Corruption among the local politicians was rampant, and Ricky knew there was currently an FBI investigation going on.

The town's public servants had a long history of breaking the law. With a ninety-eight percent Hispanic or Latino population, Eagle Pass residents were not proponents of the wall. They considered themselves more Mexico than U.S. citizens. The federal government was forced to sue them for access to build the wall along the Mexico-United States border.

At the luncheon, Christine again discussed the prosperity the increase in border patrol personnel and supporting agencies would bring to the area.

Ricky looked around the room. She spotted several men who had been at the dinner in Laredo. "We have a following," she said softly into her transmitter.

The senator intently listened as women talked to her about the violence and carnage perpetrated on Eagle Pass citizens by the drug cartels.

As they were walking to the buses, authorities detained a woman who was desperately trying to reach the senator.

"My daughter, my daughter," the woman cried. "El Monstruo took my daughter. Please, help me, Senator Richmond."

Christine turned to see who was calling to her. A well-dressed Latino woman was struggling to break free from the two policemen restraining her.

The senator nodded to Ricky. The ranger walked to the woman and took her by the arm. "I must pat you down for security reasons if you want to meet with the senator."

The woman nodded and held up her arms so the ranger could do a quick body search. She ascertained the woman had no weapons and led her to Christine.

"Thank you! Thank you, Senator," the woman shook Christine's hand. "I am Maria Alvarez. My daughter, Sofia has been taken."

"Kidnapped?" Christine frowned.

"Yes, Senator. They kidnapped her last night from our home. El Monstruo came to our home and took away my Sofia."

"The monster?" Christine raised a perfect eyebrow.

"That is what they call the soldiers of El Asesino," the mayor spoke up.

"Yes," the woman gasped. "They just break into homes and steal the young girls."

"El Asesino, the murder," Christine translated out loud. "Do you know where he took her?"

"No, Señora," the woman wailed. "El Asesino steals and rapes the young women of our town. Please, you must save my Sofia. She is only thirteen."

Maria's eyes darted around the crowd as if searching for anyone who might hurt her.

Christine turned to the mayor. "Who is this El Asesino?"

"He lives on the Mexico side of the border. We don't know who he is. He is very bad." The Mayor added. "He kills anyone who stands up to him."

"I am recording this, boss," Becky spoke through the receiver. "What do you want me to do?"

Ricky backed away from the crowd around Christine. "Tell Rhodes to have the governor contact Fort Bliss in El Paso and have the TACT team standing by for any emergency. I will talk to him tonight."

"Let's move this conversation inside the bus," Ricky recommended. She firmly grasped Maria's arm to guide her inside.

Once they were inside, Ricky gathered everyone around the kitchen table. "Are you in danger?" Ricky asked.

"I do not fear for myself," Maria cried. "I fear for my Sofia."

"Do you have other children at home?" Ricky continued.

"No, Sofia is my baby. The last of my children at home."

"So, if we take you with us, there is no one at home waiting for you?" the ranger asked.

"No, no one," Maria dried her eyes and looked at the ranger. "I can identify the men. I will testify. I will help the authorities. Please, just get my baby back."

"We will do everything we can," Christine promised the woman.

"May I speak with you alone, Senator?" Ricky addressed Christine officially.

Christine nodded and followed the ranger to her bedroom. Ricky locked the door and turned to tell Christine what she knew about the drug and human trafficking in the area.

Christine burst into tears. "This is so much worse than I ever imagined," she sobbed. "These people live in terror. Their children sold into white slavery, and anyone who protests is murdered. This should not be happening in the United States." She slipped her arms around Ricky and buried her face between the ranger's breasts.

Ricky held her tightly and stroked her back as she cried. "We are getting close to El Asesino. Maybe we can put an end to the nightmare these people face daily."

Christine tilted her tear-stained face to look in the ranger's blue eyes. Without thinking, Ricky gently kissed her. It was a sweet, loving kiss, a sharing of two battered souls seeking comfort in a world gone mad.

"Turn off your glasses, Major," Becky whispered into Ricky's earpiece.

~~~

Christine propped her back against the headboard of the ranger's bed and listened to the blonde discuss the logistics of the guard in El Paso with Director Crockett. She silently cursed herself for ending up in the ranger's bed last night. The thought of Ricky touching the other woman like she touched her made Christine's stomach lurch.

"I hope not, sir," Ricky said, "but this is a very dangerous situation down here.

"We picked up about a dozen rough-looking men in Laredo last night, and more joined them in Eagle Pass. We will spend the night in Del Rio tonight, tour the stations here, then head to El Paso.

"Sir, I have a bad feeling that there will be a deadly attempt to keep Senator Richmond from meeting with the Mexico and New Mexico governors.

"The drug cartel and the human traffickers will do anything in their power to stop the building of the wall. They are amassing a small army.

"I don't think she will do that, sir. I know. I will try.

"Yes, sir."

"What did he want you to do?" Christine asked.

"He wants to send a helicopter to pick you up and return you to Austin."

"I can't do that," Christine frowned. "Ricky, you know I have to see this through."

"I know," Ricky nodded. "I don't think the cartel will try anything in Del Rio. It is one of five cities in the United States with an FBI regional headquarters. The building is adjacent to the Roswell Hotel where we will be spending the night.

"I know some of the agents there. We will be able to pick up additional security to escort you to El Paso. I don't think the cartels will attack your caravan. We have too many law enforcement agencies involved."

Ricky sat down on the bed beside Christine. "When this is all over, we have to talk. I don't want to spend the rest of my life worrying about some assassin killing you."

"And I don't want to worry about some serial killer cutting you up into little bitty pieces," Christine spoke barely above a whisper.

"How did you find out?"

"You left your laptop on, and I read the emails," Christine grimaced. "He killed Kara, didn't he?"

"Yes," Ricky nodded. "You and I are in high-profile, dangerous jobs and if I know you, the governor's office is just a stepping stone to the presidency."

They stared into each other's eyes for several seconds, neither wanting to break the contact.

"Just...please sleep with me tonight," Christine pleaded. She hated herself for it, but she desperately needed Ricky Strong.

"Obviously, I can't help myself," Ricky sighed.

~~~

Del Rio was the most prosperous city they visited. The top employers in De Rio were Laughlin Air Force Base and the Border Patrol. The U. S. federal government supported the city.

As Ricky, had promised, the Roswell Hotel was next door to the FBI Regional Headquarters.

"I am going to take Mrs. Alvarez to the FBI and get her into protective custody," Ricky said as their bus pulled in front of the Roswell. "Crate and Barrel will stay right beside you until I get back."

"Will you be back in time to dress for the reception?" Christine smiled. "I like it when you wear those sexy cocktail dresses."

"The feeling is mutual," Ricky leaned down for a quick kiss, but the senator pulled her lips hard against her own. "I need you, Ricky Strong."

Crate and Barrel were waiting in the hallway. "Your lipstick is smeared, Major," Barrel pointed out.

"Thanks," Ricky slipped on her glasses. "You two stick to the senator like glue until I get back. Get her to her room as quickly as possible and make sure she stays there.

"I am going to see Hensley. He is going to take care of Mrs. Alvarez and get her out of harm's way."

~~~

Marcos Hensley was Ricky's first partner at the Texas Rangers. She trusted him with her life. He was also running the undercover operation within Roberto Ramos' cartel.

Marcos turned Mrs. Alvarez over to two of his most trusted agents then motioned for Ricky to follow him into his office.

"I have a problem," Marcos frowned. "I think I have a mole in my agency."

"Any suspects?" Ricky asked.

"No, but I have had safe houses compromised, and raids come up empty handed because women or drugs were moved hours before our arrival."

"Did it start with the arrival of anyone new or transferred in?" Ricky racked her brain for ways to determine who could be undermining their work.

"No. All of my team has been with me over five years," Marcos shook his head.

Ricky observed the bullpen where other agents were busy on phone calls or interviewing people. She suddenly pulled Marcos' blinds closed.

"What is wrong?" Marcos moved beside her as she lifted the blind slat.

"That guy, how long has he been here?" Ricky asked.

"You know him?"

"Yes, he was in New York," Ricky frowned. "Dave Adams. I always thought he was dirty, but couldn't prove it."

"How did you get involved with a New York FBI agent?" Marcos said.

"Long story, but the bottom line is his witness in the witness protection program died because someone leaked the location of the safe house. I always believed it was him.

"He headed a team that was supposed to protect a mafia princess who agreed to testify against her father and his mob. The mob came after her. Her cousin shot her father and brother, and she disappeared.

"Her cousin said one of the mafia lieutenants took her."

"Yeah, I read about that," Marcos gasped. "Carlos Zamboni, a nasty guy. The FBI screwed that up seven ways to Sunday. You think this guy was the leak?"

"I do. Did your leaks begin after Adams' arrival?"

"Yeah, about that time," Marcos said thoughtfully, "but he isn't on my team. He isn't privy to that kind of information. Apparently, someone higher up shares your feelings because he is just a pencil pusher here."

"Don't let him know about Mrs. Alvarez," Ricky warned. "I need her for a federal witness."

"I will inform my team of your suspicions, right now. We will keep Mrs. Alvarez safe until we can turn her over to your people," Marcos promised.

"Will I see you at the reception tonight?" Marcos grinned. "We are supposed to dance, mingle and keep an eye on Senator Richmond."

"I will be there doing the same thing," Ricky laughed.

"Good," Marcos winked, "We can dance."

~~~

The reception was one of the nicest Ricky had ever attended. The Mayor and his staff had spared nothing in their efforts to make the senator's visit a memorable one.

FBI and Border Patrol personnel were everywhere mingling with the guests and dancing with the single ladies.

"This is impressive," Christine brushed lightly against the ranger's breasts as she slid between Ricky and her chair. "So are you," she smiled.

"Umm, careful, Senator, unless you want to leave early," Ricky smiled playfully.

"Oh, I do, but you know how that goes," Christine frowned.

A waiter poured wine in Christine's glass then turned to Ricky. "Americans don't like whiskey," he said.

"They do if it is distilled correctly," Ricky smiled.

"Come, I will get you the finest," he nodded toward the bar.

Ricky walked closely beside him as they approached the bar. "The man in the white sports jacket is an informer, a mole in your FBI operation," he whispered.

"The one approaching the senator?" Ricky grimaced.

"Yes."

"One scotch on the rocks for the lady," the waiter told the bartender.

Ricky sipped the scotch and remembered how much she disliked the taste of alcohol. She sat it down on the table and took a seat that allowed her to watch the dance floor.

Dave Adams was in his early forties, average height and, ruggedly handsome with pale gray eyes. His broad shoulders and muscular build would induce any woman to trust him. Ricky could understand how a young girl in Martina's situation would have fallen for him.

Christine returned to the table with her new dance partner in tow. "Major Ricky Strong, I would like you to meet Agent Dave Adams."

"Agent Adams," Ricky ignored the hand Dave held out to her. "New York get tired of you?"

"More like I got tired of New York," Adams grinned. "Thought I'd give the wide-open spaces a try."

"How long have you been here?"

"Little over three years," Dave shrugged. "I've never gotten over losing Marta. I hoped a change of scenery would help. It hasn't."

Ricky nodded without taking her eyes from Adam's face. She had no words for how much she hated the man.

"Major Strong," Marcos strode to their table, "and I would know you anywhere, Senator Richmond," he semi-bowed, pulled Christine's hand to his lips and kissed it. "We are honored to have you in our city."

"Marcos Hensley is a man you can trust, Senator Richmond," Ricky smiled falsely, "unlike Agent Adams."

"Ricky, I loved her," Adams blurted out. "I would never hurt her."

"Yeah, but you couldn't keep her alive could you, Adams?"

The rest of the evening went without incident. Christine's presentation was well received, and many of the town's residents crowded around her seeking more details about the planned wall.

Christine kicked off her heels as the elevator door closed. Ricky smiled and leaned down for a much-welcomed kiss.

"You were wonderful tonight," she murmured against Christine's lips.

"Good enough to warrant one of your incredible foot rubs?" Christine tiptoed to kiss the ranger again.

"Good enough to warrant anything you want from me," Ricky grinned mischievously. "Anything you want, Senator."

~~~

Chapter 11

Soft lips pulled Christine from a deep, peaceful sleep. She always slept soundly in the ranger's arms. "Time to get up, Senator," Ricky kissed the hollow of her neck."

"Not right now?" Christine whispered as she pulled the blonde over her.

"Thirty minutes," Ricky grinned.

"That's enough time." Christine pulled her lover into her arms, thrilling to the soft, strength of the other woman.

"Why isn't she answering?" Daisy worried. "I need to give her this information immediately. She doesn't have on her glasses. Where does the monitor show her chip?"

"On top of the Senator's chip," Becky answered in hushed tones.

"On top of the...Oh! My gosh." Daisy gasped. "That is not good."

After breakfast, Christine thanked her hosts for their graciousness. Ricky stood off to the side talking with Marcos.

"You may be right, Major," Marcos frowned. "After the reception, last night, Adams went back to the agency and surfed the computers trying to find Maria Alvarez."

141

"I am concerned for the senator's safety," Ricky confided in her friend. "More men joined the ones who have been following us. We picked up a few followers at our first stop, and everywhere we stop we pick up additional characters.

"It is 425 miles to El Paso. You know these cartels. Do you think they would attack our buses between here and El Paso?"

"They've done worse," Marcos frowned. "They have staged all-out wars on the police in several towns. I can send a team of agents with you if it would make you feel better."

"It would," Ricky nodded. "I have picked up reinforcements in each town, but I am sure their numbers are increasing faster than ours."

"Give me thirty minutes, and I will have a team here to escort you," Marcos said.

Ricky explained to the senator what was happening. "I don't like the delay," Christine frowned. "Surely you don't think the cartel would attack a Texas senator."

"Look around you, Senator Richmond," Ricky spoke softly. "See many familiar faces?"

"I see what you mean," Christine grimaced as she identified several rough looking characters that had followed them from town to town. "As usual, you are right. Can we wait on the bus? It is sweltering out here."

"Yes, I need to report into headquarters, Ricky nodded."

Once they were alone in Ricky's room, Christine voiced her concern about the buildup of fire power the ranger was amassing.

"The last thing I need is a border war," Christine frowned. "Please, be careful, Ricky."

"That is what I am trying to avoid," the ranger nodded. "I believe a show of power will keep the DTO's from attacking us.

"DTO's?" Christine raised a quizzical eyebrow.

"Drug Trafficking Organizations," Ricky replied.

"Ranger Company E is headquartered in El Paso. They are on their way to meet us now. They will accompany us to El Paso. I believe we will be safe once we are there.

"I have the Austin Ranger Reconnaissance Team shadowing us. They are always within fifty miles of us. The helicopter you occasionally hear buzzing the caravan is from my people. They are a highly trained tactical team."

As promised, Marcos' men arrived in six pickups armed with heavy artillery guns mounted in the pickup beds. "These puppies are almost as good as tanks," Marcos grinned as he patted the hood of his truck. "This baby is mine. We will put three in front and three behind your caravan. I will be accompanying you to El Paso, Major."

"Thanks, Marcos,' Ricky nodded. "I guess we better get started."

"I'll ride with Marcos at the front of our group," Crate said. "Barrel will be in the last truck."

Just as they had done since the beginning of the trip, Ricky and Christine watched out the window as they rolled past the border fence.

"What the? Stop the bus," Christine commanded.

"Wait," Senator," Ricky caught Christine's arm and pulled her close. "It is a bad idea to get off the bus out here in the middle of nowhere."

"Look out the window," Christine commanded. "Is that a woman's head on the spike of that fence?"

Ricky looked out the window and gritted her teeth as she saw the depravity of the cartel on display. The head of a young woman had been raggedly severed close to the shoulders and mounted on the fence. Blood still dripped from the macabre exhibit. "Keep moving," she yelled as Christine hid her face in the ranger's arms.

"You can't help her now," Ricky whispered, "and you don't want to join her. We can't stop the buses."

Christine pulled herself together. "We will stop in Presidio in a couple of hours," Christine informed her staff. "The American Legion Auxiliary is hosting a luncheon for us."

"I would advise skipping that stop," Ricky frowned. Presidio isn't much to look at, and it doesn't have much of a police department. It is a border crossing into Ojinaga, Mexico. The school district and border patrol are the major employers. It is out in the middle of Bum -humped Egypt."

Christine looked at her watch. "Major Strong, I couldn't just drive through and not stop. That would be a definite snub to the people who are supporting me."

Ricky hated it when Christine addressed her by her official title. That meant she was establishing her authority and wouldn't change her mind.

"Whatever you say, Senator Richmond," the ranger scowled. "Just promise me, if I say run to the buses, you will run as if your life depends on it."

Ricky checked her map. "It is a little over two-hundred-and-fifty miles from Presidio to El Paso. We will be traveling thru the most godforsaken country you will ever see."

Christine couldn't suppress the shudder that ran through her body. "Even worse than what we have already been through?"

"Godforsaken," Ricky repeated.

~~~

The American Legion Hall was a stand-alone building with only a parking lot around it. *Not a good place to make a stand*, Ricky thought.

Local police and the Mayor greeted Christine as she stepped off the bus. "Leah, you stick with the senator," Ricky said under her breath.

Marcos approached her. "I don't like the lay of the land here," he frowned. "There are several pickup trucks parked one street over. I am pretty sure they are here up to no good."

Ricky looked around. "Let's encircle the Legion Hall with the buses and news vans. Place one of your trucks every other vehicle. We will have her covered from all sides, and anyone who is coming after her must go through us.

"Boss," Becky spoke through Ricky's glasses. "Rangers from El Paso are approaching your location."

"Thanks, Becky, tell the helicopter to make itself known. Just hover around us until I get her back on the bus."

"Ten-four, Major," Becky giggled at her response.

"Crate, Barrel come back to my bus, please," Rick instructed as she boarded their bus.

For the first-time Ricky pulled her heavy duffle bag from under her bed.

"I want you to keep these with you at all times. Here are extra magazines." She handed each ranger a Colt AR15 and slung one over her shoulder.

"Sweet, Major, how did you score these babies?" Simultaneously Crate and Barrel shoved a magazine into their gun.

"Compliments of Senator Richmond," Ricky smiled. "They were in the budget she approved last month."

"So were these." She tossed each man a set of body armor and a bullet-proof vest. "Keep these on. I know it is hot, but things could get hotter before we meet up with our team from El Paso. We are heading into the Texas badlands. A perfect place for an ambush."

Christine was nervous without Ricky by her side. She looked over the people that had crowded into the American Legion Hall to see her. As in earlier towns, she identified many faces she did not consider friendly.

For the first time, Senator Richmond was afraid. She felt like a target standing in front of the crowd. A slight commotion at the door on her left made her cringe and almost duck behind the podium. Then she saw Crate and Barrel enter the hall. They wore tactical gear. Each man cradled a destructive looking weapon. They stood on either side of her as she gave her speech.

Outside Ricky and the others stood guard. "Major," Becky's voice came through her glasses, "the helicopter pilot says the gang in their pickups are moving out. They appear to be leaving."

"We're coming out, boss," Crate informed her.

Ricky was standing with her back to the Legion Hall when Christine and her entourage emerged. Christine clutched Crate's arm for support. The sight of the blonde in tactical garb and a rifle slung over her shoulder brought home to the senator the seriousness of their situation. It also sent a warm sensation throughout her body. Ricky turned, and her crooked smile told Christine she hated all the drama but knew it was necessary.

They settled beside each other as their caravan began to roll. "We have a gang in pickup trucks somewhere ahead of us," Ricky leaned down and spoke softly into the brunette's ear.

"Umm, Major, do you have any idea how sexy you are in your SWAT outfit and that big gun?"

"This isn't a SWAT outfit," Ricky laughed. "It is our tactical dress. Thanks to you we received these armor vests and the AR15s just before we started this trip. They will probably save our lives."

"How good are you with that thing?" Christine asked, touching the barrel of the rifle.

"I am perfect," Ricky grinned.

"I will check that out later," Christine's dark eyes searched the ranger's looking for a promise that there would be a later.

Ricky nodded.

"You know, if I have a choice, I choose to get to El Paso without a border war," Christine leaned hard against her lover.

"You and I share the same goal," Ricky assured her. "I don't think these clowns will attack us with all the firepower we have around you."

"Boss, the helicopter pilot reports a roadblock ahead," Becky said softly.

"Crate?" Ricky whispered.

"Looks like they have dragged a dead tree across the road and anything else they could find to stop us," Crate responded.

"Can Marcos destroy it?"

Ricky listened as Crate and Marcos discussed the damage Marcos' guns could do.

"Yeah, Boss, we got it handled. We are speeding up so we can have it cleared by the time you get there."

After several minutes of silence, the afternoon was filled with the rapid fire of Marcos' PKT Machine Gun, mounted in the rear of his pickup.

The buses slowed as they passed over the splintered remains of the trees the heavy artillery guns had reduced to toothpicks.

"Major," Becky said softly, "the El Paso Rangers have joined your little party."

Ricky called Christine's attention to the cloud of dust rolling toward them. "Reinforcements are here. The El Paso Rangers just joined us."

The rest of the trip was uneventful. The tired senator and her retinue departed their buses and entered their hotel.

"I am dying to take a shower," Ricky said as they boarded the elevator. Dirt is caked on every inch of me."

"I am going to soak in a nice hot tub," Christine said wistfully.

~~~

Ricky dressed and went downstairs to meet with the men who had formed Christine's impromptu army. The local police reported that the DTOs had arrived in El Paso ahead of the senator's party.

Marcos informed her that his men were taking turns standing guard at the elevators and stairwells. Anyone trying to get to the senator would have to go through them.

The local ranger team had placed snipers in buildings around the hotel. The Austin Tactical Squad was close by if needed. Local law enforcement officers stood at every entrance and exit of the hotel. Their presence in the lobby was very evident. The FBI team had checked into the hotel one at a time and made themselves at home in the hotel bar and dining room. They vanished into the hotel's clientele.

Ricky's room adjoined the senator's. Crate and Barrel had rooms on either side of the hallway leading to Christine's suite.

Ricky was glad that all the pomp and circumstance was scheduled for the next day. Right now, all she wanted was a good night's sleep.

Christine had opened the door between their rooms and was waiting for her when she entered her room. A slow, soul searing kiss made the blond forget about sleep. "I had room service bring dinner," Christine mumbled against Ricky's lips. "Do you want to eat while it is still hot?"

"Probably should," Ricky murmured as she pulled the brunette tighter against her. "But then I always did like cold food."

Christine kissed the hollow of the blonde's neck and trailed her hands down the ranger's sides to her hips. "I need you in my life, Ricky Strong."

Ricky's teeth nibbled at the senator's full lower lip. "God, I love your lips," she sighed.

Christine ran the tip of her tongue along the ranger's lip then slowly slipped between her teeth. As their tongues languidly explored each other's mouth, Ricky moved the senator to the bed.

She kissed her way down Christine's neck as she removed her blouse. Christine's soft hands slid under Ricky's pullover. She gasped as she explored the soft silkiness of the ranger. In one effortless move, she pushed the blonde's shirt over her head exposing perfect breasts straining against the bra that stood between them. She slipped her hands behind Ricky's back and expertly released the bra, letting it fall to the floor without breaking their kiss.

Ricky pushed Christine's blouse to the floor and unfastened her bra. Christine's eyes had gone from brown to black with desire, and the ranger knew their food would get very, very cold.

～～～

The intrusive tone from Ricky's cell phone broke through the deep sleep of the ranger. Reluctantly, she released the woman sleeping in her arms and rolled over to answer the phone.

"Yes sir, I understand," Ricky spoke softly into the phone to keep from waking Christine. "As soon as the dinner is over. Yes, sir,"

...

"Major Strong," Deputy Director Rhodes grumbled, "why are you whispering?"

"I am surrounded, sir."

"Oh, okay," Rhodes spoke softer. "I will personally pick you up at the airport tonight. I want a full debriefing before the local press rips into you."

"Yes, sir. Goodbye, sir."

"I can tell by all the 'Yes, sirs,' that was your boss," Christine snuggled closer into the blonde. "Umm, you smell incredible."

"He doesn't want us to spend the night here tonight. He wants us to leave immediately after the dinner."

"That is fine with me," Christine teased the blonde's nipple with her teeth.

"Oh, God," Ricky gasped. "Do you know what you are doing to me?"

"Yes," Christine hissed.

~~~

"What is the schedule for today?" Ricky asked as she dressed.

"Breakfast this morning," Christine backed up to the blonde so she could zip up her dress. "Then meetings until the luncheon. After lunch, we will cuss and discuss some more then vote on items, we have worked out. All the players sign the agreements. Dinner tonight where I thank everyone for their gracious hospitality, and then I am in your hands to get me home."

Ricky grinned mischievously. "I am looking forward to that. Since all the meetings will be in this hotel, all our security will remain in place until we depart. A helicopter is parked at a helipad about two blocks away. We will be escorted to the chopper and on our way home."

"Can't happen fast enough," Christine sighed.

~~~

Christine looked like a million dollars. Her dark burgundy business suit set the serious tone for the meetings; fitted skirt, barely-pink silk blouse and a fitted jacket that somehow hugged her perfect figure yet allowed her the freedom to be as animated as she wanted to be to make a point. She let her dark hair fall loosely around her shoulders. Dangling earrings sparkled whenever the light hit them. In short, she was breathtaking and in her element.

Ricky gave up the pretense of being anything but a Texas Ranger. Dressed in a black jumpsuit and a bullet-proof vest with Ranger emblazoned across the back, she was obviously the lead security director for the senator. She wished she could put a bullet-proof vest on Christine, but knew the woman would never allow such an intrusion on her perfect attire.

The day went smoothly with only a few disagreements about the wall. Roberto Ramos and his father had traveled to El Paso to have input in the meeting.

The governors of the smaller towns wanted open borders that allowed for the easy exchange of traffic from one side to the other. The towns often ran together oblivious of the imaginary border that separated their countries. The senator's finesse and diplomacy finally won them over, and everyone signed the pact to construct the wall.

There were no signs of the threatening gang that had shadowed the senator for the past week. A fact that made Major Strong extremely uneasy. She liked knowing the location of her adversaries.

"One more function and this nightmare will be over," Christine groaned as she fell onto the sofa and kicked off her heels. "When this is over, I may wear tennis shoes for the rest of my life."

"I have a meeting with our lead agents in five minutes," Ricky leaned down and kissed Christine. "Why don't you take your shower and I will give you one of my famous foot massages when I return?"

"Promise?" Christine slipped her hand behind Ricky's neck and pulled the ranger's lips back to her own for a serious kiss. "Hurry, please, I want the VIP massage."

~~~

"Crate, Barrel, you two stay with her at all times," Ricky instructed her go-to agents. "Marcos, your team is awesome. I can't tell you how much we appreciate your help. I'll leave the coordination of everyone else up to you."

She handed out new earbuds. "Make certain everyone has these on so we can communicate.

"As soon as she finishes shaking hands and making nice with everyone, we will disappear behind the panels my men have erected at the front of the room. Our doubles will walk out the other side and hurry to the elevators. We will take the stairwell to the parking garage, meet our ride and head for the chopper a block away.

"Look me up next time you are in Austin. Dinner and drinks are on me."

~~~

The farewell dinner for Senator Christine Richmond was elaborate and entertaining. Elegantly dressed performers presented Mexican Folk Dances and received a standing ovation. An excellent Mariachi Band had everyone clapping and singing along as they sang some of the most popular Mexican songs.

Christine's presentation was well received as she praised the Texas and Mexican politicians for laying the groundwork for securing the borders of both countries.

By the time the evening was over Christine was certain she had danced with every male in the room. It took all the self-control she had to keep from limping from the room when the function ended.

As they stepped into the stairwell leading to the parking garage, Ricky pushed a pair of slip-on tennis shoes into Christine's hands. She patiently waited as Christine removed her heels and blissfully sighed as she slipped on the comfortable shoes.

"Oh," the senator moaned, "these shoes feel wonderful. I think I am in love with you, Major Strong."

"You know what they say?" Ricky grinned, "The way to a woman's heart is through her feet." She quickly stuffed Christine's heels into her backpack then led Christine down the stairs.

"Two flights of stairs, then you can sit down in the car," Ricky promised.

As they descended the dimly-lit stairs, something bit Ricky on the neck. "Ouch," She gasped as she reached to the spot of the sting.

"Oh," Christine hissed as she felt the same sting.

"Are you okay?" Ricky whispered.

"I think so. Something bit me," Christine frowned as she rubbed her neck. "I've been hit with a small…"

"Me, too. Let's get out of here," Ricky growled.

They reached the door to the garage. It was locked.

"What the hell?" Ricky raged. "I will have someone's head for this."

"Why don't you take mine?" Roberto Ramos stood in the shadows under the stairwell.

"Boss, what is going on?" Becky's anguished cry startled the ranger. "Major, we can't see a thing. The lighting is too dim."

Ricky reached for her gun, but her movements were slow and jerky. Everything was beginning to move, running together forming one big warped landscape. Something was wrong. She caught Christine as the brunette lurched forward then slid to the floor. The ranger struggled for her gun but soon joined the senator in a heap on the floor. Her glasses flew across the floor and landed under the stairs.

"Drag them into the boiler room," Ramos ordered the two men who joined him. "You hit them with enough Diazepam to kill them or knock them out for a very long time. Hide their bodies; we will come back for them when the furor dies down."

The men followed instructions then all three of them disappeared into a door hidden beneath the stairwell. They locked it from the inside then quickly followed the long hallway that led to the building's electrical maintenance area. After ascertaining that no one was in the hallway outside the room, they slipped into the hallway and ran to the loading dock at the back of the hotel.

Local police officers stopped the men as they exited the hotel. "Have you found them?" Ramos demanded. "Please tell me you have found them."

"No, sir, not yet," the rookie policeman answered.

"Has anyone checked the service elevators?" Ramos asked.

"Yes, sir, the FBI made a sweep of every floor. They have disappeared into thin air."

"Officer," Ramos hailed a border patrolman, "Is there any news?" Ramos and his two henchmen jumped from the loading dock and joined the patrolman.

"No, sir. We have sealed off every entrance and are making a floor by floor sweep. The Mayor has called in all officers to help. Not to mention all the Texas Rangers swarming this place."

"Surely, we will find them," Ramos fell into step with the patrolman as he walked to the front of the hotel. "If we don't, we will have an international incident on our hands."

"Trust me, sir," the patrolman snorted, "A Texas Ranger and a State Senator kidnapped, we will have more than an incident on our hands. We will have a major catastrophe. Countries have gone to war over less."

Ramos and his bodyguards followed the patrolman into the hotel, then mingled in with the rest of the detained guests.

~~~

Ricky could tell she was moving. It took her a few minutes to determine she and Christine were in a wire dog kennel in the back of a truck. The four-by-four-by-four cage was too small to allow her to stand. She had no idea where they were going.

A quick check of the senator's pulse told Ricky the brunette was alive but still unconscious.

"Is anyone else in here?" she called.

"Yes! Yes!" Several voices whispered anxiously.

"Do you know where we are?" Ricky asked.

"In a truck," a voice close by answered. "We are being transported over the border to be sold."

Ricky discovered her badge and gun were gone. So were her glasses and earwig. Her people had no idea how to find her. *How the hell did I let this happen?* She cursed herself. She was surprised to find her ankle holster still held Martina's Beretta Nano. *They probably took my service pistol and looked no further.*

"Do you know where they are taking us?" she asked the voice.

"Probably to the warehouse district in Juarez. I overheard one of the guards say they would hold us for a few days then export us in a shipping container.

"I think they are bringing in other women so they will have a full load."

A soft moan beside her indicated Christine was regaining consciousness. *I would almost trade my gun for a bottle of water*, Ricky thought.

"How long have we been traveling?" Ricky asked her new source of information.

"Two, maybe three hours," the woman answered softly.

Christine shook her head, then sat up. She looked around trying to ascertain any images in the darkness.

The ranger touched her gently. "We've been kidnapped," Ricky said softly. "We are in a truckload of women headed to a warehouse. Are you okay?"

"I think so," Christine moved closer to the blonde. "I have a bitch of a headache."

"They drugged us," Ricky said.

The truck slowed then stopped entirely. The double doors at the back of the truck opened, and a man a little taller than Ricky climbed into the vehicle.

"Lay down," Ricky whispered. "Pretend you are still unconscious." To her surprise, Christine obeyed immediately.

The man swept the beam of a strong flashlight over the cages. It came to rest on the cage containing Christine and Ricky. "Ahh," he grinned maliciously. "I have been thinking about you. I like palominos."

Ricky caught her breath. She was afraid he had come for Christine, but he wanted her. The ranger glared at the man as if he were garbage.

"Come on Lucho," his compadres called. "We are ready to go."

The man walked to the truck's open doors. "I think I will ride back here. Have a little fun."

The other two men hooted and catcalled to him as he pulled the doors to and shoved the lever into place to secure them. He turned his light back on Ricky.

"Your friend is dead," he grinned.

"I know," Ricky agreed loudly.

"Then she won't disturb us." The man cautiously approached the cage. He flashed his light around the truck over the other women. Ricky made a quick guess that the truck contained about twenty women, all locked in the dog-kennel type cages.

Ricky pushed her back against the cage wall and pulled her knees against her chest. If he wanted her, he would have to get on his hands and knees to pull her out.

"I'm going to shoot your friend just to make certain she is dead," Lucho pointed his gun toward Christine. "Or you can come out of the cage, so I won't have to worry about her."

Ricky quickly scooted to the cage door as he fished a ring of keys from his pocket. Christine's hand touched her back.

Lucho opened the cage and stepped back. Ricky crawled out and started to stand. The man shoved her back down. "On your knees is a good place to start," he callously laughed as he unbuckled his belt. He held the light on her face. She wondered where his gun was.

"Pull down my pants," he commanded, grabbing her hair and shoving her face between his legs.

She nuzzled the zipper of his jeans, then stroked the inside of his leg. He threw back his head and groaned as she rubbed him through his jeans.

"Pull down my pants," he demanded, roughly pulling her hair.

She unfastened the brass button and slowly unzipped his jeans. She almost gagged when she realized he had on no underwear. The stench from him was unbearable. She pulled down his jeans and tried to keep from puking on him.

"Suck me," he growled.

Ricky's mind was running through scenarios a mile a minute. No solution presented itself. If she was going to keep them alive, she had to do as he dictated.

159

A loud sound like the truck backfiring rang out. Ricky watched in amazement as a hole opened between Lucho's eyes and spurted blood in every direction. The man's eyes went wide as he crumbled to the truck floor.

Ricky grabbed his flashlight and looked around. Christine was kneeling in the cage. The Kimber was still pointed in the direction of the man.

Neither woman spoke. They didn't need to.

Ricky searched the criminal and found the keys to the cages and his gun.

She pulled Christine to her feet. "Great shot, Babe."

"Babe..." Christine's indignation was cut off by the ranger's lips on hers.

Christine put the Kimber back in her thigh holster. They unlocked the cages and helped the women out.

"You have a name?" Ricky asked the voice that had been giving her information.

"Sofia Alvarez," the woman said.

"Maria Alvarez's daughter," Ricky raised a quizzical eyebrow.

"Yes," Sofia grinned. "Is my mother okay?"

"She is," Ricky assured her. "She is very worried about you."

The women gathered around Christine and Ricky. "Our only chance is to take the other two by surprise," Ricky said. "Hopefully wherever they are taking us won't be guarded."

"These three have moved us all along the border," Sofia informed her. "They are the only gang members we have seen. But I am certain they are taking us to Juarez. There may be others at the warehouse."

160

"That's a chance we must take," Ricky shrugged. She pulled the dead man's gun from her shoulder holster, dropped the magazine and examined the bullets in it. "Full," she grinned.

~~~

The traffickers' truck pulled into the dimly-lit warehouse district. A single light burned at each end of a long row of storage buildings. The truck stopped long enough for the one riding shotgun to jump out and open a couple of storage unit doors.

"Back the truck up until I tell you to stop," he yelled at the driver. "We don't want to carry the cages any further than we have to."

The truck backed up then stopped, and both men pounded on the vehicle's doors.

"Hey, Lucho, stop screwing around and open the door. The boss will be here at midnight. We want to take a turn, too."

One of the truck doors swung open, and Lucho stood motionless. Both men stared up at him. "Hey man, get that damn light out of our faces," they shielded their eyes from the flashlight.

Ricky shoved Lucho with all her strength as Christine kept the bright light trained on the faces of the men. Ricky fired two shots. Each shot killed a trafficker. She jumped down from the truck bed and surveyed their surroundings. The three dead men were all she saw. She searched their bodies and added two more 9mm's to her gun arsenal. "Help me drag their bodies into the storage unit," she yelled.

Several women jumped from the back of the truck and pulled the men into the unit and locked the door.

"What now?" Christine whispered.

"We should split up," Ricky frowned. "We will be spotted too easily if we all travel together.

"Sofia, can you use a gun?"

Sofia nodded, yes.

"You take ten of the women," Ricky directed as she handed a pistol to the young woman. "Anyone else good with a pistol?"

A tall, statuesque woman stepped forward. "I am."

A car stopped at the gate and keyed in a passcode to enter the warehouse area.

"Quick, everyone back into the truck and hold on." Ricky yelled. "We are going to make a run for the Juarez crossing.

"I can drive," the tall woman volunteered. "You may need to provide firepower."

All the women scampered into the back of the truck, and Ricky closed the door. "You got a name?" Ricky asked their driver as the woman slowly edged the truck toward the gate.

"Lorinda," she grinned. "Hold tight, as soon as the car clears the gate; we are going through."

As the car rolled toward the truck, Lorinda eased down on the foot pedal and dragged the truck down the side of the town car, ripping off one of its wheels. "That should slow them down," she laughed as she rolled through the gate and onto the highway.

The women were only a few miles from the border crossing when a tractor trailer pulled across the road impeding their travel.

"God," Lorinda gasped, "if they stop us now, we will never get away." She checked her side mirror. Another one is behind me," she cried.

"I'll move the one in front of you," Ricky yelled as she opened the door and jumped from their truck. She ran around the front of Lorinda's truck and emptied her gun through the side window of the truck blocking their way. She yanked open the door and pulled out the dead driver, taking his place. As soon as the opening was large enough, Lorinda started the big truck rolling, again. Ricky waited until she passed then pulled the truck back across the road, blocking their pursuers. Taking the keys, she jumped out the passenger side and ran for the truck carrying Christine. She leaped onto the running board. "Gun it," she yelled as shots rang out.

"How much further?" Christine screamed.

"Couple of miles," Lorinda downshifted as the truck started down a steep grade.

"Can't you go any faster?" Christine cried. "She is a moving target hanging off the side of this truck."

"This ain't exactly a candidate for the Indie 500," Lorinda growled as she shifted gears on the lumbering truck. "Don't worry, your highness, we're gonna' make it."

Christine placed her hand over Ricky's hand that was clinging to the door frame. Ricky smiled and mouthed, "I love you."

Bullets peppered the truck as the traffickers drew closer to them. One minute Ricky was grinning crazily at Christine, and the next minute she was flying off the side of the truck as a bullet ripped through her right shoulder.

"Stop! Stop," Christine screamed beating on Lorinda's back.

"Then she will die in vain," Lorinda shook her head as she floored the accelerator.

Christine threw open the truck door and jumped from the truck. *Not my best idea*, she thought as she plowed through the sand beside the road.

Checking to make sure she was in one piece; the senator lay still as the truck sped away. Cars flew by in hot pursuit. One car pulled to a stop in the middle of the road, and armed men jumped from it looking for the figure that had jumped from the truck.

~~~

Christine shook her head trying to clear the cobwebs. She was in a small, dark room. The only light came through ill-fitting slats that formed the sides of the lean-to.

A bloody body lay twisted beside her. It took her a minute to realize the body was Ricky's. "Oh, no, God, please?" she whimpered as she searched for the ranger's wrist to see if she had a pulse.

A door burst open spilling bright daylight into the room. "The senator is awake," a rough voice called out in Spanish. "Tell el jefe. He has been waiting for her." The door slammed, and she heard the door bolt jam into position.

"Ricky, Ricky, baby, please say something." She kissed the ranger's bloody face. "Please, Ricky, I can't lose you."

The blonde laid lifeless. Christine checked to see if Ricky still had a gun. She did not. A quick touch to her own thigh told the senator she still had the small Kimber in her thigh holster. Obviously, her captures thought she was harmless. She pulled it out and took off the safety. It was ready to fire. If Ricky were dead, she would go down fighting, too.

She heard the slide bolt groan as someone unlocked the door. She put her hand, holding the gun, on the floor between herself and Ricky. Weak fingers closed around the gun, and it disappeared beneath the ranger.

Two men entered the shack. "See, El Asesino, I told you we have the Texas Senator," Roberto Ramos leered.

"You!" Christine glared at the man they called El Asesino.

"You seem surprised, Senator," the drug lord smiled.

El Asesino walked to the two women. He nudged Ricky's body roughly. "She is dead," he grunted.

"Well done, Roberto," El Asesino's voice was soft but vibrant. "We will soon be rid of the meddling senator, too. When will you ship out the next load of women?"

"Tomorrow morning," Roberto answered.

"Humm," El Asesino hummed thoughtfully, "perhaps you would like to have the senator until then."

"Yes, El Jefe. I would enjoy that very much."

"Make certain she goes to Syria," El Asesino snorted. "She won't live long there. She can identify me."

The man looked hard at Christine. "On second thought, don't take any chances. Use her until you get tired of her, share her with your men, then kill her yourself."

The two men exited the shack laughing about their plans for Senator Christine Richmond.

An hour later Roberto returned alone.

"Ah, we meet again, Senorita," Roberto Ramos sneered as he focused his flashlight on them, "and under circumstance more to my liking."

Moving faster than Christine could imagine, Ramos grabbed her by the shoulders and yanked her to her feet.

"Are you crazy?" she yelled. "Do you know who I am?"

"Yes," Ramos snarled. "You are my whore. At least until I get tired of you, then I will sell you repeatedly to the highest bidder."

Christine fought with all her strength, but she was no match for the bigger man. He roughly shoved her back against the door as he ripped off what remained of her dress.

"Don't fight so hard, Senator Richmond," Ramos cruelly laughed as he pinned her against the door. "You will like this, I promise."

She spat in his face and yanked her hand loose long enough to drag her fingernails down his face. He slapped her hard. Blood ran from her lip as she cried out.

"You like it rough, Senator?" he glared. "I figured you would." Crushing her wrists against the wall above her head, he unbuckled his belt and let his pants slide down to his knees. "This will just be a quickie, to let you know what you have to look forward to later. Tonight, I will take my time with you."

Christine closed her eyes and clenched her teeth as she felt him move against her.

Ricky was scared to take a shot left-handed but had no choice. Her right arm was useless. She struggled to her knees and tried to stop her arm from shaking as she sighted the Kimber. She wanted a kill shot. She would either kill Ramos or Christine. She knew the brunette would rather die than endure what Ramos had planned for her. Ricky squeezed off the shot.

Christine's knees buckled, and she slowly slid down the wall of the shack. She wasn't strong enough to hold up the dead weight of Roberto Ramos. She struggled to shove the dead man off her, then scampered across the floor to Ricky.

"Can you walk?" Christine whispered as she peppered the blonde's face with kisses. "You can lean on me. Wait a minute."

The senator stripped Ramos' shirt from him and tied the sleeves around the ranger's neck. She gently pulled Ricky's injured arm into the makeshift sling she had fashioned.

"Get his gun and flashlight," Ricky said hoarsely.

Christine realized that Ramos had ripped her dress off and she was only wearing panties and a bra. She stripped Ramos of his undershirt and slacks. She quickly dressed in the dead man's clothes, cinching the waist tight with the belt and rolling up the pants legs.

They slipped from the shed, locking it behind them. A full moon outlined an old farmhouse and a ramshackle barn in the middle of the most Godforsaken country Christine had ever seen.

Lights in the farmhouse told them it was inhabited. With Ricky's good arm around her shoulder, Christine moved them toward the barn. "We need to find transportation," she whispered.

Ricky gritted her teeth to suppress a groan as movement caused pain to rip through her shoulder. She had lost a lot of blood and was growing weaker by the minute. She tried to keep her weight off Christine but stumbled almost pulling them both to the ground.

"Lean on me, dammit," Christine hissed. "I can hold you up. You don't always have to be the strong one."

With no choice, Ricky rested her weight on the brunette and allowed herself to be half-dragged, half-walked to the old barn.

"Nothing," Christine sighed disheartened. "I was hoping they had a vehicle in here. I'd even settle for a horse."

"Over there," Ricky nodded toward the corner of the barn. "A motorcycle. Can you ride it?"

"I haven't since I was a teenager," Christine loudly exhaled. "I will probably kill us both. Can you ride one?"

"Normally, a piece of cake," Ricky groaned as she shifted her weight from Christine back to herself. "No way, today. I'd rather take my chances with you in the driver's seat."

"It's up to you, Babe," Ricky weakly grinned.

"When we get home, we are going to have a talk about this 'Babe' business," Christine looked at the blonde threateningly then kissed her gently.

Christine straddled the dirt bike. "Get on behind me, so we can take off as soon as I get this thing started," Christine steadied Ricky as the ranger struggled to get her leg over the bike.

Christine thanked her God as she realized the key was in the ignition and the motorcycle had an electric start. The bikes she had ridden in the past had required kick-starting, something that was difficult for her.

Christine pulled off the belt she was wearing and passed one end of it to the ranger. "I am going to belt us together she explained as she wrapped the belt around their small waists. "I don't want to lose you."

"You ready?" she asked Ricky as the ranger wrapped her good arm around the brunette's waist.

"As I'll ever be," Ricky's lips against her ear made a shudder run through Christine's body as she leaned back into the woman so the blonde could get a better grip on her waist.

"Here goes." Christine gripped the throttle, pulled in the clutch and pushed the start button. The machine roared to life humming much quieter than the senator expected. She gave the bike the gas and let off the clutch.

Ricky hung on for dear life as the bike's front wheels lifted from the ground, fell back into the dirt and the bike shot forward. "Go east," she spoke into Christine's ear.

Christine followed the road east. A quick look in the side mirrors told her she had company as two black cars pulled in behind them. "Hold on," she yelled.

"Get off the road," Ricky talked into her ear. "Go straight east. Sooner or later you will hit the wall."

Christine opened the dirt bike full throttle, running as fast as it would go. She wondered how far they were from the wall.

~~~

Chapter 12

"I've located them, sir," Becky said excitedly. "Looks like they are in a shack in the middle of nowhere, on the Mexico side."

Deputy Director Dusty Rhodes looked over Becky's shoulder at the satellite map that linked to the chips embedded in Senator Richmond and Major Strong.

"Damn," Rhodes huffed. "We can't send in a rescue team. We'll start a war with Mexico. Are they moving?"

"The senator is," Becky said softly, "but the Major hasn't moved. The woman that drove the truck across the border said the cartel shot Ricky. She may be dead, sir."

"Not Ricky," Rhodes barked. "She is too strong to die." He didn't even want to consider the possibility of losing Major Strong.

"Crate, Barrel, are you hearing this?" Rhodes addressed his agents at the border.

"Yes, sir," Crate answered. "You want us to take a dark team across the border and bring them back?"

"No, if you get caught it would be a cluster fu...uh, foul up." Rhodes cleaned up his language in front of Becky and Daisy. "You stay right there. We will keep you informed of their location."

"Sir, Daisy squealed, "Senator Richmond's chip is moving. She is walking away from the Major. Oh, God, Ricky isn't moving. She is dead."

"Look," Becky yelled, "Ricky is moving. The senator is going back for her. They are both moving."

"There, on the satellite feed, they are moving toward another building," Daisy added. "It looks like the senator is carrying or dragging the Major."

"Oh, my God," Rhodes gasped. "They are on a motorcycle."

"Don't worry, sir," Crate laughed, "The Major knows her way around a motorcycle."

"Two cars are chasing them," Daisy pointed out.

"Which direction are they headed?" Crate asked.

"Due east," Becky said, "They have left the road and are making a run for the wall."

"Damn, the cartel will capture them when they reach the wall," Rhodes growled. "They can't get through."

"Give me the coordinates of their location and your best guess at the spot where they will hit the wall," Crate yelled eagerly.

Daisy gave him the information he requested. "Crate, it looks like they will hit the wall in about twenty minutes at a point five miles from where you are. There is no opening there."

"There will be by the time they arrive," Crate yelled as he motioned for Marcos and Barrel to follow him. "Bring your heaviest artillery truck, Marcos."

Driving as fast as the dirt road would allow, the rangers and Marcos headed for the spot they expected Ricky to reach the wall.

"A little further," Becky advised Crate. "They are in a straight line for you. Now! Stop now!"

The trucks screeched to a stop. "Carve out a hole big enough for a small car to pass through," Crate directed.

Marcus opened fire on the wall, shelling it with his heaviest artillery.

"It's not working," Barrel yelled.

Crate revved the engine of the truck he was in and rammed the wall as hard as he could. Steam shot from under the hood as the radiator ripped from the truck, but the wall remained intact.

Crate backed up further from the wall, praying the overheating engine wouldn't die on him. He floored the gas pedal and hit the wall with everything the truck had. He shot thru to the other side.

"Get it back! Get it back," Marcos screamed.

Crate threw the truck into reverse and shot backward, scraping the sides of the truck on the opening. The vehicle bucked, heaved and died, stuck in the hole.

Barrel grabbed the cable on the winch attached to the front of Marcos' truck and hooked it to the bumper of Crate's truck. Marcos slowly backed up tightening the tension on the cable. Crate's truck began to move backward.

"Hurry," Becky screamed into Crate's ear. "They are only a couple of minutes away."

~~~

"Stay with me, baby," Christine yelled as she felt Ricky's arm slip from her waist. "Hold on. We are almost there." *I wish I knew where the hell 'there' was*, she thought.

172

The headlights were still behind them and gaining fast. Christine tried to turn the throttle more, but the bike was already running at maximum speed.

Flying across the badlands, Christine prayed she would see the wall in time to stop the motorcycle. Bullets zinged around them as she leaned low on the bike pulling Ricky down with her.

The incredible heat from Ricky's body told Christine the ranger was running a dangerously high fever. *Infection has set in*, the thought. Tears streamed down the senator's cheeks. She didn't know if they were from the stinging sand blowing into her face or the thought of losing the woman strapped to her.

Suddenly, the wall sprang up from nowhere. Christine gasped. It was high and black. *Where can I get through this thing?*

Ricky's arm was slowly slipping from around her waist, and the ranger's weight on her back told Christine that Ricky couldn't hold on much longer.

Two lights switched on as Crate and Barrel provided light to lead the women through the hole in the fence.

"They are here! They are here," Crate almost jumped for joy.

"You better get out of the way," Becky warned Crate. "They will run over you."

"I'm not worried," Crate laughed, "The Major can handle a bike."

"That's not the Major driving," Becky chuckled as she watched the chips embedded in Crate and Barrel scramble out of the way.

The bike sailed through the opening. "Ricky," Christine screamed, "how do I stop this thing?"

The ranger's silence told the brunette that the other woman was no longer conscious.

Closing her eyes and saying a quick prayer, the senator released the throttle to the motorcycle. The bike stalled, bucked several times, then fell over in the sand. *Thank God, Texas sand*, Christine thought as she and Ricky skidded through the red dirt.

"They are belted together," someone yelled as they tried to pick up the two women. "Unfasten that."

Strong hands lifted them into the medical helicopter that was waiting. Darkness enveloped Christine.

~~~

Chapter 13

Christine looked around the pristine room. White sheets and blankets told her she was in the hospital. The I.V. in her left arm confirmed her thoughts.

"Christine, darling," her mother was instantly at her bedside. "How do you feel?"

"Like hell," Christine said hoarsely. Her mouth was dry and felt like it was full of the sand she had skidded through in the desert.

Lady Richmond held a straw to her daughter's lips. The water was the best thing Christine had ever tasted.

"Ricky," she jerked as she recalled the dead weight of the ranger belted to her. "How is Ricky? Is she okay?"

"She is here in the hospital," Lady Richmond snorted. "I don't know how she is."

Christine grabbed the remote and pushed the nurse's call button frantically.

"Senator," Dr. Cassie Warren entered the room. "It is good to see you awake."

"Ricky, how is Ricky?" Christine demanded.

"She is in intensive care right now," Cassie frowned. "We almost lost her."

"Can I see her?" Christine tried to sit up, but was restrained by her I.V. "Can you take this out?" She dared Cassie to say no.

"I will disconnect you, but leave in the I.V.," Cassie scowled. "You need to listen to me before you go storming into the ICU."

Christine sat up on the side of her hospital bed and glared at Cassie.

"Both of you were very badly dehydrated," Cassie said. "Since we admitted you, we have had you on an I.V. to rehydrate you. Ricky was almost dead from loss of blood, and the gunshot wound was badly infected.

"We have pumped antibiotics into her to fight the infection. Our very finest surgeon fixed her shoulder, and it will be good as new in a few months, but we have a problem with the blood. She is type O negative, a very rare type. We only had one quart on hand. We have sent out a call for help to locate…"

"I am type O negative," Christine cried out. "I can donate to her. Both of my parents are type O if she needs more."

"You would do that?" Cassie studied the woman that she had chalked up as selfish and uncaring.

"Yes, yes, of course. Take all Ricky needs. Why are we wasting time?" Christine demanded.

Cassie handed her a bottle of water. "Keep drinking water," she said as she rolled a wheelchair to Christine.

"I can walk," the Senator scoffed.

"Hospital rules," Cassie smiled.

~~~

"When can I see her?" Christine demanded as the nurses completed the blood draw.

"Three, maybe four hours," Cassie frowned. "Let us do the transfusion and give it a chance to work. In the meantime, you need to rest. I have ordered you reconnected to the I.V. Keep it in until you can see her."

Christine laid her head back on the pillow. She suddenly felt exhausted. Sleep slowly engulfed her.

~~~

Christine jerked awake when a nurse touched her to take her vital signs. "What time is it?" She asked.

"Six in the morning," the nurse smiled.

"I've been asleep for twelve hours?" Christine scowled incredulously. "Your doctor sedated me, didn't she?"

The nurse stuck a thermometer into her mouth and checked her pulse. "Everything is normal," she said as she checked the thermometer.

Cassie appeared in the doorway. "You look much better," she smiled. "I think we can do away with this." She removed the I.V. needle from the back of Christine's hand and placed a band-aid over the puncture.

"Ready to go see Major Strong?" she asked as she pulled the wheelchair close to Christine's bed.

##

Christine was unprepared for the beeping of the machines hooked to the blonde. She swayed as she appraised the ranger. She was thankful Cassie had insisted on the wheelchair. Her entire body was weak. "What are all these machines?"

"Heart rate monitor, ventilator, I.V. drip, and a drug dispensing machine for morphine," Cassie explained.

"Has she awakened?" Christine whispered.

"No."

"May I sit with her?" Christine's eyes pleaded for permission to stay with the ranger.

Cassie nodded and left the room.

Christine kept her vigil at Ricky's side for fourteen days.

Ricky grew stronger daily but remained in a coma. She didn't respond to anything.

Christine read and talked to Ricky constantly. Hourly, she ran Ricky through the exercises the physical therapist had taught her. She cried, but most of all she prayed to a God that she knew existed.

"She is going to be the most toned coma patient I have ever treated," Cassie teased the senator.

"Can't you do something?" Christine asked as they watched Ricky sleep.

"She will come out of it," Cassie smiled. "She lost a lot of blood. The body will sometimes shut down as it loses blood. The brain will shut down first to operate on less blood sending it to other parts of the body. Her blood count is good. All her vitals are excellent.

"Don't worry," Cassie placed a comforting hand on Christine's shoulder. "I know Ricky. She is too strong to die."

Christine's phone vibrated. She waved goodbye to Cassie as she answered the mobile phone. "No, Deputy Rhodes, I will come to your office."

Christine frowned as she ended the call. She didn't want to leave Ricky very long. In the past fourteen days, she had only left long enough to go home to shower and change clothes. She had no idea how her office was running without her and didn't care.

Rhodes had been hounding her to debrief her on what had happened in Mexico. She shuddered as she recalled the treatment they had suffered at the hands of the drug cartel.

She leaned over and kissed Ricky's soft, full lips. She was living for the day Ricky would kiss her back. Today wasn't the day.

~~~

Ricky Strong fought daily to return to the land of the living. Trapped somewhere between light and darkness, she couldn't quite pull herself from the hazy limbo in which she now existed.

She was aware that someone was reading to her, talking to her, begging her to come back. The same voice hummed as soft hands massaged cream all over her body, then moved all her limbs in the same routine many times a day.

Christine! She was certain the hands and voice belonged to the woman she loved. The woman who had saved her life. She had to get back to Christine.

The struggle was too difficult, too exhausting, too painful. Ricky slipped back into the darkness.

~~~

"She moved her hand," the nurse smiled at the dark-haired woman as she entered the ranger's room. "She may rally today."

The beauty sat down and took Ricky's hand in hers. She leaned forward and brushed her lips against the ranger's cheek. "Time to wake up, Mi Cara," she whispered.

Christine Richmond stood transfixed in the doorway. It was her. The woman from the airport.

179

The woman Ricky had chosen to spend three days with before their border trip.

Christine numbly stumbled back into the hallway. "Who is that woman in Major Strong's room?" she hissed to the desk nurse.

"Senator," the nurse frowned, "I thought you were with Major Strong. Only her significant other is cleared to be in her room."

"Did that woman sign in?" Christine demanded.

"Yes, ma'am. I didn't look at her closely. I thought she was you. Her name is Martina Strong."

"What is her relationship?" Christine softly said, dreading the answer.

"It says, 'wife,'" the nurse whispered.

"Oh," Christine almost doubled over. Wife! The word was like a physical punch in the stomach. The stunned look on her face was heartbreaking. She walked toward Ricky's room then wheeled around and got back on the elevator.

~~~

Ricky clutched the soft hands holding hers. She willed herself to open her eyes. The effort was too much. Her head felt as if it would split open any second.

Soft lips brushed her cheek, "Time to wake up, Cara," the woman's voice encouraged her.

Ricky's eyes shot open. "Christine, where is Christine?"

"It is me, Cara," Martina smiled. She, too, wondered where the senator was.

"Martina," Ricky exhaled and closed her eyes again.

Doctors and nurses rushed into the ranger's room when the machines, monitoring vital signs began to go crazy.

"Did she wake?" Cassie demanded.

"Yes," Martina smiled. "She opened her eyes and said a few words then closed her eyes again."

Dr. Warren shook Ricky, "Major Strong, can you hear me?" she raised her voice as she shook Ricky.

"Yes! Yes," Ricky mumbled. "I hear you. Please don't shake my head."

Cassie laughed gleefully. "Thank God," she cried as she checked all of Ricky's vital signs.

~~~

"I am a fool," Christine chastised herself all the way home. "I should have known anyone as wonderful as Ricky would belong to someone else. I can't believe she lied to me. Told me she loved me."

For the first time in her life Senator Christine Richmond got drunk: mind-bending, memory-erasing, pain-killing drunk.

The next morning arrived around noon when the senator discovered her head had turned wrong-side-out and was exposing her brain to all the elements of the universe. The pain was unbearable. *Why did I do this to myself?* She thought. Then she remembered, and the pain moved to her heart.

Christine lay in her bed and cried. She cried for all the times she had touched Ricky Strong, all the times Ricky's strong, gentle hands had caressed her body as she whispered words of love into her ear. She cried for all the times they had shared, the love, the laughter, and the terror.

Christine let her pity party go on until the next morning then slid from her bed and stepped into the shower. A very different woman emerged from the shower. A wiser woman, a colder woman, a woman who had locked her heart and thrown away the key. No one would ever hurt her again!

She looked in the mirror and wiped away a single tear that slid from her eye. "That is the last tear I will ever cry for you, Ricky Strong."

~~~

Chapter 14

Major Ricky Strong stared out the window of the BMW. She was glad to be going home. She rubbed the spot where Cassie had removed the ID chip. She didn't want anyone tracking her to her home.

"Are you okay, Cara?" Martina softly said as she touched the blonde's arm.

"I am fine," Ricky gave her a weak smile. "My arm is much better. I should be back in the saddle by Christmas."

"You had a horrifying ordeal," Martina nodded. "Do you want to talk about it?"

"Not today," Ricky said softly. "I have to go into headquarters next week. If you drive me, you can sit in on the debriefing. That way, I will only have to relive the nightmare once."

"I will be happy to drive you, but perhaps I should wait in the car. I don't want to run into Agent Adams."

"He is assigned to the border," Ricky smirked, "He shouldn't see anything but dust and tumbleweeds until he dies."

"If you think it is safe," Martina nodded.

Ricky spent all her time in her home gym or riding her favorite stallion, Mercury, whose name she shortened to Merc. When she wasn't working out or riding Merc, she was practicing on her homemade shooting range.

Tex had stacked several bales of hay to form a safe place to shoot into a target. Ricky was almost back to one hundred percent. Sometimes Martina joined her. "I need to keep up my marksmanship," the Italian woman grinned. "One never knows when they will need to shoot their way out of danger."

During the day, it was easy to keep busy and drive the thoughts of Senator Christine Richmond from her mind, but the nighttime was a very different matter.

Every time she closed her eyes, she saw Christine's face. Christine, laughing. Christine's eyes, dancing as she gave her that sultry look that said: "Come on Major, show me what you've got."

The look on Christine's face when they made love. The soft smile when Christine touched her cheek with her fingertips just before she kissed her.

Christine Richmond was driving her crazy.

How could she just walk away and leave me alone in that hospital? Ricky thought a million times. *How could she not visit me or ask about me?*

Ricky had called the brunette at least a hundred times. Each time, Christine was busy or in a meeting or flying to Washington. Each time she didn't return Ricky's call. Each time Ricky died a little inside.

The main thing that kept the ranger going was Troy Hunter. When she was able, she immediately renewed their friendship through email. She explained that she had been in the hospital. She was thankful that Troy hadn't turned his affections toward another unsuspecting woman.

Ricky opened her laptop and logged onto her Facebook alias. She typed a line she had stolen from some lovesick fool's Facebook page:

Puff a cigarette daily, you will die ten years early.
Drink alcohol daily; you will die 30 years early.
Love someone who doesn't love you back; you will
die daily.

Ricky read what she had typed. Whoever wrote the prose was correct, Ricky would never write something like that for the public to see. She died daily in her own personal, very private hell.

"Hey, Sunshine," Troy took the bait. "Why so down? I love you."

"You don't even know me," Ricky typed back.

"I would like to get to know you," Troy typed. Where do you live? We can meet halfway."

"Fort Worth," Ricky typed.

"Awesome, I live in Austin," Troy informed her. Ricky was certain he was telling the truth.

"We could meet in Waco," Troy suggested. "That is about half way. A little further for me, but I don't mind. We can make a day of it. If you are a history buff, we can have lunch, tour the Texas Ranger's Museum and the Dr. Pepper Museum. Did I mention I love Dr. Pepper?"

"LOL, no you didn't," Ricky responded. "So, do I."

"See, we have a lot in common." Troy typed as he congratulated himself for reeling her in. "So, want to set a date to meet?"

"How does Saturday sound?" Ricky typed. She was getting bored and could think of nothing she would rather do than handcuff the killer.

Troy gave her the name of a restaurant on the river, a place she had dined before. "See you there at noon," she typed. "Goodnight, for now, my sweet prince."

She almost gagged on the last phrase but knew Troy would think she was even more lovesick than most.

~~~

"Thanks, Becky," Ricky pushed the button on her steering wheel to disconnect the call. "There, see, Agent Dave Adams is in Del Rio riding a desk."

Martina smiled, it was good to see Ricky back in command of the situation.

"You can sit in on my debriefing without worrying about that scuzzball.

"Martina, I have to warn you the story is not a pretty one. It is pretty rank." Ricky frowned as the vision of Roberto's attempt to rape Christine flashed through her mind. "Not pretty at all."

##

"Major Strong," Deputy Director Rhodes crossed the room in four long strides to gently embrace his finest ranger. Ricky Strong had already become a legend in the annals of Texas Ranger history, and she wasn't even aware of it.

Ricky introduced Martina, "My sister-in-law," she smiled. "Tex has all the luck. I haven't related our border experience to anyone. I only intend to tell this story once. My family wants to know so I would like Martina to sit in on the debriefing, if that is okay with you, sir."

"Of course, it is okay," Rhodes nodded.

The door opened, and a sophisticated-looking man entered the room. A slight graying at the temples complimented his dark hair. His intelligent eyes and perfectly fitting suit gave the appearance of a man who could hold his own in any situation.

"Director Crockett," Ricky almost saluted. "I wasn't told you would be here, sir."

"I wouldn't miss this for the world," Crockett smiled. "I have heard Senator Richmond's tale of your little tour de force. I am anxious to hear your version."

I wish, to hell, she had discussed her version with me, Ricky thought. *She had no idea that almost everything we did was videoed through my glasses. Oh, damn, this may be worse than I thought.*

"We have everything set up in the conference room," Becky informed the group.

"I don't believe I have been fortunate enough to meet this young woman," Crockett smiled at Martina.

"Director David Crockett, this is my sister-in-law, Martina Strong," Ricky made the introduction.

As Martina charmed the Director, Becky slipped a thumb drive into Ricky's pocket. "Thought you might like to have the unedited version, Major," she whispered.

Ricky slowly exhaled as the band that had tightened around her chest relaxed. Thank God, she didn't have to explain the love scenes between Christine and her.

"First, we will watch the video recorded during your assignment. You can interject any pertinent information you feel necessary." Rhodes said as he turned off the lights and nodded for Becky to start the computer playback.

187

The room was silent as everyone watched the scenes leading up to the kidnapping of the two women. The video ended and Becky turned on the lights.

"You don't think much of FBI agent Dave Adams, do you?" Rhodes watched Ricky's eyes as she contemplated his question.

"No, sir," Ricky answered, squeezing Martina's hand under the table.

"Why not?"

"I believe Adams is on the payroll of the New York Mafia," Ricky frowned. "I believe he is responsible for the near death of our protected witness in the Carlos Zamboni case. Adams was the only one who knew where she was. No one else could have sent them there."

"Yes, I remember that case," Crockett stroked his chin. "She was Carlos' daughter as I recall. They called her the Mafia Princess. Her testimony would have brought down the entire organization. A real shame."

Martina dug her nails into Ricky's hand.

"Do you have any proof that Adams was the traitor?"

"Not yet," Ricky said hoarsely, "but I will sooner or later."

"Why don't you pick up where the video left off?" Crockett directed her. "Tell us the rest of the story."

Ricky relived the hell she and Christine had gone through to get back to Texas. "The senator saved my life," she finished her tale. "If not for Senator Richmond, I would have died in some filthy shack in Mexico."

"The senator said you two took turns saving each other's lives," Crockett said knowingly. "It took a lot of nerve for her to jump from a moving truck to stay with you when you were injured."

"Yes," Ricky said softly. "Senator Christine Richmond is a remarkable woman, sir."

What the hell happened? Ricky thought. *She was willing to die for me, and now she won't even talk to me.*

"Have you read the senator's final report?" Crockett asked.

"No, sir."

Crockett looked around the room. He studied each person briefly then his eyes rested on Martina. "Ma'am," he smiled. "I must ask you to leave the room for a few minutes. What I am about to discuss with Major Strong requires security of the highest level."

"I understand," Martina nodded.

"Becky, please take her to my office," Ricky asked.

An hour later a shell-shocked Ricky emerged from the meeting. Director Crockett and Deputy Director Rhodes were subdued. "You will give us your answer by the end of the week?" Crockett raised his eyebrows.

Ricky nodded sullenly, shook hands with the two men then disappeared into her office.

"Mi Cara," Martina jumped up from the sofa and rushed to Ricky. "You look like hell."

"Thanks," Ricky chuckled half-heartedly. "I must look like I feel."

"Can you tell me what is wrong?" Martina's dark eyes danced in anger as she observed the anguish of the blonde.

"We need to go," Ricky frowned as she opened the door to escort Martina from the office.

"I don't care if she isn't officially back at work yet," an angry voice filled the room. "I want to know what is being done to find my sister's killer."

Even though she wanted to shake the woman throwing a fit, Ricky's heart skipped a beat as she stepped into Becky's office. "I am very close, Senator Richmond," the ranger said.

Christine tossed her hair back, lifted her chin in that haughty way that made a tremor run through the blonde. She smirked as she held Ricky's gaze. *God, I love her*, Ricky thought as she moved slowly toward the brunette.

"We should have Kara's killer in custody by next week."

"Thank you," Christine looked down at her hands. It took all her strength to keep them from trembling. More than anything in the world she wanted to touch Ricky Strong.

"Mi Cara," Martina stepped from the office and took Ricky's arm.

Anger scorched Christine's soul as she watched the raven-haired beauty loop her arm thru Ricky's.

"Martina," Ricky said as she placed her hand on the woman's arm, "I would like to introduce you to..."

"Don't you dare," Christine growled, "you son-of-a-bitch. Don't you dare introduce me to your..."

"Major!" Director Crockett entered the room. "I am glad to see you are discussing our conversation with the senator.

Crockett did a double take as he saw the fury in Senator Richmond's eyes. He didn't know what he had stepped into, but he certainly wanted to get out of it.

Christine turned on her heel and stomped from the office.

"What was that all about?" Crockett looked crestfallen. "I take it she wanted no part of our plan."

"I think she wants no part of me, sir," Ricky groaned.

~~~

Christine was almost blind with anger. *Now she brings her harlot to the office for everyone to see. Why wasn't she flashing her around before—before I fell in love with her!*

Christine tried her hardest to cross that thin line between love and hate, but no matter what she did she knew she loved Ricky Strong. She wondered if every encounter with the blonde would illicit the aching pain she was now suffering.

The senator tossed and turned all night. Awake she fantasized about ways to humiliate the beautiful ranger, but asleep her dreams filled with Ricky's lips on hers, Ricky's laughing eyes as they discussed things, Ricky's soft touch and gentle way of taking her to heights she had never dreamed existed.

I can't live like this, Christine thought. *I must get away from her, away from this town.*

~~~

Troy Hunter turned on his computer and checked his email. There was nothing from Alessa Morris. He sent her a message and was delighted with her immediate response. *She must sit on her computer just waiting to hear from me,* he thought.

They planned their date for the upcoming Saturday. "I am very excited, "Alessa typed, "I am about to go to pieces. LOL!"

You don't know the half of it; Troy thought as he typed, "I hope I can live up to your expectations."

Ricky signed off with some sappy phrase she had stolen from another woman's self-centered Facebook page.

She poured herself a glass of wine and inserted into her computer the thumb drive containing Christine's debriefing. She noted the date and time that ran along the bottom of the video. It was recorded the same day Ricky awoke from her coma.

Christine had detailed their journey only leaving out their after-midnight activities. She raved about how capable Major Strong was and how Ricky had engineered the small army of escorts that prevented a border war.

She talked about how calm and collected the ranger had remained in the face of danger. "Her presence was very reassuring and appreciated," Christine said. A faint smile played on her lips. "Major Strong did everything possible to make certain I was taken care of properly."

She described what they had been through and how ecstatic they had been as the truck approached the border crossing. She almost cried when she described watching the ranger being shot and flying off the truck.

"You jumped from the truck?" Rhodes said, "Didn't you know you were jumping to certain death at the hands of the cartel?"

"I never gave it a second thought," the senator said. "I just knew I couldn't leave her alone. She was there for me. I wanted to be there for her."

Christine described how she had shot El Monstruo to save Ricky and how an injured Ricky had managed to put a bullet into the base of Roberto Ramos' skull to save her.

As she finished her description of their harrowing escape across the badlands to the border, Crockett slowly asked her, "Did you see El Asesino? Do you know who he is?"

"Yes," Christine nodded.

Ricky played the last minute of the interrogation over and over. She tried to bridle the panic that was surging through her body. If Christine could identify El Asesino, her life wasn't worth a wooden nickel. She was a dead woman.

Ricky looked at her watch. It was after midnight. She grabbed her cell phone and dialed Christine's number. A smoky, sleep-laden voice made her stomach turn over. She loved that voice. Loved waking up beside its owner.

"Christine, please don't hang up on me," Ricky rushed. "I know you hate me for whatever reason, but this is serious life and death."

"What do you want, Major?"

"Did you give them El Asesino's name?"

"No," Christine inhaled deeply.

"This is important, who was in the debriefing? Who knows you can identify the cartel leader?"

"I...I'm not sure," Christine whispered. "I didn't think..."

"Christine, you are in grave danger," Ricky warned. "Do they have a guard on you?"

"Yes, some woman who looks like me."

"That is all? One woman? What is her name?"

"I don't know. I don't want to know," Christine said vehemently, "A female Texas Ranger, she would probably only lie anyway. Isn't that what you players do?"

The venom in Christine's voice stunned Ricky.

A long silence ensued. "Goodnight, Major Strong." The line went dead.

"Damn! Damn!" Ricky cursed aloud as she threw her wine glass across the room. "Why does she have to be so damn bullheaded about everything?"

Ricky played Christine's debriefing again. *She loved me enough to give her life for me*, she thought. *What went wrong? What made her hate me so much?*

~~~

"Tex is coming home Friday," Martina brilliantly smiled as she walked through Ricky's back door. "He has almost concluded all our business with the Beef Buyers of America.

"You will be pleased with the contract he negotiated," she beamed as Ricky filled a cup with coffee for her. "One more meeting with the Restaurants International Group and you two won't have to worry about who is going to purchase your cattle, only how you are going to fill their orders."

Ricky grinned. "Is he still planning to take Brady to the Fort Worth Fat Stock Show?"

"Oh, yes," Martina laughed. "I am glad he understands that I don't like tramping around in sawdust and manure."

"Neither do I," Ricky laughed. "That is why I leave the ranching up to him."

"I do miss the theater and fine dining," Martina said wistfully. "Of course, Tex would be more than happy to accompany me, but I have to keep a low profile."

"Why don't you put your hair up in braids or something to disguise yourself," Ricky grinned, "and I will take you to dinner and see *Mama Mia* at Dell Hall tomorrow night? I'd like to get out, too."

"Oh, Cara, I would love that," Martina gushed.

Ricky watched her drink her coffee. She wondered how the woman had managed to go from the bright lights of New York to the blue skies of Texas. Martina never complained. She seemed to be very happy with her current life. *Thanks to Tex, I am sure,* Ricky thought.

"Why are you up so early?" Martina asked.

"I have an eight o'clock appointment with the doctor. I am hoping she will release me to return to work. I have a serial killer to catch.

"I will get my release then run by Dell Hall and pick up the tickets for tomorrow night."

Martina clapped her hands like a delighted child. "I am very excited," she exclaimed.

~~

Chapter 15

"Major," Becky hugged Ricky when she entered the office. "Sorry, I have just missed you so much."

"It is good to be back," the ranger grinned as she handed Becky her doctor's release. "Please let DD Rhodes know I am back. I have a few phone calls to make."

Ricky had been disappointed when Rosie Garland's computer hadn't turned up any Facebook contacts with Troy Hunter. She decided to push her contact with the man to the limit.

Ricky scrolled through the Ranger database until she found an attractive brunette, Ranger Kay Dawson. Kay had worked with her team before. She called Dawson's commanding officer and requested the brunette for an undercover job.

She called Crate and Barrel and asked them to come to her office. The men were delighted to leave the boring assignment they had worked during Ricky's absence.

Becky entered Ricky's office and placed a stack of papers in her in-tray. "These need your signature," she grinned. "Daisy and I were very concerned about you, boss."

"I wanted to thank you for editing the border video," Ricky blushed. "It could have been very embarrassing to Senator Richmond and me."

"We only removed the scenes that were not pertinent to the investigation," Becky said.

"You were in a coma while all the news coverage was going on," Becky grinned. "Crate and Barrel are like rock stars. They have always been chick magnets, but now they really have to fight off the women."

Ricky laughed at the thought of her two handsome rangers plagued by strange women. "I am sure they can handle themselves," she smiled.

"Major," Crate and Barrel chorused as they entered her office.

"Man, it is so good to have you back. We are ready for some action. They pulled us off Senator Richmond's security detail," Crate informed her. "I told Captain Trout you wouldn't like it."

"You are right about that," Ricky laughed. I want you back with the senator, but right now I have a case we are closing this weekend."

"Anyone we know?" Barrel asked.

"Umm, the Hacker," Ricky beamed. "I have requested Kay Dawson's help on this one. She should be here soon. I will brief all of you then."

"She is very good," Barrel noted. "We worked with her on the prostitution murders last year."

"You okay, Major?" Crate asked gently.

"I am fine now that I am back in the office," Ricky smiled.

Becky brought Kay Dawson into the office.

"This is like old home week," Kay smiled as she shook everyone's hands. "How did I get so lucky to work with the Premier Texas Ranger Team?"

"Premier?" Ricky raised a perfectly arched brow.

"That is what the news media is calling you and these two losers," Kay's eyes twinkled as she teased the two men.

"Well it is just going to get better, or worse," Ricky frowned as she began filling in the ranger on the Hacker case.

"So, I will be undercover as your Facebook victim, Alessa Morris?" Kay reiterated. "The three of you will be close by when the perp makes his move?"

"Right," Ricky nodded. "We have to let him make a serious move on you. We must catch him in the act. We have no evidence to connect him to the other murders. He cuts off their hands, so we have no DNA under their fingernails and no fingerprints to identify them."

"So, this could get dicey," Barrel noted.

"What a great choice of words," Kay laughed.

"I am going to email him and tell him I am getting a room to spend the night in Waco, so I don't have to get up so early in the morning," Ricky detailed her plan.

"We will have control of the situation when he suggests going to your room. We will have hidden cameras and mics to record everything.

"Your job will be to get a confession from him. The three of us will be in the next room. We will come through the door as soon as we have enough to convict the bastard."

"Piece of cake," Kay nodded. "Which one of you lucky fellows get to take me to dinner tonight?" she laughed. "I want to hear first-hand about your border fiasco. Would you join us, Major?"

"I will take a raincheck," Ricky said. "This is my first day back. I have a ton of paperwork to complete.

"There is one more thing, Kay. Do you mind being chipped? It saved my life in Mexico."

"If it comes out when the case is over," Kay shrugged.

~~~

Ricky was pleased to see that Becky had filled out the paperwork for Crate and Barrel to receive overtime pay for the duration of the border tour. She had also filled out the forms to nominate both men for the Texas-Ranger-of-the-Year Award.

The blonde went online and filled out forms that would give Becky and Daisy the same benefits. They had watched over her and her team night and day during the trip.

She was surprised to see that Senator Richmond had authorized an additional budget for general use, allowing Director Crockett to use the money where he needed it the most.

Ricky knew that part of the money would be used to replace the truck Crate had rammed through the border wall. The rest would probably go to repair the wall.

She signed forms until she had writer's cramp then drove to Dell Hall to pick up the tickets for Mama Mia. She was glad Martina was getting to see the musical.

She promised herself she would concentrate harder on Dave Adams. Once he was out of the way, Martina could breathe easier. Of course, she would never be truly safe until they took down her brother's criminal network.

Ricky needed to find someone in the FBI she trusted. The last FBI director had destroyed everyone's faith in the Federal Bureau of Investigation, hers included.

Martina had left dinner for her in the refrigerator with a note that said, *don't stay up too late, Cara. Remember, you are supposed to take it easy.*

Ricky microwaved the chicken and rice casserole Martina had left her, grabbed a bottle of water from the fridge and settled in front of the television. *Time to catch up with the rest of the world*, she thought as she turned on FOX news.

One of the talking heads was giddy over his next guest. Ricky choked on her food when Christine's beautiful face filled the screen.

"We are delighted to have Texas State Senator Christine Richmond with us tonight," the man beamed. "Senator, I know the president asked you to spearhead building the wall along the Texas-Mexico border. As I understand it, you were kidnapped by the drug cartel."

Christine nodded. "Yes, Texas Ranger Ricky Strong was shot and captured by the cartel, also. They were shipping us out of the country with a load of women. Human trafficking is running rampant in our country, and I intend to do everything I can to stop it.

"Along the border, young women are being taken from their homes and forced into prostitution. It is disgraceful the way the former administration turned a blind eye to what is going on down there."

Ricky stopped listening to the political discussion, but she couldn't tear her eyes away from Christine's eyes and her lips. A dull ache spread through her entire body.

"Yes, I am considering a run for the U.S. Senate," Christine said.

Ricky's entire body jerked. *U.S. Senate. That means she will live in Washington.* For the first time in her life, Major Ricky Strong hyperventilated.

She couldn't breathe. Her hands shook, and her chest felt as if it would explode. She wanted to throw up.

"I know there was the talk of you running for governor of Texas," the idiot interviewer babbled, "what made you decide to run for the U.S. Senate?"

"My reasons are personal," Christine said. "I feel that I can contribute to the overall benefit of our entire country. I can influence laws that govern this country and help rebuild America."

"Have you made up your mind for certain?" the interviewer asked.

"No," Christine smiled that shy smile that made everyone fall in love with her; the one that showcased the little dimples at each corner of her lips. "I am weighing all of my options. In the end, I want to do what is best for America."

Ricky hugged her knees to her chest and willed herself to breathe slowly.

"Rather than ask you to retell your story," the interviewer said, "we are going to play excerpts from the debriefings of you and Major Strong."

The Texas Ranger's public relations department had taken parts of Christine's debriefing and parts of Ricky's and spliced together a hair-raising tale of their exploits.

For the first-time Christine watched the video on the large-screen TV in the newsroom. The look on her face told Ricky the senator was disturbed by the video. The ordeal was still too real, too raw and too painful for them both. The most painful part of all was that they were no longer together.

Ricky showered and slipped between the cool sheets. She couldn't get her mind off Christine. It was after midnight, but she didn't care. She sent a text to the brunette.

"I watched you on FOX tonight. Great job! I miss you."

A four-word text came back. "I miss you, too."

"May I call you," Ricky texted.

"Please don't. Don't make this any harder for me than it already is. Goodnight."

I don't understand, Ricky thought. *I must make her talk to me.*

~~~

Ricky awoke to the smell of freshly brewing coffee and bacon frying. She smiled. Martina was in her kitchen.

"Good morning, pretty lady," she grinned as she kissed Martina on the cheek. "Don't forget our date tonight."

"Why do you think I am cooking you breakfast?" Martina laughed. "This is my thank you!"

The Italian beauty watched the ranger as she poured coffee for them and sat down at the kitchen island. "You look tired, Cara."

"Sleepless night," Ricky deeply inhaled, then let her breath ease from her body.

"I saw your senator on the news last night," Martina glanced at her friend. "You are in love with her!"

It wasn't a question. Martina knew it was a fact. "Does she love you?"

"I don't know," Ricky dragged her hands down her face as if trying to tear away a veil. "I believe she does. I know she did, but she won't talk to me. She acts as if I have horribly wronged her somehow. I don't know what to do.

"She is barely civil to me in public. It is as if she hates me. You saw how she acted when I tried to introduce you to her."

"Yes, I did think she was extremely rude," Martina agreed.

~~~

Ricky left work early and went to her apartment to get ready for her night out with her sister-in-law. She examined herself in the mirror. She knew she was beautiful. The dress she had selected showcased all her best assets. Tall and athletic, her toned arms and legs were the envy of other women. Her long blonde hair had enough natural curl to allow her to wash it and scrunch it, so it loosely curled around her shoulders, almost reaching her taut breast. All-in-all Ricky Strong knew she was the whole package. What she didn't know was why Christine Richmond no longer wanted to unwrap the package.

Martina was gorgeous in a stunning red, fitted dress. "You were supposed to be inconspicuous," Ricky smiled as she appraised her friend. "not catch the eye of every man and woman within a hundred yards of us."

"I wanted to dress up," Martina coyly said. "I haven't been out in a very long time."

"I am trying to fix that," Ricky nodded. "If I find someone I can trust, would you testify against the mob in a RICO case?"

Martina thought about the question for a long time. "If you are the one protecting me," she frowned.

"The only way I see for you to be completely free is to take down the entire organized crime syndicate your father built," Ricky explained. "Carlito took over after your father died in the shootout with the FBI that almost cost your life. He thinks you are alive. I know he has a contract out on you."

The women discussed the ramifications of taking down the rest of the crime family as they drove to the restaurant.

Martina smiled warmly. "Mi Cara, this is beautiful."

"I hope you like it," Ricky smiled shyly. "It is as close to a New York restaurant as I could find."

"It is perfect," Martina nodded.

Martina was right, dinner and the musical were perfect. For the first time in a long time, the ranger relaxed and enjoyed herself. For a few seconds, Christine Richmond didn't torment her mind.

"Would you like to go for a drink before we head home?" Ricky suggested.

"That would be the perfect ending to a perfect evening," Martina laughed. "I don't know when I have enjoyed myself so much."

"Tex loves the theater," Ricky said. "He pesters me all the time to take you on a real date. He wants to show you off. I don't blame him. Hopefully, we can make that happen."

"Umm, I would like that," Martina linked her arm through Ricky's as she thought about her handsome husband. "I am ready for him to be home. I miss him so much when he is gone."

Ricky agreed and led them to the valet stand. "They are pretty quick," she informed Martina. The man and woman in front of them turned at the sound of her voice, and she found herself face-to-face with the woman of her dreams.

Christine cast a scathing look at her then turned her attention to Martina. "Did you enjoy the musical?" She spoke to Martina.

"Oh, yes, very much," Martina smiled her brilliant smile. "Rēēcky was kind enough to get me out of the house tonight."

Christine cringed inside as she noticed the way Martina's accent made the ranger's name come out Rēēcky. *I would like to get my hands on Rēēcky*; she thought as she raked her gaze from the top of the blonde's head to the flattering high heels she wore.

"Your car, Senator," a young valet held the door open for Christine as her escort walked to the driver's side of the car.

"Goodnight, Senator," Ricky said as Christine looked straight ahead, never speaking to her.

Ricky was careful to keep up her spirits as she and Martina finished their evening.

"She is desperately in love with you," Martina informed the ranger on the ride home.

"She has a funny way of showing it." Ricky shrugged. "I don't know what made her go from willing to die for me to unwilling to speak to me. What makes you think she loves me?"

"She was furious when she saw you with me. Women only react that way when they love someone. Don't be stupid enough to let this continue," Martina said forcefully. "Even if you must handcuff her and carry her off, make her talk to you."

"You do know it is against the law to kidnap a senator?" Ricky laughed at the idea. "Knowing Christine, she *would* press charges."

"The news media would have a field day with that," Ricky grinned. "They would depict me as a best friend turned stalker."

"Listen to me, Cara," Martina insisted. "I am right!"

It was after midnight when the pair reached home. Ricky dropped Martina off at her house and drove slowly to her own sprawling adobe ranch house.

Christine looked gorgeous tonight, she thought. *No offense to Martina, but I would have given anything to go home with Christine.*

Ricky showered and slid between the cool sheets naked. The soft coolness of the sheets felt good against her skin. She picked up her cell phone and dialed Christine.

"I wondered if you would call," the soft, luxurious voice hummed.

Ricky's heart jumped. *That is the most she has said to me in weeks*, she thought. *I need to be careful not to make her mad.*

"You looked gorgeous tonight," Ricky said softly.

"So, did you," Christine answered slowly. "So, did she."

It suddenly occurred to Ricky that perhaps Martina was right.

"Maybe I need to explain her to you," Ricky said.

"No need," Christine hissed. "She is beautiful. Just your type." The phone line went dead.

Damn, Martina is right. She is jealous. Ricky thought gleefully. She dialed Christine's number again. No answer.

Ricky looked at the clock. It was after two in the morning. *I will resolve this first thing in the morning;* she happily thought as she drifted off to sleep.

~~~

The ranger hummed a tune from *Mama Mia* as she dressed. *Today is going to be my day;* she thought as she ran through various scenarios with Christine Richmond. *I will make her listen to me.*

She called her office and informed Becky she was running by Senator Richmond's office.

"Don't waste your time," Becky said. "She flew to Washington this morning with that slimy senator from New Mexico, Hud Heimlich or something like that."

"Are Crate and Barrel with her?"

"Yes! They think you will kill them if they let her out of their sight."

"They are right," Ricky chuckled. "In that case, I will be in the office early."

Ricky wondered why Christine was cavorting with Heimlich. He was a Democrat and sleazy to boot. She had recognized him as the senator's escort last night.

Becky put her finger to her lips signaling Ricky to be quiet. "Senator Richmond's mother is in your office," she whispered.

"Why?" Ricky frowned.

Becky shrugged. "She is in a foul mood. Or maybe she is always like that."

"Umm," Ricky nodded.

The ranger wondered why Christine's mother was visiting her. She was certain it was not a social call. She put on her best official face hoping Lady Richmond wouldn't see her displeasure at her visit.

"Lady Richmond," she enthusiastically burst into her office. "It is a pleasure to see you. How can I help you?"

"Have you caught Kara's killer?" Lady jumped straight to the point.

"Almost," Ricky answered evasively.

"What is that supposed to mean?" Lady demanded.

Ricky studied Christine's mother. Like her daughter, she was beautiful. She had aged well with the help of hair dye and a nip and tuck job. "It means I will have the killer in custody after this weekend," Ricky said sternly. "I can't tell you any more than that right now."

"Not to change the subject," the ranger frowned, "but how are you handling all of this?"

"I was just fine until you almost got my only daughter murdered in some running battle with the Mexican drug cartel," Lady Richmond scowled.

"My team protected Senator Richmond," Ricky frowned. "They did a darn good job."

"She saved your life," Lady pointed out.

"Yes, she did," Ricky agreed. "How is she doing?"

"I'm not sure," Lady shook her head. "She is dating that crook from New Mexico, Hud Henlick, or something like that."

"Heimlich," Ricky corrected her. "She is dating him? How long?"

"After you got out of the hospital," Lady said thoughtfully. "She sat with you around the clock when you were in a coma then as soon as you left the hospital she began dating that poor excuse for a man."

"She stayed in the hospital with me?" Ricky repeated in disbelief.

"She sat with you around the clock, only leaving long enough each day to shower and change clothes." Lady Richmond tilted her head and surveyed the ranger. "Didn't you know?"

Ricky shook her head, no.

"She read to you and talked to you. She even did your physical therapy hourly so your muscles wouldn't atrophy."

I have missed something somewhere, Ricky thought.

"Why Heimlich?" Ricky asked.

"She thinks he is handsome. I find him repulsive," Lady stormed returning to her condemnation of the New Mexico senator. "He is helping her line up support in Congress. She is considering a run for the U.S. Senate. Personally, I'd rather see her sleeping with a rattlesnake."

"Sleeping," Ricky choked. "Is she sleeping with him?"

"Well, she is a woman," Lady huffed. "She has needs, even if she is my daughter. I suppose I should be happy she isn't gay like Kara."

"Yes, you should be thankful for that," Ricky rose to show Lady to the door. "I will be in touch soon."

Ricky closed her door and collapsed onto the sofa. She leaned her head back and fought the urge to have a screaming fit. Just the thought of Christine with someone else, made her stomach turn over.

She had gleaned two things from her conversation with Lady Richmond: Christine had been there for her in the hospital, and Christine was sleeping with Heimlich. She wanted to puke.

~~~

Chapter 16

Senator Christine Richmond slipped into her pajamas. Her meeting with a few of the movers and shakers in Washington had been successful. She received promises of campaign funds and support for her run for the U.S. Senate. All she had to do was vote for an occasional pet project they supported.

She had met with both Democrats and Republicans. There wasn't a dime's bit of difference between them. They all had been willing to throw money and influence behind her in exchange for her votes. They were supposed to be serving the voters, not acting as lobbyists for special interest groups.

Heimlich had escorted her back to her room. He was insistent that she invite him in, but she begged off, telling him she was exhausted. He had grabbed her and kissed her hard before she knew what was happening.

He had overpowered her so easily; it scared her. She spent over an hour under the scalding hot shower trying to wash away the feel of his touch.

She slipped into bed and turned out the light. As always, she closed her eyes and conjured Major Ricky Strong. Ricky's dancing blue eyes, gazing into her own. That cocky smile that said, "I know what you want, Senator and I'm going to give it to you." Ricky above her, blonde hair falling around them, forming a place that held only their faces, their lips, their love.

Dear God, help me, she prayed. Help me be strong enough to do what is right. The phone rang.

"Hello," she whispered.

"Are you alone?" Ricky asked.

"Of course," Christine snapped. "It is one in the morning. Why wouldn't I be alone?"

"Sorry, your mother told me you were sleeping with Heimlich," Ricky choked.

"Would that bother you?" Christine asked.

"More than you could ever know," Ricky whispered into the phone.

"Would that make you crazy?" Christine continued. "Make you want to kill something or someone? Make you wish you were dead?"

"Yes," Ricky hissed.

"Good! Then you know the hell I have been living in." The line went dead.

~~~

"Are you ready, Kay?" Ricky asked as she handed the ranger a pair of camera glasses like the ones she had worn during the border operation.

"Ready and able," Kay Dawson nodded.

"Remember we will have eyes and ears on you at all times. We have no evidence that ties this guy to the other murders. You have to get him to confess."

"Four Rangers are already in place in the restaurant," Ricky explained. "Two of them are working as waiters, one is the hostess, and one will be dining. Everyone has electronics like ours. I am going to step into the other room and test our receivers and transmitters."

212

Ricky entered the room adjoining Kay's and closed the door. Becky and Daisy were monitoring the glasses worn by all members of the team. "Can you hear me, now?" Ricky smiled as she repeated the words made famous by some cell phone company.

"Yes," Kay laughed. "These things are great."

"We are all interconnected," Ricky explained. "Everyone sound off."

Each team member checked in.

The phone in Kay's room rang. "Hello," she said cheerfully. "No, I will meet you in the lobby."

"He called from the lobby phone," Kay informed her listeners.

"Showtime," Ricky said softly. "Stay alert, everyone."

Kay had read all of Ricky's emails to Troy Hunter, so she was familiar with their discussions. Hunter looked nothing like the picture he had posted on Facebook. He was tall and gaunt. A beak-like nose reminded her of an eagle. His eyes were small and close together. Only his sensual lips kept him from looking ordinary. He smiled revealing perfect white teeth. He was almost handsome.

There was nothing about Troy Hunter that would lead one to think he was a serial killer.

"You must be Alessa?" he gleefully grinned as he approached her.

"You must be Troy?" she smiled warmly. "You don't look like your picture on Facebook."

A frown settled over his face.

"You are more handsome than your photo," she laughed. "Much more handsome."

The dazzling smile returned to his face as he held out his hand to shake hers.

"You are even more beautiful than your photo, too," he shyly said.

She continued to hold his hand in hers. "Shall we eat?" she grinned. "I am starving."

To Kay's surprise, Troy Hunter was a remarkable conversationalist. He loved computers, wrote software programs and loved animals.

His antidotes about his nieces, nephews, and Charlie kept her in stitches. He was very entertaining.

When the check came, Troy insisted on paying it. "We should split it," Kay suggested.

"Sorry," he grinned, "Gentlemen never let ladies pay. And you are a true lady." He placed enough cash in the receipt book to cover the check and tip.

They left the restaurant and drove to the Texas Ranger's Hall of Fame and Museum. Troy was extremely interested in the history and heroics of the Rangers. He purchased two books on the history of the Rangers. "Before we talk again," he smiled as he handed one of the books to Kay, "we will read this and discuss it." Kay noticed he paid for everything in cash.

"I applied to be a Texas Ranger," he grinned shyly. "I didn't make it. They are very selective."

Kay was surprised to find Ricky's photo in the current Ranger Heroes' Room. She glanced around the room to see if Ricky was anywhere in sight. She was relieved to see that she wasn't.

"That was fascinating," Troy said as they walked to his car.

Kay nodded in agreement.

"Did you see that blonde female ranger?" he asked.

"Yes," Kay said. "Do you know her?"

"No," Troy laughed, "but she is the one that saved the senator in that border battle a few months back. She is very attractive."

"Yes, she is," Kay agreed. "What was that senator's name? Katherine...or..."

"Christine Richmond," Troy supplied the name. "She lost her sister last year. I think I read the Hacker got her."

"Oh, my goodness," Kay feigned terror. "I did read something about that. They were twins, weren't they?"

"Yeah," Troy glanced sideways at her. "That was a real shame."

"Enough about murder," he grinned. "I am going to take you to a restaurant recommended by my friends."

~~~

Kay had to admit that she found Troy Hunter to be enchanting. She was beginning to think Major Strong had gotten this one wrong.

"I had a wonderful day," Troy shyly smiled as he walked Kay to her room.

It is now, or never, Kay thought. "Would you like to come in for a nightcap?" she said coyly.

Troy gazed into her eyes; then he bent to kiss her on the cheek. "I'd better not," he sheepishly smiled. "I am not certain I could make myself leave. You are a very beautiful woman."

Kay sighed. "Who said anything about you leaving?"

"I'd like to get to know you better," Troy frowned, "before we take this to the next level. I've been hurt before. I am taking things slowly."

Kay nodded, tiptoed to kiss him sweetly on the lips and then opened the door to her room. "Email me," she whispered as she closed the door.

Troy quickly slipped his foot between the door and the frame, preventing it from closing. "I will call you," he smiled and held his phone out to Kay. "Give me your phone number."

Kay keyed her number into his cell phone.

"I love the sound of your voice. Goodnight, Kay." He walked to the elevator.

"Crate, Barrel, follow him," Ricky ordered. "Stick with him until you find out where he lives."

Kay flopped onto the hotel bed. "You know I feel bad," she laughed. "I couldn't even entice a serial killer to enter my room."

Ricky scowled. "Maybe I am wrong. Maybe he is just trying to pick up a date. God, I need a break in this case."

"I read the case files," Kay said. "You have nothing on the other four victims. No names or way to identify them."

"Correct," Ricky nodded. "We did identify Rosie Garland, but could find no connection between her and Troy other than the Facebook flirting. If I could just get an ID on the women, I could get their laptops and see if they communicated with him on Facebook. Right now, I am basing my entire case on picking him up from Kara's computer. That doesn't prove he murdered her. He seemed like a nice guy."

"He certainly didn't come across as a creepy killer," Kay agreed.

Kay's phone rang. "Hello. Oh! Hi Troy," she enthused. "I am glad you called."

Kay nodded at Ricky as she listened to Troy. "Next weekend. I would love to. I had a wonderful time, too. Goodnight."

Kay checked her phone to get Troy's number. "He blocked his number," she frowned.

"I noticed Kara and Rosie were raped," Kay frowned. "I didn't see that in the other reports."

"The other three were so badly deteriorated we couldn't get much forensic evidence from them. The river and the fish didn't leave us much to work with," Ricky said. "Fortunately, Kara had only been dead about a week when some kids found her body washed up on the riverbank. Most of it was still intact. Same with Rosie."

"You want to give it another go next weekend?" Kay asked.

"Yes," Ricky nodded. "I have a gut feeling about this guy."

~~~

Wednesday was Ricky's turn in the barrel. It seemed everyone was shooting at her.

Lady Richmond made her usual demanding visit wanting to know if she had Kara's killer in jail. "Not yet," the ranger replied.

"It seems you and my daughter have become quite the heroes of Austin," Lady snarled. "The millennials are emulating you."

"I have no idea what you are talking about," Ricky frowned.

"The University of Texas is offering a law and politics course next semester," Lady scoffed. "The idea is to interest more young women in law enforcement jobs and politics. Rumor has it you and my daughter will be guest professors the first semester right after Christmas."

She sneakily glanced sideways at Ricky. "When you see my daughter, try to convince her to dissociate herself from that Henlick character."

"Heimlich," Ricky corrected. "I thought you wanted her to dissociate herself from me. You'll be happy to know she has. I doubt she would listen to anything I might say."

"Humph," Lady snorted, "I'd rather see her dating you than that weasel."

"You only say that because you know it isn't even in the realm of possibility," Ricky shook her head at the older woman as she escorted her to the elevator.

"You really should be careful what you wish for, Lady," Ricky smiled as the elevator door slid closed between them.

"Major, you have a call on line two," Becky informed her as she walked back to her office.

"Strong," DD Rhodes barked through the phone line, "we have another handless floater, washed up about an hour, ago. What the hell is going on? I thought you had this under control."

"So, did I, sir," Ricky cleared her throat. "Where is the body?"

"Austin's ME has it. You want it?"

"Yes, sir," Ricky exhaled. "Any idea how old it is?"

"Not yet." Rhodes snorted. "Keep me informed on this. The press is breathing down my neck."

"Anyone in particular?" Ricky inquired.

"That blonde from channel four," Rhodes said. "You know the one with the big…?" He stopped short of finishing his description of the busty news anchor.

"Paige Daily, Sir?"

"Yeah," Rhodes huffed.

"I will talk to her, sir," Ricky said.

After she had finished her call with Rhodes, she called the TV reporter.

"Must be my lucky day," Paige teased. "Did I rattle your boss, so you are calling to pacify me?"

"Would that work?" Ricky laughed.

"Wouldn't hurt," Paige sensuously smiled.

"We do need to talk, Paige. How about dinner tonight?"

"Is this your idea or did Rhodes tell you to wine and dine me?"

"Entirely my idea," Ricky chuckled. "Is Truluck's okay? Jen is singing tonight. I know you like her."

"You know me too well, Ranger Strong. What time will you call for me?"

"Seven," Ricky smiled. She liked Paige. She also feared her. She was a ruthless reporter and could smell a story a mile away. Right now, Ricky was sitting on a powder keg of stories.

Whoever coined the phrase *bad things come in threes* certainly knew what they were saying.

A scuffling outside Ricky's door made her look up as Crate and Barrel charged into her office. "Before you yell at us, boss, hear us out," Crate cried as he slammed the door closed behind them.

"We have been pulled off Senator Richmond's protection service." Barrel blurted out.

"Like hell, you have," Ricky jumped from her seat and stood face-to-face with her two best men.

"Rhodes told us our services were needed elsewhere," Crate continued. "The FBI is taking over her security detail."

"The FBI," Ricky stormed. "Why not the Boy Scouts. They are both about as effective when it comes to protecting someone." She rounded her desk and grabbed her phone. She didn't waste time with Rhodes. She called Crockett directly.

"Sir, I have a serious problem," she tried to breathe evenly as Director David Crockett listened to her.

She silently listened as he spoke.

"Yes, sir. I understand, sir. Thank you, Director. With the utmost discretion, sir."

"What is going on?" Crate demanded.

"It seems Senator Richmond's father is a good friend of the FBI Chief for this sector," Ricky explained. "He requested that the FBI take over Christine's security detail. He thinks they are more capable of protecting the senator than we are."

"What did Director Crockett say?" Barrel asked."

"He said I am the major over this division. I can make my own calls, but I better be prepared to live with the consequences." Ricky pushed back her chair.

"I want the two of you to continue to provide security for Senator Richmond, only in the shadows. Don't let the FBI know you are there. Same way you protected her in D.C."

"About D.C., Major," Crate motioned for Barrel to sit down. "There are some things you need to know about Senator Richmond and Senator Heimlich."

~~~

Ricky parked her car in front of Paige Daily's home. She and Paige had dated for over a year, but eventually parted ways when they mutually agreed that their careers didn't mix well together. Ricky had too many secrets, and Paige worked too hard trying to uncover them. They remained friends and occasionally answered each other's calls for help.

Ricky rang the doorbell and listened as the click of Paige's heels approached the door. Paige hungrily scanned the ranger. "God, you are gorgeous," she smiled.

"I had forgotten how beautiful you are when you dress up for a date." Paige tilted her head slightly and smiled. "Is this a date, Ricky?"

"This is two friends having dinner together," Ricky smiled. "And I need your help."

##

As always Truluck's Seafood and Steakhouse was outstanding. Their favorite local female vocalist was performing. They contentedly listened as they sipped their after-dinner drinks.

"So," Paige leaned across the table and ran her finger slowly around the back of Ricky's hand, "What can I do for you, Major?"

Ricky swallowed as the blonde's touch reminded her how soft and affectionate the woman could be. She watched the candlelight dance in Paige's green eyes and tried to recall why they had broken up.

"Jen is in rare form tonight," Paige smiled as the singer finished her set and walked toward their table.

"Ricky, Paige," the performer greeted them warmly. "It is a joy to see the two of you together again."

"It is nice," Paige nodded. "You are even better than I remember. I love your new routine."

"Jen, you do keep getting better and better," Ricky agreed. "I have missed listening to you."

"Then you two should come here more often," Jen grinned. "Liven the place up a little. Two gorgeous women always make things better."

The three visited until the singer had to return to the stage. "Want to get out of here?" Paige said softly.

Ricky nodded, paid the check and walked out into the cool night air. "Do you mind running by my place?" Ricky asked. "I have something I want to show you."

"You're not going to show me your etchings, are you?" Paige laughed.

Ricky joined her merriment. "I might. Did you *have* to wear that dress tonight?"

"As I recall, you love this dress," Paige mischievously grinned. "You said it showed off all of my assets."

"My point, exactly," Ricky chuckled.

Ricky pulled her car into the parking garage and turned to face Paige. "I need your help to catch a serial killer," she exclaimed.

"Wow, Major Strong, you sure do know the way to a girl's heart." Paige caught Ricky's hand. "How can I help?"

"Come on; I'll pour us a glass of wine and show you what I've got." Ricky laughed. "That wasn't a come-on line."

As Paige poured their wine, Ricky brought a box from her bedroom and began to spread photos on her dining table. Paige leaned over Ricky's shoulder, careful to drag her ample breast across the ranger's arm, and placed the wine glass in front of her.

"Oh, my God," Paige gasped as she saw the photos Ricky had spread out.

"Gruesome," Ricky nodded.

"You sure know how to kill a mood," Paige huffed. "What is this?"

"The victims of the Hacker," Ricky shrugged. "I brought everything I have so you could pick out the best things for you to use. I am desperate to identify these four women."

"This is the first victim," Ricky began to line up the photos in order of their deaths. "This is Kara Richmond, Senator Richmond's twin, this is Rosie Garland, and this is the one we fished out of the river this morning."

"Who are the other women?" Paige asked as she shuffled the photos around.

"I have no idea," Ricky sipped her wine.

"As you know, the Hacker chops off their hands. The first three were in the river for a long time before being discovered. We were only able to identify Kara because the senator brought us hair and fingernail clippings to match DNA. Jane Doe 4 matched.

"Rosie Garland was a woman I watched him court on Facebook, but she had no emails from him on her computer. It appeared they simply stopped communicating on Facebook. Next thing I knew we were fishing her out of the river."

"Our forensic art department put together these computer-generated drawings of the other three victims. I thought I had tracked down the killer, but while I had him under surveillance, another victim was dumped into the Colorado. Here is the morgue shot of her."

"They all look alike," Paige frowned. "Your guy definitely has a type."

"No one knows about our latest victim," Ricky said. "This would be exclusive for you."

"What do you want me to do?" Paige asked.

"Broadcast an appeal asking for anyone who recognizes or think they may know any of these women to call me. If I can identify even one of these women, I can prove my theory about the murders."

"This one is the senator's sister," Paige picked up Kara's photo. "She was married to Blaize Canyon, right?"

Ricky nodded. "Yeah, Blaize is a piece of work."

Paige laughed and agreed. "Would it be possible to get Senator Richmond to make a passionate plea for help? That would be a real coup for me and a boost in my ratings."

"I will talk to her in the morning," Ricky said. "Now I better get you home."

"I might be willing to spend the night," Paige sensuously smiled, "You know, for old times' sake."

Ricky ran her tongue between her lips and inhaled. "You have no idea how tempting that is," she slightly smiled, "but I am afraid I am committed."

"Anyone I know?" Paige raised a perfectly arched brow.

"You will be the first to know if we ever go public," Ricky grinned. "Which of these photos do you want? I'll line up the senator. Anything else you need from me?"

"Apparently, not," Paige shrugged.

～～～

Ricky dropped Paige off at her home then headed for Christine's house. She rehashed the information Crate and Barrel had given her about Christine and Heimlich.

The senator had confided in the two rangers that she was certain Heimlich was a front man for the Mexican drug cartel. She was pretending to like him to get information from him.

Ricky called Crate's mobile. "How is it going?"

"Senator Richmond and Heimlich just arrived at her house," Crate said softly. "I don't see the FBI guy anywhere. They are walking to the door of her home. Boss, it looks as if he is pushing his way inside."

"I am almost there," Ricky chuckled. "I will send him packing."

Ricky pulled her car alongside Heimlich's rental car and made a note of his license plate. She looked around for the FBI agent that was supposed to be guarding Christine. He was not there. *Typical*, she thought.

As she reached to push Christine's doorbell, a scream came from inside the house. Ricky turned the doorknob and was surprised to find it unlocked.

"Get off me, you oaf," Christine was yelling.

"Surely you don't think you can tease me all night then send me home?" Heimlich said as he pinned the brunette against the sofa. He swiftly pushed down his slacks and began pulling up the skirt of Christine's dress.

"No! Stop," Christine cried. "I will file rape charges against you." She bucked and fought the man trying to slide from under his weight.

"Who do think they will believe?" Heimlich grunted.

Ricky racked her Sig bringing a stillness to the room. "Get off her nice and slow," she said into the deathly silence.

Heimlich didn't move, obviously considering his options. Ricky poked the barrel of the pistol into his ear. "Now!"

Heimlich stood, and his slacks fell around his ankles. He made a move to pull them up. "No, no," Ricky hissed. "Step out of them."

Heimlich hesitantly obeyed.

"Now take off your shirt," Ricky growled. The man stood naked. "Looks like rape to me," Ricky snorted as she shoved Heimlich toward the front door. "Today is your lucky day. If you disappear in two minutes, I am not going to arrest you."

She shoved him out the door, closed and locked it. She called Paige, "Get to this address with a camera crew quickly. I have a surprise for you."

Ricky called the local police. "There is a nude man prowling around the Casa Linda Heights area. Please send a patrolman. He was last seen at this address."

Christine and Ricky watched from the upstairs window as the police and Paige arrived at the same time. Heimlich was hiding in the shrubbery across the street from Christine's house.

Paige's cameraman flooded the shrubs with light as he filmed the police dragging the naked man into the yard. Neighbors came out to see what was going on.

Paige gave a detailed description of what her viewers saw live.

Ricky's phone rang. "You alright, boss?" a laughing Crate asked.

"Yes," Ricky chuckled. "You two go home and get some rest. I will guard the senator until morning." She slid her phone into her pocket and turned to face Christine.

"What makes you think I want you here?" Christine weakly said.

"Do you want me to leave?"

"No!" The brunette was in the ranger's arms, smothering her with kisses. "I know this is wrong," she whimpered, "but I can't help it."

Ricky wasn't sure what Christine thought was wrong, and she didn't care. Everything about holding the brunette in her arms felt right.

The rest of the night was filled with exquisite sensations as Ricky did everything she knew to let Christine know how much she loved her. Gentle kisses turned into desperate pleadings as their lips and tongues tangled when their need to claim more of each other raged out of control. Christine clung to her, pulling her tight against her, begging Ricky to love her more.

"I have missed you so much," the brunette whispered as she nibbled Ricky's lower lip. "How can I love you so much when you hurt me so badly?"

"Baby, please tell me what I did wrong," Ricky pleaded as Christine slid her hand up the blonde's leg and touched her. The question disappeared in the sounds of passion.

Ricky awoke the next morning to an empty house. The note on the dresser said, "Please get rid of Heimlich's car."

Ricky eyed the dress she had worn the night before. It laid in a wrinkled heap beside Christine's bed. *Time for the walk of shame,* she thought.

She checked Christine's closet on the chance that some of her clothes might still be there. She was surprised to find one of her dress suits and a pair of low heels. She showered, borrowed clean underwear from Christine, dressed and went downstairs. She called Crate.

"Where are you?" she asked as she gathered Heimlich's clothes and found his car keys.

"Senator's office," Crate whispered. "Her FBI bodyguard showed up around eight this morning. I have no idea where he was last night."

"Stick with her," Ricky said. "I will talk with you later."

Ricky called Christine. Her call went to voice mail.

"Please call me," she said.

~~~

"I need to speak with Senator Richmond," Ricky informed Christine's receptionist. "Please tell her it is official business and extremely important."

228

As she waited for Christine to see her, Ricky thought about Martina telling her she should handcuff the senator, drag her somewhere and make her talk to her.

I had her alone last night, Ricky thought. *Unfortunately, we didn't do much talking.*

"The senator will see you now, Major," the receptionist led Ricky to Christine's office.

Ricky steeled herself. She never knew in what mood she would find her lover.

The brunette didn't move from her desk. Instead, she raised her eyes slowly from the papers in her hand, scanning the ranger's body. A slight smile played on her lips. "What can I do for you, Major Strong?"

Let me spend the night with you tonight, Ricky thought but said something entirely different.

"I need your help catching Kara's killer," Ricky got right to the point. "I also need to know what is going on with Heimlich."

Christine's brown eyes darkened. "How can I help catch Kara's killer?"

"Are you familiar with Paige Daily?" Ricky asked.

"The television reporter," Christine frowned slightly. "The one with the big breasts on channel…"

Ricky cut in, "She has agreed to help me."

"Of course, she has," Christine snarked. "Is that her real name? Sounds more like a newspaper reporter, you know, read this page daily. I bet more than one person has turned that page."

Ricky ignored the senator's catty remark. "If I can identify our other Jane Does, I can catch the killer. I need to find a common thread between the victims."

"She has agreed to air a special on the Hacker. She will show the artist's drawings of the slain women and request her viewer's help in identifying the victims.

"We just pulled another woman from the Colorado. Her body is relatively fresh. We have an actual morgue photo. It will be the first time we have taken the entire story to the public."

"What do you need from me?" Christine asked.

"Paige wants an interview with you," Ricky shuffled her feet. "Since your sister was a victim of the Hacker, she feels having you on the special will give it a personal touch and great credibility."

Christine nodded. "When does she want to film the special? I will clear my calendar."

"Tomorrow?" Ricky raised her eyebrows questioningly.

"Will you be there?"

"I can be," Ricky said.

"I would like that," Christine softly said.

"Now, tell me about Heimlich and why you are dating him?" Ricky pulled a chair closer to Christine's desk and sat down.

Christine took a deep breath. "You do know I have never slept with him, right?"

Ricky nodded. "I know you have a great deal of integrity. I can't see you stooping that low." She didn't add that Crate and Barrel had given her the same information the day before.

"When the cartel was dragging us from place to place in Mexico, I saw Heimlich at one of the warehouses. It was briefly. They thought I was unconscious so weren't worried about anyone seeing him.

"After our return, he called me to express his appreciation for my efforts to move the wall project forward. He volunteered to be on the committee I am forming to spearhead the project.

"I knew he was a mole for the cartel and I was hoping he would take me around his close friends. He introduced me to some shady characters last week.

"After last night, I am sure he will be drummed out of office. Last night was some of your best work, by the way." Mischief danced in her eyes as a smile produced the dimples Ricky loved.

"Are we talking about Heimlich's arrest?" Ricky raised a sculpted eyebrow.

"Oh, that, too," Christine seductively smiled.

Chapter 17

"If you will sit here, across from me, Senator," Paige smoothed her skirt. She rarely interviewed women as poised and gorgeous as Senator Christine Richmond. The reporter was a little self-conscious.

After the filming, Paige explained how her station would handle the special. "We will edit out things like where I dropped my iPad, and you looked down the front of my dress when I bent over to pick it up."

"I did no such thing," Christine protested. "You should wear high-necked dresses," she meekly added.

"We will run teasers, and ads promoting the special then air it on Monday night," Paige continued. "That will guarantee a large audience for the show."

"Where is Major Strong?" Christine looked around the set for the blonde.

"I think she is in the ladies' room," Paige said.

"She has worked hard on this case," Christine noted. "She should get some credit."

"She doesn't like publicity," Paige smiled knowingly. "She is more of a behind the scenes kind of gal."

"Have you known her long?" Christine asked.

"About five years. I have tremendous respect for Ricky. She is the most dedicated law enforcement officer I have ever met."

Both women watched Ricky as she strolled toward them. A member of the film crew stopped to shake hands with the ranger.

"It is a shame she is off the market," Paige wistfully said.

"What do you mean?" the senator frowned.

"She told me she is in a committed relationship," Paige whispered.

Paige's words hit Christine like a kick in the throat. She had almost forgotten that Ricky belonged to the dark-haired Italian beauty.

"I must go," Christine gathered her purse and jacket. "Thank you, Miss Daily for helping bring my sister's killer to justice. Let me know if I can be of any further assistance."

"What did you do to her?" Ricky watched as Christine made a hasty exit from the set.

"Nothing," Paige frowned. "She suddenly was in a hurry to leave. Probably had another appointment. Want to buy me a drink?"

"Sure," Ricky nodded. *I have nowhere else to go*, she thought.

~~~

Christine threw down her book and rearranged the pillows on her bed. She turned out her lights and tried, again, to sleep.

The night before immediately filled her mind. She berated herself for so quickly jumping into bed with Major Ricky Strong. She cursed herself for being so weak where the ranger was concerned.

Even though she was disgusted with herself, she couldn't help recalling the soft, gentle way Ricky had made love to her. She could almost feel Ricky's hands on her, caressing her, touching her, whispering her name, driving her crazy. Her need for the woman was overwhelming. She toyed with the idea of sleeping with Ricky until self-loathing became stronger than her desire to be in the ranger's arms. She looked at her bedside clock. It was after midnight. She hoped Ricky would call. She didn't.

~~~

Ricky scanned her appointments for the day. It was before eight, and she wanted to get some work finished before her first appointment. She wondered what Crate and Barrel wanted that was so important they had made an appointment to see her.

The men showed up at eight o'clock on the dot. They nervously shuffled as they greeted their boss.

"Sit down," Ricky gestured toward the chairs in front of her desk. "Who is guarding Senator Richmond?"

"Two of our buddies," Crate answered. He hesitantly glanced at Barrel.

"Okay," Ricky grinned. "What is going on? What are you two up to?"

"This," Crate slammed a thick manuscript onto Ricky's desktop.

She pulled the book toward her and thumbed through it. After several minutes, she looked up from the papers. "What is this?"

"We started writing it to chronicle your activities," Barrel blurted out.

"Then things got out of hand," Crate frowned. "Honest Major, we never intended for things to get this far."

"What are you talking about?" Ricky scowled as she glanced at the book, again.

"Let me start at the beginning," Crate cleared his throat. "When you accepted the border detail to protect Senator Richmond, we instantly realized that it was a hot assignment.

"We decided to keep a journal on our day to day activities.

"When we returned to Austin, and you came through the ordeal in one piece, we showed it to Vander Cameron, the movie producer.

"He suggested we try to get some publishing house to publish it."

"We would like to do that, but only if you approve," Barrel added.

Ricky laughed. "Hey, if you guys want to do this it is okay with me. I seriously doubt you will find any takers, but knock yourselves out."

"Thanks, Major," both men beamed. "We already have a publisher. All we needed was your permission."

"What is the title?" Ricky grinned.

"Too Strong to Die!" Both men chorused as they exited the office.

~~~

"Major," Rangers Lee Phillips and Tim (Tank) Tanksly stood as Ricky entered the room. "We have a full report on your suspected rapist."

They followed Ricky into her office.

"We followed him to this address," Lee slid a sheet of paper in front of her. I checked county tax records to see who owns the house."

Your guy is Scott Winslow," Tank joined in.

235

Ricky frowned, the name was familiar. "Did you run a background check on him?"

"He is the head of the National Republican Committee," Tank said.

"Damn," Ricky cursed. "This case just can't get any worse. You guys up for some overtime this weekend?" Both men nodded enthusiastically.

They discussed rendezvousing with Kay Dawson, Becky and Daisy for dinner the next evening. Ricky called Kay and was glad the brunette was excited about the opportunity to make another run at Troy Hunter.

After the men had left her office, Ricky called Christine, again. She left a message but didn't expect any response. For the thousandth time, she wondered what she had done wrong. She was very concerned that Christine spent a lot of time with Winslow.

She checked with Crate and Barrel who assured her the senator was safe. "That FBI clown is camping out in her waiting room," Crate said. "He has no idea we are shadowing her.

"Are you going to relieve us tonight?"

"Probably not," Ricky said. "I have some arrangements to make for our stakeout on Hunter this weekend. Tim and Tank are on their way to relieve you.

"Crate, you two keep an eye out for Scott Winslow, the National RNC chair. We believe he is our killer posing as Troy Hunter."

~~~

Using her Alessa Morris Facebook account, Ricky logged on to the social media and typed *I may have met my destiny this weekend. Planning a second date next weekend. Wish me luck. Very happy.*

She posted the information and waited. Her email box dinged in less than a minute.

"I saw your Facebook post," Troy wrote. *"I hope it was about me."*

"I was definitely about you," she typed back. *I had a wonderful time and am looking forward to seeing you again."*

"Same place, same time?" Troy typed.

"Sounds good. Why don't you bring Charlie? I would love to meet him."

"Traveling makes Charlie nervous. I would have to give him valium or something, LOL. He shakes so hard his hair falls out."

"Poor baby," Ricky typed. *"I guess I should wait to meet him in his home."*

"Charlie would love that," Troy typed back. *"So, would I. Would you feel safe visiting Charlie at my home, then we can go out to dinner?"*

"I would like to get to know you better," she typed back. *"That is a big step."*

"I understand completely," Troy answered. *"You are very wise to wait until you feel safe with me. So, I'll see you in the same place Saturday morning."*

Ricky closed her computer and made a list of the surveillance items they would need for the weekend. She would sign everything out in the morning. She, Crate and Barrel would drive to Waco and set up the cameras and equipment they would need to track and protect Kay Dawson.

Her cell phone dinged a message from Christine. "May I take you to dinner tonight?"

The text was an answer to her prayers. She desperately wanted to discuss Scott Winslow with Christine. She also wanted to see the woman.

"I'll pick you up at seven," Ricky responded.

"Perfect. Thank you, Ricky."

Ricky inhaled deeply then called Crate. "Change in plans. I will take over security for Senator Richmond tonight. You two get some rest. We will leave for Waco around ten in the morning."

"You got it, Major," Crate welcomed the prospect of a good night's sleep. "Is Kay going with us in the morning?"

"She can," Ricky said, "Why don't you call her and tell her to report to my office in the morning? See you all at ten."

Ricky smiled to herself. She was surprised that Crate was interested in Kay. He was a confirmed bachelor.

Ricky had just enough time to get to her apartment, shower, and change. She had no idea where they were going, so she slipped on a simple dark burgundy dress that hugged her curves and dropped stylishly below the knees. Low heels and a strand of pearls completed a look that would impress in a bar and grill or one of Christine's uptown dining places. She was excited about seeing the brunette. Maybe they could have a meaningful conversation over a nice quiet dinner.

~~~

Take a right on Fourth," Christine instructed. "I appreciate you picking me up at my office. My car is in the shop. The restaurant is on the corner of Fourth and Colorado."

As Ricky turned off Congress Avenue onto Fourth Street, she realized their destination was Truluck's. Ricky debated if she should inform the senator that she had dined at the restaurant a few days ago, with Paige Dailey. "Truluck's is one of my favorite restaurants," she said.

"Do you come here often?" Christine smiled as Ricky parked the car.

The ranger nodded yes.

Christine made small talk as the waitress took their order and returned with their drinks.

"I need a favor," she said then sipped her wine.

Ricky raised her eyebrows quizzically but said nothing.

"The University has asked us to be guest professors next semester to introduce a new course on law and politics."

"Us?" Ricky frowned.

"You and me," Christine smiled innocently.

"I think you are quite capable of handling the class by yourself. I am not sure I can commit the time it will require. I do catch criminals for a living, you know?"

"They are trying to reverse their liberal, left-wing reputation," Christine shrugged. "It seems you and I are the current symbols of law and order. The conservatives' darlings."

Ricky nodded. She wasn't sure she could stand a semester of the emotional rollercoaster ride on which the senator always took her. "Let me think about it?"

Christine watched the lights dance in Ricky's blue eyes. She wanted to reach across the table and hold the woman's hand.

"Tell me about Scott Winslow?" Ricky asked as the waitress placed their orders before them.

"Straight arrow," Christine frowned thoughtfully. "He runs a tight ship. Pretty much decides who gets to run for what office. He is grooming me for Governor. He wants me to do the UT course for the publicity. I want to do it to help put some sense of normality back into higher education.

"For some reason, he seems to like me and helps me whenever he can."

"For some reason, hum?" Ricky teased. "Could it be because you are drop-dead gorgeous and extremely desirable?"

Christine hung her head and blushed at Ricky's compliment. She looked up at the ranger through long lashes. A seductive smile played on her lips.

"Can we discuss us?" Ricky inhaled deeply.

"Us?" Christine tilted her head to the side as if she had no idea what Ricky was referencing.

"You know this on again, off again, game you keep playing," Ricky said softly. "One minute you can't stand to be in the same room with me, and the next minute you are tearing off my clothes.

"I never know if I am meeting Christine the Temptress or Christine the Terrible. Dating you is like dating two different women.

"On the border tour, you were wonderful even under fire. You saved my life. I saved your life. We were a team, and we were in love."

"Are we dating, Major?" Christine asked.

"I am certainly not dating anyone else," Ricky declared.

"Ricky," the restaurant's entertainer stopped at their table. "It is so good to see you, again."

Jen scanned Christine, "Senator Richmond, it is a pleasure to have you dining with us tonight."

"Thank you," Christine smiled. "We are looking forward to your next set."

"Then let me get started," Jen smiled and made her way to the band.

"I love to hear her sing," Christine looked away from Ricky.

Jen started her first song, and Ricky knew Christine was not going to answer her question.

They drove to Christine's home in silence. Ricky pulled her car in front of the house. "I had a good time," she said sullenly.

"So, did I," Christine nodded.

"The senator unfastened her seatbelt then turned in the seat to face the ranger. "When I met you, you took me by surprise," Christine said softly. "You don't look gay. You don't act gay, except in bed. What would happen if the world found out you were gay? Would your career be ruined? Would you lose your job or be put back on patrol?

"I didn't intend to fall in love with you. You are the only woman that has ever attracted me. You aren't like other gay women I have met. You are very feminine and confident. You truly have it all together. That is one of the things I love about you."

"Look," Ricky said, "I don't wear a burr haircut or march in every gay pride parade that goes down the street. My personal life is my own business. My sexuality does not define me. I am an outstanding law enforcement officer. I don't rub my sexual preference in anyone's face because that is not how I want to be judged. I want people to think of me as a good person, a good ranger and a good friend. That is all that matters. My sexuality isn't important except between me and my significant other.

"Would I lose my job? No. Thanks to you we function under the archaic 'Don't ask, don't tell' policy. Those close to me know my proclivity for women. The ones that matter to me don't care. Those that care don't matter to me."

"I would be run out of office if anyone ever learned of my relationship with you," Christine said sadly.

"I guess that is something we will never know for certain," Ricky exhaled slowly. She leaned across Christine and opened the car door. "Goodnight, Senator."

"Don't you want to come in?" Christine almost begged.

"No," Ricky sighed. "I've answered my last booty call from you, Senator."

~~~

Ricky pulled her car from Christine's drive. She was concerned that she hadn't seen the FBI security detail all night. She drove around the block and parked her car at the end of the street. The man was nowhere in sight. She waited an hour then drove back into the senator's drive. She kicked off her shoes and settled in to watch the house.

She was glad she had gotten some answers from Christine. Now she knew what was wrong with the woman; Christine felt she had to choose between being in politics or being with her. Obviously, the senator had chosen politics.

Chapter 18

A soft knock at the door drew everyone's undivided attention. "Showtime," Kay said into the ears of those monitoring her. She took a deep breath and opened the door. A smiling Troy Hunter stood in the doorway holding a beautiful bouquet of flowers. He shyly held them out to Kay. "For you," he grinned.

A sincere smile lit up the undercover agent's face as she accepted the flowers. "These are beautiful, Troy. Thank you."

"I will just wait here while you put them in water." He smiled, obviously pleased with her warm reception of the flowers.

"Oh, no," Kay laughed. "I refuse to leave you standing in the hallway. Please, come in. I won't be but a minute."

Kay fumbled around in the bathroom, giving the man plenty of time to check out her room and take a quick look in her suitcase. She had black lingerie laying on top of her clothes.

From the other side of the wall, the team of rangers watched and listened. "He is looking in your suitcase," Ricky said softly. "Give him time to get a good look at the lingerie."

Kay opened and closed cabinet doors. "Surely there is a drinking glass here somewhere," she called out.

"He has walked away from your suitcase," Ricky whispered.

"This should do until I can get them home," Kay smiled as she walked from the bathroom.

A shy Troy was standing close to the door as if prepared to bolt from the room.

"I will have these all week to remind me of you," Kay sensuously said as she placed the flowers on the desk.

"Hopefully, you will give me something to remember you by," Troy smiled slightly and made himself blush.

"Maybe," Kay said in a sexy kittenish tone.

"Damn, she is good," Ricky whispered to her team. Everyone agreed.

"Are you hungry?" Troy changed the direction of the flirting. "I want to take you to a new place my friends recommended. I hope you don't mind? I made reservations."

"That sounds wonderful," Kay grinned. "What is the name?" She knew she needed to give the team a head start on them.

"Río de Sueños," Troy rolled the Spanish off his tongue as if it were his first language.

"River of Dreams," Kay translated. "That is beautiful."

Waiting in his car, Crate pulled up the restaurant on his cell phone. "I got it, boss. We are on our way there now."

Kay languidly gathered her purse and pretended to search for her cell phone. "Would you mind calling my number?" she frowned at Troy. "I have misplaced my cell."

"I have you in my favorite persons' list," he smiled.

Her ringtone sounded in the bathroom. "Ah, there it is," she grinned at Troy and walked to the bathroom. "Give me just a minute while I powder my nose. I hate using public facilities."

Troy took the opportunity to search through her suitcase. He slipped a pair of her black panties into his inside jacket pocket.

Ricky nodded as she watched him. He had to be her man.

~~~

The entire day was uneventful. Troy took the agent to lunch, a few more museums and dancing at a super club. Kay was beginning to believe they were looking at the wrong man for the murders. She decided to push him.

As he backed the car from the parking lot, she slid her hand onto his thigh. She felt him jerk at her touch; then he covered her hand with his. "I love your hands," he said.

The warmth spreading from his leg to her hand told her she was affecting him. She leaned over and whispered in his ear, "I have had a wonderful time tonight. I wish it didn't have to end." She was careful to let her soft breath envelop his ear. Her lips lightly touched it.

It was almost midnight when they returned to the hotel. Troy walked her to her room, holding her hand. She swayed against him. "I think I over-indulged in the wine," she giggled.

She unlocked her door and invited him in. He took both her hands in his and held them gently. "You have beautiful hands," he smiled. "They are so soft and warm. Very sexy."

"The rest of me is the same way," Kay murmured.

He pulled her to him and leaned down to kiss her lips. "I am looking forward to next weekend," he said. He whirled on his heel and walked down the hallway. He got on the elevator without looking back.

~~~

Kay closed the door and locked it. Ricky, Daisy, and Becky joined her in her room.

"Jeez," Kay exclaimed. "I did everything but grab him by his privates. The guy is a monk."

"He does seem more scared of you than you are of him," Ricky frowned. "I can't figure his game."

"Do you still think he is your guy?" Becky asked.

"I am beginning to wonder," Ricky shrugged. "Let's all get a good night's sleep and head back to Austin in the morning."

~~~

Ricky tossed her gun and badge on the dresser of her apartment, stripped and stepped into the shower.

She replayed Kay's date with Troy in her mind. She waited until the water was almost scalding before adding cold water to temper it. She wanted to wash away the dread she was feeling. She had been so positive that Troy Hunter was her killer, but he certainly wasn't acting like a killer. He was acting more like a lovesick kid that had just discovered the girl of his dreams liked him.

She towel-dried her hair and slipped on an old college t-shirt that was so threadbare her breasts were visible through it. A pair of bicycle shorts completed her attire. The warm apartment belied the driving rain that was pelting her windows. *A perfect night for hot chocolate*, she thought.

When she and Christine had been fighting for their lives in the Mexico badlands, she had conjured visions of the two of them snuggling in front of the TV with hot chocolate, sharing the day's events.

She snorted and pushed the remote-control button to bring her television to life. She skipped to the local news station and sipped her cocoa as Paige Daily revisited the Hacker story. Paige ran a clip from her original interview with Christine.

A distressed look crossed Paige's lovely face as someone off camera spoke to her. The program broke to a commercial. When the show returned, Paige was chewing on her lower lip and seemed disconnected from what was going on around her. She was holding her cell phone away from her as if it might burn her.

"We are live, Miss Daily," a cameraman called to her.

"To my viewers," Paige blurted out, "A man who claims to be the Hacker has called me on my personal cell phone. Sir, are you still on the line?"

"Yes," a mechanical voice erupted from Paige's speaker phone. Ricky knew it was coming through a voice changer. "I want to get a message to Major Ricky Strong."

Ricky felt a wave of nausea sweep over her. He knew she was on to him, but how?

"Would you like to speak directly to Major Strong?" Paige asked brilliantly. "I can call her on my assistant's cell phone and put her on speakerphone. The two of you can talk."

"Ye-e-s." The man dragged out the word as if thinking about it.

Ricky jumped when her phone rang. She grabbed it and breathlessly answered it as she turned on her iPad and texted Becky Paige's phone number. "Trace the call," she ordered. She prayed Becky was watching the show.

"Major, are you watching this?" a young female voice almost whispered.

"Yes," Ricky hissed. "Give the phone to Paige. I will be happy to talk to him." She wondered why he had chosen now to speak out.

"Major Strong, thank you for taking our call," Paige said loudly.

"I am always happy to speak with cowardly killers," Ricky challenged the caller. "How do I know you are the Hacker? Do you know any details that haven't appeared in the news media?"

"Kara Richmond had a tattoo around her ankle," he chuckled.

"Anyone could know that," Ricky said calmly. "What kind of tattoo?"

"A chain," the man barked. "I left that so you could identify her for her sister."

"Still nothing others wouldn't know," Ricky said lightly. "Why don't you tell me why you cut off their hands?"

"Umm," the caller hummed. "I love ladies' hands. They are so soft and warm. Very sexy."

Now he is playing with me, Ricky thought. *His words were the exact words Troy Hunter said as he held Kay's hands.*

"What do you do with them?" Ricky asked. "Do you collect hands from beautiful women? Are they still soft and warm when you play with them? You do play with them, don't you? Perverts do that sort of thing."

"You think you are smarter than me," the man raised his voice.

A text from Becky appeared on her iPad. "Got him, boss. Crate and Barrel are headed for him right now. Keep him talking."

"I know I am smarter than you," Ricky taunted Troy. "I will catch you."

"I think not, Major Ricky Strong," the man growled. "I will kill one more time, then move on. You will have no idea what state I will visit next. Maybe Florida. Florida is nice this time of the year."

Suddenly loud shouting and gunfire came from the cell Paige was holding. She jumped almost dropping the phone.

Crate's voice came on the line. "You're not going to believe this, Major. Get over here. Becky, text her the address."

Ricky pulled her jeans on over her shorts, slid into her boots and grabbed her leather jacket as she charged out the door. She couldn't wait to see the pervert who had been butchering women in her town.

The ranger put Crate on her car phone as she sped to the address Becky had provided. "This isn't our killer. No way," Crate yelled. "Boss we left Senator Richmond unprotected."

~~~

Christine shuddered as she watched the televised exchange between Ricky and the Hacker. Dread spread through her as the man vowed to kill one more time. She wondered how close Ricky was to catching him.

She hung on Ricky's every word. She admired the ranger's calmness under such duress. That was just one of the many things she loved about Ricky Strong. Even under such terrifying conditions, she found herself longing for Ricky's touch. She wondered if she would ever get over Major Ricky Strong.

The storm outside doubled its efforts to get into her house. The driving rain pelted her windows and blew tree limbs against the house. She almost missed the sound of her doorbell as the howling winds overpowered any other sound.

She moved slowly to the door, wondering who in their right mind would be out in this weather. *Probably the FBI agent who took over my security.* She knew that Crate and Barrel continued to guard her. The TV show she had just watched told her Ricky would dispatch them to the Hacker's location.

She looked at her security camera and was surprised to see Scott Winslow on the screen. *What could be important enough to bring him out in this awful weather?* She pulled open the door slightly, giving him just enough room to slip in and keep the rain out.

"Scott, what are you doing out in this storm?" Christine demanded.

"I was worried about you," he frowned. "I was watching that news show and realized you were unprotected."

Christine briefly wondered how he knew Crate's voice on the show indicated she had no security. "There is an FBI agent in the car outside," she said.

"Yes, I know," Scott nodded. "He stopped me. I thought I would drown before he let me ring your doorbell."

Christine relaxed. The agent knew Scott was in her home. She chided herself for feeling uneasy with the man who had been her mentor for the past eight years.

"As you can see, I am fine," the senator smiled. "You should have called. You are drenched. Come into the library; I have a fire going in the fireplace. You can dry off. Would you like a drink? Brandy, Scotch..."

"Brandy would be great," Scot smiled as he removed his overcoat and hung it on the hall tree.

He frowned when Christine handed him his drink. "Aren't you joining me?" he smiled as he held up his glass.

"No, I am not much of a drinker," the brunette grinned as she returned to her chair in front of the fire.

"Surely on an evening like this you could have a glass of wine with a friend," Scott insisted. "Let me get a glass for you."

He quickly walked to the bar and poured a glass of Merlot for the senator and handed it to her.

"Why do you still have security?" he asked as he sipped his Brandy. "Are they afraid the Hacker will come after you?"

"It has to do with the border trip," Christine grimaced. "Homeland security, you know." She flipped her hand as if dismissing something insignificant. For some reason, she didn't want to confide in him that she could identify the drug cartel leader that traveled freely from Mexico to the U.S.

Scott stared into the fire and carefully chose his next words. "I have always admired your strength," he said. "The way you fight for what you believe in and the way you won't back down. You will make a superb governor."

"Thank you," Christine smiled sweetly. "That means a lot to me coming from you."

He grinned. Her obvious admiration for him and the Brandy gave him courage. "I know this is awkward, but would you be open to dating me?"

Christine's mouth dropped open slightly as her eyes darted to his. His question took her completely off guard. "I...I don't think that is a good idea," she frowned. "I find that professional and personal lives don't blend very well."

The front door swung open, and Ricky charged into the house. "Christine, are you okay?" She ran into the study to find Christine and a stranger sharing drinks. She skidded to a stop as they looked at her as if she had three heads.

"That was quite an entrance, Major," Christine scanned the blonde. A slight smile played on her beautiful lips. "What brings you out this late at night in such awful weather?"

"The fact that we pulled away your security detail," Ricky glared at the man calmly sipping his drink in front of Christine's fire. "But I see you are just fine." The ranger wondered if she would ever overcome the twinge of jealousy she felt whenever she found Christine spending time with someone else.

"Major Ricky Strong, I don't believe you have met the RNC Chairman Scott Winslow," Christine stood and moved closer to the fireplace as she made the introduction.

Ricky scrutinized the man as he stood and extended his hand to shake hers. "It is a joy to meet the newest Texas Ranger Legend," he smiled.

"Scott Winslow," Ricky repeated as they shook hands. The man looked nothing like Troy Hunter. A hundred questions ran through her mind.

"As you can see, we are safe and dry," Winslow's smile didn't reach his eyes. "Nothing for you here." Ricky knew he was dismissing her.

Christine's sudden move to stand beside her told her otherwise. "Scott and I were just sharing a drink before he braves the storm," the brunette held Ricky's gaze. "Won't you join us?"

"Thank you, Senator. A nip of Brandy might be good," Ricky sweetly smiled at Christine. "It is an atrocious night."

A night I'd like to spend in bed with you, Christine thought as she sensuously walked to the bar.

Ricky pulled her eyes from the senator's gently swaying hips and looked at Winslow. She was not surprised to see the lust in the man's eyes as he followed Christine's movements. It was almost sinful for a woman to walk that seductively.

"Why don't you remove your wet jacket?" Christine suggested as she handed Ricky her drink. "You are soaked to the bone."

"I, umm, uh, am not properly dressed," Ricky blushed. "I was dressed for bed when Paige Daily made me a participant in her newscast. When I realized, you might be in danger; I just threw my jacket and jeans over my clothes. For modesty's sake, I need to keep on my jacket."

Ricky didn't miss the way Christine ran the tip of her tongue along her lips for moisture, then pressed them together. She took a step toward the senator, momentarily forgetting there was another person in the room with them.

Christine tore her eyes away from Ricky's lips and returned to her chair by the fireplace. Ricky stood beside her so she could watch Scott Winslow. "I'll just stand," Ricky wrinkled her nose. I don't want to ruin your furniture."

Winslow studied the ranger. She was tall for a woman and very shapely. Her long blonde hair was wet, curling wildly around a beautiful face, hosting the most piercing blue eyes he had ever seen. Her wet jeans molded to her body like skin. He wondered what he would see if she removed her jacket. He drained his Brandy glass.

Christine stood to take his empty glass. "Scott, thank you so much for coming to check on me. As you can see, I am well protected." She began to walk toward her front door. "With the FBI agent outside, and Major Strong in here, I feel very safe."

Winslow reluctantly stood. The night was ending very differently from what he had planned, thanks to Major Strong. Christine held his coat so he could slip into it. He had no choice but to leave.

Christine locked the door behind Scott Winslow, turned and leaned back against it. A faint smile played on her lips as she surveyed Ricky. She quickly closed the space between them. "You look like a drowned puppy," she grinned, as she unzipped Ricky's leather jacket and slid it off her.

The senator gasped as she saw Ricky's t-shirt. "Your shirt is drenched, too," she huskily said as she scanned the threadbare shirt pulled tightly across the ranger's taut breast. She wore no bra.

"You look like the winner of a naughty Wet T-shirt Contest," Christine grinned.

"Come upstairs and let me get you some dry clothes." She grabbed Ricky's hand and pulled her to the staircase leading to her bedroom.

Ricky stopped at the bottom of the stairs. Christine raised questioning eyebrows. "We both know this is the point of no return." A slight smile twisted the ranger's lips.

Christine tugged her hand, pulling the blonde up the stairs.

~~~

"Dry your hair," Christine tossed Ricky a towel. "I'll find you something to wear." She opened an armoire and brought out a UT sweatshirt and a pair of jeans. "The jeans will look like pedal pushers on you," she smiled, but the sweatshirt should be a perfect fit."

She tossed the clothes on the bed and turned to face Ricky. Holding the ranger's eyes with her own, Christine slid her hands under the wet t-shirt and lifted it over Ricky's head. She caught her breath sharply as she stared at the blonde's perfect breasts. She couldn't stop her hand from caressing the right one. She dropped the wet t-shirt and slipped her other arm around Ricky's waist.

"I truly didn't initiate a booty call," she whispered as she brushed her lips against Ricky's.

256

"I'll take the blame for this one," the ranger murmured as she pulled the senator against her.

The storm raging outside paled in comparison to the one raging in Senator Christine Richmond's bedroom.

~~~

Chapter 19

"Don't leave me," Christine whispered as the sun filtered through the drapes. "Stay a while longer."

Ricky pulled the woman tighter against her and kissed the top of her head. The sensation of Christine's warm, pliable body molded into hers was almost unbearable. "Nothing in the world feels as good as holding you," Ricky whispered.

Christine pulled herself up to kiss Ricky's lips. "I love you, Ricky." She moved her full, soft lips slowly against the ranger's lips. Her tongue sweetly explored the blonde's lips, tracing them before thrusting into her mouth.

Ricky tightened her arms around the soft, loving woman and lost herself in the pure joy of making love to Christine Richmond.

Much later, Ricky fell back onto the bed beside her lover. "You have no idea what you do to me," she rasped, trying to catch her breath. "Or what you make me want to do to you."

"After last night and this morning," Christine giggled, "I think I have a pretty good idea. May I say the feeling is mutual?"

"Honey, we have to find a way to work this out," Ricky said hoarsely. "I want to be with you all the time. I don't want to show up when I am no longer strong enough to stay away from you."

"I want that, too," Christine raised up on her elbow and looked deep into Ricky's mesmerizing blue eyes, "but you have commitments..."

Ricky's phone went crazy as the ring tone for Crate rattled the room.

The ranger sharply exhaled as she located her phone on the floor. "Strong!"

"Major," Crate shouted in obvious distress, "God, Ricky we have another floater."

Ricky closed her eyes and took a deep breath. "I'll be right there."

"Major, it is Kay," Crate sounded as if he would burst into tears.

"Oh, my God," Ricky bolted from the bed and pulled on the sweatshirt Christine gave her. "Where is she?"

"Under the Congress Avenue Bridge. Barrel and I just arrived. We have the area roped off. It looks like this is the kill site."

Ricky pulled Christine into her arms. "I love you so much," she whispered. "I have to go. One of my officers has been murdered."

"Who?" Christine rushed to the closet and began throwing on clothes.

"Kay Dawson. She is the undercover agent that has been meeting with the man we suspected as the Hacker."

"I'm going with you," Christine declared.

Ricky hesitated, then nodded. As much as she hated admitting it, she needed the other woman with her.

On the way to the crime scene, Ricky dispatched Lee and Tank to pick up the man they knew as Troy Hunter.

"Take him to the station for questioning," she instructed. "Hold him until I get there."

She then called Becky. "Call Judge Hartford, get a search warrant for this address, asap."

"Can you fill me in?" Christine said softly. She rested her hand on the ranger's thigh.

"Yes," Ricky nodded as she related their undercover operation to catch Troy Hunter. "Until last night I have never met Scott Winslow. We thought he and Troy Hunter were the same people, but Scott looks nothing like Troy. Apparently, Troy rents a house from Scott."

"On Paige's show, he said he would murder one more woman, then disappear," Christine said. "Ricky, what if he just disappears? What if he moves to another state and starts killing all over, again?"

The ranger dragged her hand across her face. "I must catch this son-of-a-bitch."

Ricky parked her truck and held Christine's hand as they walked down the slippery slope to the gathering of police and Lane Mason's CSI team.

Crate met them as they reached level ground. He eyed Christine. "I am not sure she should see this," he nodded toward the senator. "This is the murder site. There is a lot of blood, and the hands are gone."

"Perhaps you should wait here," Ricky said softly.

"I want to be at your side on this one," Christine said stubbornly.

Ricky nodded then led the way to the gurney where Lane Mason had secured the body.

"Ricky," Lane scowled, "I am sorry. Crate told me she was one of yours."

"May I see her?" Ricky asked as she began unzipping the heavy body bag.

"Of course," Lane frowned. "This is the freshest victim we have recovered from the Hacker. I want to get her body back to the lab as soon as possible. Hopefully, I can learn a lot from it."

Ricky stared at the dead woman's face. "She was one of the best I have ever met. I can't imagine him getting the drop on her. Be sure you run a tox panel on her."

"Lane, did you see this?" Ricky pointed to Kay's lips. "There is something in her mouth."

Lane leaned in and looked at the dead ranger's mouth. "Looks like she bit a chunk out of him. Let's load her up boys," he ordered.

"The sooner I get her on a table the sooner I can provide you with facts," he said to Ricky.

Crate and Barrel joined them. "How are you doing, Senator?" Barrel greeted Christine.

"I have had better days," Christine smiled. "I don't know how you deal with this day in and day out. I truly appreciate the security you two provide me."

"Our pleasure," Crate exclaimed.

"I will have Senator Richmond with me until around two," Ricky informed them. "Then I will turn her back over to you two."

Crate pulled Ricky aside. "You need to change into your own jeans. This is not a good look for you."

Ricky laughed. "Since when did you become a fashion expert?"

~~~

Christine fastened her seatbelt as the ranger backed her pickup from the parking lot.

"We have a little over two hours," Christine glanced sideways at Ricky. "What do you have in mind?"

"Breakfast," Ricky grinned. "I am starving."

"Umm," Christine hummed as she rested her hand on the ranger's thigh. She smiled as the blonde trembled at her touch.

"I need to run to my place and change clothes," Ricky said. "I don't look very official in a sweatshirt, pedal pushers, and riding boots."

"After breakfast, I want you to look at video footage of Troy Hunter. See if you know him. Lane should have a preliminary report for us by then."

Ricky covered Christine's hand with her own. "I like your hand on my leg," she smiled shyly.

"As do I," Christine said huskily.

~~~

"We got a break," Lane grinned as Ricky and Christine entered the lab. "Leave it to Kay to go down fighting. She bit a piece out of him. I am running a DNA match now."

"It looks like she took a chunk out of his forearm," he informed them as the computer flashed through its searches.

"He is usually meticulous," Ricky frowned. "I am surprised he left that evidence behind. In the past, he has cut off women's hands and breasts to keep them from being identified. I can't imagine him leaving behind a piece of himself."

Crate and Barrel joined them. "We thought we would pick up the senator here," Crate said. "Are you having any luck?"

"We are searching the DNA databases now," Ricky shrugged.

"Damn," Lane cursed. "Something is screwed up, or your killer is even more devious than we imagined."

"What is it?" Ricky craned her neck to look around the ME.

"We have a match on the DNA."

"Awesome," Ricky beamed.

"It matches the DNA of a dead man." Lane shrugged and looked at Ricky for an explanation.

Lane's announcement knocked the air from the ranger. She had been hoping against hope that they would finally get a break.

"Someone up there hates me," she mumbled.

~~~

As she followed Crate and Barrel to their car, Christine wondered why Ricky hadn't insisted on taking her home. *I will catch up with her tonight*, she thought.

Ricky Strong slowly walked back to her office. She couldn't believe the Hacker had gotten to her best undercover agent.

Judging from the amount of blood at the crime scene, he had somehow lured Kay Dawson to the meeting spot under the bridge. Apparently, he had been scared away before he could toss Kay's body into the water. Ricky prayed that Lane would find something on Kay's body to help them identify the killer.

At least Kay's body had been fresh enough to give them a clue on how the Hacker managed to get the jump on his victims. The killer injected Kay with an almost lethal dose of narcotics. It was enough to assure she didn't awaken while he was removing her hands.

Ricky picked up two files and headed to the interrogation rooms. She had two people to question. The first was a stupid teenager who was posing as the Hacker on Paige Daily's show. The other was Troy Hunter.

Ricky sat down across from Dane Trip. She stared at him for a long time. He began to wiggle as he grew more uncomfortable under the ranger's glare.

"I thought it was a joke," the pimple-faced teen squeaked. He cleared his throat then repeated his statement in a little deeper voice.

"A joke?" Ricky said incredulously, "You think men cutting off women's hands and letting them bleed out is a joke?"

Dane shrugged. "Ranger, sir, uh, ma'am, I didn't know I was helping a serial killer. Honest. I don't watch the news."

"How did you know what to say?" Ricky scowled.

"He was on the other cellphone." The boy looked like he was about to cry. "He was watching the show. Whenever you asked me a question, he gave me the answer."

Ricky looked through the file. The boy had spoken to her through a phone connected to a voice changer. She knew the serial killer had changed the rules of his game. Before he was killing women for the perverted joy of it; now he had added the excitement of matching wits with the ranger.

"What did he look like?" Ricky asked.

"I never saw his face," Dane croaked. "I answered an ad on Craig's List for an assistant private detective. It specified ages fourteen to eighteen."

"Yeah, no one else would be that stupid," Ricky growled.

The boy nodded, then continued. "He met me in the motel room where you arrested me. He wore a mask like the Lone Ranger. At first, I thought I had been lured into a sex ring and decided not to go into the room; then he showed me the hundred dollar bills.

"He gave me the money, stayed with me until I contacted Ms. Daily. He called me on another cellphone and left."

"I swear, ma'am, I had no idea I was helping a killer." Tears began to run down Dane's face.

Ricky pushed a box of tissues to the boy, read him the riot act about answering items on Craig's List then told him to go home.

"What about my money?" the teen hiccupped. "It belongs to me."

Ricky nodded. "We are pulling hundreds of fingerprints from the bills. It is a long shot, but we might get lucky. When we are through, we will return the money to you. I'll have an officer take you to fingerprinting so we can disregard your prints on the bills. He will give you a receipt for the money."

Ricky thought about Christine as she moved from one interrogation to another. She sent the gorgeous brunette a text. "May I take you to dinner?"

The immediate reply was, yes. Ricky smiled. Life with Christine was certainly more pleasant than life without her. A slight tremor ran through her body as she recalled how good it felt to hold the senator.

Ricky slapped the file onto the interrogation table and stared at Troy Hunter briefly. The man wasn't at all intimidated. She sat down across from him and introduced herself.

"I know who you are," Troy grinned hesitantly. You are famous, Major Strong."

"Where were you last night?" Ricky asked casually.

"On a date," Troy shrugged.

"I need a name and phone number," Ricky smiled. "I need to check your alibi."

"My alibi for what?" Troy's eyes darted around the room.

"I need to know where you were at the time Kay Dawson died." Ricky's eyes were glued to his face. She didn't want to miss his reaction when she informed him Kay was dead.

"I don't know a Kay Dawson," he declared.

"You know her as Alessa Morris."

"Alessa," his eyes bugged out as if she had gouged him in the throat. "No, no, she was my date last night. She can't be...Oh, my God, I am the last one to see her alive."

"I swear, Major Strong, I didn't kill her."

Ricky had one of her gut reactions. She knew Troy Hunter was telling the truth.

"Why don't we start with your real name?" she said.

"Wayman Cross," the man said miserably. "I am an accountant for American Airlines. I live in Austin."

"How did you end up meeting Kay?"

"I received a promotion which required me to move to Austin. About a month ago, I flew to Las Vegas for the weekend to celebrate my new job. I met a man on the plane, and we struck up a conversation.

"When he found out I was moving to Austin, he suggested I look at a house he had for lease. He leased it to me for almost nothing."

"He told me his mother was constantly setting him up with blind dates and she had arranged one with the daughter of a very wealthy customer. He said that would be fine except he was gay.

"He told me he was supposed to meet the woman in Waco and show her a good time." Wayman sighed. "He said that under no circumstance could I have sex with her.

"He offered me three thousand dollars to take his place. He said he had never met the woman so she wouldn't know I wasn't him."

"What was his name?" Ricky asked.

"Troy Hunter," Wayman shrugged.

"How did you end up on a date with Kay, uh Alessa, last night?"

"Troy called me and suggested that I call Alessa. He said he had made reservations for us at the Texas Roadhouse, and that our check was already paid. I had her cell phone number on my phone, so I called her. She seemed delighted to hear from me and agreed to meet me at The Texas Roadhouse. We had dinner and a couple of drinks. I walked her to her car, and she drove away.

"I swear, Alessa was alive when I left her."

Ricky's phone rang and Christine's face graced her screen. She let the call go to voicemail.

"Look, Major, I will take a polygraph," Wayman pleaded. "I would never hurt Alessa. I was falling in love with her."

"Can you describe the man you met on the plane?" Ricky asked.

"He was just average," Wayman shook his head. "Brown hair, brown eyes, average height—about five-ten—weighed about one-seventy-five. I think he was a nice-looking fellow. It was hard to tell. He wore an eyepatch, and he had a mustache. He reminded me of a pirate."

Ricky inhaled then slowly exhaled. She rubbed the bridge of her nose with her thumb and forefinger. "Would you go through a mug shot book and see if you recognize anyone?"

"Sure," Wayman nodded. "I'll do anything you ask, Major."

"Wait here."

She closed the interrogation room door and slowly walked to her office. She pulled out her phone to return Christine's call. She noticed she had two voicemails. One of them was from Kay Dawson.

She sat down in her office and played back Kay's message. *Major, I just had dinner with Troy Hunter. Are you sure we have the right man? He is so sweet and shy. I know you are probably going to kick my butt tomorrow for doing this on my own.* Kay laughed, *but I took it as a personal insult when I couldn't even tempt a sex-crazed serial killer. I am almost home. See you first thing in the morning. Goodnight.*

That pretty much exonerates Wayman, Ricky thought.

She dialed Christine's number. "Hello," the senator said breathlessly.

"What are you doing and who are you doing it with?" Ricky teased.

"I am making you a home-cooked meal," Christine giggled. "And you know, I only do it with you."

"I am leaving here in about five minutes," Ricky smiled into the phone. "Can't wait to see you."

"Umm, me, too." Christine hummed.

When she returned to the interrogation room, Wayman had his head resting on his arms. Ricky thought he was crying. "Are you okay?"

The man jerked. "Yes, ma'am. I just can't believe she's dead."

"Neither can I," Ricky said. "Ranger Lee is going to show you the mug-shot books. After you go through them, you are free to go. Don't leave town. I may have more questions for you after we complete the autopsy."

"I will help in any way I can," Wayman reiterated.

Ricky stopped by the CSI office on her way out of the building. "Was Kay's cell phone in her purse when we found her body?"

The Agent in charge pulled an evidence bag from a box marked Dawson and emptied the contents onto the table. "This is all we found, Major. No cell phone."

~~~

Ricky approached the car containing the FBI agent running security on Christine. The man was asleep. She slammed her boot into the side of his car.

He jumped, hitting his head on the roof of the vehicle. He flapped his hands around as if unsure what to do with them. Ricky yanked open his door and dragged him out of the car onto his knees.

"You were asleep," she raged. "There are people trying to kill Senator Richmond, and you are getting your beauty rest. Where the hell do you go when you aren't here?"

"I...I, uh," the agent stuttered.

"What is your name? Let me see some I.D.," Ricky demanded. "Better yet turn around and put your hands on top of the car." She unholstered her gun and shoved it into his back as she searched his pockets.

She pulled out his I.D. wallet and flipped it open. "Agent Bobby Day," she read. "Agent Day, you haven't answered my questions."

"Look, Major," Day accepted his wallet as she shoved it into his hands. "I've got no back up here. I watch the senator twenty-four/seven. My boss considers the threat to her minor, so he isn't taking this whole thing seriously.

"When I disappear, it is to shower and change clothes. When I sleep, I sleep here. We both know your men are watching her, too."

"First, the threat to Senator Richmond is extremely serious," Ricky scowled. "She is in danger from more than one faction. The liberal left and unions would like her head on a stake, and the Mexican drug cartel is itching to kill her. Make no bones about it; she is always in danger, so are you. When they make their move, her security will be the first thing they will take out.

"Second, my men and I will always be nearby. Maybe your boss doesn't care if she dies on your watch, but by God, she is not going to die on mine.

"Third, go get a good night's sleep. I will be here the rest of the night. Be back here by nine in the morning. My Rangers are Clyde Barrel and Roger Crate, introduce yourself to them in the morning. The three of you work out an arrangement so you can get some sleep."

"Yes, ma'am" Day saluted.

"Saluting is not necessary," Ricky grinned. "If I were you I wouldn't let my boss know I was working with the enemy. Your boss will throw a fit, and I will get into a pissing match with him. I guarantee you; he won't win. I will be forced to document your absences and sleep habits."

Day nodded and climbed back into his car. "I will see you at nine in the morning, Major."

~~~

Oh, Lord, something smells wonderful, Ricky thought as she walked into the senator's house. She followed her nose to the kitchen and watched from the doorway as Christine removed a dish from the oven.

The brunette moved to the sink to wash her hands and jumped when Ricky slipped her arms around her waist and pulled her back against her.

"Dinner smells delicious," the ranger whispered into her ear before trailing kisses down her neck to her shoulder, "and so do you."

Christine turned in Ricky's arms and slid her hands around the blonde's neck. "You are going to like dessert even better she murmured against the ranger's lips.

Ricky tightened her arms around the voluptuous woman and kissed her languidly, savoring the feel of her soft lips and body pressed hard against her. Their tongues danced a waltz, slow and easy as Ricky's hand moved from Christine's back to her sensitive breast.

"Um, Major," Christine murmured. "You should eat dinner first. It will get cold. I promise you I will not."

Ricky grinned and kissed her one more long, hungry kiss.

They discussed the Hacker and Ricky's frustration with the case. "He knows I am after him," the ranger said, "and he seems to stay two steps ahead of me."

"He said he would make one last kill then move on," Christine frowned. "Do you think he will leave our state?"

"Part of me hopes he does," Ricky nodded. "Another part of me wants so badly to apprehend him."

"I know, baby," Christine caught the blonde's hand and kissed her knuckles. "Why don't you get a shower, while I clear away the dishes? I will be up in a few minutes."

Ricky's eyes danced as she leaned in for a kiss. "I won't be long," she promised.

~~~

Christine lay motionless in the bed beside Ricky. She loved the warmth of the ranger and the soft slumbering sound she made as she slept.

Ricky had fallen asleep shortly after they made love. Christine knew it had been a difficult day for her lover. Losing Kay Dawson to a maniacal murderer was haunting Ricky. She had tossed and turned all night fighting imaginary killers in her sleep. Christine had held her tightly and soothed her, kissing away silent tears.

Ricky stirred and wrapped her arm around the brunette, pulling her closer against her. "Are you awake?" Christine whispered.

"Yes," Ricky breathed into her ear, sending a slight tremor throughout her body.

"You had a restless night," the senator softly said.

"I am sorry," Ricky let her hand wander from the woman's ribcage down to her firm, round hips. She pulled her tightly against her abdomen. "Did I keep you awake?"

"Not really," Christine lied. She kissed the valley between Ricky's breasts and smiled as the ranger moaned contentedly.

"Don't start something you can't finish," Ricky smiled as she kissed Christine's full, warm lips.

"I believe I am very capable of finishing it," the senator chuckled as she pushed closer to the blonde.

An obnoxious ringtone filled the room. "That's not my phone," Ricky mumbled.

"It's mine," Christine snorted. "My mother."

"Your ringtone for your mother is *The Good, The Bad and The Ugly*?" Ricky laughed as she rolled over and handed Christine her phone.

"Hello, Mother. Yes, I know Thursday is Thanksgiving." Christine rolled her eyes. "Yes, I remember I promised to spend the day with you and Daddy. No, Mother, don't do that. If you invite him, I will leave. Yes, two o'clock. I will be there with bells on."

"Wow," Ricky grinned. "I forgot about Thanksgiving. You have to spend the day with your folks?"

"Um," Christine hummed. "What will you do?"

"Work," Ricky answered. "I haven't made plans for Thanksgiving."

"Join us," Christine beamed. "Having you with me will make the day enjoyable instead of unbearable."

"I don't know," Ricky stroked Christine's arm. "I don't think your mother likes me. Why do you call her Lady, anyway? Is she royalty or something?"

"Lady is her given name," Christine smiled. "My grandparents actually named her Lady."

"Oh," Ricky said sheepishly. "I didn't mean to make fun of her. It is just unusual."

"You are avoiding my question," Christine kissed the top of Ricky's breast, then trailed her tongue to her nipple.

"If I say yes, may I spend the night again tonight?" Ricky grinned mischievously. "I will need something in the morning to remind me why I agreed to enter the lion's lair for Thanksgiving."

"I could begin working on that right now," Christine said against her lips, "and all night and in the morning."

"I would love to go," Ricky laughed out loud as she pulled the brunette on top of her.

~~~

"I am on my way to pick you up," Christine said into the cellphone. "I will be there in fifteen minutes. Umm, I love you too."

The senator watched the blonde as she walked toward the car. Ricky looked like a model for classy, casual clothes. Dressed in a pair of gray slacks, a pink V-necked sweater, and heels, she was gorgeous. Her curly blonde hair cascaded over her shoulders and rested on her breasts. Breasts that Christine had caressed earlier in the day. *She looks more like a runway model than a Texas Ranger*, Christine thought.

They had practically lived together for the past week. Kay Dawson's death had spooked Ricky. She seldom let the senator out of her sight. Although Christine couldn't locate it, she knew there was a Sig on the ranger's body somewhere.

As they pulled into the drive of the Richmond mansion, Ricky looked at herself in the visor mirror. She alternated between smiling gleefully and looking deadly serious.

"What are you doing?" Christine laughed.

"I am trying to get the appropriate expression to stay on my face," Ricky grinned. "After awakening at your side for a week, I can't get this happy look off my face. I need to look more serious, or you mother will know I am sleeping with her daughter."

Christine threw back her head and laughed. "Keep the happy countenance, dear. It will drive my mother crazy."

Ricky checked to make certain no one was watching them, then leaned down for a kiss. Christine slipped her hand behind the blonde's neck and pulled her lips harder against hers. "Let's leave as soon as possible," she whispered.

"Your folks," Ricky smiled, "you call the shots." She gently wiped a lipstick smear from Christine's lower lip with her thumb.

~~~

The Thanksgiving gathering was a combination of family, friends and important customers. Ricky wondered if all of Christine's holidays had been this impersonal. At least twenty people milled through the Richmond mansion.

A man in his late thirties rushed to Christine. "Chris, it is good to see you," he planted a lingering kiss on the senator's cheek.

"It is good to see you, too, Cranford. Christine turned to Ricky. Cranford Ward this is my friend Major Ricky Strong. Ricky, Cranford is Daddy's junior attorney."

Ricky wasn't certain what a junior attorney was, but smiled as she shook hands with the man.

Armand Richmond took Christine's elbow and guided her from guest to guest. It was obvious he was proud of his successful daughter.

"Beautiful isn't she?" a quiet voice startled Ricky. She turned to see Scott Winslow at her side.

"Yes, she is," Ricky agreed. "She is also extremely intelligent and capable."

"Christine said she was bringing you," Lady Richmond barked as she spotted Ricky.

"I appreciate you allowing me to share the holiday with you," Ricky smiled.

"I suppose we have to befriend people from all walks of life," Lady wrinkled her nose. "Have you and Christine collaborated on your Spring curriculum?"

276

"You will be proud of us, Mother," Christine and Armand joined the three. "Major Strong and I have had a great deal of intercourse about our curriculum." She turned her brilliant smile on Ricky. "Haven't we, Major?"

Ricky fought the pink blush that moved up her neck to her cheeks and swallowed the tea that threatened to shoot out her nose. "We have definitely penetrated the mysteries of politics and law enforcement." The ranger mischievously grinned as Christine's eyes widened and a slight blush colored the woman's olive completion.

"That is good to know," Armand hugged his daughter's shoulders and turned to his wife. "Isn't it, dear?"

Lady Richmond glared at Ricky. "Yes, that is what every mother wants to hear," she snarled.

"Mr. Winslow," Ricky changed the conversation, "I understand we have you to thank for the opportunity to influence young minds."

"I believe it will give the senator a great deal of good publicity." Scot frowned slightly. "We will launch several positive initiatives before announcing Christine's campaign for the governor's mansion."

The butler announced that dinner "was served" and the small crowd moved toward the huge dining room.

Christine quickly switched nameplates with a local banker, moving her own to sit next to Ricky. "Mother never misses an opportunity to make others uncomfortable," she whispered in Ricky's ear as everyone took their seats.

Thanksgiving Dinner was a pleasant affair. Politics and the election of the new president were the main topics of conversation.

Maids were serving coffee and dessert when the doorbell chimed throughout the house.

"Sir, sir, you can't go in there without an invitation." Scuffling sounded outside the door as the butler tried to impede the entrance of a handsome, dark-haired man.

Silence fell over the diners as they watched the man confront Armand Richmond. "You didn't respond to my letters, Father," he pointed an accusing finger at the shipping magnate.

"I am not in the habit of corresponding with prisoners," Armand stood to face his son. "You are not welcome here."

"Afraid I will embarrass you in front of your fancy friends?" Randall was obviously controlling his rage, "Or hurt my sister's illustrious political career?" His eyes searched the face of each person at the table, coming to rest on Ricky.

"Well, what do we have here?" He leered. "Is she yours?" He asked Scott Winslow.

"Randall," Christine jumped up from the table and moved quickly to hug her brother. "It is good to see you."

The man seemed shocked at the warm welcome from his sister. He hesitated then embraced her in a grateful hug. "You are the one I have missed the most, Chris," he beamed.

Ricky stood, "Please take my seat next to your sister."

Randall scanned the blonde again. "No, please finish your meal."

"Nonsense," Christine smiled. She turned to one of the maids, "Please serve the three of us in the breakfast room."

She took her brother's hand and nodded for Ricky to follow her to another room. As they left, Ricky could hear conversation begin around the dining table.

"How are you?" Christine linked her arm through her brother's and caught Ricky's hand with her free hand.

"Much better," he smiled a smile that reminded Ricky of his sister. A small dimple danced mischievously on each side of his lips.

"Randall this is Major Ricky Strong. She is a Texas Ranger," Christine introduced the two. "She is my lo...yal bodyguard." She ducked her head. She had almost introduced Ricky as her lover to a man she barely knew.

Ricky shook hands with the man. "It is a pleasure to meet you."

"Why do you need a bodyguard?" Randall frowned. "Is your life in danger?"

"The senator has had threats against her life," Ricky answered.

"I certainly hope someone threatens me," Randall grinned. "Maybe you could protect me, too."

Ricky shook her head, no. "I belong to the senator," she smiled.

Indeed, you do, Christine thought.

"Major Strong has been assigned to protect me until the imminent danger has passed," Christine said.

"You look good," Christine said. "Daddy said you were in prison."

"I was, several years ago," Randall nodded, "but I have been out and living the good life for over five years."

"Why didn't you come home?" Christine asked. She raised her hand and traced a scar that ran from her brother's eye down his cheek.

"I wanted to," Randall frowned. "Father told me his son was dead to him and he never wanted to see me again. I wrote several letters but never received a reply."

"Oh, Randall, why didn't you contact me?" the senator asked.

"I tried, but it is impossible to get within a hundred yards of you."

"So, what gave you the courage to show up today?" Ricky asked bluntly.

"I...I have truly gotten my act together," Randall smiled sheepishly. "I don't blame Father for not believing me. I was horribly addicted to drugs, but I have been clean since prison. All I ask is a chance to prove myself to him.

"For the past four years, I have worked in a shipyard in California. I wanted to learn the business from the ground up."

Ricky glanced at the man's hands. They were no stranger to manual labor. Of average height and muscular, he wore brown slacks and a tan sweater over a dark brown shirt that was open at the neck. His taste in fine clothes matched his sister's.

Everything he wore fit flawlessly. The long sleeves of his shirt peaked just below the sleeves of his cardigan. The shirt collar rested perfectly outside the sweater. He looked like casual money. Ricky wondered how he could afford the expensive clothes he wore.

"Let me talk to Daddy," Christine smiled sadly. "I will convince him to give you a second chance."

He smiled thankfully. "I can't tell you how much that would mean to me."

"Are you staying in Austin?" Christine asked.

"The Courtyard downtown," he answered. "I thought I would look for an apartment after Thanksgiving."

He turned to Ricky. "Perhaps you could help me locate something reasonable in a good part of town."

"You do know Austin is a college town?" Ricky chuckled. "There is no such thing as a reasonably priced apartment in any part of town.

"I am afraid I am not available anyway. When I am not providing security for your sister, I am sleeping." *With your sister*, she concluded in her mind.

"I can have one of my staff help you," Christine volunteered. "They like to do anything that gets them out of the office."

"Do you need money or a car?" Christine asked, eager to help her brother.

"No, I am fine financially. The shipyards in California paid very well. Except for buying a car, I still have the first penny I made."

"I thought I would visit Kara tomorrow," Randall smiled. "Since she isn't here today, I assume Father's renouncement declaration because she is gay is still in effect."

A dark cloud passed over Christine's lovely face. "Kara is dead," she whispered.

The look of disbelief on Randall's face was heartfelt. "How? When?" He collapsed into the wing-back chair and buried his face in his hands.

"A serial killer murdered her," Christine said gently. "That is why the Rangers have such close security on me."

"Oh, dear God," Randall gasped. "Do you have any idea who killed her?"

Both women shook their heads, no.

"I own an apartment building in downtown Austin," Christine said. "You are welcome to live in one of the apartments. Kara had lived in the penthouse before she died."

"Only if you let me pay you rent," Randall insisted.

The three talked until darkness settled outside. "I'd better get you home, Senator," Ricky said.

"Take a picture of Randall and me before we leave," Christine pulled her cell phone from her purse.

"Let me use mine," Ricky insisted. "I know how to operate it." She took a photo of the two and forwarded a copy to Christine's cell phone. "How about you, Randall? Want me to forward the photo to your cell phone?"

"A cell phone is a luxury I haven't allowed myself," he smiled apologetically.

"I should be going, too." He hugged Christine again then turned to Ricky. "I feel like we are family," he grinned as he pulled her into a too-friendly hug.

~~~

Lady entered the foyer. "Did he leave?" she asked.

"Yes, Mother. You and Daddy treated him heartlessly."

"You have no idea what he put us through," Lady shrugged. "Don't trust him, darling. He is no good."

"How can you say that? He is your son and my brother," Christine cried.

A maid entered the foyer carrying a take-out bag.

"I had the cook fix you some leftovers," Lady said tiredly. "There is enough for you and Major Strong to have dinner." She handed the sack to Ricky.

For the first-time Ricky thought that Lady Richmond looked her age. Her face seemed to sag and wrinkles creased her forehead. It was obvious that Randall's appearance was adversely affecting her.

Christine was quiet all the way home. She went upstairs while Ricky put the food in the refrigerator.

Ricky checked all the rooms downstairs making certain the windows and doors were locked. She armed the alarm system, turned out the lights and went upstairs.

Christine was in the shower. Ricky undressed and slipped under the hot spray with her. Christine collapsed into Ricky's arms crying against her shoulder. The ranger stroked her back, murmuring comforting words to the brunette. "I love you more than you will ever know, Christine Richmond."

~~~

It was dark outside when Ricky woke. She lay still for a long time, listening to Christine's soft slumber. Her body was completely relaxed. Christine had loved her until she was almost boneless. All the tension had left her body.

Christine moaned beside her. "Are you okay?" the brunette asked as she kissed Ricky's shoulder.

"A little sore," Ricky chuckled. "You know you would kill a lesser woman?"

"A lesser woman wouldn't keep begging for more," Christine giggled as she burrowed deeper into the ranger's arms.

"You are addictive," Ricky brushed her lips lightly across Christine's. "I can't seem to get enough of you."

The ranger started laughing. "I can't believe you told your mother we had a great deal of intercourse. I almost choked."

Christine chuckled, "I almost died when you spouted off about penetration."

"I just wanted to give as good as I was getting," Ricky laughed.

"Oh, you do, baby. You always do," Christine sighed.

~~~

Chapter 20

Major Ricky Strong turned on her computer. Becky brought her a cup of coffee and sat down with her own steaming cup.

"How was your Thanksgiving?" the younger woman asked.

"Perfect," Ricky smiled. "We have a lot to be thankful for."

Becky nodded. "Some of us more than others," she smiled.

Ricky raised a questioning eyebrow.

"Bruise on your neck. Right there where it meets your collarbone," Becky grinned.

"Damn," Ricky blushed and went to check in the mirror.

"You could wear a bandana like the old west Rangers used to wear," Becky suggested gleefully. "I guess the body you were guarding got up close and personal."

"Don't you have anything to do," Ricky smirked, "like debride a skeleton or something?"

Becky laughed as she left the office. "A lot of makeup will hide that."

Ricky pulled up the files on Randall Lane Richmond. The man had been in and out of jail from the age of sixteen until his thirtieth birthday when he was incarcerated for six years.

Most of the charges had been drug related. The six-year sentence was for assault. *Probably a bar fight*, Rick thought as she scrolled to the next page.

She was shocked to see the pictures of Randall's victim. It was a young Latino woman he had molested, beaten senseless and left for dead. The girl's brother had found her and rushed her to the hospital.

Supported by her family, the girl had filed assault charges against Randall. He had pleaded guilty and served his time. He had been an exemplary citizen since his release from prison.

This guy could be dangerous, Ricky thought. She texted the picture of Randall and Christine to Crate and Barrel then called Crate.

"I just sent you a picture of Senator Richmond and her brother. He could be dangerous. Don't leave her alone with him."

"Sure thing, Major," Crate said. "You know the FBI fellow, Agent Day?"

"Yeah," Ricky said slowly.

"He has returned to his headquarters, and Dave Adams has been assigned to guard the senator."

"Son-of-a..." Ricky stopped short of cursing. "Watch him like a hawk. I am certain he works for the mob. Man, that is like throwing a fox into the henhouse. Find out who made that call."

"Right, boss," Crate answered.

"Oh, and Crate do it without arousing any suspicions."

Ricky continued to peruse Randall's file. She couldn't tell what his job entailed, but he wasn't a dock hand. He was active in the International Longshore and Warehouse Union.

A call from Christine lit up Ricky's phone. "How is the love of my life?" Ricky crooned.

"Better now," Christine smiled into the phone. "I am picking up Randall and taking him to see the apartment. Can you join us?"

"I would love to," Ricky answered. "Pick me up first. That will give us a few minutes together alone." Truthfully, she didn't want to leave the senator alone with Randall Richmond.

"Pick you up in twenty," Christine laughed.

Senator Christine Richmond was ecstatically happy. She could not recall ever being so happy. Everything was right in her world. The woman she loved without reservation, loved her. Her brother was back in her life, and she was a shoo-in to win the governor's race.

Of course, there were some drawbacks to all the things that made her happy. Apparently, Ricky had chosen her over the Italian beauty. She had an uneasiness about the way her parents were treating her brother, and she would be dumped from the Republican ticket if her constitutes ever found out she was gay.

All bridges I will cross when I get to them, she thought as she watched Ricky walk toward her. *I can take on the world with her at my side.*

~~~

Randall loved the penthouse. Christine quoted him the "family" rate. He smiled knowingly and humbly accepted.

Over lunch, the man broached the subject of his parents. "Chris, how can I make them believe that I am a different man?"

287

"Talk to Mother," Christine advised. "Although she is the most vocal, she is the softest. Daddy is so tied up in the shipping company he doesn't pay much attention to what is going on around him. He is sometimes very difficult to reach."

Randall shook his head. His sister had always given him sound advice. He could understand how she had become so powerful in politics. Being governor would be another feather in her cap.

"Why don't you go through the regular hiring process with Richmond Shipping and get a job with the company?" Ricky suggested. "Prove to your father that you are capable of making it on your own."

"That is a brilliant idea," Christine smiled coyly at the ranger.

"I must get back to the office," Christine said. "I am speaking to the National Chamber of Commerce tonight, and my speech isn't quite finished.

"Will you be there, Major?" she raised a perfectly arched eyebrow at Ricky.

"Wouldn't miss it for the world," Ricky smirked.

"Perhaps I could escort you," Randall smiled at the blonde.

"She is being facetious," Ricky chuckled. "She knows I will be there. My team is providing her security tonight."

"Oh!" Randall was crestfallen.

"You can come as my guest," Christine suggested. "Mother and Daddy will be there. Unfortunately, there are no empty seats at their table, but I will find some nice people to sit next to you."

"Probably not a good idea to see our parents in public," Randall shook his head. "I think I will take the advice both of you have given me.

"If you will drop me back at my hotel, I will move my belongings into my new penthouse." He smiled warmly at Christine. "Thank you, Chris."

A Texas thunderstorm loomed on the horizon as the women dropped Randall at his hotel. Fat drops of rain were falling by the time they parted. Ricky leaned over and kissed the brunette. "I will pick you up at seven."

~~~

As always, Christine's speech was flawless, and she received a standing ovation from the attendees. It was captivating to watch. She smiled and laughed in all the right places. Her self-deprecating anecdotes were designed to give her audience an enthralling view of her daily life as a Texas Senator. Listening to Senator Christine Richmond talk, one felt as if they were best friends with the senator who needed their help and by God, they would be there for her.

After her speech, Christine mingled with the crowd and spent time with her parents. Armand was extremely proud of his daughter and dragged her to meet every wealthy customer he had.

Lady Richmond stood beside Ricky and watched her husband parade their daughter around the room.

"He wants her to take over Richmond Shipping when he retires, and she gets tired of politics," Lady smiled.

"He wants her to be CEO of their company, and she wants to be President of the United States," she added.

"President of the United States," Ricky echoed. She had forgotten Christine's political ambitions.

"Of course, dear," Lady smirked. "Being Governor of Texas is simply a steppingstone to the presidency."

Ricky nodded. She wondered if their love would survive a long-distance relationship.

~~~

Ricky pulled her car into the garage next to Christine's. "You look tired," she said softly to the brunette.

"Sometimes these gatherings are hard for me," Christine inhaled deeply. "I don't mind the speeches and mingling with my constituents, but I get so tired of Daddy dragging me around the room like a prized pony. He should have to wear these heels. I bet he wouldn't be so eager to crisscross the ballroom."

"A very beautiful prized pony," Ricky leaned over and gently kissed the senator. "When we get inside, I will rub your feet."

"That is the best offer I have had all day," Christine laughed.

Christine reclined on the love seat in her bedroom and slipped her feet into Ricky's lap. "You have the softest hands," she looked up at Ricky from under long, dark lashes.

"Senator," Ricky smiled, "you have the smoothest feet I have ever touched."

"Um, and just how many feet have you touched, Major?"

"Honestly," Ricky shrugged, "only yours. I am not in the habit of giving women foot massages."

"I am glad," Christine whispered a gleam dancing in her eyes. "I was afraid you had a foot fetish."

An hour later, an exhausted Christine was asleep on the love seat. Ricky slipped the senator's feet from her lap, pulled a soft throw over the brunette and went to take a shower.

The sound of the shower pulled Christine from a light sleep. An unfamiliar ringtone told her Ricky had left her cell phone downstairs.

She walked downstairs to Ricky's jacket on the coat tree in the foyer. *Please don't let it be the Rangers*, she thought. *I want her to myself tonight. I need her.*

She pulled Ricky's phone from her jacket pocket to take it upstairs with her. The ringtone had stopped. A ding told her the caller had left a voicemail.

I shouldn't do this; she thought as she pushed the button to play the voicemail.

"Rēēcky," Martina's voice assaulted her ears, "I need you. Call me."

The woman's sexy accent on Ricky's name made Christine furious. She considered putting the phone back into the ranger's pocket. The sound of the Italian beauty's voice reminded Christine that *she* was the other woman in this relationship.

Why do I keep falling into bed with Major Ricky Strong? Christine chastised herself. *Why can't I get her out of my mind and out of my system?*

"Honey, are you coming up here or do I need to come get you?" A smiling Ricky appeared at the top of the stairs.

"You have a phone call," Christine flatly said as she held the phone out to the ranger.

Ricky quickly skipped down the stairs and took the phone. She looked at the call registry then pushed the button to play back the message. She held the phone to her ear. Her eyes darted wildly around the room as she listened to it.

Ricky pushed the button to call Martina. "Are you okay?" she asked when Martina answered.

"Rēēcky, I am probably acting like a baby," Martina whispered into the phone, "but Tex and Brady are at the stock show in Houston, and all of the electricity just went off."

"I'm on my way," Ricky darted upstairs and dressed in record time. Christine was still standing in the foyer when she returned.

"I have to take care of this," the ranger frowned.

"Of course, you do," Christine said bitterly.

Ricky leaned down to kiss the brunette goodbye. Christine backed away from her.

"I'll be back as soon as I can," Ricky frowned.

"Don't bother," Christine scowled.

"Christine, I... Lock this door behind me," Ricky said as she called Crate. "I have an emergency at home. I need you to watch Senator Richmond." The ranger ran out into the cold, stormy night.

"Be there in five, Major," Crate responded.

Christine locked the door and leaned against it. The torrential downpour made her feel even more alone. She wondered how Ricky could drop her like a hot potato when Martina called. "This will never happen to me again," she said out loud.

～～～

Breaking every speed limit, it took Ricky forty-five minutes to reach the ranch. She worried that

292

Agent Adams had somehow tracked down Martina. She turned off her lights as she approached the curve that would take her out of the trees onto flat pasture land and full sight of the ranch houses. She reached her home first where she left the pickup and moved toward Martina and Tex's home on foot.

All the lights on the ranch were off: the barn lights, the security lights that flooded the arenas, and all the house lights.

Ricky turned her jacket collar up against the driving rain and relentless wind. She knew the temperature was below freezing. She moved stealthily around her own home looking for a flicker from a flashlight. She saw nothing.

Damn Adams, she thought, *if he is on my property, I will shoot him.*

She ran the half mile to Martina's home. Careful to stay low and slip behind any cover she could find. Finally, she was at Martina's back door.

Ignoring the steps that led up to the porch, Ricky easily hauled herself over the side of the rails that surrounded the porch. The electric transformer between the two houses was spewing electricity in all directions.

Listening for any sound, she moved toward the door. It was locked. Backing away from the door, she slid her cell phone from her pocket and called Martina.

"Rēēcky, hurry," Martina whispered. "Someone is trying to get in the front door."

"That is me," Martina. "Unlock the door."

Ricky heard the deadbolt slide back, and the Italian beauty flung open the door. Ricky slipped inside.

"Cara, you are soaked," Martina cried.

"Yes, but the good news is I think the transformer blew. That's why the lights went out."

"Thank, God," A deep chuckle escaped Martina's throat. The relief in her voice was palatable. "I was afraid Dave Adams had found me."

"I didn't see any sign of anyone," Ricky said. "Jeeze, it is freezing in here. I am going to start a fire."

Martina nodded. "First let's get you into some dry clothes. You look like a drowned rat. I will be right back."

As Martina found clothes for the ranger, Ricky stacked firewood in the fireplace and started a fire. She stood in front of the fire, shivering as she started peeling off her soaked clothes.

Martina gave her a sweatshirt and a pair of flannel sweatpants. "I think my bras will just hang on you," she mischievously smiled as she handed Ricky a pair of panties.

Ricky sneezed three consecutive times. "I can't stop shaking," she chattered, trying to keep her teeth from chipping each other.

Martina brought a wool blanket from the bedroom and wrapped the ranger in it. "Sit here in front of the fireplace. I will make you some hot chocolate."

"Where is my cell phone?" Ricky asked, eyeing her wet clothes on the floor. "I need to call Christine and let her know everything is okay."

Martina retrieved the phone from the wet pocket of the ranger's jacket. She dried it off, handed it to Ricky then headed to the kitchen.

It was almost two in the morning. Ricky wasn't surprised that Christine didn't answer the phone. She left a message, "Hi honey, I just wanted to let you know I am spending the night here tonight. Everything is okay. I will see you in the morning."

Martina placed two steaming cups of hot chocolate on the coffee table and sat on the floor next to Ricky. She handed Ricky the cup along with four aspirin. "Here, drink this it will help warm you, and the aspirin will make you feel better. You are chilled to the bone."

They finished their hot chocolate, but Ricky was still shivering. "You have caught a bad cold, Cara," Martina said. "I am going to get an electric blanket. I must get you warm."

"No electricity," Ricky tried to smile, but her trembling lips wouldn't let her. "When will Tex be home?"

"Before noon tomorrow," Martina said softly. She went to the bedroom and returned with a thick, down comforter. She sat down behind Ricky and wrapped her legs and arms around the ranger. Pulling Ricky into her bosom, she clutched the blonde tightly against her. She pulled the comforter around them and let her body heat warm the shivering woman.

Martina could tell that Ricky had a raging fever. She hoped the aspirin would bring it down. As Ricky's tremors lessened, they both fell asleep.

As the sun peeked into the room, Martina opened her eyes. Ricky's fever had broken. The ranger was sleeping peacefully. Sometime during the night, they had lain down on the floor. Martina was cradling Ricky's head between her breasts. She wondered if she could extract herself from their entanglement without waking the ranger.

Martina moved slightly, and Ricky tightened her arms around the woman's waist. "Christine," she murmured, "don't go."

Martina touched her cheek lightly, "Rēēcky, it is me, Martina."

Ricky scrambled away from her as if she had been zapped with a cattle prod. She gaped at Martina. "I... Martina...I,"

"Nothing happened, Cara," Martina laughed. "Except that, I may have saved your life."

Ricky looked down at her clothes as the night before came back to her. Suddenly exhaustion overcame her, and she slumped back against the sofa.

"How do you feel?" Martina asked.

"Like a herd of cattle stampeded over me," Ricky smiled weakly.

'You are still weak," Martina helped her stand and sit on the sofa. "Keep the comforter around you. You had an awful chill and then a raging fever. You were very sick."

"I feel very weak," Ricky scowled. "I don't think I have ever felt this weak."

"I am going to put on the coffee. What would you like for breakfast?" Martina stood and brushed the wrinkles from her slacks.

"Do you have any of those cherry Danish, I love so much?" Ricky looked up at her from under long, dark lashes. Martina thought she looked like a little girl.

Ricky fell asleep right after breakfast. She slept the entire day and into the early morning hours of the next day. She hadn't been this tired since the border tour.

Voices from the kitchen pulled her completely awake. She recognized Tex's voice. "Is she going to be alright? Should we take her to the hospital?" The concern in his voice was evident.

"I think she will be fine," Martina's warm Italian accent hummed. "She is tough, like you."

Ricky could tell from the silence that they were kissing. She waited until they resumed conversation then stumbled into the kitchen.

"We have electricity," Ricky grinned as she entered the warmly lighted kitchen.

"Yes," Martina cast an adoring glance at her husband. "Tex had the transformer replaced first thing this morning."

Ricky rolled her head on her shoulders as Martina placed a steaming cup of coffee in front of her.

"I am going to have an automatic generator installed," Tex grinned. "I don't want my women endangered because of the weather."

"Your women?" Ricky croaked. Everyone laughed. It was a line Tex always used to get a rise out of his cousin.

"It is good to see you are almost back to yourself," Martina patted the blonde's arm.

"Have you seen my cell phone?" Ricky looked around the kitchen.

"It is dead," Martina handed it to her. "We didn't think to charge it."

Ricky dragged both her hands down her face. "I will charge it in the truck," she nodded. "I need to call Christine. She will be worried."

"Use my phone, Cara," Martina held out her cellphone to the ranger.

"No way," Ricky huffed. "I am pretty certain the FBI has a tap on the senator's phone. A call from a strange phone would get their attention. With Adams in Austin, I don't want to take any chances with your safety."

"Are you strong enough to drive?" Tex frowned. "Martina said you had a rough couple of days."

"All I need is a shower, and I will be a new woman," Ricky grinned. "Apparently, I needed the rest."

##

Chapter 21

As soon as Ricky's phone had a small charge, she called Christine. The call immediately went to voice mail. "Hey, honey," she said brightly, "I am almost home. I need to change clothes. Would you like to go to dinner tonight?"

As she pulled into her parking garage, Crate called her. "Major, Senator Richmond is leaving for a speaking engagement in Fort Worth. Should we go with her?"

"Of course, you should," Ricky hissed. "Crate, tell her to call me."

Ricky spent the day going over the Hacker files. She was missing something. She just didn't know what. She was thankful the killer hadn't struck again. Kay was his last victim.

Ricky ran the killer's MO through international NCIC. The files started flashing by as the National Crime Information Center's computers compared Ricky's data to data nationwide.

Killing time, Ricky logged onto her personal email. She hadn't checked it in a week and dreaded cleaning it out. She gasped as she saw multiple messages from Troy Hunter.

His first emails were gloating, shaming her for letting him kill her best undercover agent.

His later emails were furious, cursing her and daring her to interact with him.

She re-read some forty emails from the man. He was obviously more deranged than she had originally suspected.

As she finished reading the emails the second time, a new one dinged into her inbox.

"You and I have the same taste in women," Troy taunted her. "We both like beautiful brunettes, five-six or five-seven, like Senator Richmond."

Ricky did not engage him in an email conversation. She knew he was threatening Christine.

Her computer beeped and filled her screen with cases identical to the Hacker. Oklahoma authorities called him the Handy Man because he cut off their hands. In Arkansas, he was dubbed the Mangler. In New Mexico, he was the Cutter. Louisiana nicknamed him the Butcher. Ricky noticed the perp had spent a year in every state surrounding Texas. He always killed eight victims then disappeared. He had killed 32 women plus the seven in Texas. One more kill would give him 40 kills

He has only killed seven in Texas, Ricky thought. *He hasn't moved on. Serial killers rarely deviate from their patterns. He will kill one more time in my state.*

Crate's ringtone pulled Ricky from her morbid thoughts. "We are heading back to Austin, Major. Should be in around nine tonight."

"Did you tell the senator to call me?" Ricky asked.

"Yes, Major," Crate replied.

"Crate stay very close to her. Don't take your eyes off her for a minute. I just received an email from the Hacker threatening Christine."

"Major," Becky's voice came over the intercom, "you have a visitor, Randall Richmond."

"Send him in," Ricky frowned. She wondered why Richmond was at her office.

"Randall," she stood as the handsome man entered her office, "how are you doing?"

"Good," he beamed. "I was in the area and thought you might have dinner with me."

Ricky considered his offer. Maybe he could shed some light on Christine's sudden coldness.

"I would love to," she smiled.

~~~

"I did as you suggested," Randall smiled, "and I now work for Richmond Shipyards. I had lunch with mother yesterday."

"That is terrific," Ricky beamed. "I am very proud of you. You'll see, Armand will come around."

"I hope so," Randall shrugged. "I think mother is ready to accept me back into the fold, but father is a tough nut to crack."

"What made you return to Texas?" Ricky asked as the waitress placed their dinner in front of them. Ricky was drinking iced tea. Randall was drinking bourbon.

"I discovered I missed my family, Randall frowned. "I got into drugs in college. Like a fool, I was certain I could handle hard drugs. You know, could stop whenever I wanted. I quickly found I couldn't make it through the day without a hit. Things went downhill from there. Father disowned me.

"I would do anything for drugs. I stole and conned women out of their life savings. I was a male prostitute.

"I woke up in jail and realized I had hit rock bottom. I tried to contact Father, but he wouldn't accept my calls." A faraway look filled Randall's eyes. "He could have kept me out of jail, hired me a good attorney instead of a court-appointed loser."

"He probably saved your life," Ricky said. "You got clean in jail, completed your degree, and came out a better man."

"I definitely came out a different man," Randall snorted.

"All of that is behind you," Ricky smiled as she squeezed his left forearm.

He yanked his arm away from her as if she had hurt him.

"I am sorry," she frowned. "Did I hurt you?"

"That is the arm that took most of the needles," Randall hung his head. "It is still very tender."

After six years, Ricky thought. She wondered if the man was using again.

Ricky sipped her iced tea. "Your end goal is to redeem yourself with your father and accept some of the responsibility of running Richmond Shipping?"

"Something like that," he harrumphed.

"I think you and Christine will be a dynamic duo," Ricky smiled.

"Christine?" Randall looked at her questioningly. "All Christine cares about is being President of the United States."

"True," Ricky chuckled, "but she can only be president for eight years then she will return to the private sector. Although she is in politics, I know she keeps her finger on the pulse of Richmond Shipping."

"Mother said she ran the company when Father had a heart attack," Randall nodded. "She is incredible."

"Yeah, she is," Ricky sighed. "She is one of the most brilliant women I have ever met. She is tireless and fearless. She never runs out of energy."

"I am sure I can learn a lot from my sister," Randall smiled. "It is good to be back in her life."

"She is very fond of you," Ricky said.

"She is very fond of you, too," Randall swirled his drink then downed it in one swallow. "She talks about you constantly. To hear her talk, one would think you are superwoman."

"I am fortunate to call her my friend," Ricky laughed. "She does have a temper, though."

Randall threw his head back and laughed out loud. "She does twist off sometimes," he said.

"Yes, and most of the time I have no idea what I have done to set her off," Ricky frowned.

"She told me how you saved her life in Mexico," Randall grimaced.

"Did she also tell you that she is the one that got us out of Mexico alive?"

"No," he shook his head.

"I was half dead. One of the drug dealers shot me. She strapped me to her and drove a motorcycle across the badlands back into the U.S. I was dead weight. She saved both of us."

Randall's eyes shone with pride. "I had no idea. My sister is a woman of many talents and extremely modest."

"Yes, she is," Ricky smiled. *I wish she would see me. I wish I knew why she runs hot and cold toward me,* she thought.

Crate's ringtone sounded on Ricky's cellphone. Strong," she answered.

"The senator is safe in her home, Major," Crate reported. Lee and Tank are relieving us. That creep Adams is parked in front of her house."

"Thanks, Crate. I will see you in the morning."

"Is everything okay?" Randall asked.

"Yes," Ricky nodded.

"Are you having any luck finding Kara's killer?" Randall signaled the waitress for another bourbon.

"It is one of the most puzzling cases I have worked," Ricky frowned. "The guy is like a ghost. We don't have a shred of evidence from the murders."

"I read the last one was your undercover agent," Randall sipped his drink.

Ricky nodded silently.

"I must be going," the ranger said as she signaled for the check. "I have an early day tomorrow."

"I hope I didn't upset you," Randall placed a gentle hand on Ricky's arm.

"No, you just reminded me how far I am from catching the Hacker."

~~~

The busy hubbub between Thanksgiving and Christmas made the days pass quickly. Christine accepted every speaking engagement she received. It helped take her mind off the blonde woman who haunted her dreams.

After a week of not returning Ricky's calls, the ranger had stopped calling. Sometimes in the early hours of the morning, the senator wished the blonde would kick in her door and crawl into her bed.

Occasionally—when the danger was high— Ricky would be on the security team protecting the senator. She made a point to stay away from Christine.

The Hacker was dormant. Ricky knew he was still in town but was thankful that he wasn't killing. She had requested a female undercover agent from the County Sheriff's department. She was unprepared for what she received.

Nicole Weil was a fiery brunette with flashing blue eyes and a ready smile. Of Swedish and Jewish decent, the combination of characteristics was striking. Ricky couldn't take her eyes off the woman when she glided into her office.

"I have studied the files you sent over," Nicole said. "I volunteered to help you catch this guy." She held out her hand as she introduced herself. "Special Agent Nicole Weil," she smiled, placing her file on Ricky's desk.

"Major Ricky Strong," Ricky shook the firm hand Nicole offered.

"I know a lot about you," Nicole smiled. "I jumped at the chance to work with you."

"I am flattered," Ricky tilted her head and gazed into the most brilliant blue eyes she had ever seen. Nicole Weil was mesmerizing.

Ricky studied Nicole's file as the agent wandered around the office reading Ricky's plaques and awards.

"You have a law degree," Nicole said as she read the Certificate from the University of Texas.

Ricky nodded, studying Nicole's file. "As do you."

"A good grasp of the law comes in handy in our line of work," Nicole grinned. "I did a stint in the public defender's office, but that wasn't my cup of tea. I found I'd rather put away criminals than set them free."

"This is very impressive," Ricky said as she closed the file. "You need to know this guy was able to kill my best undercover agent."

"I heard," Nicole nodded.

"First thing we need to do is get some sexy photos for the internet. Come on I will show you where the photo room is."

Ricky left Nicole with the photographer with instructions to get some provocative photos. No nudes, just suggestive. Three hours later, the blue-eyed beauty tapped on the ranger's door.

"That took longer than I expected," Ricky said as Nicole spread the photos out on her desk.

"Whoa, these are gorgeous," Ricky grinned. "These photos will have half the males in Texas befriending you on Facebook. Whose idea was this?" Ricky held up a photo that showed Nicole turning to look over her naked shoulder. Right down her spine *Miss Me Yet?* was written in black marker.

"I got the idea from a posting I saw last night," Nicole laughed. "It is amazing what women will put on Facebook for all the world to see."

"I have been pretty shocked," Ricky agreed. "We are lucky more women aren't molested every day."

They spent the next two hours setting up Nicole's Facebook page. Then they invited as many friends as allowed to follow her. Just as Ricky had predicted, Nicole quickly had over 250 Facebook friends.

"Let's let it sit overnight," Ricky grinned as they looked at the page with satisfaction. "We will save the back shot for later. Our guy likes pathetic women whose boyfriends have dumped them. We will collect more friends tomorrow, then send him a friend request."

For the first time, Ricky noticed it was dark outside. "It seems we have spent the entire day on this," she noted.

"Do you have dinner plans, Major?" Nicole asked. "I would like to pick your brain a little more."

"No, I am free tonight," Ricky smiled. *Without Christine, I am free every night,* she thought.

"Let me check in on my security team," Ricky called Crate to make sure everything was okay with Christine.

"She is home right now," Crate informed her, "but I think she is going out with her brother tonight."

"Stay close to her. Don't let Randall be alone with her," Ricky warned.

"Why don't we go in my vehicle?" Ricky suggested. "We can visit on the way to the restaurant, and I can drop you back here after dinner."

"Works for me, Major," Nicole said agreeably.

~~~

Ricky maneuvered her truck into a parking place close to Truluck's.

"I love this place," Nicole grinned. "This is where I make all my wealthy dates take me."

"Where do your poor dates take you?" Ricky laughed.

"Texas Roadhouse," Nicole smiled.

They spent the next hour with their heads together, discussing the Hacker case. Nicole asked specific, in-depth questions. Ricky was impressed with her knowledge and grasp of the situation.

"Once we engage Troy Hunter, we will put two guards on you around the clock," Ricky informed her.

"Is that necessary?" Nicole frowned.

"Yeah, it is. Kay was the best undercover agent I have ever had, and he killed her. I still haven't figured out how he got the drop on her." Ricky studied the woman next to her. "I am not taking any chances with you."

Nicole placed her hand on Ricky's forearm. "I will be careful, Major. I want to catch this creep as much as you do."

~~~

Christine and Randall had just ordered their drinks when the senator spotted Ricky and Nicole. The two women were sitting at a secluded table in the corner.

If she isn't cheating with me, she cheats with some other woman, Christine thought. *How could I be such a fool? Why can't I hate her?*

Occasionally Ricky's soft laughter would float to their table. Christine tried to ignore the two but couldn't keep her gaze from returning to them. When the brunette placed her hand on Ricky's forearm and leaned into her, Christine thought she would throw up.

"Are you okay, Sis?" Randall inquired. "You look pale."

"I am fine," Christine barked.

The band started to play, and the singer walked through the crowd speaking to the diners. She stopped at Ricky's table. Christine could tell the ranger was introducing her latest paramour to the singer. She could imagine the conversation: *"Jen, I want you to meet my current lover, not to be confused with Senator Richmond, the fool."*

Ricky's phone dinged a text from Crate. *"Senator Richmond at three o'clock."*

"Damn," Ricky muttered.

"Is something wrong?" Nicole asked.

"Nothing serious," Ricky smiled timidly. She located Christine and realized they would have to walk by her table to exit the restaurant. *Maybe we can wait for them to leave*, she thought.

"The Hacker has overtly threatened Senator Christine Richmond," Ricky informed Nicole.

"He has already murdered her twin sister," Nicole gasped. "What are you going to do?"

"I have a security team on her around the clock," Ricky frowned. "Fortunately, the senator knows she is in danger and cooperates with us. Some people are fool enough to try to evade their bodyguards."

"Yes, I worked with a woman like that. She got her wish. She died." Nicole shook her head. "There is no accounting for the stupidity of some people."

"Or the contrariness of them," Ricky scowled as she saw Christine walking toward them.

"Senator Richmond," Ricky stood.

Christine motioned for Ricky to lean down so she could whisper something in her ear. "I hate you," she growled, then slapped the ranger as hard as she could. Ricky and Nicole stared after the woman as she walked out of the restaurant.

Ricky quickly took her seat trying to draw as little attention as possible. She rubbed her face where Christine had slapped her. *Damn, that hurt.*

"What was that about?" Nicole gaped at the ranger.

"I wish, to hell, I knew," Ricky mumbled.

~~~

Chapter 22

Troy Hunter hadn't engaged in communications with anyone since he killed Kay Dawson. The thrill of outsmarting Major Ricky Strong and murdering her undercover agent had lasted longer than any of his other highs.

He had emailed Strong at her email address, but she hadn't responded. Obviously, she had taken him at his word and believed he had left town. She wasn't even checking her emails. He decided he would email her daily to taunt her. Sooner or later, she would open the emails.

Last night she had appeared on that Daily woman's show and assured the citizens of Austin that the Hacker had moved on. It had taken all the self-control he possessed to keep from calling her on the air and mocking her. It was best she believed he was no longer a threat. She would pull the security team off Senator Richmond.

Matching wits with Ricky Strong had taken his murders to a new level of excitement. He had never contacted anyone in the other states where he had killed. Ricky Strong was an added bonus. He wouldn't kill her, but he would kill the person she was responsible for protecting. That would be an insult to her, both professionally and personally.

After he killed the senator, it might be a thrill to date Major Ricky Strong. Although he preferred brunettes, Ricky Strong was one good-looking blonde.

Troy logged onto his Facebook page and scoured posts. The nice thing about Facebook was he could search for victims in California or New York while sitting in Texas.

Several women caught his eye, and he sent them friend requests. Several of them responded immediately. He was disappointed the one named Rachel Winn hadn't responded to his request. From what he could see of her home page, he couldn't tell where she lived. Her blue eyes were incredible. She was beautiful. He would check on her again tomorrow.

~~~

Christine Richmond drained her wine glass and threw it into the fireplace. The fire hissed as the remains of the wine fell into it. This wasn't the way she had envisioned her Christmas holidays. She had planned on Christmas shopping with Ricky Strong then snuggling with her at night. She hadn't seen Ricky since right after Thanksgiving. She didn't count the time she slapped the ranger at Truluck's.

She was furious when she saw Ricky with a woman that resembled her. No doubt about it, Ricky had a type. She hadn't intended to slap the ranger, but when she stood with that goofy smile on her face, Christine couldn't resist the urge to slap her. Thankfully no busybody with a cellphone had recorded it, or it would be all over the internet.

She had lost more sleep over Ricky Strong than anything else in her life. She hated to admit it, but she was only happy when she was with the blonde.

Her phone played Scott Winslow's ringtone. "Senator," Scott said, "I just called to remind you that you are supposed to host the Christmas luncheon at UT tomorrow. It is their last school function before school is out for the holidays."

"I will be there, Scott," Christine replied listlessly.

"You don't have to sound excited," he teased. "You know, the students voted on their speaker, and they selected you. It is good to know the next generation is in the Christine Richmond camp, too."

"I'm sorry, Scott. I am just a little down tonight."

"I can come over and bring wine," he offered gleefully.

"No," Christine faked a laugh. "The last thing I need tomorrow is a hangover."

~~~

As everyone dined, Christine looked over the crowd waiting to hear her speech. Crate and Barrel flanked her. FBI Agent Dave Adams sat at the table in front of her. Being surrounded by bodyguards had become a way of life for her. She scanned the crowd for Ricky but didn't find her. She did see the blue-eyed woman Ricky had been with at the restaurant. Christine's face slightly burned as she recalled her own actions.

The Chancellor introduced Christine, and the applause was deafening. The senator smiled, took a deep breath and began talking. "As many of you know, the past year has been both exciting and terrifying for me." A titter ran through the crowd as people nodded their heads encouraging her to go on.

"I had interesting experiences on both sides of our southern border and…" Suddenly a loud crack echoed throughout the hall, and Christine found herself lying beneath agent Barrel.

"I'm hit, Crate. Get her out of here." Barrel rolled off Christine. "Stay low, Senator. Crawl to Crate."

Crate yanked her through the drapes behind the head table, and blue eyes grabbed her other arm. Between the two of them, they practically dragged her from the hall, down a dimly lit hallway into a parking garage. Ricky was waiting for them.

"Nicole, into my truck," Ricky yelled.

She turned to Christine and grasped her tightly by the shoulders. "A black Beemer will be here any second. Get into it and lay down in the floorboard. Your life depends on it."

"But…" Ricky cut off Christine's argument with a firm kiss. "For once in your life, don't argue with me."

Crate pulled Christine behind a low wall as Ricky jumped into her truck with Nicole and burned rubber leaving the parking garage. Two other vehicles raced down a ramp and fishtailed in their efforts to overtake the ranger.

A black BMW skidded to a stop. Crate opened the back door and shoved Christine onto the floorboard. "Stay down, Senator," he barked.

Christine lay quietly on the floorboard as the car drove the speed limit leaving Austin. She knew she had just lived through an assassination attempt.

The driver's phone rang and the driver answered using the car's phone. "I have her, Rēēcky. She is safe."

"Martina, she has a location chip in her," Ricky said breathlessly. "You are going to have to remove it. Otherwise, they can trace you to the ranch."

"I don't carry around surgical implements with me," Martina huffed.

"Don't you have a manicure kit with you?"

"Yes, Cara," Martina answered. "I will take care of her."

After several miles and what seemed like hours, Martina pulled into a roadside rest area. "You can move up here beside me now."

Christine did as she was told, locking the door as she closed it.

The two women faced each other. "It is in my left shoulder," Christine said, "right here."

Martina pulled a German-made manicure kit from her purse. "Nice set." Christine smiled slightly.

"You know this is going to hurt, Senator?" Martina said.

Christine took a deep breath and nodded. She wondered if the beautiful Italian woman knew they were sharing a lover.

Christine deeply inhaled as Martina used manicure scissors to cut a small opening over the chip. She used a pair of tweezers to catch hold of the chip and extract it. Tears ran down Christine's face, but she made no sound.

When Martina finished, she gave Christine a tissue. "Hold this over the wound until the bleeding stops," she instructed. "I am going to dispose of this."

Martina returned to the car and drove away from the rest stop.

"What did you do with the chip?" Christine asked.

"Flushed it," Martina grinned. "The environment it is in will dissolve it in no time."

They drove a long way in silence.

"Do you know about me?" Christine asked Martina.

"You mean about you and Rēēcky?"

Christine nodded shamefully.

"Yes, Rēēcky told me how she feels about you." Martina stared straight ahead constantly checking her rearview mirror to see if anyone was following her.

She turned off the highway and traveled up a gravel road about half a mile. An automatic gate opened as she approached and the gravel turned into pavement.

Christine looked around. Everything she saw was beautiful. The pristine setting looked like a picture from a calendar. A red barn was in the distance. An enormous herd of Black Angus grazed all around her.

"Where are we?" Christine asked.

"This is our home," Martina smiled. "This is where Rēēcky comes to unwind."

I bet you help her unwind, Christine thought.

Martina pulled her car behind Ricky's home and led Christine into the house. "Come, I need to sterilize your wound. Rēēcky would never forgive me if I let you get an infection."

Martina went straight to the cabinet that held the alcohol and first aid kit. She carefully cleaned Christine's wound and put a clean white bandage over it.

Christine followed the woman to the kitchen where Martina put on a pot of coffee. "Rēēcky will be here soon," she informed the senator.

"How did you happen to be there today?" Christine asked.

"It was no coincidence," Martina smiled. "Every time you make an appearance Rēēcky considers dangerous, we are standing by to do as we did today. Rēēcky and Nicole led the assassins away from you, and I brought you here."

Screeching tires told Christine that Ricky had arrived. "Are you both okay?" she asked as she charged through the door.

"We are fine, Cara," Martina smiled. "Your senator will live despite my limited surgical skills."

Martina wet a cloth and headed out the door. "That reminds me, I need to wipe the blood from my car seat."

"How can she be so okay with everything? About us?" Christine grimaced.

"I thought there was no longer an *us*," Ricky said softly.

"Do you have any idea what a living hell my life has become since I met you?" Christine switched into tirade mode. "How many sleepless nights I have spent crying for you? All the hours I sat at your side in the hospital, not knowing if you would come back to me? You even have my blood in you. How can I love a woman who cheats on someone like her?"

"What?" Ricky looked aghast.

More screeching of tires told them another vehicle had arrived. Ricky grabbed Christine by the wrist and pulled her to the back door.

Christine watched as a handsome man and little boy ran from their truck to the dark-haired woman. The man embraced the woman then scooped up the child. "Mama," the boy laughed as he hugged the woman.

"My cousin and his family," Ricky grinned.

"Your cousin?" Christine whispered.

"Yes. Tex is married to Martina and Brady is their son." Ricky chuckled.

"I...I thought..." Christine turned away from the ranger. "All this time, I thought she was your...You told Paige Daily you are in a committed relationship."

"I am," Ricky shrugged. "The minute I saw you, I was committed to you."

Christine couldn't hold back the tears. Her jealousy and distrust of Ricky had caused all the misery she had endured. She had no one to blame but herself.

"I thought you knew Martina was my cousin-in-law," Ricky frowned. "You thought I was with her. That explains the rude way you acted around her."

"I am extremely embarrassed," Christine hid her face in her hands. "She must think I am the most ungrateful human alive."

"She did ask me why I always liked the bitchy ones," Ricky laughed.

"Ones," Christine growled. "How many others have you liked?"

"None enough to make a commitment," Ricky backed away from the brunette. "You're not going to slap me, again, are you?"

Martina opened the back door then stopped. Christine was in Ricky's arms. "There is a casserole in the refrigerator, Cara," she said before pulling the door closed.

~~~

"I think we need to talk," Ricky said.

Christine nodded sheepishly.

"What made you think Martina was my significant other?" Ricky asked as she poured coffee for them.

Christine sipped the coffee recalling when Ricky had broken her heart the first time. "The morning we met at the airport to leave for the border. You left me three days before we departed and that gorgeous woman dropped you at the airport.

Ricky shook her head, "Why didn't you ask me about her then?"

"I didn't have to ask you. I saw you kiss her," Christine frowned.

"N-o-o-o-o, I am certain I have never kissed Martina," Ricky tried to hide her smile. "Tex and I share almost everything, but I am certain that would never include his wife. He'd take off my head."

"You walked to the rear of your car and raised the trunk lid. I saw her step close to you and..."

"Kiss me on the cheek," Ricky completed Christine's sentence. "She has never kissed me on the lips. She wouldn't do that."

"It could have been on the cheek," Christine sheepishly mumbled. "She signed the hospital register as your wife!"

"That was the only way they would allow her to see me," Ricky shrugged.

"Then you showed up at Mama Mia with her. She said you were getting her out of the house."

"I was," Ricky's smile was insuppressible, "out of her house, not mine. Tex and Brady were exhibiting cattle in Colorado. She was out here alone.

"I tried on several occasions to explain to you my relationship with Martina. Each time you pushed me away and assured me you knew our relationship."

"I couldn't stand the thought of hearing you say she was your significant other," Christine almost whispered. "If I didn't confront it head on, I could almost justify being with you. I hated being the other woman, but I couldn't stay away from you."

"So, you went against everything you believed to be with me," Ricky said seriously. "You must love me a lot."

"I do," Christine bowed her head.

"We have a lot of problems to overcome," Ricky said softly. "Your political career and our relationship will be a problem. You, living in Washington and me living in Texas. Long distance relationships rarely work."

"I know," Christine gazed into the ranger's blue eyes. "I am willing to try if you are."

"I am more than willing," Ricky slowly smiled. "But you have to talk to me. You have to let me finish sentences even though you think you don't want to hear the information I am sharing with you."

"I will," Christine nodded. "I know how to communicate with a crowd and win in politics. I know how to run a Fortune 500 company, but I am not very good at intimate relationships. Being in politics and business has taught me to be suspicious of everyone. Trust is not one of my strong suits. You are just too good to be true. I keep expecting to find a fault in you, but I don't."

"Believe me, I have plenty of faults," Ricky kissed her gently. "Cheating isn't one of them."

"I want to be with you Major Ricky Strong. Please help me trust in you."

"Then why are we standing here?" Ricky grinned. "I need to give you a tour of our home. I think you will like the room at the end of the hall."

"Is it your bedroom?" Christine smiled suggestively.

"Yes."

"I was hoping it was," the senator wrapped her arms around the ranger's waist. "Let's see it last."

~~~

Christine dozed happily in the arms of the woman she loved. Her night with Ricky had been like nothing she had ever experienced. The open communication between them—both verbally and physically—had been amazing. They held back nothing from each other.

"I love your bed," she whispered into the ranger's ear.

"Our bed," Ricky pulled her closer. "I don't ever want to fall asleep again without you."

"Umm," the brunette hummed, trailing her fingers down the blonde's side.

"When I awoke in the hospital, and you weren't there," Ricky said huskily, "I thought you had deserted me. Then you wouldn't see me or talk to me. I felt used."

"I was there for…"

A soft kiss cut off Christine's words. "Martina told me you had been with me night and day. That you had provided the blood for the transfusion that saved my life. I couldn't reconcile the woman you were in Mexico with the woman I was butting heads with in Austin."

"I was trying to get my head on straight," Christine whispered, "but I couldn't stay away from you."

"Please don't ever do that again," Ricky murmured as she pulled the senator on top of her.

~~~

It was late afternoon when Christine reached for the blonde and discovered a cold, empty bed. She lay still listening. The sounds from the ensuite told her Ricky was showering. She joined her.

Later they walked hand in hand to the kitchen. "I don't believe my jeans and sweater have ever looked as good," Ricky appraised the other woman. "My shoes even fit you."

"I am starving," Christine declared, as Ricky opened the refrigerator door.

"We are in luck," Ricky grinned. "Martina left us lasagna, bread sticks, and a salad." She handed the items to Christine then turned on the oven.

"As much as I hate to let the outside world into our sanctuary," Ricky kissed Christine gently, "I guess we should turn on the TV and see what they are saying about the attack on you."

Every channel clamored with reports of what had transpired during Senator Richmond's Christmas luncheon at UT. Reports ranged from her seriously injured to her demise.

"The mainstream media has its head stuck so far up their…"

"Shush, darling," Christine turned up the sound as Texas Ranger Director David Crockett answered questions at a press conference.

"Senator Richmond is in protective custody," Crockett informed the news people. "We anticipated the attempt on her life, and we were able to immediately extract her from the scene without any injury to her.

"Where is she now?" an idiot newsman asked.

"We wouldn't be very protective if I told you that," Crockett said scornfully.

"The assassin shot one of your men during the attack," a woman said. "How is he?"

"Ranger Clyde Barrel is doing fine," Crockett replied. "He was shot in the shoulder. The shot went through without hitting any bones. He was lucky."

"If he hadn't jumped in front of Senator Richardson, the bullet would have hit her in the head," another newsman blurted out.

"More than likely," the director nodded.

"Where is Major Strong?" a blonde newswoman asked.

"Major Strong is at Ranger Headquarters directing the interrogation of the two gunmen we arrested," Crockett stared directly into the camera. "I am certain we will know more when she completes her questioning of the suspects."

"Oh, that is my cue to get my butt back to work," Ricky sighed. "Will you be okay here for a few hours?"

"I'd rather go with you," Christine pretended to pout.

"Okay, we will wait until after dark then drive into headquarters." Ricky pulled the brunette into her arms. "I don't like being away from you, either."

"Give Martina my compliments," Christine smiled as she loaded their plates into the dishwasher. "That was the best lasagna I have ever eaten."

Ricky rummaged in a drawer and pulled out a set of car keys on a rabbit's foot key chain and two ponytail bands. They put their hair in ponytails and shoved it up under the caps Ricky pulled from the hall closet.

"What do the keys fit?" Christine frowned.

"Your chariot for the evening, Senator," the ranger laughed.

They drove to the barn in Ricky's pickup. Inside, Christine was surprised to see an older, black Chrysler 300. "That looks like a mafia ride," she laughed.

"Wait until you see the inside."

"Oh, my gosh," Christine giggled as she surveyed the dice hanging from the rearview mirror and the black velour seats. A carpeted dash completed the look. "I take that back. It's a pimpmobile."

"What better disguise for a couple of law-abiding citizens?" Ricky laughed.

They stopped to tell Tex and Martina they were leaving. "We will be back around midnight," Ricky informed them.

~~~

On the outskirts of Austin Ricky called Becky.

"Major, we have been worried sick about you," Becky gasped. "Do you have the senator?"

"I sure do," Ricky winked at Christine. "I am headed your way. I'm in the pimpmobile, so you will need to open the gate to the garage for me."

"Call me when you turn onto our street," Becky said. "You won't believe who we have in custody."

"Give me a hint."

"Ex-senator from New Mexico," Becky chirped. "Out on bail for attempted rape."

"Hud Heimlich," Ricky and Christine chorused.

"This just keeps getting better and better," Ricky chuckled. "I can't wait to get there."

~~~

Ricky and Christine pulled off their caps and tossed them on Ricky's desk. "Which interrogation room is holding the disgraced senator?" Ricky asked. She quickly perused the file on Heimlich's arrest.

"Wow! We *actually* caught him with the smoking gun?"

"Yep," Becky nodded eagerly. "He was casually leaving the hall when Crate bumped into him. You know Crate has a nose like a bloodhound and smelled gunpowder. He frisked Heimlich and confiscated the gun used to shoot Barrel.

"GSR test proved that Heimlich was the shooter. He had gunshot residue all over his clothes and hands." The more Becky talked, the more excited she became.

"My man nailed his sorry ass."

"Your man?" Ricky quizzically raised perfect eyebrows.

"Ah…um…I mean Crate," Becky blushed.

They entered the observation room and watched Heimlich. The man was checking his perfectly manicured nails and humming to himself.

"Have we made any announcements about who we have arrested?" Ricky asked.

"Oh, no, Major," Becky looked appalled. "We would never do that without your approval."

"Just making sure Crockett hadn't approved it."

"No. No one knows we have Heimlich or that creep who tried to kidnap you," Becky turned to Christine. "That guy will never see the light of day again."

Crate joined them. "This clown isn't talking," he huffed. "I have threatened him with everything, but he just keeps saying he isn't talking until his lawyer arrives to make him a deal."

"I have an idea," Ricky smiled as she pulled out her phone and touched Paige Daily's quick dial number. "Paige, I have an exclusive for you."

An hour later the team had set up a scene like Paige's set. They set up a live feed into the Smart TV bolted to the wall in Ricky's office.

Ricky and Christine relaxed in the two visitor's chairs while Paige prepared to interview them on the faux set. "You are okay with me recording this for real?" Paige asked.

"Yes," Ricky and Christine nodded.

"You can't air it until we give you the green light," Ricky grinned.

"We are ready to go," Ricky informed Crate.

Crate sauntered into the interrogation room and grinned at Hud Heimlich. "You are being discussed on the evening news." He informed Hud.

"What are you talking about?" Heimlich croaked.

"Come on; I will show you." Crate led the handcuffed man into Ricky's office. "This is Major Strong's office, but she isn't here."

Heimlich stared in horror as the two women appeared on the screen. Paige Daily was interviewing Major Strong and Senator Richmond.

"I want to thank both of you for being on the show tonight," Paige smiled. She turned to face the camera.

"My guests tonight are Senator Christine Richmond and Major Ricky Strong of the Texas Rangers." Paige beamed as if she had just pulled off the biggest scoop in news history.

"Senator, let's start with you," Paige nodded. "I understand that you dated Hud Heimlich for a short time."

"Very short," Christine grimaced.

"What the hell is going on?" Heimlich demanded.

"Not sure," Crate grunted.

"As I understand it," Paige continued, "he was out on bail for assaulting you, and now he has tried to shoot you?

"What is going to happen to him now, Major?" Paige asked seriously.

"He has finally gotten smart," Ricky smiled. "He has agreed to turn state's evidence and has been singing like a nightingale.

"He is naming names and providing dates and locations. He has given us directions to several bodies. His information is invaluable. We will be able to shut down several undesirable entities in Texas and other states.

"Of course, we will put him into the witness protection program. I believe the FBI will handle that."

"No! No! Heimlich began screaming. "You fools will get me killed. They'll slice me into small pieces and feed me to the fish."

"Huh," Crate snorted as he turned off the TV. "I believe your lawyer is here. He probably has taken care of your bail."

"No! You don't understand," Heimlich squeaked, "he isn't my lawyer. He is the lawyer for the cartel."

"Look, Jackass," Crate grasped the front of the man's shirt and shook him. "We have one spot open in witness protection. You can have it, or Manuel Juarez can have it. Whoever talks first gets it. I truly don't care."

"Okay, okay, I'll tell you what you want to know." Sweat poured down Heimlich's face.

Crate handed him a paper towel. "That is probably the wisest decision you have ever made."

~~~

Armed with insurmountable evidence provided by Hud Heimlich, the Texas Rangers very stealthily lined up their arrest warrants. Rangers were working stakeouts on each warrant recipient waiting for the word to start rounding them up and hauling them into headquarters. More than fifteen hundred law enforcement officers were standing by for the *go* command.

Ricky propped against the front of her desk as Christine leaned into her for a kiss. "This is scary," the senator exhaled. "What are we waiting for?"

"You," Ricky gazed into the darkest eyes she had ever seen.

Christine bowed her head. "You will have to catch him on the American side of the border."

"I know. It will make it much easier for me if you tell me his name." Ricky kissed the brunette on the forehead. ""I was fading in and out, but I know you recognized El Asesino when we were captives. Don't be scared, baby. I would die before I would let anything happen to you."

"That is what scares me the most," Christine whispered. "I can't lose you."

"You won't," Ricky reassured her. "You are not protecting me by withholding his name from me. May I have the name?"

"Lucho Rivas," Christine mumbled.

"Lucho Rivas, the governor of Chihuahua, Mexico? The guy you were sitting across from during the negotiations on the wall?" Ricky stared at her incredulously.

"Yes," Christine nodded. "I have never seen such cruelty in a human's face. Ricky, he is pure evil."

"We need to come up with something, quickly to draw him to this side of the border." The ranger frowned. "It won't do any good to cut off all the tails if the head is still alive. "

"His twin daughters attend UT under assumed names," Christine said thoughtfully. "Maybe we could…"

"You're a genius," Ricky laughed exuberantly, "God sent me a gorgeous genius. I love you!"

"What are you going to do?" Christine was anxious to hear the blonde's plan.

"Give them and their boyfriends free trips to Las Vegas," Ricky said thoughtfully. "I'll call our undercover division and see if they have tails on them. I am betting they do."

"I'll call Marcos and see if he still has deep cover agents in Roberto Ramos' organization. I am betting he does since Roberto's father is the one that truly runs the slave trade."

An hour later Ricky relayed the information she had learned from their various departments.

"One of our undercover agents is dating one of the twins, and we still have two deep-cover people in Ramos' mob.

"I have a private jet standing by to take our partyers to Vegas, the ranger continued. "As soon as they are airborne Paige will announce that the twins have been kidnapped and held for ransom.

"An agent is sending a ransom note to Lucho Rivas' home. As soon as Rivas enters America, he is ours."

~~~

Ranger Marcos Hensley very quietly arrested Lucho Rivas as he attempted to enter the U.S. at six in the morning.

Ricky gave the order to serve the warrants and agents fanned out across Texas slapping handcuffs on criminals and taking them to jail.

After all the drug cartel members had been processed and placed in cells, Ricky called a meeting in the Austin Convention Center in facilities made available by Senator Richmond's office.

She cautioned the Rangers to stay alerted and swiftly move if they heard any rumors of cartel members anywhere in Texas.

"We have to be certain we have them all," Ricky said. "The lives of the people who will testify against these thugs depend on us."

The operation took a week of non-stop arrests and relocating prisoners to Austin. "I want them all here," Ricky informed her team. "In one location, they will begin to feed on themselves. Then we will get enough evidence to put them all away for life or on death row."

~~~

"Nothing will happen until after the first of the year," Ricky stroked Christine's smooth back. "Then the feds will swoop into town and begin interrogating them one by one."

"Are you okay with handing your case over to the FBI?" The movement of Christine's lips against her breast made tremors run down Ricky's body."

"Yes. We will continue to provide protection for those testifying. U.S. Attorney Peyton Myers will run the RICO case against them. She is top notch. Very capable and cagey as a fox. If anyone can line up all the cartel criminals for prison, Peyton can." Ricky felt Christine stiffen in her arms.

"Let me see," the ranger feigned thought, "Peyton is a couple of years older than me. A gorgeous blonde with a killer body and more street smarts than a New York taxi driver."

Christine was getting stiffer by the minute.

"I slept with her the first time right after I had my left leg amputated and then twice before having my right leg removed. Then I..."

Christine slapped the ranger's arm, "You are not funny, Ricky Strong. What an awful thing to say."

"I just wanted to show you have ridiculous you are being. You instantly had a jealous reaction to me working with a woman I respected," Ricky pointed out.

"Baby, before you entered my life, I was almost a nun. I haven't been with anyone but you for the past five years. If it takes the rest of my life, I will prove to you that you can trust me to love only you."

"I am sorry," Christine cooed. "I love you too much, but I won't let the green-eyed monster come between us."

"I do have a slight problem," the senator continued to run her fingers over the ranger's abdomen and down to her thigh.

"I think I can help with your problem," Ricky pulled her on top and kissed her sweetly as she ran her hands down the other woman's firm, silky back.

Christine raised her head and looked into the pools of blue. A happy light danced in Ricky's eyes. "I am certain you can," she smiled slyly. "My problem is Mother."

"Oh," Ricky exhaled sharply. "You certainly know how to take the wind out of one's sails. What does Lady want?"

"Her daughter home for Christmas," Christine leaned down and kissed her lover.

Ricky moaned and gently shoved Christine off her. "This needs to be a *dressed conversation*," She grinned as she walked to her closet.

Christine instantly felt the cold, space left by the ranger and pulled the covers tighter around her. Sitting up so she could recline against the headboard, she continued. "I know I need to be in hiding until this case is over, but I can't stop living. I am a State Senator, Chairman of the Budget Committee. I have to continue to work for those who elected me."

"You need to continue to stay alive for those who love you," Ricky scowled, pulling on a loose-fitting sweater. "I don't think your mother was overly thrilled with me showing up for Thanksgiving. How is she going to feel about Christmas?"

"It doesn't matter," Christine said honestly. "She has to get used to seeing you at family gatherings sooner or later."

"I can put a heavy security presence on you in addition to myself," Ricky thought out loud. "As you go about your Senate work, I can station a six-man guard team on you while you are working. After hours, you will be mine."

"Um, I like the sound of that," Christine grinned.

"I want you to be fully prepared," Ricky smiled a crooked smile. "A guard team will be dressed in tactical response gear complete with AK47's, and Glock 22's."

"Machine guns?" Christine asked wide eyed.

"Some people call them that," Ricky nodded. "They will be armed with as much firepower as possible. The cartel has been known to storm a police station and murder everyone in it. I doubt a senator's office would deter them."

"Things like that don't happen in Austin," Christine frowned.

"My call," Ricky grinned that lopsided grin that drove Christine crazy.

"Whatever you say, Major," Christine acquiesced. "Armed guards don't bother me half as much as dining at my mother's."

"Are you going to tell your Mother about us?" Ricky watched as a dark scowl crossed the senator's face.

"I'm not pushing you to tell her. I just wondered how you intend to handle, *us*?" Ricky continued.

"Are you going to tell your staff?" Christine asked.

"They already know," Ricky grinned. "Of course, my family knows."

~~~

Chapter 23

Christmas Eve was a typical Texas day; warm and sunny. Few Texans identify with the song *White Christmas*.

"Do you ride?" Ricky asked as she placed a plate of bacon and eggs in front of Christine.

The senator tilted her head slightly, surveyed the ranger with a gleam in her eye and answered. "I do."

"Want to go for a ride after breakfast?" Ricky kissed the back of her neck, then sat down beside her. "I would like to show you around the ranch."

"That sounds like fun," Christine nodded. "How long have you lived here?"

"All of my life."

"There is a great deal I don't know about you, Major Strong."

After breakfast, they walked the quarter of a mile to the barn. A shrill whinny welcomed the couple as they entered the barn. Ricky caught Christine's hand and pulled her toward a magnificent dark bay stallion.

"He is beautiful," Christine smiled as she held out her hand for the horse to sniff her. A chestnut in the next stall stretched her neck, asking to be included in the petting.

"So are you, sweetheart," the senator laughed as she scratched around the horse's ears.

"Honey, meet Bonnie and Clyde," Ricky grinned.

"Bonnie and Clyde," Christine shook her head. "What awful names for such glorious horses."

"Oh, they have some fancy names and lineage," Ricky chuckled. "Tex can tell you all about them and their sires and dams. I just ride them."

"You just do the fun stuff," Christine glanced at her sensuously.

"Every chance I get," Ricky nuzzled the hair at Christine's neck.

"There you are." Martina entered the barn. "You haven't come out of your house in days. We were afraid you had died in there," Martina teased.

Ricky slid her arms around Christine and rested her chin on the senator's shoulder. It felt good to wrap herself around the brunette's back. "Ricky has been sharing things with me," Christine smiled innocently.

"Um hum, I am certain she has," Martina grinned.

Trying to ignore the sensation of Ricky's soft breasts pressed into her back, Christine said, "We are going for a ride. Want to join us?"

"No, I am making chicken parmesan. If you two can leave your house long enough, we would love to have you dine with us tonight."

"I guess we could do that," Ricky replied reluctantly.

"You don't have to," Martina raised a dark eyebrow.

"We would love to," Christine smiled.

"Around six," Martina grinned. "We are letting Brady open his presents from us tonight. Of course, Santa's gifts won't be until in the morning."

"I would love it if you would attend midnight mass with us," Martina said.

"I don't think that is a good idea," Ricky frowned. "As much as I would love to attend, I need to keep her undercover for right now."

Martina laughed. "I wouldn't touch that last line with a ten-foot pole. Have fun on your ride." She sashayed from the barn.

"She is very sexy," Christine murmured.

No way was Ricky going to respond to that comment, either.

~~~

"I love the ranch," Christine beamed as they returned to the barn. "How many cattle do you run on it."

"Tex keeps between 400 and 450 at all times," Ricky answered. "He turns 200 or more every year. He is an excellent cattleman. Martina has taken to ranch life. She loves it here, too."

"It is a wonderful place to raise a little boy," Christine smiled.

"It was a fun place to grow up," Ricky recalled. "Tex is two years older than me, so he was my big brother. God has never made a better man than Tex."

Christine glanced sideways at Ricky. "Martina isn't from Texas, is she?"

"No. She's from New York."

"How did she end up here?" Christine asked.

"It is a long story," Ricky grimaced. "One I am not at liberty to divulge."

Ricky quickly dismounted and held the headstall on Christine's horse until she was safely on the ground.

Christine slid her arms around the ranger's neck and kissed her tenderly. "I love being with you," she whispered against Ricky's lips. "I want to be with you always."

"We share a mutual goal," the blonde returned the kiss with more passion, gently running her tongue along the senator's full lips, inviting the brunette's tongue to dance with hers. An offer Christine gladly accepted.

~~~

Brady fell in love with Christine. At dinner, he asked permission to sit beside her which Ricky reluctantly granted, taking a seat next to Martina.

Christine was just as taken with the small boy. She attentively listened as Brady told her about feeding an orphaned calf with a baby bottle.

Sitting across from her is not as good as sitting next to her, the ranger thought, *but the view is beautiful*. Ricky blushed when she realized Christine was tormenting her with eye sex.

"You are an incredible cook," Christine complimented Martina. "Where did you learn to cook like that?"

"Old family recipes," Martina smiled warmly. She could see why Ricky was so enthralled with Christine Richmond. The woman was gorgeous and gracious. Martina hadn't missed the hot looks the brunette was giving the ranger.

"...and sometimes Mama gets mad," Brady informed Christine. "Dad says a mad Italian woman is worse than a Texas twister."

"Um, Brady," Tex blushed slightly. "I think you are about to get me into trouble with Santa Claus."

"You mean you won't get any presents tonight?" the wide-eyed boy gasped.

"Yeah, *something* like that," Tex cringed.

The laughter of the adults around the table puzzled Brady, but he decided he was the cause of their merriment so he must be doing something right. He beamed at Christine who hugged him tightly.

Christine and Ricky walked hand in hand back to their home. "That was delightful," the senator smiled as she leaned against the ranger. "I wish my family gatherings were that intimate and loving.

"Our holidays have always been a show for clients or some politician. Not really about family. Now Kara is gone, and my parents refuse to welcome Randall back into the family."

"Will he be there tomorrow?" Ricky asked.

"I don't know. You took away my cell phone, so I haven't spoken to anyone since you took me into protective custody."

"I know first-hand how ruthless the drug cartels and mobsters can be," Ricky frowned.

Christine nuzzled the ranger's neck, "I think you are just keeping me here for your own enjoyment." The moonlight danced in her brown eyes as she looked up at the blonde.

"That, too," Ricky whispered.

~~~

Christine awoke to the sound of Ricky dragging a tall trunk from her closet. "What are you doing?" she asked.

"Getting you a disguise so you can have Christmas dinner with your mother," Ricky grinned. She opened the trunk exposing several wig heads sporting long blond hair, curly red hair and multi-colored brown hair streaked with purple, red, green and yellow.

"You want to be a blonde, redhead or party-girl brown?" Ricky held up each head as she spoke.

"I have heard blondes have more fun," Christine smirked impishly. "Although, I don't think I could possibly have any more fun than I am right now."

"Oh, the fun has just begun," Ricky grinned a predatory grin as she crawled on all fours up the bed.

Christine squealed and feigned fear just before she grabbed the ranger and dragged her on top of her. "Um, this is more like it," she said huskily.

Later they lay in each other's arms trying to slow their breathing. "You are just perfect for me," Christine nibbled at Ricky's ear. "So, perfect."

"The more time I spend with you, the more I want to be with you," Ricky raised up on her elbow and looked down at Christine's face. "When we leave this house, you aren't going to turn back into a cold-hearted bitch, are you?"

"Why, Major Strong, you say the sweetest things to a girl," Christine smirked. "What do you think?"

"I think I am scared. I fall harder for you every day," Ricky confessed. "There is no going back from where I am now."

Christine caressed Ricky's face gently then slid her hands around the ranger's neck, pulling her lips down to hers. "I will never hurt you, again," she promised.

~~~

As they approached the Austin city limits, Ricky handed Christine a burner phone. "Better call your Mother and let her know we will be in attendance."

Lady Richmond sounded relieved and grateful that her daughter was joining them for Christmas dinner.

"Of course, Major Strong is welcome," the matriarch enthused. "She saved your life.

"I am so glad you will be here. That handsome lawyer from the DA's office is coming, too."

"Mother, stop trying to fix me up with men," Christine huffed. "I don't..."

"Well, I can't fix you up with women," Lady said indignantly.

"Why don't you just not fix me up at all," Christine growled. "Did you invite my brother?"

A long silence greeted her question. "Really, Mother, you invite people you barely know, but leave out Randall?"

Ricky laid her hand on the senator's leg and calmed her. "Say goodbye," she whispered.

As Ricky accepted the phone, she smiled slightly at Christine. "Don't let them ruin our holiday, honey. We will have dinner, and I will insist on sweeping you away for your safety."

"You think my mother cares about that?" Christine inhaled deeply. "All she cares about is appearances."

"I can't wait for her to see you decked out like Lady Gaga," Ricky laughed.

"Look who's talking, Cher," Christine giggled. "I do have fun with you, Major Strong."

"That is all that matters, sweetheart."

~~~

"Christine, this is Christmas, not Halloween," Lady Richmond hissed when she opened the door.

"I can leave, Mother," Christine threatened. "I am supposed to be hidden away somewhere. I talked Ricky into bringing me here."

"Against my better judgment," Ricky added.

"Let's go, Senator," Ricky took Christine's arm and pulled her away from the door. "I don't like this anyway."

"No, wait! Don't leave," Lady begged. "I was just shocked by your attire and hair. Believe me, darling, blonde is not your color.

"I have a surprise for you."

"Please, Mother, not another..."

"Oh, my gosh, look at you," Randall pulled Christine into a warm bear hug, "and you, Major Strong."

"You two will certainly liven up an otherwise dull and boring gathering," he beamed as he included Ricky in his hug.

"Father, come see what the cat just dragged in?" Randall called.

Armand strode to the foyer and embraced his daughter. "What is this?" he grinned.

"My disguise," Christine laughed. "Major Strong insisted on it."

Armand chuckled. "It should be good conversational material over dinner. Come, Mother, don't look so distraught. We have both of our children home for Christmas."

Lady Richmond smiled and nodded.

A dozen or so people milled around the great room and were excited to see Senator Richmond. Most of them were there because of her.

Ricky quickly checked out the crowd. There were no strangers. She had seen all of them come and go from the senator's office.

Scott Winslow quickly staked his claim on Christine. "Senator Richmond, we have been worried to death about you."

As Scott led Christine to the sideboard for a drink, Randall caught Ricky's arm. "Is she okay?" He asked.

Ricky wanted to say *she is just perfect*, but settled for, "She is holding up okay. Witness protection is hard for her."

"I am sure it is," Randall agreed.

"She has a fit to get back to work, but I don't think that is a good idea."

"Where are you keeping her? May I visit her?" Randall's concern was obvious.

"We have her in a safe house," Ricky shook her head. "I can't tell anyone where she is. That would be a serious breach of protocol. I shouldn't have let her come here, but you know Christine. I either had to let her come or handcuff her."

"That sounds promising," Christine giggled as she slipped her arm through Ricky's and squeezed tightly.

"So," she beamed, "Mother and Daddy have decided you are a good guy after all?"

"I am sure the jury is still out," Randall bowed his head slightly, "but they are giving me a second chance. I promise I won't blow it, Sis."

"I am glad," Christine slipped her other arm through her brother's, "Mother beckons."

Dinner was a joyous affair. Everyone insisted on hearing about Christine's near brush with death. They queried Ricky about the statewide roundup of drug dealers and murders.

"Do you know U.S. Attorney Peyton Myers well?" Scott asked.

"I have worked with her on several cases," Ricky nodded. "She will make us proud."

"I know you and Christine have certainly made us proud," Randall raised his wine glass. "A toast to Senator Christine Richmond and Major Ricky Strong."

Approval ran around the table as the diners joined in the toast.

Christine insisted they stay until the bitter end. She helped her parents and brother bid goodnight to their guests then walked into the study.

"Must I continue wearing this dreadful wig?" Christine asked.

"Yes," Ricky nodded. "You promised."

"It does grow on one," Randall smiled as he refilled his families wine glasses.

"That is what I am afraid of," Christine laughed.

"Mother, Father, Christine," Randall stood in front of the fireplace, "thank you. Thank you for welcoming me home and giving me a second chance. I promise you won't regret it."

"Tell me how this came about," Christine smiled brightly at her brother.

"Your brother went to work in our warehouse district," Armand started the story. "I kept getting reports of how great the new man was doing.

"A position in administration opened, and his supervisors recommended him. "Imagine my surprise when I found out they were all ecstatic over my son."

Armand bowed his head. "I admired his willingness to start in the warehouses. He has been excellent in the administration part of our operations, too.

"Chris, your plea to give him a second chance convinced me I should. It will be good to have both of you running our conglomerate."

"Both of us?" Randall questioned. "I thought you were married to politics, Sis."

"One can only spend so many years in politics," Christine smiled knowingly. "It is a job with a high burnout rate. My plan is four years as governor, eight as president, then go into the private sector, Richmond International."

Randall glanced away then back at his sister. "I had visions of me being the private sector and you in politics."

"Christine has always planned to take the helm of Richmond," Armand explained. "She owns it."

Randall's head jerked as if his father had slapped him. "Christine owns the family business?"

Armand nodded. "Of course, you were away during that time, but Christine married the owner of the second largest shipping company in the U.S. He died in a Teamsters' brawl. He left everything to Christine. When we incorporated Christine's company into Richmond International, I simply made Christine the owner of all Richmond stock. We are a privately held company, so she is the sole owner of the business."

"I see," Randall said softly then raised his glass toward Christine. "A toast to the Queen!"

Ricky walked out the back door of the Richmond home and moved silently around the grounds searching for anyone observing the family home. She scanned Martina's Beemer for explosives and found none. She had waited a long time before she decided it was safe to bring Christine out to the car.

The ranger breathed easier as they left the Austin city limits behind them. Christine had been strangely silent since leaving the Richmond's.

"Are you okay, honey?" Ricky pulled Christine's hand onto her lap.

"I think I am," Christine said softly. "I…I felt sorry for Randall. I think he was shocked to learn I own Richmond International, thus the entire Richmond conglomerate."

"He did seem surprised," Ricky agreed.

"I need to talk with Father. When he retires, and Randall and I take over the company, I will give my brother half the stock."

"That is very generous of you," Ricky shrugged.

"You and Tex did the same thing," Christine smiled. "I want to have the same relationship with Randall you have with Tex."

"I understand that," Ricky nodded. "Still let him prove himself. Tex and I grew up side by side. There is a lot about Randall you may not know."

"Do you know things about him I don't know?" Christine pulled her hand from Ricky's and turned to face her.

"I checked into his background. Why he went to prison? That sort of thing. It looks like he paid his dues and managed to stay out of trouble. I am not saying don't trust him. I am just saying let him earn his place in the company."

Christine leaned over and kissed the ranger's cheek. "You give good advice, Major Strong."

"I give good back rubs, too."

"Um, how quickly can we get home?"

~~~

Chapter 24

Christine snuggled into her blonde lover for warmth. The late December temperature had dropped drastically overnight.

She had forgotten her concern over Randall. Loving Ricky always made everything else fade into the background. All that truly mattered was being with the ranger. Christine was thankful that neither of them had commitments until after New Year's when Peyton Myers would begin building her cases. Christine was looking forward to meeting Peyton.

Christine kissed the blonde lightly on the lips. "Wake up and pay me some attention," she whispered.

"Wake up and what?" Ricky kept her eyes closed as she teased the brunette.

"Pay attention to me," Christine giggled as the ranger rose above her.

"And what, exactly does that mean?" Ricky's eyes danced as she kissed the woman.

"You know," Christine whispered.

~~~

Troy Hunter was going crazy. He couldn't locate Senator Richmond or Major Strong. The thing that disturbed him most was that Rachel Winn had not responded to his third friend request on Facebook.

He logged onto his Facebook page, scrolled down the home page and gasped. A large photo of Rachel

Winn's naked back sent a shudder through his body. Down her spine was written in black marker, *Need Someone to Love*. Her face was looking back over her shoulder, and those gorgeous blue eyes danced sensuously. He sent her another friend request.

To his surprise, she accepted.

Hi, just wanted to say you have the most beautiful eyes, he posted.

Thank you.

Do you have big plans for New Years? He typed.

Not really.

God, he hated women of few words. He decided not to communicate with her anymore tonight. He wasn't letting her go, just playing with her. He decided she would be his next victim.

Hi, Rachel. David, here. *Want to go to a New Year's Eve party with me?*

Damn, someone else is courting my girl, Troy thought.

Sure, why not. Give me a call. You have my number.

I hope you have fun New Year's Eve, Troy wrote. He was desperately trying to get her attention now.

Thank you, was all he received.

~~~

January second, they hit the ground running. Ricky drove Christine to her building where six heavily-armed guards were placed strategically in the senator's office.

Christine checked her meeting calendar and printed a copy for Ricky.

Crate and Barrel entered her office. "Happy New Year," the pair chorused.

"You, too, fellows," Ricky laughed.

"You think we have enough firepower?" Barrel raised an eyebrow.

"Consider them your personal army," Ricky grinned. Six of them and two of you ought to be able to protect my...uh the senator. Follow me; I will introduce you."

As the door closed behind Ricky and her team, a cold loneliness dropped over Christine. It was the first time in over three weeks she had been away from the blonde. It hurt, both physically and mentally.

Ricky introduced Crate and Barrel to the small militia she had assembled. She asked them all to meet in Senator Richmond's office in five minutes.

"Your security team is coming in to meet you," Ricky informed the brunette. "I want you to know their faces. If the faces change, let Crate or Barrel know immediately. Under no circumstances should you see anyone protecting you but the men you are about to meet."

The six men quietly filed into the room. Christine studied their faces as Ricky introduced them. All of them were over six feet tall with broad shoulders. They were extremely intimidating.

One of the men stepped forward. "We just want you to know that it is a privilege to serve you, Senator. We need more people like you in politics.

"We will keep you safe, ma'am."

A smile caressed Christine's lips. "Thank you. I am grateful for you."

The men returned to their stations. "They will accompany you everywhere you go," Ricky said. "You will be transported in an armored Hummer."

"We discuss very confidential subjects in the budget meetings," Christine frowned. "I don't think the security team will be allowed in the chambers."

"They have two choices, Senator," Ricky scowled. "They can allow your security team to be with you at all times or I can hide you away in a safe house. You already know my preference."

"Can't you stay with me?" Christine almost whined.

"Honey, you know I want to, but I must take care of some things first."

"Where are you going?"

"Back to headquarters. Peyton has set up her command station in our facility. I promised her I would go through the files and give her all the information I have on the players. She will probably want to talk to you tomorrow."

"Can I go with you?" Christine blurted out.

"Of course, you can. I thought you had a meeting this morning."

Christine crossed her arms. "I do, dammit."

Ricky walked to the door and locked it. The senator was instantly in her arms.

"I am acting like a baby," Christine mumbled against her lips, as Ricky gently kissed her.

"Um, but you are my baby," the ranger whispered. "Go to your meetings. The security team will bring you to meet us for lunch. Okay?"

Christine nodded her head. "I am having withdrawal. It is hard to go cold turkey after spending every minute with you for almost a month."

"I am just a phone call away," Ricky kissed her one more time. "God, I love your lips."

~~~

U.S. Attorney Peyton Myers was a no-nonsense woman. In a gray world, things were black and white to Peyton. You were either guilty or innocent. Being a little bit guilty was like being a little bit pregnant. In the end, one had to suffer the consequences of their actions.

The RICO case she was building had two good things going for it: she would put a lot of bad guys in prison, and she would be working with Texas Ranger Ricky Strong.

She looked up as her secretary led two sleazy-looking men into her office. "What can I do for you gentlemen?"

"We have extradition papers for Señor Lucho Rivas." One of the men rattled some papers in front of her.

Peyton yanked the papers from his hand and quickly scanned them. She looked the man in the eye as she ripped the papers in half and tossed them on the floor. "The U.S. doesn't recognize Mexican extradition papers," she grinned ruefully. "Good day, gentlemen."

"Is there a problem, Ms. Myers?" Ricky calmly entered the room.

"I don't think so," she said. "Do we have a problem, gentlemen?"

The men shook their heads and left the office.

"What was that about?" Ricky asked.

"Nothing important," Peyton scanned the ranger's lean, muscular body. "You work out every day, don't you?"

"I wish," Ricky laughed. "I am lucky if I get to the gym three times a week. You look great. How is the Attorney General's office treating you?"

"I can't complain. I get to do what I like best, put away criminals. Thanks for this case, by the way. It is almost a slam dunk. You and Senator Richmond did your homework on this one."

"I was hoping to meet the senator today," Peyton added.

"She will join us for lunch," Ricky nodded. "She had meetings all morning."

Ricky and Peyton spent the morning going over the files. Peyton made notes as Ricky told her everything she knew about the various gang members. Ricky had painstakingly taken detailed written and video confession from Heimlich along with details of crimes committed by others that had been witnessed by Heimlich.

Ricky's phone signaled a text from Crate. *We will leave in ten. See you in twenty-five.*

"Senator Richmond is heading to the restaurant for lunch. You ready to go?"

"I am," Peyton grinned. "I'm starving."

Ricky and Peyton arrived early. The restaurant had set up a private room for the diners. The ranger checked out everything in the restaurant, then stood outside the door with Peyton waiting for Christine's arrival.

"I have seen her on TV," Peyton commented. "Is she as gorgeous as they make her look?"

"Even more so," Ricky smiled.

"Oh! Wow!" Peyton exclaimed when Christine stepped from the Hummer.

Ricky couldn't tell if she was in awe of the security or the woman they were guarding.

"You were serious when you said she has a small army protecting her," Peyton whispered as she watched Christine glide toward them.

"Senator Christine Richmond, this is U.S. Attorney Peyton Myers." Ricky made the introductions.

"Major Strong has told me so much about you," Christine extended her hand to Peyton. "It is a pleasure to meet you."

"The pleasure is all mine," Peyton smiled.

Ricky spent the next hour watching Peyton fawn over Christine. She was obviously enamored of the senator.

Christine sat across the table from Ricky and Peyton was seated beside the senator.

"Senator Richmond saved my l-i-f-e," Ricky warbled as Christine hooked the toe of her shoe behind the ranger's calf and slowly raked it up and down her leg. A scarlet blush crawled up the blonde's neck as she looked up at the senator. Christine's sensual eye contact only made matters worse.

"I saw the documentary on you two," Peyton nodded. "It was very impressive."

"Major Strong is very impressive," Christine smiled. She was pleased with the effect she was having on her lover.

"That took a lot of nerve to strike off across the badlands on a motorcycle with an injured woman strapped to you," Peyton rhapsodized.

The alarm went off on Christine's phone. "I must run," she smiled. "Another meeting. I have enjoyed meeting you, Peyton and look forward to working with you."

Peyton stood and nodded.

"Major," Christine smiled at Ricky, "I will see you in my office at four."

"Yes, ma'am," Ricky almost saluted. *Sometimes I get very excited around her,* she thought.

Peyton sat down and ordered a cocktail. Ricky got a refill on her Dr. Pepper.

"She is something," Peyton thought out loud.

"Yes. Yes, she is," Ricky nodded.

"She's not married?" Peyton asked.

"Widow," Ricky replied.

"Oh," Peyton sounded deflated. "That is a shame."

"Do you know much about her?" Ricky asked.

"I've heard she is a real hard ass," Peyton sipped her drink. "Single-handedly defeated the same-sex marriage bill when it came through the Senate. A proponent of the Right-to-work bill, and strong supporter of open carry.

"Didn't she go to jail for handcuffing herself to the doors of an abortion clinic?"

"You have done your homework," Ricky laughed. "She also cares about America and Americans. She will make certain the wall gets built."

"What does she do for fun?"

"Ask her," Ricky shrugged.

By the end of the day, Peyton had two cases ready to file. "This is slow going," she frowned. "but I want to make certain we dot our I's and cross our T's. I don't want some thug walking away free because we failed to do our due diligence."

"I agree," Ricky nodded. "I have to go with my team to move Senator Richmond."

"Why don't we go to dinner together?" Peyton suggested. "See if she wants to."

Ricky called Christine. "Are you on your way?" the senator said anxiously. "I miss you."

"Peyton asked me to see if you wanted to go to dinner tonight," Ricky said.

"You know what I want," Christine hummed, "and it doesn't include Peyton Myers."

"Okay, Senator," Ricky smiled. "No, we understand you have a lot to do. Yes, ma'am, I am on my way to change out the security team now. Yes, ma'am, I will be glad to stop and pick up some very personal feminine items for you. Just text me the list."

"You little, shit," Christine laughed into her phone. "Hurry."

Ricky slipped her phone back into her pocket. "Sorry, the senator has other plans for tonight."

"Do you want to go to dinner after you get her settled?" Peyton asked.

"No, I'd better pass," Ricky grimaced. "My partner wouldn't like that."

"Partner," Peyton studied her. "You mean ranger partner or significant other."

"Committed relationship," Ricky nodded. "Very committed."

Damn, Peyton thought as she watched the ranger walk away, *this isn't going to be as much fun as I had hoped.*

~~~

Chapter 25

"I want to interview this man," Peyton tossed a file onto Ricky's desk.

"Manuel Juarez," Ricky sneered. "He's the thug that tried to kidnap Senator Richmond from the parking lot."

"Yes. What was she doing alone in a place like that anyway?" Peyton frowned.

"Roscoe's isn't bad," Ricky defended her favorite dancehall.

"It is if a woman is unaccompanied," Peyton snorted. "I know."

"Oh, yeah, I recall you experienced their hospitality," Ricky grinned. "It is a good thing you had a gun."

"It wasn't funny, Strong. No one told me it was ladies' night when I went."

"I'll have someone bring over Juarez for interrogation," Ricky nodded. "Probably take a couple of hours. You want to break for lunch?"

"Sure. Why don't you see if Senator Richmond wants to join us?"

Ricky called Christine. "Would you like to join us for lunch?"

"I am having lunch with Randall," Christine informed her.

"Under no circumstances are you to get out of sight of your security team," Ricky reminded her.

"I love it when you are overly protective," Christine teased her. "Can we go home early tonight? I have had a rough day already, and it isn't even half over."

"Of course," Ricky said eagerly.

"I love you," Christine said softly into the phone.

"Same here," Ricky smiled.

~~~

Manuel Juarez was in the interrogation room when they returned from lunch. Ricky followed Peyton into the room. By the time, they were through interviewing Juarez, Peyton had more than enough evidence to bury Lucho Rivas.

They watched Juarez through the one-way glass. "I hope the FBI can protect him," Ricky frowned. "His testimony is crucial to the case against Rivas."

"I think I will move Rivas' trial forward as fast as possible," Peyton wrinkled her forehead in thought. "With Senator Richmond's eyewitness account and the evidence Juarez has given us, I will have no problem getting a conviction.

"Once the rats see Rivas go down, they will plea bargain their hearts out. I will put them away for twenty to thirty years and save the taxpayer billions."

"Have I ever told you how much I admire you?" Ricky said. "You and Senator Richmond are truly public servants. Few politicians give the citizens a second thought. To them, taxpayers are just a bottomless piggybank."

A text message from Becky dinged into Ricky's cellphone. *Senator Richmond headed your way.*

Ricky opened the observation room door and stepped into the hallway. Peyton followed.

"Senator Richmond," Peyton rushed to meet the beautiful brunette. "What a delightful surprise."

Christine looked past Peyton and flashed that little smile that always melted Ricky. The ranger was surprised to see Randall behind his sister. The security team was behind them.

"Randall is insisting on talking to you," Christine addressed Ricky. "I told him he is wasting his time. You are very stubborn."

"I am having dinner at Truluck's with mother and father tonight," Randall smiled. "Everyone will be thrilled if you and Christine can join us. We miss our superstar." He cast a loving glance at his sister.

"I don't think so," Ricky frowned. "That is too public. She needs to go to the safe house. I don't want her in the open any more than necessary until after Rivas' trial."

"Which I plan to commence immediately," Peyton assured the senator.

The guards entered the hallway to take Juarez back to his jail cell. Ricky stepped back so she could watch everything going on in the hall.

The guards escorted Juarez from the room. The thug stopped in his tracks when he saw Randall's profile. Ricky stepped between the two men before Randall saw Juarez and pushed the Latino back into the interrogation room. "Keep him here until the senator leaves," she instructed.

"Please, Major Strong," Randall flashed his sweetest smile.

"No way," Ricky growled. "Don't you have someplace to be, Senator?"

Christine scowled but nodded. "I will finish around three," she said curtly. "I will call you so you can oversee the changing of the guards."

"It was nice to see you, Peyton," Christine smiled slightly. "You, too, Major."

"What is going on?" Peyton asked as Ricky led her into the interrogation room with Juarez.

"How do you know that man?" Ricky scowled at Juarez.

"No, no senorita," Juarez pretended to be stupid.

"Peyton, why don't you go get us a cup of coffee?" Ricky frowned. "There is some in the room next door."

Peyton nodded and went to the observation room.

Ricky turned off the camera recording their session. "The camera is off. You can speak freely," she told Juarez.

"I have nothing to say," Juarez smirked.

"Let me put this another way," Ricky opened the drawer on her side of the desk and pulled out a thick telephone book. "Either tell me what you know about that man or I will beat the hell out of you with this phone book."

Juarez placed his hands on the table and laughed in her face. He howled in pain as the ranger slammed the heavy phone book down on his hand. "Punta, you broke my hand," he cried.

"Hum, I don't see a mark on it," Ricky grinned maliciously. "Sometime during the night, you will probably die from internal bleeding, and there won't be a mark on you."

"You are one crazy bitch," Juarez whimpered as he held his useless hand.

"You want matching hands?" Ricky leered as if she would enjoy the process.

"I don't know his name," Juarez said. "He is an enforcer for the cartel."

"How do you know that?"

"He was in Oklahoma when I was there." Juarez squirmed in his chair as he tentatively bent the fingers of his injured hand. "We were handling shipments for distribution all over the U.S."

"He lives in California, but does the cartel's business all over the states."

"You're positive that's him?" Ricky demanded.

"I'd know that scar anywhere," Juarez nodded. "He was knifed during a brawl we had with another cartel on the New Orleans docks.

"We highjacked their shipment, and one of them knifed him."

"See how much nicer it is when you cooperate," Ricky smiled. "Your hand isn't broken. Just keep moving your fingers. You will be fine."

"What was that about?" Peyton met her in the hallway as Ricky signaled for the guards to take Juarez back to his cell.

"I am not certain," Ricky scowled. "I am not sure Randall is entirely honest with his family."

"He sounds like one bad dude," Peyton shrugged. "Do you trust him around the senator?"

"No, that is why I tell my men to never leave her alone with him."

I am ready, dinged into Ricky's phone.

"The Queen beckons," Ricky laughed.

~~~

The changing of the guards—as they called it—was very convoluted on purpose. The Hummer that appeared to be carrying Christine pulled into the Texas Rangers' parking garage. Agent Nicole Weil exited the vehicle under heavy guard and entered the facility.

Across town, Major Strong was already on the top floor of the parking garage of the building that housed Senator Richmond's office. Ricky stood outside the elevators as Crate and Barrel delivered Christine to her. They slipped into a nondescript car and headed for the ranch.

"What a day," Christine softly said as she leaned over for a kiss.

"It was interesting," Ricky placed her hand on top of Christine's. "Did you and Randall have a nice lunch?"

"It was good," the senator nodded.

"…but," Ricky prompted.

"He seems different. I think it bothers him that I own the company."

"Did you discuss it?" Ricky asked.

"Yes. I told Randall I was going to talk to Daddy about making him a partner."

"If something happened to you, who would inherit Richmond International?" Ricky said casually.

"Eventually, Randall. After the death of Mother and Daddy, of course. Why do you ask?"

"Just curious," Ricky squeezed her hand. "I missed you today."

"I can't wait to get a nice hot bath then slip into your arms," Christine grinned impishly.

"My thoughts, exactly," Ricky laughed.

~~~

Ricky waited on the line until New Orleans Detective Phillip Taylor picked up his extension. She explained her situation and asked if he could supply her any additional information on Randall Richmond.

Taylor scrolled through his personal files on Richmond. "Mean son-of-a-bitch," he announced. "He was into everything bad: prostitution, drugs, white slavery. Nasty piece of work.

"He would wear out his welcome, then move on to another state. I am not certain what he did for a living. Nothing legal I am sure."

"That was before he did prison time?" Ricky noted.

"No, that was after he got out of prison," Taylor said. "He must have gotten smarter in prison because he managed to stay one step ahead of the law after he got out of the pen."

"Do you know where he went when he left New Orleans?"

"Arkansas, I think," Taylor replied.

"I can't figure out how the guy was constantly in trouble, spent six years in the pen and we don't have a DNA sample on file anywhere," Ricky said.

"You're kidding?" Taylor huffed.

"I wish I were," Ricky snorted.

"Hang on a minute," Taylor opened and closed drawers in his desk. "Yeah, here it is. Call this guy in Arkansas. He is a detective in the Little Rock Police Department. He called me about Richmond. Maybe he can help you."

Ricky dialed the number for Little Rock Detective Mike Wales. "Wales, here," a deep baritone voice announced.

Ricky went through her story again.

"I handled him a couple of times," Wales said. "He liked to knock around women. Nasty mother."

"Do you have any idea where I can locate him?" Ricky asked.

"No, last I heard he was in Oklahoma City, I think."

The sinking feeling in Ricky's stomach threatened to push up her breakfast. She pinched the bridge of her nose between her thumb and forefinger and prayed. *God, things are good between Christine and me, please don't let Randall be the Hacker.*

A dozen calls to the Oklahoma City Police Department netted her a voice mail for Senior Detective Macy Lane. She left her name, number, and a brief message.

Ricky logged onto her phony Facebook page and became Rachel Winn. *My New Year's resolution is to give up men*, she typed. She posted one of the shots of Agent Weil exposing a lot of her very attractive breasts.

A dozen perverts texted back telling her they were different from other men and she should give them a try.

Men really like Nicole, Ricky thought.

I am thinking about giving up women, Lonely Boy posted, accompanied by a cute puppy picture.

Cute puppy, she posted.

364

His name is Charlie, Lonely Boy posted. *He loves beautiful women. I am certain the two of you would hit it off.*

Ricky spent the next fifteen minutes exchanging pleasantries with Lonely Boy aka Troy Hunter.

She logged off when another man posted a lewd comment about Nicole's breasts.

She searched the internet and found a precious female, Poodle-Chihuahua mix. A Poohuahua, she laughed at the mixed-breed name. *Come to mama, Princess*, she thought as she copied the picture. *Tomorrow you will meet Charlie online.*

Christine texted that the security detail was leaving her office in ten minutes. Ricky hurriedly left her office and drove to the top floor of Christine's parking garage.

She toyed with the idea of telling the senator that her brother might be the Hacker but decided not to implode her world. She had a good idea how the brunette would react to her news.

She locked the car doors as Christine buckled her seatbelt.

"Where do you get all these different vehicles?" Christine surveyed the Jeep Wrangler. "Thank God it has a good heater."

"From the impound lot, so we are never in the same vehicle twice." Ricky smiled as she leaned down to kiss the brunette. Christine pulled her harder against her. "I hate it when we are apart," she mumbled against the ranger's lips.

"I do, too," Ricky kissed her again. "How was your day?"

"Busy, we are gearing up for the final jump over the first hurdle. The primaries are in March."

"Piece of cake," Ricky laughed. "You know you will win the primary. Which reminds me, Paige Daily wants to do a shoot with us teaching our UT class. Should be good publicity for you."

"Should be," Christine smiled. "I appreciate you agreeing to do this. I know how busy you are."

The senator chatted as they drove to the ranch. She was cognizant of the ranger's silence but chalked it up to her preoccupation with the RICO case.

"Per the news media, Peyton is winning her court case," Christine said.

"Looks that way," Ricky nodded.

When they arrived home a note from Martina informed them there was a beef stew in the refrigerator and crackers in the cabinet.

"You take your shower," Christine slipped her arms around Ricky's waist. "and I will make a salad and tea.

The ranger hugged her tightly for a long time then left the room.

"It smells great in here," Ricky smiled as she entered the kitchen. Christine was stirring the stew as it warmed on the stove and salads were on the island counter. She looked over her shoulder at the blonde.

Ricky stood behind the brunette and slipped her arms around her waist. She nuzzled the woman's neck and held her tightly against her. "I love you so much," she whispered.

Christine turned in her arms. "Tell me what is bothering you, baby."

"I am just holding my breath until a verdict comes in on Rivas." Ricky kissed her softly. "This is the most important case Peyton will handle this year. It will determine the fate of the other cases. If she gets a guilty verdict, in this case, the others will fall like dominoes."

"I have faith in Peyton," Christine smiled. "I am sure she will win the case."

"How is Randall doing at Richmond International?" Ricky asked as she placed their tea and crackers on the counter with the salads.

"I am not certain," Christine frowned. "Daddy left a message that he needs to speak with me about Randall. I was so busy I never had the opportunity to return his call.

"I thought that we might go to his office in the morning if you don't mind."

"Works for me," Ricky nodded.

~~~

Ricky was always awed by the opulence of the offices at Richmond International. The walls showcased original art worth millions. Prized statuary graced gracefully arching niches.

"This place looks more like an art museum than a shipbuilding conglomerate," she said softly.

"Mother and Daddy built this company from nothing," Christine smiled proudly. "They love fine art, so they indulge themselves. They deserve it. They worked hard for it."

"Senator Richmond," an attractive receptionist beamed at them as she stood to greet them, "your father is expecting you."

"Good morning Rose," Christine smiled. "Sit back down. I know the way to Daddy's office."

Armand greeted his daughter warmly and shook Ricky's hand. "Thank you for keeping my girl safe," he said.

"She is a top priority for us, sir," Ricky replied.

"How is the campaign going?" Armand asked his daughter.

"It is good, Daddy. Just six more weeks until the primary."

"I appreciate your visit," Armand nodded. "I know how swamped you are. I just wanted to give you a report on your brother so you can rest easy and give the race all of your attention."

"I assume he is doing well," Christine smiled.

"He is excellent," Armand grinned. "Chris, he has taken to this like a fish to water. I am glad he was man enough to confront me. I have a new respect for him. He is not at all like he used to be."

Christine hugged her father. "I can't tell you how happy that makes me."

Christine's alarm sounded on her cell phone. "I have to run, Daddy. I have a big budget meeting this morning. Thank you, again for putting my mind at ease."

Ricky was silent as she drove Christine to the Ranger Headquarters to meet her security team.

The brunette placed her hand on the ranger's thigh. "You are very quiet, darling. Is everything okay?"

"Yes,' Ricky smiled weakly. "I have a lot on my mind." She couldn't reconcile the Randall Richmond she knew with the reports she was receiving from other law enforcement agencies.

368

"I know you do, but things are moving fast." Christine pulled her hand to her lips and kissed her knuckles. "Hopefully, all of this will be over before the primary, and we can get on with our lives."

"Where do you plan to live when things return to normal?" Ricky asked.

"Where ever you are," Christine squeezed her hand. "I don't care where we live. We can live in our house in Austin or at the ranch."

"Should I get rid of my apartment?" Ricky raised a questioning eyebrow.

"Definitely," the brunette laughed.

"People will figure out we are living together," Ricky warned.

"I know," Christine said softly. "We will cross that bridge when we come to it."

"I have never lived with anyone," Ricky shrugged.

Christine scrutinized her lover's face. "Never?"

Ricky shook her head, no. "I have never cared enough about anyone to share my day-to-day life with them."

"I am glad," the senator slowly smiled. "I have never lived with a woman. It will be an entirely new and wonderful experience we can share the rest of our lives."

~~~

Chapter 26

Ricky sat in the courtroom behind Peyton Myers as the jury returned to the jury box. Peyton was fidgeting with her pen as they waited for the decision. Christine had testified in the trial but had no desire to be on hand for the verdict.

The jury foreman quietly stood as silence fell over the courtroom. The judge addressed the jury. "In the case of the Federal Government versus Lucho Rivas, how does the jury find?"

"The jury unanimously finds Lucho Rivas guilty on all counts, your honor. It is the desire of the jury that he serve life without parole."

Peyton and Ricky exhaled sharply. Peyton turned and hugged the ranger. "We did it, Ricky! We did it!"

Rivas was immediately handcuffed and led from the courtroom. "I should have killed you myself," he screamed at Ricky. You and your..."

The deputy yanked Rivas' handcuffs hard and dragged him from the room.

"I think you owe me a drink, Major," Peyton grinned.

"And a steak," Ricky nodded. She called Christine to give her the good news.

"We are going to Ruth's Chris Steakhouse for drinks and dinner to celebrate," Ricky was euphoric.

"May we pick you up? Great, be there in twenty. Same here."

~~~

The sommelier had filled their glasses, and Ricky proposed a toast. "To the finest U.S. Attorney in America," she laughed as their glasses clinked together.

Peyton looked around the table. "I could not have accomplished this without the two of you," she smiled.

"Although Rivas was found guilty of several murders," Christine frowned, "you didn't ask for the death penalty. Why not?"

"The death penalty would have resulted in an automatic retrial," Peyton scowled. "I'd rather see him rot in jail than take a chance on his sentencing being overturned."

"Um, I didn't think about that," Christine nodded. "Excellent work counselor."

Peyton's phone constantly dinged as they dined. "The rats' attorneys," she grinned as she turned it off. "Soon this entire mess will be settled, and the two of you can resume a normal life."

"Whatever that is," Christine laughed. "I am looking forward to moving around without a small army." She rested her hand on Ricky's leg.

A slight blush colored the ranger's face. Ricky bowed her head to hide the rush of happiness she felt sitting beside the senator.

~~~

Detective Macy Lane in Oklahoma had related the same information as the other detectives Ricky had spoken to about Randall. Her last call would be to

Detective Paul Wright in Santa Fe, New Mexico. Unfortunately, Paul Wright was on extended leave.

"Does he have a partner or someone else who can talk with me about Randall Richmond?" Ricky asked.

"No, ma'am," the officer answered her. "His partner died two weeks ago, that is why Detective Wright is taking a leave of absence."

"I am sorry to hear that," Ricky mumbled. "I know how hard it is to lose a partner. When he feels like it, would you have him call me."

The man took her number then hung up. Ricky spun around in her chair and studied the many awards and certificates hanging on her office wall. The latest was the Governor's Award for Valor. She leaned her head back in her chair and closed her eyes.

Images of Christine on the border tour flashed through her mind. Christine in killer heels dancing with Roberto Ramos. Christine, lying beside her, their lips touching. Christine's sincere concern for American citizens along the border, who were suffering. The look on Christine's face as Ricky squeezed off the shot that killed Ramos. Christine's determination to get them back on U.S. soil.

Senator Christine Richmond was a true American hero. The senator had also received the Governor's Award. Ricky briefly wondered if her relationship with the senator would hurt Christine's chances in the gubernatorial election.

The Hacker dove into her thoughts like a dark demon diving from hell. She wondered if she could string him along on Facebook for two weeks.

Sitting with her eyes closed and thoughts running through her mind, she had an epiphany. She called ME Lane Mason.

"Lane, would you run Kara Richmond's DNA against the DNA we pulled from the skin found in Kay Dawson's teeth?"

"If they match," Lane said, "it should have shown up when we ran the skin DNA through the system. Kara's was already in the system."

"Humor me and run them against one another," Ricky asked.

"I'll call you, Major."

If Randall Richmond was the Hacker, his DNA should be a sibling match to Kara's. If the skin they pulled from Kay Dawson's teeth didn't match Kara's, DNA they were right back to zero. She jumped when her phone rang.

"Strong."

"Major, I am sorry, but the DNA isn't even close," Lane informed her.

Ricky blew out the breath she was holding. "Thanks for double checking," she said.

That lets Randall off the hook, Ricky thought as she hung up the phone.

She was glad she wouldn't have to tell Christine her brother was the Hacker but disappointed that she had come up empty handed.

She called back to Detective Wright's office and told them to cancel her message. She had found the answer to her question.

~~~

Troy Hunter smiled when an email from Rachel Winn dinged into his inbox. Another photo of

Princess was attached. Rachel had gone from stone cold to very warm with the introduction of Charlie. They had been corresponding daily for the past six weeks. He read the email.

Charlie and Princess would look so cute together. Princess is two-years-old this month. Is Charlie neutered?

Troy thought about getting a little risqué. He didn't want to scare Rachel away but wanted to remind her he was very interested in her. He debated, then finally wrote: *No, he is in perfectly good working condition. So am I.* He attached the photo of Charlie lying between his legs. He had padded himself to make certain she didn't miss the size of his package.

Oh my, was her only comment.

Would you like to arrange a play date for Charlie and Princess? Troy typed. *Charlie has impeccable manners, so do I.*

Let me think about it, Rachel replied.

Ricky was certain Troy Hunter was still in Austin. She hoped she could string him along as Rachel Winn then get him to make a mistake. She had no clue who he was.

~~~

January was a blur. Christine was keeping a grueling campaign schedule, holding rallies all over the state. Her security team was still with her everywhere she went. Ricky had insisted that they guard her until Peyton had everyone securely behind bars.

Secretly, Ricky was also protecting the senator from the Hacker. She knew he was still at large and was communicating with him as Rachel Winn. Somehow, she had to draw him out into the open.

Most of the time Ricky accompanied the senator to provide extra security. Honestly, it was also to sleep with her at night. Christine felt safer with the ranger by her side.

Today was Friday. During the last two days, Christine had given speeches in Waco, Fort Worth, and Arlington. She was scheduled to speak at Southern Methodist University tomorrow. She would return home Saturday night. Ricky had slept without her the last two nights. She didn't want to wait another day to see the senator.

Ricky checked her watch. It was four o'clock. Driving the seventy-five-mile an hour Texas speed limit, she could be in Arlington by eight p.m. Just in time to catch the end of Christine's speech at the University of Texas at Arlington and take the beautiful brunette to dinner.

Friday traffic from Austin to Fort Worth was always heavy with A&M and UT students driving home for the weekend. Ricky kept to her schedule by pushing her speed to eighty.

She parked her car at the rear of the auditorium and placed her Official Texas Ranger permit onto her dash, so it was visible.

She slipped into the standing-room-only auditorium and smiled as she watched the senator field questions from the audience. An attractive young woman made her way to the microphone to ask the senator a question.

"Hello, Senator Richmond," the young woman began. "My name is Holly Brandt, and I appreciate you taking the time to visit with us today."

"Thank you, Holly," Christine smiled her sweetest smile. "I appreciate you attending my rally. How can I help you?"

"You are my hero. What you did in the RICO drug case took a lot of nerve. What you did during your border tour is spellbinding. I believe in you and almost everything you stand for, but I want to know why you worked so hard to defeat the passage of the same-sex marriage bill?" Holly gazed steadily at Christine waiting for her answer.

"At the time, I felt I was right," Christine said clearly.

Holly leaned down to the microphone and said, "Don't you think it is wrong for the government to tell people whom they can and cannot love?"

"Holly, I think you are aware of my stance on same-sex marriage. I won't debate it with you." Christine turned her smile on the entire audience and thanked them for coming then disappeared behind the curtain at the back of the dais.

Her security team formed a wall around her and quickly moved her from the podium to the hallway leading to the rear of the auditorium. As the team passed her, Ricky slipped into the security ranks protecting Christine.

"Thank you," Christine smiled hesitantly. "I am glad you are here." She fought the desire to grasp the ranger's hand.

The team rushed Christine into Ricky's car, and the ranger sped away while the guards gathered around the black limo that had driven the senator to the rally.

They rode in silence until Christine released the death grip she had on Ricky's hand. "You heard the last exchange I had with that student?"

"Yes," Ricky squeezed her hand.

"I feel like such a hypocrite," Christine exhaled slowly.

"Changing a lifetime philosophy isn't easy," Ricky smiled. "Unless you feel it is wrong enough you can't live with it. Maybe you can't change it."

Christine buried her face in her hands. "I don't...the only thing I am certain of is that I want to be with you. Do I think it is right? I don't know.

"I do know I can't live my life hiding who I am and hiding you."

Ricky glanced at the senator's face lit by the blue hues of her dash light. She looked tired and distraught. The ranger pulled the brunette's hand onto her lap. "We don't need to have this conversation now. You are exhausted and have another rally in Dallas tomorrow."

"Let me take you to dinner then give you one of my famous foot rubs. I plan to drive you back to Austin tomorrow."

Christine gave her a thankful smile. "I love you more than you can ever imagine, Ricky Strong."

~~~

"Major, there is a tall, handsome cowboy asking to see you," Becky announced through the intercom. "He says his name is Tex Strong."

377

Fear drenched Ricky as she raced to open the door. Tex had never visited her office. *God, let Martina be okay,* she thought.

"Tex, is everything okay?"

"Yes," Tex nodded. "I just need to talk with you in private."

Ricky motioned toward a chair as she closed her door. Taking a seat behind her desk, she watched her cousin. "Is everything okay with you and Martina?"

"It...Ricky, she is wonderful," Tex said. "She is every man's dream. I...I just worry about her.

"She never leaves the ranch. She can't travel with Brady and me for fear of being seen and recognized. She was so thrilled that you took her to see *Mama Mia.*

"She never complains, but I know she misses going out. I would love to take her to a nice restaurant for dinner. I want to take her dancing. She loves to dance. She loves the theater. I want to share those things with her. It seems like she is only living half a life. Can't you do something?"

Ricky was quiet for a long time. She had racked her brain for a way to free Martina from the ever-threatening menace of one of New York's most powerful crime families.

"You know about her brother," Ricky frowned. "He is three steps to the left of crazy. He would kill her in a heartbeat and not bat an eye.

"Martina's testimony put away half the family. Unfortunately, the prosecutor made too many technical errors, and Carlito walked. I am certain it was intentional. Now Carlito has a contract out on Martina."

"Ricky, you must do something," Tex begged. He bowed his head then looked up at the ranger. "We are expecting our second child in seven months." He couldn't hide the smile that spread across his face. "She is extremely happy. We both are.

"Ricky, she deserves more from life than being a shadow citizen."

A huge grin broke across the ranger's face. "Congratulations, Tex. Do you know if it is a boy or a girl?"

"Martina likes to be surprised," Tex grinned. "You know me, if it makes her happy, I am happy."

"I think about Martina's situation all the time," Ricky frowned. "In the meantime, keep her out of the spotlight. Dave Adams is in Austin. He is the FBI agent that I am certain is working for the mob. He has been assigned to guard Christine. That is why I keep my men with her all the time.

"I am certain Adams will kill both the senator and Martina if he has the chance."

Tex shook his head. "I am sorry I bothered you with this. You have your own problems. I... I just love Martina more than I can say."

"Believe me, Bro, I understand."

After Tex had left her office, Ricky sent a text message to Christine who was in Amarillo. *Two nights is too long.*

Can you fly here tonight? Christine responded.

Ricky had already checked the flight schedule from Austin to Amarillo. *I can be at your hotel by midnight*; she added a smiling emoticon to her text.

I miss you so much. Can't wait to see you. Christine added a smiling emoticon of a cute, smiling devil with horns holding up a halo.

Ricky suppressed the rush of heat that engulfed her body. *Even hundreds of miles away the woman drives me crazy*; she smiled to herself.

Still trying to fit the pieces of the puzzle together, to guarantee Martina's safety, she called the only person she trusted in the FBI. Then she called Peyton Myers and arranged to have dinner with her.

~~~

"How did I get so lucky?" Peyton teased as she slid into the circular booth and scooted close to Ricky. "I am surprised you aren't on the road with Christine."

"She's in Amarillo," the ranger shrugged.

"So, while the cat is away," Peyton grinned, "does the mouse want to play?"

Ricky laughed. "You know me better than that."

Peyton nodded

"I need your help," the ranger informed her.

"What can I do?" Peyton asked.

"Help me bring down a New York crime family," Ricky shrugged.

"Oh, is that all?" Peyton laughed. "I was afraid you would ask me to do something difficult."

Ricky chuckled.

"You do know I have no authority in New York," Peyton frowned. "I can't prosecute crimes there."

"What if I bring the criminals to you?" Ricky said slowly. "What if they are caught committing crimes in Texas?"

"My backyard, my bailiwick," Peyton grinned. "Tell me what you have in mind?"

For the next three hours, they discussed Martina and the New York Crime syndicate that was trying to find and kill the beautiful Italian woman.

"How do you know her?" Peyton asked.

"I escorted a prisoner extradited from Texas to New York," Ricky explained. "Once I turned him over to the New York authorities I had the opportunity to ride along on a takedown of the Zamboni crime syndicate.

"Martina was the state's major witness. She had dates, transactions, names of killers and those killed. She even had videos of some of the murders and drug deals. With her help, the U.S. Attorney in New York took down most of the family. Just before Carlito Zamboni's trial, the attorney was gunned down on the street. The attorney that tried the case made so many technical errors; the court threw out the case. I believe it was intentional.

"Carlito is Martina's brother. He rebuilt the syndicate and put a contract out on Martina. Martina went into witness protection and has been in hiding for the last seven years. She can't go out in public for fear of being seen or photographed. With today's social media someone would post her on Facebook. She is incredibly beautiful. She is tired of being a shadow citizen."

"Are you sleeping with her?" Peyton frowned.

"What? No," Ricky barked. "I have no romantic interest in her. I simply think she deserves better than the life she is living. Besides, she is pregnant. I promise you; I had nothing to do with that."

Peyton laughed, "But she is important to you. Why?"

"I think the FBI agent responsible for her safety works for the mob. The mobsters located her in witness protection and were moving in on her. I helped her escape. I am the only one who knows where she is."

"Obviously, one other person knows," Peyton teased. "She *is* pregnant."

Ricky was silent for a long time, debating on whether to tell Peyton the entire truth. "She is married to my cousin," Ricky finally said.

Peyton nodded, "Tell me your plan."

~~~

Christine Richmond paced the floor. She had hoped Ricky would be in her hotel room when she arrived, but she hadn't heard from the blonde.

The senator opened the complimentary bottle of wine the hotel had provided. She sipped the red liquid. *Not bad*, she thought. She placed the second glass beside her own and poured a glass for Ricky. Red wine was always a little better after it breathed.

She considered walking onto the balcony, but late February was cold in Amarillo. She settled on the sofa and turned on the TV.

Her Republican opponent, Roy Bennett, was on a local talk show. Publicly they shared many of the same views, but she knew he was pro-big labor and against the wall between Mexico and the United States.

He held forth on abortion and gays in general. He was so fanatically homophobic; Christine suspected he was gay.

Christine replayed the ongoing argument that continually tormented her. Did she believe it was wrong to love Ricky as she did? The answer was a resounding, no.

Did she think it was wrong to hide her relationship with the ranger? Yes!

In her heart, she knew her life with Ricky Strong would destroy her political career. Was she willing to give up the governor's mansion and the White House for the blonde?

A soft knock on her door told her Ricky had arrived. The thrill that ran through her at the thought of opening the door and falling into the ranger's arms answered her last question.

~~~

"Wow," Ricky inhaled deeply, trying to slow the beating of her heart. Christine snuggled tighter into her arms and kissed her way down the blonde's throat to her taut breasts. "Let me catch my breath," Ricky begged.

Christine pulled the covers over their naked bodies. "I miss you so much when we are apart," she breathed softly into Ricky's ear. "I hate sleeping without you. Honestly, I *don't* sleep much without you. I can't stop thinking of how it feels to fall asleep in your arms."

"I know, honey," Ricky exhaled slowly. "My nights are sleepless without you."

"This will be my last tour," Christine said. "The primary is Tuesday. We have a televised debate Monday night."

"Then the general election in November," Ricky reminded her.

"I have to win the primary first," Christine laughed. "I could make a major faux pas during the debate."

"You will win by a landslide. Everyone on the UT campus is already wearing a t-shirt that says, *Love our Gov. Christine Richmond.*" Ricky gently rubbed her hands up and down the brunette's back.

"Have you caught your breath?" Christine nibbled at Ricky's lips.

"I have. Are you going to take it away again?"

"I am going to do my best," Christine giggled as she pulled herself on top of the ranger.

~~~

Chapter 27

Ricky had added another security team. Christine moved in a bubble of armed men. The ranger was taking no chances. Metal detectors were at every entrance to the campaign headquarters.

Ricky had personally supervised the sweep for explosive devices. It was time to let Christine's adoring fans into the massive room that had been set up to house the debate and the next day's election results party.

A stage was at one end of the room for the TV anchors who were moderating the debate. Scott Winslow was everywhere giving orders and making certain everything was set up properly for his candidates.

It was no secret Scott favored Christine, but he tried to appear neutral until one of the candidates was selected to represent the Republican party in the gubernatorial election.

Lady, Armand, and Randall Richmond sat in the front row.

Ricky stood backstage with a nervous Christine. She leaned over and whispered in the senator's ear. "I can't believe you wore those, *fuck me heels*," she grinned.

"I wore them just for you, darling," Christine smiled. "Remember that."

Scott introduced Christine. She glided onto the stage and took her place behind the podium. Ricky watched her from the wings. Security flanked the candidates on all sides. There was always someone close enough to Christine to die for her.

Ricky scanned the audience as the debate began. Christine bested Roy Bennett on every point discussed. More than once the audience had to be silenced after one of Christine's remarks.

"That concludes our questions for tonight," the announcer said, "but we will give each of our candidates the opportunity to give their closing remarks. You each have two minutes." He nodded to Christine's opponent. "You go first."

Bennett rambled about gays, welfare, unions, and education. Then it was Christine's turn.

"Thank all of you for coming tonight," Christine said. "I have always told you that I would never lie to you or stoop to trickery to win an election. I have always felt that it is important that you know who I am and what I truly stand for as your representative and as your governor.

"Therefore, I want you to know that I have fallen in love with a remarkable person."

Christine stopped as the crowd went wild, clapping and wolf whistling. "Thank you," she smiled.

"Before you go to the polls tomorrow it is important that you know that I have fallen in love with another woman."

A stunned silence fell over the hall, then Holly Brandt stood. "We love our Gov., Christine Richmond," she yelled. A titter went through the crowd as others stood, then more of the crowd got to their feet. Finally, the entire room was filled with people on their feet, yelling "We love our Gov."

Christine bowed her head for a long time then leaned into the microphone. "Thank you."

"Becky," Ricky nudged her assistant. "I think Lady Richmond has fainted. Please help Armand and Randall."

Christine walked off the stage as dignified as she had walked on to it. Ricky took her elbow and steered her to a private room and locked the door.

"You know you probably just destroyed your career?" Ricky frowned. "You didn't have to do that for me."

"I didn't do it for you," Christine's eyes glistened with tears. "I did it for me. I chose you, Ricky Strong. I chose you over politics, over my family, over all others."

Ricky wrapped the brunette in her arms. "I promise I will spend my life making you glad you did," she murmured as their lips met. As Christine pulled the very essence of the ranger into her soul, she knew this was the feeling she wanted to have for the rest of her life.

Loud knocking pulled them from their kiss. Christine wiped her lipstick from the ranger's lips then nodded for her to open the door.

"What the hell was that?" Scott Winslow stormed into the room.

"The truth," Christine said adamantly.

"You could have waited until after the gubernatorial election to drop that little bomb." Winslow's face was so red Ricky thought the man would explode.

"I owe it to my constituents to give them the opportunity to vote for the person they feel most represents their values.

"I don't want people to elect me then find out I duped them. They get enough of that on the national level."

"You can kiss the governor's mansion goodbye," Scott howled. "Damn, Roy Bennett is such a flawed candidate. The guy is downright stupid. The Democrats will walk away with this election. We will have a Democratic governor for the first time in twenty years, thanks to you.

"Who could you possibly love so much you would destroy the most promising political career to materialize in thirty years?

"Why didn't you confide in me?" Scott continued. "I could help you cover it up. I could…"

"I didn't need your help to cover it up," Christine glared. "I have been covering it up for over a year. I don't want to cover it up. I am tired of lying and hiding. I am proud of the woman I love."

Scott swung his furious gaze to Ricky. "You," he growled. "This is all your fault. You were supposed to protect her. Who did you let get that close to her?"

Ricky pulled her most innocent face and shrugged.

Randall charged into the room. "Mother and Father left," he declared as he hugged Christine. "Gosh, Sis, you could have shared that with us in private before declaring it to the world. We will stand by you."

"Will you?" Christine grimaced. "Where are Mother and Father? They won't stand by me," she almost whispered. "They will try to talk me out of it."

"I better go see about them," Randall frowned as he hugged Christine's shoulders. "We will talk later." The look he cast at Ricky was unreadable.

Ricky caught Christine's elbow. "We need to get you out of here for security's sake."

The security team circled them as they moved from the room to the back door where their cars were parked. Ricky opened the door and helped Christine get settled. "We're good for tonight, fellows," she grimaced. "Get some sleep. Tomorrow will be a long day."

Becky, Crate, and Barrel hugged the ranger. "Call us if you need anything," Becky said. Crate and Barrel nodded.

~~~

They drove in silence until the Austin city limits sign disappeared from Ricky's rearview mirror.

"Are you okay?" Ricky asked as she placed her hand on top of Christine's.

"I am better than I have been in a very long time," Christine softly said.

Tex and Martina greeted them as Ricky pulled her car to a stop behind the house.

"Come inside," Ricky smiled. "It is colder than blue blazes out here."

Martina pulled Christine into a solid hug. "Ricky is lucky to have you," she smiled.

Tex pulled all three women into a Texas size hug. "I am the lucky one," he grinned. "Three gorgeous, amazing women in my life."

"Did you know she was going to make her announcement?" Martina asked Ricky as she poured fresh coffee into the cups Ricky had placed on the kitchen counter.

"No," Ricky grinned. "I was so busy looking at her shoes; I thought I misunderstood her at first."

The look Christine gave Ricky made Martina glance at the senator's shoes. "Oh, those heels," she smiled knowingly.

Tex looked at the heels then grinned at Ricky who simply shrugged.

"I didn't discuss it with anyone," Christine volunteered. "I just wanted to stop hiding."

"What about you?" Tex asked Ricky. "Will this cause problems for you at work?"

"I intentionally didn't out Ricky," Christine frowned. "It is not my place. I didn't know how it would affect her and her job."

"Everyone I work closely with knows I am crazy about you," Ricky smiled. "I don't know about my superiors."

"Let's catch the late-night news and see what people are saying," Martina suggested.

"Where is Brady?" Christine asked.

"Sleepover with a little boy from church," Martina grinned. "His first. I think I am the only one disturbed that my baby wants to spend the night away from home."

Ricky pushed the buttons on the remote and went to Fox News. She wanted to know if Christine's announcement had been picked up by the major news media.

"Our viewers will remember Republican Texas State Senator Christine Richmond," the TV commentator said. A beautiful photo of Christine attending the president's inauguration filled the screen. "During her time in the Senate, Senator Richmond single-handedly defeated two major bills in the Texas Senate, the abortion bill, and the same-sex marriage bill.

"Listen to what Senator Richmond had to say at tonight's debate." The station ran Christine's announcement in its entirety. Ricky switched to other news stations who were running the same clip.

"I believe you have gone viral," Ricky grimaced.

Martina stood as Ricky turned off the TV. "We will leave you two," she smiled as she caught Tex's hand. "We need to take advantage of having the house to ourselves tonight."

Ricky locked the door behind them then slowly wrapped her arms around Christine. "We need to hold on tightly to one another," she smiled. "I think we are in for one hell of a ride."

~~~

"Director Crockett wants to see you in his office at nine," Becky greeted Ricky as she walked through the door. "Where is Senator Richmond?"

"In her office," Ricky shrugged.

"That was quite an announcement she made last night," Becky smiled.

"Yeah," Ricky nodded as she closed her office door.

In all her years as a ranger, Ricky had only been called into Director Crockett's office three times. All three times it was to congratulate her for some honor she had been awarded. Somehow, she had a feeling this was not going to be one of those times.

She looked around her office. She wondered what she would do if she weren't a Texas Ranger. She wondered who would catch the Hacker.

She closed her eyes, and Christine's smiling face filled her mind. Suddenly she realized she didn't care what she did just as long as she was with Christine Richmond.

Her phone dinged the arrival of a message. *Going to campaign headquarters at five to await results. Want to join me? We may be the only ones there.*

May I take you to a late lunch around two, Ricky texted back.

I would love that.

I'll pick you up at two. Love you.

Love you, too.

Ricky realized it was the first time either of them had committed words of endearment to their cell phone messages.

~~~

Ricky fidgeted in her chair as she waited to see Director David Crockett. She had arrived early. She fought the urge to play a game on her cellphone.

"Major," the receptionist said, "Director Crockett will see you now."

Ricky opened the door and stepped into the lion's den. Director Crockett was behind his desk, leaning back in his chair. He studied her as she entered and sat down across from him.

Both sat in silence for a long time.

"You wanted to see me, sir?" Ricky broke the silence.

"Yes," Crockett nodded. "Did you see the announcement Senator Richmond made last night?"

"Yes, sir, I was there for the debate."

"Humph," he snorted. "What did you think?"

"I think Christine Richmond is the bravest woman…no, individual I have ever met."

"Are you intimately involved with Senator Richmond?" Crockett's gaze was stoic and unwavering.

"Yes, sir," Ricky raised her chin slightly. "I am."

Crockett shook his head and turned his chair around, so his back was to Ricky. He sat that way for several minutes then swiveled his chair around to face the ranger.

"I hope you have enough influence with Senator Richmond to make her change the ridiculous *Don't Ask Don't Tell* malarkey we are currently observing. Don't be foolish enough to announce to the world your relationship with Senator Richmond. My hands are tied under the current law. I would have no choice but to relieve you of your badge. Just between you and me, Major, I don't give a hoot about with whom you sleep.

"What I do care about is the Hacker. I want him captured. Do you understand me?"

"Yes, sir," Ricky saluted him. She was proud to serve under a man like David Crockett.

"Go help her win this damn election," Crockett stood and extended his hand. "Good luck."

~~~

Christine laughed as Ricky related her visit to Director Crockett. "I thought he was calling me in to fire me," she finished.

Ricky moved, so their thighs were touching. "Have you heard from your parents today?" she asked softly.

"No," Christine bowed her head. "I am not surprised by Mother, but I thought Daddy would stand by me."

"You know you don't have to go to the election watch," Ricky suggested. "Although, I predict the voters might surprise you."

"What do you mean?" Christine tilted her head in that way that made Ricky want to hold the brunette in her arms.

"I mean, the only thing that has changed is your preference for women...

"A particular woman," Christine interjected.

"Yes, and thank heaven for that. But that is the only change. You are still one bad-ass senator that knows how to get results for her constituents. You are still all the right things: conservative, support the constitution, freedom of speech, right to carry, anti-abortion except in cases of incest or rape. You are a strong supporter of the military, law enforcement, building the wall, immigration reform. You are on the right side of everything important.

"I predict the voters will rally behind you."

Christine smiled a pitiful smile. "You are very sweet, darling." She leaned in and kissed Ricky lightly.

"I will go to the election watch party. I refuse to hide as if I am ashamed because I am not."

Ricky nodded in agreement.

~~

Chapter 28

"Senator Richmond," Holly Brandt ran to greet Christine. "I have been saving a table right in front of the big-screen TV for you. Your family is already here."

"Thank you, Holly," Christine smiled. "I love your shirt. It is very flattering."

"We really could leave off your name," Holly beamed. "Everyone knows our governor will be you."

I wish I had just half her confidence, Christine thought.

Armand Richmond stood and walked to meet his daughter. He engulfed her in a strong hug. "I am so proud of you, Chris," he smiled.

"For announcing to the world that I am gay?" Christine frowned.

"For having the strength of your convictions," Armand nodded. "For being woman enough, to tell the truth. You know how I hate lies."

"I do, too, Daddy," she smiled. "Is mother speaking to me?"

"She is miffed that she now has to stop promising her friends their sons can date her daughter," he laughed. "Watch out she will be trying to set you up with their daughters."

"Not a chance," Christine chuckled. "I am a one woman, woman." Her eyes swept the hall, and she smiled when she located Major Strong.

"You have chosen wisely," Armand followed her gaze. "She is a remarkable young woman."

Ricky caught the senator watching her and walked to her table. "Fox News is starting the countdown," she smiled. "The first precincts are in."

Figures flashed on the screen showing her Republican opponent, Roy Bennett ahead by a thousand votes in his home county. Christine looked down at her hands. Ricky moved her chair closer to the senator and whispered in her ear.

"You have on those shoes, again," she smiled. "I cannot be held responsible for my actions later tonight."

"Regardless of the outcome," Christine murmured, "I do expect a reaction to my heels, from you."

"Count on it, Senator," Ricky whispered.

"Votes that were cast by early Texas voters have been counted," the newswoman announced. "Senator Christine Richmond is leading by a large majority in the early voting. Of course, it is the voters who voted after her announcement that will determine the next governor of Texas."

The news team went on to replay Christine's announcement made the preceding night. The campaign headquarters began to fill up as Christine's supporters entered the room. Soon it was standing room only.

Results came in for Dallas and Harris counties. Roy Bennett jumped ahead. Christine bowed her head.

She wanted to leave, run somewhere and hide with Ricky."

Fox News called Hill and Travis counties for Bennett.

Tarrant County reported their count and Christine jumped in votes, but Bennett still led.

Bennett was on TV bragging that Christine had handed him the governor's job. "Shouldn't be screwing around," he said in his whiny, uneducated voice.

Denton, Montgomery, Williamson and Galveston rolled in. Christine surged into the lead. Earth-shaking yells and applause went up from those watching in the campaign headquarters.

At midnight Roy Bennett called Christine to congratulate her on a landslide victory. She had won by a wider margin than any candidate in a primary.

"You did it, honey," Ricky hugged the brunette. "You won the primary."

The crowd began chanting "Governor Richmond! Governor Richmond!"

Christine walked to the microphone and smiled as she waited for her enthusiastic fans to quiet.

"I truly do not know what to say," Christine said humbly. "I came here tonight to give my *You did a great job, but I lost* speech. I cannot tell you how proud I am that I can say 'You did a great job and we won!'"

The applause and roar shook the hall.

"Thank you," she grinned.

~~~

All the lame-stream media could talk about was the fact that Republican Golden Girl, Senator Christine

Richmond was gay. There was continuous speculation about who the other woman was. They failed to point out that Christine had won the primary by a landslide. National news teams flocked to Austin to do interviews with anyone who could name the senator's significant other.

Christine steadfastly refused to do TV interviews with anyone but Paige Daily.

The fake news stations finally settled on Peyton Myers as Christine's partner.

Peyton Myers was beautiful, they reasoned. *Didn't Senator Richmond work closely with the U.S. Attorney to bring the drug lords to justice? Didn't Christine and Peyton appear together on newscasts after Peyton won the RICO case?*

Peyton accepted an interview with the worst news station in the U.S. The interviewer was famous for making up fake news. Supposedly the station wanted to discuss her success with the RICO case. Peyton wasn't naive enough to believe that.

"They will crucify you," Christine warned her.

"I don't think so, Senator," Peyton smiled as she pulled her car fob from her purse. "I am ready for this."

～～

The unsavory news team quickly reviewed their attack on Peyton. They would congratulate her on a job well done and say that she had single-handedly broken the backbone of the Mexican drug cartel operating in the U.S. After putting her at ease, they would slam her with questions about Senator Christine Richmond.

Snuggled up on the sofa in Christine's home, Ricky and the senator watched the interview.

The news personality smiled and preened as she led Peyton through the interview. They discussed the RICO case then the woman said, "U.S. Attorney Peyton Myers are you the woman Senator Christine Richmond is involved with?"

"I wish," Peyton laughed. "Christine is gorgeous, brilliant and extraordinarily honest. We need more people like her in politics. Could use them in the news media, too."

"But she is gay," the announcer shrieked.

"So is your lead anchorman," Peyton sweetly smiled. "I thought you people loved gays. Or do you just love left-wing zealot, liberal progressives, that are gay and stupid enough to swallow the bull you espouse?

"Senator Richmond has always represented the people of Texas to the best of her ability. She is the one that broke the RICO case. Without her, we could not have put so many criminals behind bars. She is spearheading the building of the wall to secure the boundaries of the United States.

"She teaches a course in politics at the University. Students stand in line to register for the course. She is tireless, dedicated and trustworthy.

"Sadly, I am not her significant other, just as you are not a legitimate news station."

Peyton unclipped the microphone from her collar, stood and made a regal exit as the interviewer was begging to cut to a commercial.

~~~

A whistle on Ricky's phone told her Troy Hunter had just sent an email to her pseudo, Rachel Winn.

Ricky opened her laptop and logged onto her email.

Good day, lovely lady, Troy wrote. *I wanted to let you know I may be away from my computer for a few days.*

I will miss you, Ricky posted. *Are you going out of town?*

Yes. I must go to Colorado. I will email you when I return. Maybe we can get together and let Charlie meet Princess, and you meet me.

How long will you be gone? I miss you already, Ricky wrote desperately trying to find some inkling to his whereabouts.

My job will keep me in Colorado for three weeks.

You can still email me, Ricky wrote trying to sound desperate. *I look forward to our daily chats.*

I will try. I am not certain I will have Wi-Fi, Troy responded. *I will be extremely busy. Bye for now.*

Bye, Ricky closed the conversation.

Ricky rubbed her eyes. She knew Troy Hunter was up to something. She just wasn't certain what it was.

A Facebook notice dinged into her email. It was a posting from Troy Hunter. A beautiful blonde had responded to a cute video he had posted of Charlie playing with a cat.

I have a little dog that looks just like Charlie, the blonde said.

Post a photo so that I can see him, Troy posted.

The blonde posted a photo of a dog that could be the identical image of Charlie.

Wow! Troy answered. *They could be litter mates. Where did you get yours?*

PetSmart in Springfield, CO. The blonde posted.

Got mine in Trinidad, Troy responded.

Do you like to fish? Troy typed.

Very much, the girl typed.

I love fishing the Mundell Reservoir, Troy posted.

Do you have a boat? The blonde asked.

I do, Troy responded. *A real nice one.*

Another woman posted on their conversation.

Let's take this private, the blonde suggested. She and Troy disappeared from Facebook

Ricky scanned earlier dates on Facebook and discovered the pair had been Facebook friends for about two months. *Blondes aren't his type*, Ricky thought. *I wonder what has changed.*

Ricky pulled the blonde's photo from Facebook and sent it to Daisy. Then quickly walked to the forensic lab.

"Daisy, I just sent you a photo of a pretty blonde. I think she is in Springfield, Colorado. See if we can get an ID on her."

Daisy initiated the facial recognition software, and the two waited.

"Have you talked to Crate and Barrel lately?" Daisy asked.

"Not really," Ricky exhaled. "We have been busy. I just seem to pass them in the night."

"Crate said it was a full-time job keeping up with Senator Richmond," Daisy said.

"I have to do something nice for them when this nightmare is over," Ricky thought out loud.

The computer beeped, and the driver's license of a pretty, blonde woman appeared on the screen. It was a match to the photo Ricky had pulled from Facebook. The woman's name was Lillian Dawes.

"She looks like you," Daisy commented as they scrutinized the photo of Lillian Dawes.

Ricky had a sinking feeling the Hacker was headed to Colorado. She returned to her office and called the Springfield, CO police department.

She passed all the information she had to one of the city's four detectives. Springfield was a city with a population of about fourteen thousand.

Detective Pete Jordon had been thrilled to get the case. The Hacker's infamy had spread, and Jordon could see a promotion to a bigger department if he could apprehend the serial killer.

"I am sending you the woman's name and address along with a photo of her and her driver's license," Ricky said.

"I will put out the word to be on the lookout for any strange men entering our town," he informed Ricky. "This isn't a very large town, Major—only fourteen thousand folks here. We should be able to catch him."

"Do you want me to come up there?" Ricky volunteered.

"No, ma'am, that won't be necessary," Jordon assured her. "I think I can handle this."

"Please, immediately warn Ms. Dawes of the danger she is in," Ricky encouraged Jordon.

Ricky glanced at her wall clock as she tried to call Lillian Dawes. She received no answer and no answering machine. She made shorthand notes in her

Hacker file: *Cld Dawes @5:30 p.m.* She documented her conversation with Detective Pete Jordon then slid the file to the corner of her desk.

She sat silently trying to ascertain the source of the scraping and giggling sounds at her office door. She smiled as the door opened and Christine put her head into the office.

"Come in," Ricky jumped to her feet, anxious to see the senator.

Christine flung open the door, and half a dozen people flowed into Ricky's office. Christine, Crate, Barrel, Daisy, Becky and Peyton filled her office. Christine's security team filled the doorway.

"What is going on?" Ricky asked cautiously.

"We are going to party," Peyton laughed as she pulled the ranger into the crowd.

"What are we celebrating?" Ricky grinned. *God, I want to kiss you,* she thought as she smiled shyly at Christine.

Christine reached for Ricky's hand and pulled her beside her. "Peyton has just won the last of the RICO cases," the senator smiled. "And I can drop the Dream Team that follows me everywhere. No offense, fellows."

"None taken, Senator," the security team chorused.

"That does call for a celebration," Ricky laughed. "Where are we going?"

"My celebration," Peyton grinned. "I get to choose. I want to go to dinner and a movie."

"I'm in," Ricky smiled as she thought about sitting next to Christine in a dark movie theater.

"We want Christine's security team to join us," Peyton wiggled her eyebrows and Daisy giggled. "They are the ones that kept our star witness safe."

Dinner was steaks, drinks and a lot of happy chatter. It had been a long time since Ricky and those around her had felt safe enough to relax and have a good time.

Christine insisted on picking up the check. "It is the least I can do to repay all of you for protecting my life."

"Movie time," Peyton raised her voice above the merry makers.

"I suppose you choose the movie, too?" Ricky grinned. "What kind of movie is it? Please, no sappy, sad shows."

"A chick flick with a happy ending," Peyton laughed.

"All chick flicks have a happy ending," Ricky rolled her eyes.

"Obviously, you never watched *Out of Africa*, darling," Christine smiled sensuously.

To Ricky's surprise, three limousines were lined up at the curb waiting for them as they exited the restaurant.

"Okay, who got drunk enough to order three limos," the ranger laughed as the limo drivers opened the doors and her party piled into the vehicles.

The limos pulled in front of the Alamo Drafthouse Cinema on East Sixth Street. A red carpet covered the path from the limos to the theater entrance. Crowds gathered on both sides of the barricades and cheered as the partyers exited the limos.

"Wow," Ricky laughed as Christine clung to her arm. "Someone told them you were coming, U.S. Attorney Peyton Myers."

Peyton pointed to the marquee. Ricky stared in shocked silence as she read the name of the movie they were going to see. She whirled around to face Crate and Barrel.

"You...you...did this? This is your movie!" She fought back the tears as she hugged the two men she trusted with her life.

Too Strong to Die spread across the marquee in the largest letters possible.

"Everyone loved our book," Crate grinned. "We were on the best seller's list for months. Of course, you have no time to read for fun, so you weren't even aware of it."

"The book was such a success," Barrel chimed in, "a movie producer wanted to make a movie of it."

"Who plays Christine," Ricky laughed, "and me?"

"Lana Parrilla is the senator and that new actress...what's her name," Crate wrinkled his forehead in thought. "You know Rebecca Romijn. She played in *King and Maxwell* and *The Librarians*. Two pretty powerful actresses, boss."

"Kate Upton auditioned for the part, but they cut her at the last minute," Barrel added. "They thought she was too busty to play you."

"You certainly know how to make a girl feel desirable," Ricky teased.

Everyone laughed as Barrel blushed a deep red when he realized what he had said to the ranger.

"Today is the release day for the movie," Becky said. "This is the official premier. Director Crockett arranged for the stars to attend. He is hosting them. The movie is showing in all the Alamo Drafthouse Cinemas and all the AMC theaters in the U.S."

"I can't wait to see the reviews and attendance numbers tomorrow," Daisy added.

Christine and Ricky were content to stay in the background as Crate and Barrel accepted the accolades for their book and movie. Romijn and Parrilla graciously signed autographs on the covers of *Too Strong to Die*.

Martina and Tex met the group at the theater and sat with them.

As the party left the theater, Paige Daily stopped them on the red carpet. Her cameraman videoed a quick interview with Crate and Barrel. Paige grabbed Martina's arm and pulled her in front of the camera. "As you can see, Austin's most beautiful women have turned out for this premier."

Ricky was slow to react. Paige spoke with Martina for over a minute on national TV before the ranger stepped in front of the beautiful Italian woman.

"This interview is over," Ricky glared at Paige as she pulled Martina away from the cameras. Everything had gone as planned.

~~~

"That was the most exciting movie I have seen in a long time," Christine said as Tex drove them home.

"I believe the boys embellished the fight scenes," Ricky laughed as she slipped her arm around Christine's shoulders and pulled her closer. "It was heart-stopping when you jumped from that truck after the cartel shot me."

"I can't believe you two lived through that experience," Martina said. "I heard your report, but to see it on the big screen in living color. I wanted to cry. I am so proud of you both."

"Aww shucks…" a soft kiss stopped the ranger's silly impersonation of a bashful hillbilly.

"Don't downplay it, darling," Christine whispered. "You were amazing."

"You are braver than anyone I have ever met," Ricky murmured against her lips.

"Uh, my back seat," Tex cleared his throat, "no making out in it."

Everyone laughed, and Christine settled against the ranger's shoulder.

Ricky's phone rang. "It's Peyton," she whispered as she answered. She listened in silence as Peyton talked.

"You are certain," Ricky asked. "Okay, you know what to do."

"Is that what I think it is?" Martina frowned.

"Yes, your family is officially in Austin," Ricky nodded. "Carlito is with them."

"It didn't take them long," Tex squeezed Martina's hand that was resting on his leg.

~~~

Chapter 29

Martina put on coffee as Ricky placed cups on the counter. Everyone took a seat on the barstools circling the island.

"Will she be safe?" Tex asked as he scooted closer to his wife.

"She will have the same security team we had on Christine," Ricky nodded. "They are the best.

"We will observe Carlito's henchmen for a few days and get an idea of how they operate. They will be looking for Martina."

"She stays here until you get everything nailed down tight," Tex scowled.

"Will someone tell me what is going on?" Christine demanded.

"She doesn't know about me?" Martina frowned. "I thought you would tell her."

"It is not my tale to tell," Ricky shrugged.

"Why don't you and Tex check on the horses?" Martina looked at Ricky. "I want to talk to Christine alone."

After her husband and the ranger left, Martina picked up her coffee cup and motioned to Christine to move to the sofa.

"Rēēcky never told you much about me because I am in the witness protection program. Carlito

Zamboni is my brother. He is cruel and crazy. He would rather kill something than eat.

"Nine years ago, I turned state's evidence against my family; my father, cousins, and Carlito. I went into the FBI witness protection program.

"I fell in love with the FBI agent who was my handler. He told me he loved me, too. I was a fool.

"My father, his lieutenants and several cousins were killed in an FBI raid on a warehouse filled with drugs. I had given the federal agents a tip that the drugs and the family would be at the location the night of the raid."

"You were responsible for the death of your father?" Christine's eyes opened wide as she contemplated such an action.

"My only regret was that Carlito got away," Martina snarled.

"I'm not sure I could..." Christine stopped mid-sentence as she witnessed the hatred in Martina's eyes.

"When I was fourteen," Martina said venomously, "my father traded my virginity to another crime boss for a favor. I have always been very beautiful and well endowed. My father found that there were many men willing to do his bidding in exchange for a night with his daughter. My father turned me into a whore."

Martina inhaled deeply then continued her story. "When my mother learned, what was happening, she threatened to go to the police and testify against my father. He beat her so badly she had brain damage and was confined to a wheelchair for the rest of her life. I think that in the end, my father killed her to get rid of her.

"I had no one to protect me, Carlito traded me to his friends for favors until I learned how to use a gun. I shot one of them in the groin. No one bothered me after that. I hated Carlito and my father with a passion."

"How did Ricky get involved with you?" Christine asked.

"She delivered a prisoner to the New York police department. FBI agent Dave Adams was coordinating the raid on the warehouse with the police. They needed all the law enforcement agents they could find and invited Rēēcky to ride along on the raid."

"I was in the car with Rēēcky and Dave," Martina continued. "After the smoke cleared my father and most of his men were dead. Carlito escaped.

"Dave put me in a safe house. I trusted him to keep me safe. I thought he loved me. Rēēcky volunteered to guard me until arrangements could be made to put me into the witness protection program.

"Only Dave and Rēēcky knew where I was hiding. Rēēcky stayed awake to guard me during the day and Dave guarded during the night.

On the third night of my stay in the safe house, Dave called Rēēcky and informed her he was tied up and couldn't get away. He asked her to stay with me until midnight.

"Rēēcky didn't like the feel of things. She moved her car to the street behind the house and hid it in the driveway of an empty home that was for sale. She lowered the folding stairs that led to the attic.

She was looking out the front window of the safe house when a black SUV parked across the street.

"She didn't even wait to see who got out of the vehicle. She grabbed me and pushed me up the drop-down stairs into the attic. She pulled the stairs up behind us, and we scooted as far into the recesses of the attic as we could.

"A loud crash told me the front door had been kicked in. Three men ran into the house and fanned out going through the rooms. They began to curse when they found we were gone. One of them said, 'Damn that Adams. That prick never gets anything right.' They left, leaving the front door standing open.

"Rēēcky insisted we wait until dark to leave the attic. She was afraid someone was watching the house. When it was black outside, she lowered the stairs and climbed down.

"We slipped out the back door of the house and climbed over a neighbor's fence to reach Rēēcky's car. She called someone who met us with a pickup bearing Arkansas license plates. Tex met us in Arkansas and brought us here. This has been my home ever since."

"Tex," Christine raised her eyebrows questioningly.

"He was wonderful," Martina smiled sweetly. "We danced around each other for two years. Finally, he told me how he felt about me and asked me to marry him.

"I told him he needed to know about my past and then make up his mind. I told him everything I just told you. He slowly pulled me into his arms and gave me the sweetest kiss I have ever known. Then he pulled a ring box from his pocket and proposed to me, again.

"My years with Tex have been the happiest of my life. I am alive today, thanks to Rēēcky."

"It seems we both have that in common," Christine mumbled.

The door opened a crack. "May we come in now?" Ricky smiled. "The horses are fine."

~~~

Chapter 30

Christine crisscrossed the state, holding rallies in any town big enough to have a polling site. Although Ricky was unhappy about her lack of security, the senator was delighted to leave behind the small army that had followed her everywhere during the past year.

Crate and Barrel still shadowed her when Ricky was unavailable. The ranger worked night and day to free up time to travel with the brunette.

Christine said goodnight to Crate and Barrel and opened the hotel door. The soft scent of vanilla, soap and light perfume told her Ricky was in her room. The soft slumbering noises emanating from her king-sized bed told her the blonde was asleep.

Silently Christine slipped into the bathroom and closed the door. It took all her self-control to keep from waking Ricky. She turned on the shower, waited for the water to get hot then stepped under the spray.

The hot water pelting her back felt good and washed away some of the day's fatigue. She shampooed her hair and stood for a long time enjoying the tingling sensation of the high-pressure spray on her body.

She towel-dried her long black hair and brushed her teeth. She debated searching in the dark for her pajamas then decided to sleep in the nude. She knew Ricky would prefer that state when she awoke next to her in the morning. She stealthily slipped into the bed and curled around the ranger. Her heart stopped beating as she realized, again, how much she loved Ricky Strong. Sleep came quickly. She always slept like a baby next to the blonde.

~~~

Soft lips on her shoulder pulled Ricky from a deep sleep. She pushed back into Christine's arms as she realized it was morning. "Why didn't you wake me when you came in last night?" she said sleepily.

"You were exhausted," Christine murmured against her skin. "I don't have to be *anyone* until this evening. We will have all day together."

"That means I can take my time worshipping you," Ricky said softly.

"You may take all day," Christine giggled as the ranger pulled her closer.

~~~

Ricky stood behind the curtain as Christine answered questions from the audience. A young woman stood and walked to the floor microphone. "Senator, I wanted to say thank you for all the things you have done for our state. I recently went to see *Too Strong to Die* with a group of friends. It was fascinating. You and Major Strong took on the Mexican drug cartel and won. I have to tell you; you are my new action hero."

Applause filled the auditorium. "Thank you," Christine said humbly.

An older woman made her way to the microphone. "The young lady is right," she said. "I forgot the movie was a true story. It was like watching *Die Hard* only with women." Laughter rippled through the ten thousand attendees. "I want to thank you for taking a stand and making things easier for women like me. We will be voting for you next week."

The audience began chanting, "We love our Gov!"

~~~

"That was an interesting rally," Ricky commented as she pulled her car away from the auditorium. A quick glance in the rearview mirror told her Crate and Barrel were close behind them.

"I don't understand the polls," Christine frowned. "I am drawing crowds like that everywhere I go, but I am down ten points in the polls."

"Maybe the polls are wrong," Ricky grinned. "It wouldn't be the first time."

"Let's talk about something besides the election," Christine said. Although she had put everything she had into the campaign, the brunette knew her numbers were falling.

"On a more positive note," Ricky smiled, "Crate and Barrel's movie has broken all box office records. I am having trouble doing my job because of the autograph seekers."

"I know," Christine agreed. "My mother is now a big fan of yours. As you saw tonight, everyone wants to hear about our heroic feats. Unfortunately, that doesn't translate into votes."

Ricky pulled the brunette's hand into her lap and laced their fingers together.

"Everyone wants to know who my partner is," Christine laughed. "How can they watch *Too Strong to Die* and not figure that out?"

"No kidding," Ricky laughed.

They drove in silence for a long time then Ricky broke the solemn mood that filled the car. "Maybe we should tell them it is me."

"What? No!" The anguish in Christine's voice was palatable. "There is no way I will let you sacrifice your career for mine."

"It is my fault you are in this situation," Ricky muttered.

"As I recall," Christine chuckled, "You didn't exactly force yourself on me."

"No, but I didn't stay away from you, either" Ricky admitted. "The truth is I couldn't."

"That is a good thing," Christine laughed. "But seriously, you know that Director Crockett would be forced to fire you. I will not let you do that, Ricky. I love you too much."

The blonde nodded and squeezed the hand of the woman that was the most important thing in her life.

"Are you making any progress with the Hacker case?" Christine changed the subject.

Ricky discussed the case, leaving out the fact that Troy Hunter was now stalking a blonde that looked like the ranger. She suspected the killer was trying to divert her attention from Christine.

The elections are next week. After they are over I will devote every waking hour to hunting down Troy Hunter, whoever he is, Ricky thought.

~~

Chapter 31

Randall Richmond reread the quarterly balance sheet then scanned the profit and loss statement for Richmond International. Armand and Christine had done an exceptional job of positioning the ship building company in the international market.

He looked at the two multi-billion dollar contracts lying on his desk. Both hinged on Christine winning the governorship of Texas. Randall had promised favors only a governor could grant in exchange for the contracts. He knew his father and sister did not do business that way, but what good was it to be governor, if one couldn't profit from it?

Over the past year, Randall had become active in several influential organizations in Austin. In his own way, he had campaigned for the senator. He knew that the fortunes of Richmond International were dependent on Senator Christine Richmond.

They would survive and continue to flourish if Christine lost, but things would be easier if she were the governor of Texas.

Armand had turned more, and more of the daily operations of the conglomerate over to him. Randall thrived on the responsibility and basked in the admiration he received from others. For the first time in his life, Randall felt pride in what he was doing. Everything was finally going right for him.

He wanted Christine to win so he could continue to run the family business. If she lost, he was certain she would take an active role in Richmond International.

~~~

Director David Crockett tossed the newspaper on his desk. A sneering photo of Raymond Tate covered the space above the fold. Crockett shuddered as he thought about reporting to the pompous ass. The man was no more governor material than a jackass.

Senator Richmond was by far the more qualified candidate. She was a hard worker, better educated, more knowledgeable and certainly more honest. Her accomplishments far exceeded Tate's.

Tate's entire campaign revolved around the fact that Christine had admitted she was gay and he was not. The man misquoted the *Bible* and spewed anti-gay rhetoric every time his mouth opened. He dismissed Christine's honesty by pointing out that she wouldn't name the woman with whom she was having an affair.

Tonight, was the final debate before the elections tomorrow. Crockett had a feeling things would change after tonight.

Crockett called his wife. "Are you ready to go, honey?"

~~~

When the narrator introduced her, Christine regally took her place behind the podium and smiled her gorgeous smile. Tate smirked as the moderator introduced him. He brushed away Christine's offer to shake hands as if she were contagious.

Christine remained calm and focused. She stuck to the issues. She answered the narrator's questions, receiving applause from the audience. The narrator cautioned the audience that they were to be quiet and not applaud the debaters.

No matter what question was directed to Raymond Tate he managed to twist it, so he referenced Christine's sexuality and refusal to name her "girlfriend."

Ricky watched from backstage. She wore a simple, fitted sapphire-blue dress that hit her mid-calf. A side slit ran up to her thigh. Her hair curled around her beautiful face and rested on her shoulders. Dangling earrings and three-inch heels completed a look any movie star would envy.

As the debate ended, each debater had the usual two-minute closing speech. Tate went first. He spent the entire time pointing out that Senator Christine Richmond was gay. He concluded by saying, "Not only is she gay, but she also is ashamed of her significant other and is not being honest with the voters."

Christine used her time to discuss solutions to some of the problems facing Texas. Midway thru her closing statement, the narrator interrupted her.

"Senator, if you want to be truly honest with the voters, why don't you tell us with whom you are involved?"

Christine glared at the narrator. "That question is completely inappropriate," Christine said furiously.

Ricky gracefully walked to the podium to stand beside the senator, "But completely understandable," the ranger said into the microphone. "I am proud to say that I am Senator Richmond's partner."

The auditorium went crazy. Ricky's first inclination was to rush Christine from the stage for her safety then she realized the audience was applauding and wolf whistling in support of them. Christine took the ranger's hand, and they walked off the stage. Tate stood gaping as saliva ran down the corners of his mouth.

Paige Daily replayed the last seven minutes of the debate on a continuous loop. She commented over and over about Raymond Tate drooling after the two gorgeous women.

~~~

Chapter 32

The ringing of a phone pulled Christine from a satiated sleep. She felt for the offending sound and answered it.

"Oh! Hello, Mother," she mumbled. She pulled the phone away from her ear to see what time it was. "Why are you calling me at seven in the morning?" She put the call on speakerphone.

"I think you have some explaining to do, Christine," Lady said accusingly.

"About what?" The brunette snuggled closer to the blonde who was now wrapped around her body.

"That...that...Texas Ranger," Lady sputtered. "Major Ricky Strong."

"Oh, give it up, Mother," Christine growled. "You and I both know you would give your eye teeth to be where I am right now." Lady was still sputtering when Christine disconnected the call.

"Now, that is a scary picture," Ricky laughed. "You need to spend the rest of the morning erasing that from my mind's eye."

Christine's laughter was light and free. "That is what I plan to do."

Scott Winslow called at noon. "Are you showing your face today?" he asked when Christine answered the phone. "Your supporters are already gathering at your campaign headquarters to watch the election results."

"Yes," Christine happily said as she put his call on speakerphone, "Ricky and I are leaving the house now."

"Must she accompany you everywhere you go?" Scott demanded.

"Yes, she must," Christine grinned wickedly and winked at Ricky. "She takes care of all my needs."

Ricky laughed out loud as Winslow choked.

~~~

"Senator," Holly Brandt met Christine at the door, "you must see this."

Christine and Ricky followed Holly to the huge television suspended behind the podium at one end of the room. Armand, Lady, and Randall were sitting with Scott Winslow at the table closest to the TV. Christine and Ricky joined them.

"They are doing exit polling," Holly informed them. "So far you are leading in traditionally Democratic counties. Judging from exit polls, you will win Travis and Dallas counties. It has been years since a Republican has carried those counties."

"Who is conducting the exit polls?" Christine frowned.

"An independent group called Democracy in Action," Holly answered. They aren't affiliated with either the Democrats or the Republicans. They are bipartisan and encourage others to be, also.

"Most of the news outlets, that are interested in the truth use them."

"That is good,' Christine frowned, "but how am I doing in the Republican precincts? If I lose them, I lose the election."

Holly nodded. "None of the large precincts have reported yet, but you are leading in the smaller precincts."

"Oh, look," Holly gasped, "Dallas County is coming in. Aww, man, Tate eked out a win in Dallas. I am sorry, Senator."

Christine smiled weakly. "It looks like Republicans are staying home and Democrats are voting the party line."

"Well, what do you expect?" Scott Winslow barked, "after your little announcement to the world."

"If that causes me to lose the election," Christine shrugged, "I have no business in politics, anyway."

"I am sure Republicans are deserting you because they are afraid you will campaign for same-sex marriage," Winslow scowled.

"I will," Christine declared.

Silence fell around the table as Winslow and Christine glared at one another.

"You just surged ahead," Ricky gasped, "It looks like you carried Bexar County; Republicans and Democrats."

The rest of the night was a constant seesaw as the two candidates jockeyed for the most votes. As the various precincts reported their votes, everyone began wondering why traditional Republican counties were so slow reporting their results. Collin and Travis counties' results were trickling in slowly. Harris and Montgomery Counties hadn't reported their numbers at all.

Harris—with one-and-a-quarter-million voters—traditionally voted Democratic. Montgomery with a million plus voters consistently voted Republican. It appeared the two counties would decide the winner of the election.

Tate called Christine. "I think you should concede, Senator," the man laughed gleefully. "The two largest counties are still out along with Travis County. Republicans have never carried Travis and Collin counties."

"We will see," Christine said more confidently than she felt.

"You have my number," Tate beamed, "just call me when you are ready to concede." He hung up laughing loudly.

"Sis," Randall moved to the empty seat beside his sister, "I just wanted to tell you that I am here for you regardless of the outcome."

"Thank you," Christine squeezed his hand.

"You were there for me when Mother and Father refused to speak to me. I will never forget that."

Christine nodded. "You are family," she smiled.

"What will you do if you don't win the election?" Randall asked hesitantly.

"Take a very long vacation," the senator smiled at Ricky, "then join you at Richmond International."

"Oh," Randall tilted his head slightly, "that will be fun. You and me working together."

"Yes," Christine laughed, "remember how we played store when we were little? You always had to be the store owner, and I was the cashier."

Randall laughed, "You have always been good with money. Of course, in real life, our positions are reversed. You are the sole owner of Richmond, and I am the employee."

Christine smiled knowingly. Maybe losing the race wouldn't be too bad, after all.

The local Fox News station returned to the screen following their endless commercials. "Well, folks, Paige Daily's stoic face revealed nothing, "we feel safe in calling the race."

The results for Travis and Collin Counties filled the screen. Tate surged ahead of Christine. The silence in the campaign headquarters was deafening.

Christine's phone rang. She looked at the incoming caller. Tate was calling to gloat.

Montgomery County's totals popped onto the screen beside Paige's head. "For the first time in history, it looks like Montgomery's Republicans and Democrats agree on the same candidate, Senator Christine Richmond. She has pulled over a million votes from the good folks there."

The campaign headquarters went wild.

Paige continued. "Harris County has traditionally been Democratic, but they like Senator Richmond this year, giving her over three-fourths of their votes."

Ricky thought the room would explode as the results for Tarrant and Johnson Counties filled the screen with overwhelming votes for Christine.

Senator Christine Richmond won the race by a large margin.

~~~

Christine slipped off her heels and gratefully accepted the glass of wine Ricky held out to her. Ricky settled on the sofa and pulled the brunette's feet onto her lap. She slowly began to massage the senator's aching feet.

"Oh, my God, that feels so good," Christine closed her eyes and surrendered to the gentle strokes of the ranger's strong hands. "That is the second best-feeling thing you do to me."

Propped against the arm of the sofa, Christine watched Ricky as she lovingly massaged her feet. "No one has ever massaged my feet," the brunette commented.

Ricky smiled. "You are the governor-elect of Texas. You will have people standing in line to kiss your feet."

"You are the only one I want to kiss my feet," Christine looked at her from beneath long dark lashes and smiled salaciously.

"You have a lot to do to prepare to move into 1010 Colorado St.," Ricky slowly smiled as Christine laid her head back and moaned sensuously.

"You know the first floor is a museum?" Christine smiled.

"Yes," Ricky nodded. "Dad took Tex and me on the tour when I was about twelve. The Governor's Mansion has twenty-five rooms."

"We will live entirely on the second floor," Christine sighed. Ricky's hands were making her entire body relax.

"We?" Ricky raised an eyebrow.

"Yes! You and me," Christine grinned a crooked little smile. "I hope you don't think I jeopardized my political future to live in the Governor's Mansion *alone*."

"I hadn't given it any thought," Ricky frowned.

Christine sat up and crawled onto the ranger's lap. She gently nibbled Ricky's lower lip. "I refuse to live there without you," she giggled as she pushed her breasts against the blonde. "Who will take care of my needs."

"Since you put it like that," Ricky grinned, "when do we move?"

～～～

"Thank God, you are here," Becky squealed as Ricky walked through the door.

"What is wrong?" Ricky asked.

"Just look at my call director," Becky gasped as she pointed to the device. Every light on the call center equipment was flashing red.

"It has been like that all morning, and we have a thousand messages wanting return calls." Becky spread her arms in dismay. "Important calls that we need to handle can't even get to us."

"I think I can fix that," Ricky smiled. She called Paige Daily and requested a favor. Within minutes, Paige was announcing on her morning talk show that Major Ricky Strong and Governor-elect Christine Richmond were vacationing in Hawaii. "The pair left early this morning after Governor-elect Richmond's grueling campaign."

The lights on the call director began going out, and the phone load returned to normal.

"Every conservative politician in town is calling Director Crockett," Becky grimaced. "They are demanding your head."

"I will go talk with him," Ricky frowned.

"No!" Becky grinned her most evil grin. "He and Mrs. Crockett are out of town. They *really* are vacationing in Hawaii. They left the night you made your grand announcement. He is taking all the accumulated vacation he has logged over the years. We won't see him for four months."

"He is a sly fox," Ricky laughed. "He truly does know how to survive in politics. He won't return until Christine is Governor."

A text message from Christine dinged into Ricky's phone. *I will be unreachable all day. See you tonight. Love you.*

~~~

Christine opened her personal laptop and logged into the private books of Richmond International. She located political donations and printed a list of the Texas politicians that had received large donations from her family. She quickly glanced at the company's profit and loss statement. Expenses were higher than usual. Something seemed out of place, but she couldn't put her finger on it. She didn't have time to look closely at the books. She would talk to her Father later.

She called the first three names on the printout and made appointments to speak with them. Her first three meetings were with the Lieutenant Governor, the Speaker of the House then the States Attorney General.

She handed her secretary the list on her way out the door. "Please call them and arrange appointments for me. I want to speak to all of them before the week is over."

Christine spent the entire day visiting her associates and pitching her case against the *Don't Ask, Don't Tell* policy of the law enforcement organizations in Texas.

By the end of the day she had spoken with eleven of her friends in the Senate. They all agreed to help her with the House of Representative. Christine would personally meet with the thirty-one Senate members and enlist their help in contacting the one-hundred-fifty house members. Their goal was to solicit support to vanquish any symbolism of the *Don't Ask, Don't Tell* policy.

~~~

Ricky was preparing dinner when Christine entered their home.

"Umm, something smells good," the brunette wrapped her arms around the ranger's waist and pushed her body against Ricky's back. "I am starving."

Ricky turned in her arms and kissed her lovingly. "Go change into something more comfortable while I get dinner on the table."

Christine couldn't resist a look at what Ricky was cooking. "Oh, my, shrimp sautéed in brandy. You are making my favorite stir-fry dish."

"Hurry," Ricky kissed her again then pushed her away, "I am adding the vegetables."

Christine quickly returned in her sweats and an old t-shirt. "How was your day?" She stole a piece of shrimp. "Oh, that is so good."

"Not too bad," Ricky answered her question. "Yours must have been very busy. I miss talking to you during the day."

"I have so much to do before I take office on January 20." Christine poured their wine and carried it to the table. "The Legislature meets the second

Tuesday in January, so technically Governor Albright will still be governor when they reconvene."

"Of course, everyone I know is calling to ingratiate themselves to me." She didn't add that she had directed her secretary to give her cell phone number to all senators who called.

Each contact went the same. The senator would congratulate her on being elected governor then mention a pet project with which they needed her help. Christine would assure them she would give their request her utmost attention. Then Christine would enlist their help to repeal the *Don't Ask, Don't Tell* law.

Christine pulled her thoughts back to their discussion. "I have less than ninety days to line up the people I want to appoint as members of boards and commissions who oversee the heads of state agencies and departments.

"My biggest decision is who will be Secretary of State."

"Do you have any thoughts on that?" Ricky asked.

"Yes," Christine nodded. "Holly Brandt."

Ricky raised her eyebrows questioningly. "Is she qualified?"

"More than you can imagine," Christine laughed. "I had my office check her out after she challenged me at that rally.

"She is a constitutional law attorney and has won two cases before the Supreme Court. She heads the state chapter of Young Republicans and is tremendously active in politics on all levels. Best of all, she is Latino. Her family has the true American Dream story to tell.

Her parents legally immigrated to the U.S. as teenagers. They met in college and married. She is a strong proponent of legal immigration."

"...and she is gay," Ricky added.

Christine raised a perfectly arched eyebrow.

"I checked her out, too," Ricky smiled. "I check out anyone who contacts you."

Christine reached out to take Ricky's hand, "Do you have any idea how much I love and appreciate you?"

"Humm, not really," the ranger grinned shyly. "But I am certain you can remind me."

Christine smiled seductively. "Let me take a quick shower, and I will show you."

"I'll clear the dishes," Ricky smiled. She wondered if the brunette would always make her heart beat double time.

~~~

By the end of the week, Christine had lined up more than enough votes to pass the legislation she wanted. Between promised donations and favor exchanges, she had lined up almost everyone in the legislature behind her. Now it was time to talk to Governor Albright. They had scheduled an all-day session so Albright could bring her up to date on the many items he was juggling.

"Christine," Albright greeted her with genuine fondness as he clasped her hands in his. "It is good to see you. We have a lot to cover before I turn over the reins to you."

Christine took a deep breath. "I have something I need to discuss with you in private before we begin," the Governor-elect smiled tentatively.

"Of course," Albright nodded. He waved his hand dismissing his staff. "How can I help you?"

"I am certain you know that I am in a committed relationship with Texas Ranger Major Ricky Strong." Christine held the Governor's gaze.

Albright nodded slightly encouraging her to continue.

"I would like you to call a special session to revoke the *Don't Ask, Don't Tell* policy the state has concerning law enforcement agencies."

Governor Albright templed his fingers as if praying. His clear blue eyes studied Christine for several seconds. "When do you want me to call the session?"

"As soon as possible," Christine breathed a sigh of relief. "I would like to have this settled before Director David Crockett returns from vacation.

"I have already lined up enough support to pass the law making it illegal to discriminate against employees because of their sexual orientation or gender identity.

"As you know, similar bills have died in committee, but I have aligned enough support to take it directly to a vote."

"Consider it done," Albright chuckled. "I might as well go out with a bang. Knowing you, I assume you have already drafted the bill and passed it out to the Legislature."

"I have," Christine smiled. "I wanted to make certain I had the needed support before I bothered you with it."

Albright called his secretary into his office. "Please take the draft Governor-elect Richmond has and send it to the entire legislature along with the notification for a special session to address the bill.

"I want to convene the session before Christmas so we can complete this before Christine's inauguration."

The secretary smiled at Christine and left the room.

"Before I begin with my items," Albright smiled, "would you give me an updated report on the wall between Mexico and the U.S?"

"As you know," Christine frowned, "the Rio Grande River forms a natural boundary between Texas and Mexico. Unfortunately, the river is very shallow in many places so that anyone can wade across it. In some places, it is completely dry.

"Construction of a wall has already started in Brownsville. It will run from the Gulf of Mexico up to El Paso. There is a three-mile area between the river and the wall that belongs to the U.S.

"Border Patrol will constantly monitor that section of the border. Anyone found between the river and our border will be shot."

Albright jumped at the word *shot*.

"Will the feds stand behind that?" he asked.

"Yes, there is already a bill in the house to protect the U.S. from the invasion of illegal aliens no matter their country of origin. It carries that verbiage. I have assurance the federal government will enforce the law."

"Congratulations on a job well done," he smiled at Christine. "The wall should be finished during your term as Governor. That is only fitting when one considers all you have done to promote its construction."

"What are you going to do about same-sex marriage?" Albright frowned.

"Nothing," Christine shrugged. "A piece of paper doesn't make one any more committed than one's word. The government can't legislate morality. We need to stop trying.

"There are civil laws in place to protect one's financial rights. People simply need to take advantage of the laws in place."

Albright nodded his head thoughtfully. "Well then, let's get down to my business."

~~~

Chapter 33

Randall Richmond stood still as his tailor checked the fit of his custom-made suit. "The fit is perfect, sir," the shop owner smiled.

Randall watched himself in the mirror. The suit was flawless. The sleeves were the perfect length. The slacks touched his Italian shoes in just the right place. The suit cost more than most dock workers made in three months.

"This is excellent," he smiled at the tailor. "I need two more in the material we selected. I will wear this one now. I have lunch in a few minutes with the Governor."

The tailor nodded his head. He had been making suits for Armand Richmond for more years than he could remember. He was pleased that Armand had sent his son to him.

The limousine ride to the restaurant was peaceful and enjoyable. Randall thought about Christine Richmond. Her election as Governor had almost doubled their business. Everyone wanted to associate with the female Governor of Texas.

He needed Christine to support a proposal to allow larger container ships carrying heavier loads to use the Galveston ports.

Richmond International already had contracts to build the larger cargo carriers that would be able to carry double the number of shipping containers now allowed.

He checked his watch and realized he was early for their lunch. He decided to get a table and order a cocktail. The hostess recognized him and led him to his favorite table.

As he sipped his wine, he thought how different his life was compared to five years ago, when he was fighting to stay alive. He closed his eyes as he recalled the death of his cellmate. His mind drifted back to how scared he had been, waiting for his release from prison.

Randall Richmond would complete his sentence in ten days. He lived in constant fear that something would happen to prevent his release. His cell mate kept complaining about how unfair it was that Randall was getting out and he had to stay in the hell hole they had inhabited for the past six years.

He had been horrified when the jailers had dragged him from the cell the morning his cellmate was found dead. After hours of grueling interrogation, the warden had declared his cellmate's death was due to a heart attack and sent him back to his cell.

Randall spent the next five days backed into the corner of his cell, his knees drawn up in front of him. He reluctantly left his cell to eat, then returned pulling the cell door locked behind him. If he could live five more days, he would be free.

He still recalled how thankful he had been to breathe the fresh, clean air outside the prison. He worked various jobs to live a meager existence. It had taken him a long time to work up the nerve to approach his family.

A commotion at the hostess' stand announced the arrival of Christine Richmond. Randall strode to her side and hugged her tightly. "I have a table and a glass of your favorite wine waiting for you," he smiled. He nodded to Christine's ever-present security detail. He wondered if Crate and Barrel ever slept.

"I am sorry I only have an hour," Christine smiled sweetly, "but I did want to see you if only for a quick lunch."

"My little sister is Governor of the great state of Texas," Randal smiled proudly. "I am very proud of you."

Christine blushed slightly at his unexpected praise. "I hope I haven't bitten off more than I can chew," she laughed. "I can't seem to catch my breath. Hopefully, things will calm down after the inauguration.

"You will be at my inauguration, won't you?"

"I wouldn't miss it for the world," he grinned.

"How are things going at Richmond International?" Christine asked casually.

"Good, but I do need your guidance on a couple of things."

Randall watched his sister's eyes as he explained the need for the larger cargo carriers and a port to handle them. "Port Galveston would be ideal to serve the larger, heavier boats, but it would require considerable investment in heavy-duty cranes to handle the large metal cargo containers" he concluded.

"Put together a proposal and present it to the Texas Maritime Division of the Texas Department of Transportation. That is their bailiwick," Christine said thoughtfully. "If they accept your proposal, they could present the final study to me along with their recommendation."

"TxDOT isn't very easy to deal with," Randall frowned. "Couldn't you just instruct them to do it?"

"I could suggest it," Christine scowled, "but it would look better if you presented it with no undue influence from me."

"Of course," Randal frowned, "it would look like you were trying to pass legislation that would be beneficial to our conglomerate."

"Exactly," Christine grinned.

"The Governor has called a special session to address the *Don't Ask, Don't Tell* laws," Randal shrugged. "Didn't you instigate that?"

"Yes," Christine nodded.

"You exerted a lot of influence to make that happen," Randal pointed out. "I don't see how that is any different."

"Repeal of the Don't Ask, Don't Tell laws doesn't line my pockets with gold," Christine smirked. "It does help those, who have always supported me, keep their jobs."

Randal shrugged and sipped his wine. "We should order. You are running out of time." He waved at the waitress.

Christine ordered then surveyed her handsome brother. "I like your new suit," she smiled.

"Thank you," he blushed slightly. "Father insisted that I have some "decent" suits to wear to New York."

"New York!" I haven't heard anything about New York."

"You have been extremely busy, so you haven't spoken to Mother and Father," Randall looked perturbed. "I guess they haven't told you we are going to New York for Christmas. Of course, they expect you to join us."

"I am certain we can discuss it at Thanksgiving when we are all together," Christine frowned slightly. "I am not certain Ricky can get away that long at Christmas."

"I don't think... they don't want to include Ricky," Randall said hesitantly.

"Then I won't be there either," Christine growled. She threw her napkin on the table and stood.

Randall jerked back. It was the first time he had witnessed the famous temper of Christine Richmond. Fury burned in the woman's eyes. He caught her wrist. "Please, don't go, Sis. Let's finish lunch. We won't discuss our parents. Okay?"

Christine inhaled angrily, tossed her long hair back from her face and sat back down.

Randal watched her closely as she fought to get her temper under control. *Major Ricky Strong is her Achilles' Heel,* he thought.

~~~

"Incoming, boss," Becky hurriedly announced as Christine burst through Ricky's door.

"How did I get so lucky?" Ricky stood as she saw the fire in the governor elect's eyes.

She is pissed off, Ricky thought. *I hope I haven't done anything to...*

Christine slammed and locked the office door. "I need you," she declared as she threw herself into the ranger's arms.

Ricky gladly allowed the Texas tornado to have her way with her. Afterward, as she lay on the sofa holding Christine in her arms, she kissed her gently and stroked her back, soothing her.

"I just want you to know this is a first for me," Ricky whispered in the brunette's ear, "and my office sofa."

Christine laughed softly. Making love to Ricky had diminished the fury she felt at her parents. "Did I hurt you?" she murmured. "I didn't mean to take out my anger on you."

"Oh, feel free to use me, anytime," Ricky chuckled. "Do you want to tell me what you are so angry about?"

"My parents," Christine sat up and looked for her blouse and bra.

"Behind my desk," Ricky directed.

"Oh," Christine shrugged and slightly smiled as she stood and pulled her skirt down then smoothed the wrinkles from it.

"Is there any chance you can remain this angry until we get home tonight?" Ricky laughed as she replaced and fastened her clothes. "Or I could call your mother, and you could talk with her as soon as we get home."

Christine burst out laughing. "I love you so much," she placed her hand on the side of Ricky's face. "I never want to spend a night away from you."

"You won't have to," Ricky pulled her tight against her and held her for a long time. Ricky's intercom buzzed insistently. "We will talk tonight, okay?"

The brunette nodded and tiptoed for one last kiss before leaving the office. Ricky followed her into the reception area. "Thank you for stopping by Governor

Richmond," Ricky mischievously smiled. "I enjoyed the exchange with you."

Christine cast her a sultry glance and disappeared out the door.

Deputy Director Rusty Rhodes stood silently in the middle of the outer office until Christine left.

"Major, we need to talk," Rhodes huffed and strode past Ricky into her office.

"Major," Becky pulled Ricky to her desk, "you have lipstick all over your face." Grabbing a tissue, she quickly wiped the telltale signs of passion from the ranger's contrite face.

"Thank you," Ricky whispered as she went to join the man pacing the floor in her office.

"Sir," Ricky extended her hand to Rhodes who shook it vigorously. She motioned to a chair in front of her desk then sat in her chair on the other side.

"Major Strong," Rhodes took a deep breath, "I am afraid I am going to need to put you on suspension until Director Crockett returns and decides what to do with you."

"Why?" Ricky demanded. She could see the sweat running down Rhodes' neck.

"Because...because you are..." he fumbled for words.

"Gay," Ricky supplied the word he was trying to say.

Rhodes nodded.

"Did Director Crockett tell you to suspend me?" Ricky asked, watching the man squirm.

"No, I am just receiving so much flak from the powers that be...I."

"Have you spoken to Crockett?" She held a tissue out to Rhodes.

"No," Rhodes grabbed the tissue to wipe his forehead and neck. "I have to do something. Crockett won't be back until after Christmas."

"You know you are putting your hands on a ticking time bomb?" Ricky pointed out.

Rhodes nodded.

"Do you have any accrued vacation?" Ricky asked.

Rhodes nodded again. "Enough to carry me through Christmas."

"Why don't you do what Director Crockett did?" Ricky smiled slightly. "Use all your vacation time. No one can fault you for that. I am sure your new boss, the Governor, will understand."

"That would leave you in charge," Rhodes frowned.

"I can handle difficult situations," Ricky grinned. "I assure you I will not suspend myself."

Rhodes nodded his head like a bobble-head doll, as he considered his alternatives. "Consider me on vacation starting immediately," Rhodes stood and shook Ricky's hand. "I will stay away until my vacation runs out, by then your girlfriend will be governor."

"Governor-elect Richmond will be Governor," Ricky nodded. She followed him to the reception area. "Sir, with all due respect, don't ever call her my girlfriend, again. Are we clear?"

"I meant no disrespect," Rhodes frowned. "What should I call her?"

"Governor!" Ricky smiled.

Chapter 34

"UPS just delivered an overnight package for you," Becky held the small container warily as she carried it toward Ricky's desk. "There is no return address."

"Let's take it to the lab to open it," Ricky scowled. "We never receive deliveries here."

Christine arrived just as the two were walking to the forensic lab. Her eyes lighted as she saw the ranger. Ricky's quick smile told the brunette her love was happy to see her.

"Do we need to return to my office?" Ricky smiled hopefully.

"Not today, dear," Christine laughed. "I received a small package via UPS. Crate insisted we bring it to you without opening it."

Crate held out the package addressed to Christine. It was identical to the one Ricky held.

"Crate is always right in these matters," Ricky frowned as she turned over the package. "Becky, let's bag these. We may need to try to pull prints from them."

The twisting feeling invading Ricky's stomach told her she wasn't going to like what was in the packages.

Raylee Ryan looked up from the microscope as the five blue aliens entered her domain. Wearing the dress required to be in the forensic lab, Ricky greeted Lab Director Ryan. She introduced those with her then handed the bag containing the packages to Raylee.

"I don't know what this is," Ricky frowned, "but it is strange that Governor-elect Richmond and I received identical packages."

"Let's go into the explosives testing area," Raylee nodded, leading the way to a soundproof room.

She placed both boxes into a 3D x-ray machine. She pushed the button and watched on the computer screen as the machine scanned the boxes.

"Oh, dear God," Raylee gasped. "The packages contain hands."

Everyone crowded around the computer screen to see the contents of the boxes. "Hands," Ricky whispered. She knew without opening the boxes that they were from Troy Hunter.

Raylee opened the packages with forceps. "We will dust everything for prints," she said. "But these hands have been bleached and scrubbed. I doubt we will find anything on them.

"I doubt it, too," Ricky frowned. "Do both hands belong to the same woman?"

"I'm pretty sure they do," Raylee nodded, "but I won't know for certain until I test them."

"Can you make any guess about how long their owner has been dead?" Ricky scowled.

"Let me run some tests on them," Raylee grimaced. "I should be able to answer all your questions by the end of the day."

"There is a note inside the one addressed to you, Major," Raylee pulled a small 3"x3" post-it note from the box and read it. "Why did you stop emailing me? This hand could belong to the Governor-elect."

Christine gasped. "That is why you kept the security detail on me?"

Ricky nodded. "He threatened you in his last email to me."

Ricky's cell phone rang. It was the detective in charge of the Hacker investigation. "Major Strong," she answered as her stomach turned over.

"Ricky, we have a fresh floater," the detective informed her.

"As soon as you can, please bring her to our forensic lab," Ricky directed. "I think we have her hands."

"Will do."

"One more thing," Ricky hated to ask the question, "what color is her hair?"

"Brunette, of course," the detective scoffed. "It is always a brunette."

The misery in Ricky's eyes made Christine's heart hurt. She touched the ranger's arm. She fought the need to hold the blonde and comfort her.

Christine followed the ranger back to her office and closed the door. She slid her arms around Ricky's neck and kissed her gently, comforting, lovingly.

The alarm on Christine's phone reminded her she had an appointment. "I have to go, baby," she whispered. "I will be home early tonight."

"Thank you," Ricky nodded then kissed her again.

~~~

Ricky called Detective Pete Jordon in Springfield, CO. She had to check on Lillian Dawes. Jordon put her on hold as he called the officer assigned to protect Dawes.

"She is alive and kicking," Jordon informed her. "My officer is watching her order coffee at Starbucks right now."

"Please tell him to stay close to her," Ricky directed. "We just pulled another woman from the Colorado. I have no idea who she is."

"Will do, Major. Thanks for the heads up."

Ricky opened her laptop and logged onto the fictitious Alessa Morris email account they had set up for Kay Dawson.

Troy Hunter had emailed the account daily. Taunting Ricky for letting Kay Dawson die at his hands.

Hunter's last email was yesterday. *How did you like my little presents?* The man jeered. *Your Governor-elect might be next, or I might just save her for last. I am certain I will entertain many women before I finish.*

Ricky paced in front of her personal whiteboard. Photos of all the Hacker's Texas victims spread across the top. Across the bottom were pictures of his victims from other states.

The mode of operation in every Texas case was the same, except in Kay Dawson's case. Every victim's hands were removed—with a hacksaw—and their body dumped into the Colorado River that flowed through Austin. Only Kay's murder had provided investigators with a DNA sample. Unfortunately, there were no DNA matches in any of the national or international databases.

Ricky had been working on the Hacker's case for almost two years and felt she was no closer today than she was when they dredged the first decomposed body from the river.

Obviously, Troy Hunter had been communicating with the latest victim at the same time he was emailing Ricky's alias, Rachel Winn.

Now the monster was threatening Christine. A shudder ran through Ricky. She had to find a way to catch Troy Hunter, whoever he was.

~~~

Fresh from a shower and dressed in a terry cloth robe, Christine stood at the top of the stairs and watched as Ricky closed and locked their front door.

A smile crossed the ranger's troubled face as she slowly ascended the stairs. She gladly slipped into the waiting arms of her lover. The dark dread of the day slipped away as Christine moved her full, soft lips against Ricky's.

"Come, let mama take care of you," Christine murmured against the warm lips. She pulled the robe's tie belt and let the garment slip from her silky, warm body.

After Christine finished with her Ricky couldn't recall anything but the incredible feel of the brunette against her. Christine made love to her in every way imaginable, leaving the ranger's mind filled with amazement and happiness. Only thoughts of Christine filled her mind. There wasn't room for anything else.

Ricky fell asleep with only one thought in her mind; how much she loved and craved the woman in her arms.

~~~

Ricky read the glaring headlines of the morning paper then called Director Crockett.

The bill to stop discrimination against all employees regardless of sexual orientation cleared the house and senate with only a few Democrats voting against it.

"Good morning, sir," she smiled into her phone. "I just wanted to let you know you can come home now."

Crockett laughed, "Thank heaven, I am going crazy with all this sunshine and ocean.

"How is everything with you, Major?"

"Hectic," Ricky chuckled. "I have made no progress on the Hacker and life is pretty crazy in the governor's mansion."

"I will be home tomorrow," Crockett said. "You can tell me all about it. Have you called DD Rhodes?"

"No, sir, I wanted to inform you first. Would you like me to meet you at the airport?"

"No, you stay there and continue to hold down the fort. I'll get myself home."

~~~

Ricky tightened the security around Christine as the inauguration neared. They sipped their coffee as they discussed their move to the governor's mansion.

"You know we don't have to live in the governor's mansion," Christine exhaled slowly.

"I will live where ever you want," Ricky smiled. "Doesn't the mansion have the reputation of being the oldest occupied Governor's Mansion south of the Mason-Dixson?"

Christine laughed. "Indeed, it does, but I don't think past governors have actually made it their home. They just stayed there occasionally for appearances."

"So, we could sleep there one night a week and spend the rest of our time here?" Ricky smiled. "You could entertain there, so we don't have to allow people into our sanctuary."

"My thoughts exactly." Christine refilled their coffee cups and kissed the blonde on the cheek. "I don't relish the idea of people touring my home while I am making love to you one floor above them."

"Might be kind of exciting," Ricky grinned. "Of course, you are rather vocal. Probably not a good idea."

"I'm the vocal one?" Christine smiled provocatively. "Perhaps we should test your theory."

~~~

January flew by with parties for the new governor. Christine and Ricky were on an endless treadmill of parties and shaking hands of people they didn't know.

Christine's inauguration was without incident. Ricky helped her move from her Senate office to the governor's office.

Christine was surprised when her secretary announced her mother was headed for her office. She looked up as Lady stormed her door.

"Mother, what an unexpected pleasure," the brunette rose to great the family matriarch.

Lady waved her back to her chair as she settled into the visitor's chair across from the governor. "I know you have been busy," Lady smiled slyly, "so I have put together a little dinner party so you can thank all the people who made your election possible."

"That is very thoughtful of you, Mother," Christine smiled mirthlessly. "I am certain you are aware that I have only been in office a little over a week. There are more important things that require my attention. I do not have time to throw a dinner party."

"Don't be ridiculous, dear," Lady grinned, "I will take care of every detail. All you have to do is show up."

"When do you plan to hold this soiree?" Christine frowned.

"The second Friday night in February," Lady beamed. "We can have a Valentine theme. You, know, thank you with all my heart."

"A little juvenile, don't you think?" Christine scowled. "I'd rather not, Mother. Maybe in May or June, when I have a chance to breathe."

"Christine, please do this for me," Lady whined. "I am so proud of you."

"Let me check with Ricky," the governor shook her head. It was easier to let her mother have her way than argue with her.

"If it is inconvenient for her," Lady smiled sweetly, "I wouldn't be offended if she can't make it."

"We come as a pair," Christine smirked. "If Ricky can't attend your party, neither can I."

"Don't be ridiculous, dear. You can't plan your life around a Texas Ranger who is gallivanting all over the state."

"I can, and I do." Christine stood to open the door for her mother. "It is what I want."

Lady ignored her daughter's attempt to move her to the door. "Call her right now and ask her if that date is good for her," the woman pouted.

Christine pushed the button to connect her with the ranger. "Hi, pretty woman," Ricky chirped into the phone.

"Darling, I have you on speakerphone and Mother is in my office." Christine smiled as her mother cringed at the term of endearment she'd used with Ricky.

"Umm, hello, Lady," Ricky said. "What is going on?"

"Mother is planning a thank you party for me on the second Friday in February. Will you be available then?"

"Let me check," Ricky groaned. "Honey, you know I have this sting going down. I'm not certain how that will work out time wise." They listened as Ricky rattled on her keyboard.

Lady glared daggers at her daughter.

"That will work as good as any day," Ricky said slowly. "For you, Governor, I will make it happen."

"We will set it as a tentative date," Christine nodded. "You and I can discuss it at home tonight."

"I've gotta run, baby," Ricky chuckled, "duty calls. Love you."

"Love you, too, darling," Christine smiled.

"You really should be more professional in the governor's office," Lady huffed.

"And you really should be on your way," Christine scowled.

Lady indignantly snorted as she left the office. Although she made a show of being offended by her daughter and the ranger, secretly she was impressed with their devotion to one another. She knew her daughter would always be safe with Major Strong.

451

Chapter 35

"We are moving Martina into my old apartment tomorrow," Ricky softly said as she settled against the overstuffed arm of the sofa.

"Why?" Christine motioned for Ricky to make a place for her to sit between her legs. Ricky did, and the brunette leaned back against the ranger, reveling in her softness.

"Umm, you smell good," Ricky murmured as she buried her face in the brunette's hair and wrapped her arms around her.

"Don't change the subject," Christine said. "Why are you moving Martina into your old apartment?"

"There are thirty-two of Carlito Zamboni's mobsters entrenched in Austin." Ricky shifted to pull the governor's back tighter against her. "Before they arrived, they leased that new apartment development outside of town. You know the one close to Slaughter Creek."

Christine nodded and lightly trailed her fingers along Ricky's leg. "The entire complex?"

"All the units that are finished," Ricky said. "There are about forty of them in all, counting Carlito and his lieutenants.

"They wasted no time embedding themselves in the narcotics and prostitution trade in this area. We have had wiretaps on Carlito's men since their arrival.

We already have enough information to arrest them for human trafficking and drugs."

"Why don't you simply arrest them?" Christine asked.

"We don't have anything on Carlito. He has kept his nose clean. I want him. Martina will never be safe until he is behind bars.

"We are coordinating with a secret FBI task force. They have enough to take down the New York branch of the Zamboni family. We want to take down everyone at once like we did the Mexican drug cartel you and Peyton destroyed."

"Is Peyton going to prosecute the Texas gangsters?" Christine asked.

"Yes," Ricky moaned as the brunette pressed her nails into her calves. She tightened her legs around Christine, enveloping her.

"Do you want to hear my report, Governor?" Ricky shifted as Christine turned in her arms to face her.

"Later," the brunette purred.

~~~

Much later, Christine snuggled into the warm body of the ranger as she pulled the soft sofa throw over their naked bodies. "I am ready to hear the rest of your report now," she murmured.

Ricky gulped and cut to the chase," The bottom line is I will need to stay with Martina until Carlito makes his move."

"What?" cold air swept Ricky's body as Christine pulled away from her taking the cover.

Glad I waited until after we made love to share that with her, Ricky thought.

"You mean to stay with her all the time like you did with me?" Christine's glare dared the ranger to say, yes.

Ricky nodded silently.

"I do not believe this," the governor stormed. "You are going to…

"Not like I did with you," Ricky choked. "I will stand watch downstairs so no one can get up to her room."

"Ricky Strong, I don't like this one bit," Christine growled.

"It won't be for long, honey," Ricky reasoned. "Once we let Dave Adams know where she is, he will report to Carlito. They should move swiftly after that."

"What if there is a shootout?" Christine worried her lower lip with her top teeth. "What if you are hurt or…?"

Ricky tried to pull the brunette into her arms, but Christine resisted. "I can't lose you, Ricky; not to another woman or a bullet."

Ricky caught Christine's face between her hands and forced the brunette to look in her eyes. "You will never lose me to another woman," Ricky declared. "You are like no one I have ever met. No other woman in the world compares to you. I love you! I always will!"

"And the bullet?" Christine raised a quizzical eyebrow. "Will you always be able to dodge the bullet?"

"Honey, I am good at what I do," Ricky said honestly. "Now that I have found you, I am not about to let myself get killed. My love for you is too strong to die?"

Christine collapsed against the ranger. "I'll kill you if you get hurt," she mumbled.

Ricky chuckled. "I will be fine."

~~~

Tex pulled Ricky aside as Martina and Christine made sandwiches in the kitchen.

"Are you sure about this, Ricky," the handsome rancher's worried look told the ranger he was dying inside at the thought of intentionally placing his wife in harm's way. "Can't I stay with her where ever she is?"

"I will be with her twenty-four/seven," Ricky reassured him. "Crate and Barrel will be with me. We won't let anything happen to her, I promise. Her family doesn't know you and Brady exist. I want to keep it that way."

Ricky was much more concerned about Christine. The ranger had pulled her most trusted men from the governor's security team to protect Martina. She had a bad feeling she was leaving Christine too exposed. She prayed the Hacker's latest kill would hold him for a while.

Lee Phillips and Tim Tanksly were taking Crate and Barrel's place on Christine's security team.

~~~

Christine and Ricky helped Martina get settled into the apartment. "You have good taste Mia Cara," Martina smiled as she looked around the ranger's former home.

"I hope you will be comfortable here," Ricky smiled.

455

"I hope you won't be here long," Christine shrugged.

"I understand," Martina smiled at Christine. "I, too, will be sleeping alone."

"I will be keeping a vigil beneath the stairs," Ricky showed the women her hiding place. "These two boards have purposely been loosened so that I will hear anyone going up the stairs." She stepped on the two stair steps that made a loud creaking sound.

"Crate and Barrel will be in the bedroom on each side of yours, and Nicole Weil will sleep on the sofa in your room.

"My FBI counterpart will *accidentally* inform Dave Adams of your location. All we have to do is wait."

"I suppose I should be leaving," Christine frowned as she walked toward the door.

"I will walk you to your car," Ricky caught the governor's hand and opened the door.

"Please be careful," Christine's downcast eyes told Ricky all she needed to know about how the brunette felt about the plan. "I would be much happier if you were staying with me, but I do understand."

The ranger placed her fingers under the governor's chin and tilted her face up to see her eyes. "I love you," she whispered as she kissed Christine's soft, red lips.

As Christine drove away, Ricky had a twisting feeling in her stomach. She felt that she was being forced to choose between the woman she loved and the woman Tex loved. She didn't feel good about her choice. She hoped Carlito made his move soon.

The first two days of their tight surveillance went without incident. Ricky was in constant contact with the agents running the wiretap. She didn't want any surprises.

Christine was staying away so she wouldn't interfere with the plot to catch the gangsters. She and Ricky talked every night, but it didn't assuage the loneliness the governor felt. Her security team went with her everywhere. A rookie was left at her home to make certain no one entered the house during her absence.

It was early afternoon when a knock on the door of Ricky's apartment sent the ranger scurrying to her hiding place beneath the stairway. Martina looked out the peephole and was shocked to see Dave Adams at the door.

Martina had fallen in love with the handsome agent—who had sworn his love for her—during their operation to bring down her father's crime family.

Dave's betrayal had been hard to accept. She had trusted him with her life, and he had left her vulnerable to her father's henchmen. If Ricky hadn't stepped in and whisked her away, she would be pushing up daisies in the Zamboni family graveyard.

Martina ran to Ricky. "It is Dave."

"Let him in," Ricky nodded and pressed her back against the wall beneath the stairs.

"Crate, you here?" Ricky said softly.

"Picking you up loud and clear, Major," Crate replied through the earpiece they wore.

Martina opened the door a crack. "What do you want?" she growled.

"Martina," Dave attempted to push the door open, but the chain lock prevented it.

"How did you know where to find me?" Martina scowled furiously.

"Please, unlock the door," Dave pleaded. "I need to talk with you. It is important."

"Setting me up to be killed was important, too," Martina hissed.

"Please, Martina," Dave looked around nervously. "You are in danger."

"From you," Martina growled.

"I have a message for Major Strong," Dave insisted.

"Let him in," Ricky instructed as she moved into the room and drew her gun. "What do you want, Adams?"

"Carlito has the Governor and is willing to trade her for Martina."

Silence hung over the room as Ricky glanced back and forth between the woman she had sworn to protect and the man who threatened the life of the woman she loved.

~~~

Chapter 36

Slipping in through the back of the house had been child's play. The lone guard was asleep in his patrol car. Troy Hunter evilly grinned as he walked thru the governor's personal home. He had considered killing her in the Governor's Mansion, but after weeks of watching the routine of Christine Richmond and Ricky Strong, he realized he would never catch the gorgeous governor at the mansion alone. The ranger guarded her night and day.

Troy didn't know why the couple had separated. He just considered it his good fortune when Ricky Strong moved back into her apartment. He was astounded when he saw the Italian beauty move in with her. Apparently gorgeous, classy women liked Major Ricky Strong.

Troy knew he was deviating from his kill routine for the first time. He hadn't established a Facebook friendship with Christine Richmond as he had with her sister. He hadn't gained her trust and made dates with her. He was going straight for the kill.

He touched the hacksaw inside his coat and the heavy dose of narcotics he had in the two syringes in his pocket. A thrill of arousal ran thru his body as he recalled the look of horror on his victims' faces as he watched them bleed out. He hugged himself as he imagined the fight Christine Richmond would give him.

After a thorough search of the mansion, he settled on hiding in a bedroom closet on the second floor. The room looked like a layout for a home-decorating magazine. Troy doubted anyone ever used it.

He practically danced down the stairs to the first floor. He knew the governor's routine and didn't expect her home until after dark. Her security team would make a cursory walk-through of the home then set up guards at the front and back doors. He giggled at his own brilliance. They would be watching outside while he killed Christine Richmond inside. Brilliant!

Noise at the back door of the home startled him. He ducked from sight as the door opened a crack. He watched through the slats in the louvered door as two dark, burly, men entered the kitchen. One was tall with thick black hair. The other was a little shorter and bald.

"We will grab her when she enters the house," the taller man said.

"Do we just whack her?" the other man asked.

"No, we kidnap her. Carlito wants to trade her for his sister then we will shoot them both."

"How will we get her out of here?" the bald man grunted as he sat on a barstool at the kitchen counter.

"Carlito has that all figured out. We just drug her and call him."

"Let's get the layout of this place," the tall man said as he led the way upstairs.

Troy looked around the small room where he had hidden. It was the pantry. To his surprise, a door was at the back of the cupboard. He stealthily moved to the door and slowly turned the doorknob. A blast of musty, cool air told him he had opened the door to the basement.

The two men returned to the kitchen. "There is a study or library or some fancy named room off the hallway," the bald man gestured, "it has liquor. Want a drink?"

"Sure, why not. You pour while I report to the boss and let him know we are safely inside the Governor's home."

The two men moved out of sight, and Troy listened. He wondered why he wasn't frightened. Obviously, the men were killers who would just as soon kill him as look at him. He smiled as he realized the men were the hunted and he—Troy Hunter—was the hunter. He almost danced with glee as he wondered how long it would take the two large men to bleed out.

It was almost sundown when Troy heard sounds of snoring coming from the other room. He quietly opened the pantry door and ventured into the kitchen. A cautious peek into the library reinforced his suspicion that the men were sleeping.

Troy removed the syringe from his pocket and plunged it into the heart of the man sleeping closest to him. The man didn't move. Within seconds his snoring ceased, and his breathing was very light.

The bald man's head rested on the back of the chair, and his mouth hung open as he snored loudly. Troy eased into position behind the man and plunged the second syringe of drugs directly into the man's heart. The thug jerked and tried to get to his feet. His body spasmed and he lurched forward.

Troy wasted no time sawing off the hands of each man. He tied their feet and tightened tourniquets around their wrists. He grinned at the crimson stain that had spread onto Governor Richmond's expensive Italian rug. He had never injected drugs directly into the heart before. He wondered how long it would take for the men to rouse.

As he waited, Troy composed a brief note to Major Ricky Strong.

Two gangsters for you, Major. Not my usual fare, but I owe you a favor for providing Agent Dawson for me.

I am leaving you one hand from each man. I am taking the other for my collection.

Maybe, next time I will leave you a little memento to remember Governor Richmond.

Until we dance again, Major,

Troy Hunter

The bald man stirred and reached for his gun. Only then did he realize he couldn't grip it. He had no hands. He willed the two hands lying on his chest to move, but nothing happened.

"Surprise," Troy laughed. "Why don't you tell me what you two are doing in Governor Richmond's home?"

"What the hell?" the man tried to pull his feet beneath him and realized he was tied.

Blood slowly oozed from the stumps at the end of the man's wrists. "Do you know what that is?" Troy used a sharp kitchen knife to nudge the tourniquets he had tied on each man's wrists. "That is all that is standing between you and certain death. If I cut the rope, blood will spurt out every time your heart beats. Until there is nothing left to pump out."

Troy beamed as he watched the horror in the man's eyes. He laughed softly. If the guard hadn't been outside, he would have thrown back his head and howled in sheer delight.

"Answer my question, or I will cut the rope." He moved toward the man who cowered away from him, trying to hide his handless arms.

"Why are you here?" Troy hissed as he pulled his cell phone from his pocket and punched record.

"To kidnap Governor Richmond and take her to Carlito."

"Why?" Troy barked.

"To trade her for his sister," the gangster fearfully watched Troy.

"Why?" Troy barked again. "Give me the details."

"Martina, Carlito's sister, testified against the family in New York. That woman Texas Ranger has her in witness protection here."

"How do you know that?" Troy frowned.

"We have spies in the FBI," the dying man answered.

"Give me a name of the spy," Troy prodded him with the knife.

"Dave Adams."

"Say it louder," Troy commanded.

"Dave Adams," the gangster screamed. "Dave Adams told us where Martina is."

"What is your name?" Troy asked softly.

"Micky Malone."

"And your friend?"

"Max Martinez. Why?"

"Just want to know the names for your tombstones." Troy swiftly cut the tourniquets on each man and watched as the life drained from them.

The Governor will be home soon, Troy thought. *I am too tired to deal with her today. I want to be fresh and at my best when I do the gorgeous Christine Richmond.*

He punched a couple of buttons on his phone. He smiled as a familiar voice came on the line.

~~~

Ricky jumped when her cell phone vibrated. She kept her gun trained on Dave Adams and glanced at the face of her phone. She gasped as she saw the name of the caller—Kay Dawson.

"Major Strong," Ricky said breathlessly.

"Major," a man's voice swarmed across the line. "Get to Governor Richmond immediately. She isn't at home. That is where I am. She is in danger. Don't bring her home. The place is a mess. She shouldn't see it. I left a present for you." The line went dead.

Ricky steadied her hands as she called Crate. She was glad she had switched Tank and Phillips to her team and put Crate and Barrel back with Christine. "Crate, can you see Christine?"

"Yes, Major, she is dining with her parents." Crate moved closer to the Governor. "I am about two feet away from her."

"Listen to me closely," Ricky spoke softly. "As soon as she finishes, take her to the address I am going to text you. My brother will meet you there. Turn Christine over to him.

"Be positive no one follows you. Take any measures necessary. Remove your batteries from your cell phones and turn off your GPS systems. Clear?"

Ricky called Tex. "I need you to meet Crate and Barrel at the address we set up in the case of emergency. They have Christine with them. You know what to do.

"Yes, Martina is fine." She quickly texted the street address to Crate and the name of the street to Barrel. They were taking no chances.

Ricky called four of her team into the apartment. She called the rookie guarding Christine's house. "Is anything happening there," she asked.

"Quiet as a grave," the rookie's cocky reply made her cringe. "We will be there soon."

"To relieve me, I hope," he said.

"Yeah, sure," Ricky retorted. "To relieve you."

"Martina, I want you with me until I find out what is going on," Ricky pulled the woman beside her. "Tank, Phillips you walk in front of us Adams and Martina will walk in the middle, Nicole and I will bring up the rear."

Ricky called the agents running the wiretap. "Any chatter?" she asked.

"One of Carlito's men called to report in several hours ago, nothing since."

"What was his location?" Ricky inquired.

"We didn't get a location on it. He wasn't on the phone long enough."

"Alert the Tactical Team to take their positions around Governor Richmond's home. I want them standing by for immediate action," Ricky frowned. "I want eyes on Carlito in case he starts to move."

"Yes, Major. We have men watching him now."

The van pulled through the mansion gates and let out Ricky, Martina, Dave Adams and the other three rangers. Then it pulled into one of several garage bays and lowered the door.

Ricky motioned for the rookie guard to pull his vehicle into one of the open bays and close the door behind him.

Ricky and Tank approached the front door tentatively. Ricky was surprised to find the door locked. She keyed in the entry code and smiled slightly as the electronic deadbolt whirred back. *No way anyone got past this lock,* she thought.

The entryway was as beautiful and peaceful as ever, but the study told a different story. The double doors opened onto the worst carnage Ricky had ever seen. Christine's beautiful Italian Rug was almost solid red. The room reminded Ricky of a slaughter house she had visited on a high school field trip. The stench of fresh blood filled her nostrils.

She stood for a moment trying to suppress her gag reflexes, then carefully moved into the room. Nicole Weil appeared at her side.

"What the fu...?" Nicole dashed for the kitchen as she threw up in her mouth. She was washing her face with cold water from the faucet when Martina joined her.

The rest of the team stood in stunned silence digesting the bloodbath that had taken place in the exquisite room. A cell phone started ringing. They glanced at one another then Ricky realized the phone was in a severed hand lying on the chest of the bald gangster.

466

The only way to the phone was through the lake of blood. Ricky pulled on plastic booties and carefully walked to the phone. She pushed the button that turned on the speakerphone.

"Hello, Major. Did you find my present?" Troy laughed diabolically.

"Why?" Ricky asked. "I thought you only butchered helpless women."

"They were there to harm Christine," Troy growled. "They were after *my* prize kill. I have waited too long for the rapture of the Governor to let some thugs harm her."

A cold shudder ran through Ricky's body as she realized the man she was dealing with was growing more insane by the minute.

"Troy, is that your real name?"

"It's as good as any," the madman giggled. "I am one of many."

"Humm, Legion," Ricky thought out loud.

"Yes," the maniac hissed, "but I prefer Troy for now."

"I left a video on the cellphone you might find interesting," Troy giggled again. "You should be able to rid our city of the New York mobsters that have infiltrated it."

"Play the recording. Even you should be able to figure out what to do with the information." The line went dead.

Ricky bagged the cellphone and moved back toward the hallway. She slipped off the booties and stepped onto the clean hall carpet. Everyone followed her to the kitchen. They silently listened as Ricky played the recording made by Troy Hunter.

Ricky pulled a chair from the dining room and motioned to Martina to sit down. "I am going to tape your arms to the chair arms. Adams is going to call Carlito and let him know he has captured you. We need to draw your brother here." The ranger placed a strip of duct tape over her mouth.

"You're crazy," Adams barked. "I'm not leading Carlito into a trap. He will kill me."

Ricky looked down at her boots then allowed her eyes to travel slowly up Adam's body. "Either help us lure Carlito here, or I will leave you handcuffed to a tree where Troy can find you. I am pretty sure he will know what to do with you."

"You wouldn't dare," Adams smirked.

"After what you did to Martina," Ricky grinned her most evil grin, "I would love to have an excuse to give you to him."

"Call Carlito now, or I move to plan B which will not include you," Ricky scowled. "Don't screw up. If you tip him off in any way this is a trap; you are a dead man."

Ricky messed up Martina's hair, so it looked as if she had struggled. Everyone stepped outside the room to keep from being seen on the cell phone.

Adams pulled his phone from his pocket and dialed the mobster. "Saluti, Mio Fratello."

Ricky quickly ran the translation through her mind, *greetings my brother*.

"I have a present for you." Adams turned his cell phone so that Carlito could see Martina bound to the chair.

"Ah, we meet again, little sister," Carlito said gleefully. "I hope my men availed themselves of your charms before strapping you to the chair."

Martina growled, throwing her head back and forth as if trying to break loose from her bondage.

Carlito laughed. "Remove the tape from her mouth."

As soon as Adams ripped the tape from Martina's lips, she gave the performance of a lifetime.

"You cowardly son-of-a-bitch," she spat on the cellphone screen. "Sent your bitch dogs to do your dirty work. You aren't man enough to face a woman. You merda di pollo bastard. I'll tear off your balls."

Adams slapped Martina across the face.

"No," Carlito screamed. "Don't lay a hand on her. I am on my way. I want to kill her myself. Text me the address."

Adams hung up. Ricky took his phone and texted the address.

"Carlito is on his way," Ricky informed the tactical team. "I have no idea how many men he will bring with him. Stand your ground until you hear gunfire from inside. Remember; if necessary, shoot to kill."

She called her FBI contact in New York. "Turn your men lose. We are good to go."

Everyone was out of site when Carlito burst through the front door. Only Martina and Adams were visible.

"So, you thought the government could protect you from me," Carlito slowly moved toward Martina. "How long have you been hiding out in this one-horse town, living in the shadows? That is no life for a mafia princess."

He ripped off the tape Adams had replaced. Martina cried out softly as the skin from her full lower lip went with it.

"Aww, did I hurt you?" Carlito snarled. "When I am through with you, you will beg to die." He held his gun to his side as he caressed Martina's cheek. "So pretty."

"You are under arrest," Ricky placed her gun against Carlito's temple. "Tell your men to drop their guns or all of you will die."

Carlito's eyes darted around the room and came to rest on Adams. "Traitor," he screamed. Before Ricky could pull the trigger, the mobster fired one bullet that hit Dave Adams between the eyes.

Ricky's bullet blew Carlito's brains out the side of his head. Carlito's men pulled their guns only to meet the same end as their crime boss.

The battle outside was quick and deadly. No law enforcement officers died. Carlito's men were dead and the ones at his headquarters were in custody.

"Not a bad day's work," Ricky grimaced as the ambulances began to fill the courtyard.

~~~

"I can't believe it is over," Martina exclaimed as Ricky ignored the speed limits to get to Christine and Tex. "Thanks to you, Rēēky."

"Thank Tex," Ricky smiled. "He is the one that moved me off high center."

"Tex?" Martina looked confused. "How was he involved?"

"He visited me at the office one day and pleaded with me to bring your case to a close." Ricky glanced at the beautiful woman beside her. "He said you never complained, but he knew you missed leading a free, full life.

"I explained the dangers of letting your family know where you are but assured him I would do everything in my power to keep you out of harm's way. When I presented the idea to you, you jumped at it. Of course, Tex was already on board."

"He never mentioned it to me." Martina seemed lost in thought.

"He didn't want to interfere in your business," Ricky explained. "He wanted the decision to be yours."

Christine and Tex were in the yard when the ranger stopped her vehicle. Tex scooped Martina up in his arms and Christine embraced the blonde as if she would never let her go. After a lot of kissing and crying, they went to their respective homes.

"Thank, God, this is over," Christine peppered Ricky's face with kisses. "We can stop looking back over our shoulders.

"We were terrified. All the news showed was the bodies carried from the mansion and... Why did this shootout take place at our home? I thought you were leading the mobsters to your apartment."

"It is a very long story," Ricky scowled. "Can I save it for later? Right now, I just want to take a nice hot shower and hold you."

~~~

Chapter 37

"Honey," Ricky pulled Christine closer and marveled at how good she felt. "I have something I need to tell you."

Christine's body became rigid. "Are you okay? I mean nothing is going to happen to you because of the shootout? You won't lose your job?"

"No, no, nothing like that," Ricky chuckled as Christine relaxed and snuggled closer. "It concerns our home in Austin."

Christine pulled back to gaze into the blonde's eyes. "It is a mess, isn't it?"

"Yes," Ricky nodded hesitantly. "I know how much you love it and..." Soft fingers on her lips stopped the ranger's speech.

"Nothing matters except that you are safe," Christine whispered. "When can we move back into the house?"

"Three months," Ricky bowed her head. "Carpets and rugs have to be cleaned or replaced. Walls need repair and repainting. Windows need replacing."

"I guess we will just have to live in the Governor's Mansion," Christine chuckled. "After the shootout, your landlord won't renew the lease on your apartment. Of course, we could move in with Mother and Daddy. They have plenty of room and..."

Soft lips stopped the words. "No way," Ricky mumbled. "The Governor's Mansion is just fine."

~~~

"Oh, my God," Christine cried out. "Oh, my God."

"Shush," Ricky whispered in her lover's ear as she pulled Christine's mouth into her shoulder to silence her. "I think there is a tour going through the Governor's Mansion below us."

"I...I can't catch my breath," Christine's chest heaved as she fought to bring her breathing under control. "How do you always do that to me?"

"Practice," Ricky chuckled.

They lay on their backs as their breathing evened out.

"Should we dress and welcome the tourists?" Christine smiled.

"After your little audio exhibition, I think not." Ricky chuckled. "It is best they think we aren't home."

"Is it okay if I shower, Major?" Christine grinned sensually at the blonde.

"Only if I can join you."

As they dressed, they discussed the party Lady was planning, to show off Christine to her friends.

"I may not be able to make it," Ricky said tentatively. "I have to finish my work with Peyton by the end of the month. As you know, we have been working night and day."

"You will make it or else," Christine threatened.

"Or else what?" Ricky teased.

"The guest bedroom for you, Major Strong." Christine realized Ricky was toying with her.

473

"I am positive I will be at the party," Ricky laughed. "Three weeks should give us time to finish filing everything."

"I am just glad your mother is taking care of all the details," Ricky noted. "A party of the magnitude she is planning would be inconceivable to me."

"Lavish parties are Mother's forte," the governor slipped her skirt over her head and smoothed its tailored lines down her svelte body. "She loves to show off."

"She loves to show off you," Ricky bent to kiss the brunette's lips before she applied makeup. "As do I. Do you have time for lunch today?"

"I will make time," Christine artfully applied her lipstick. "Right now, I have to run to my meeting."

"I am ready," Ricky quickly painted her lips. "Is the meeting at the Capitol?"

Christine nodded as the ranger followed her downstairs. "I will drop you off at the Capitol. Crate and Barrel will meet you there."

~~~

"I didn't open this one," Christine's secretary placed her daily mail in her inbox. "It is marked personal and looks like an invitation."

The governor examined the expensive envelope then smiled at the return address. It was from her mother.

"Hey, pretty lady," Ricky leaned around the door. "Ready for lunch?"

Christine couldn't hide the smile that covered her face at the sight of the ranger. "I was just about to open an invitation from Mother."

"I received one, too," Ricky nodded. "I haven't opened it."

"I guess she is still ignoring the fact that we come as a couple," Christine grinned as she slid the letter opener across the top of the envelope.

"What the...damn?" the governor cursed softly.

"What is wrong?" Ricky quickly moved to stand beside her.

"Are you kidding me?" the ranger huffed as she read the invitation out loud.

You are cordially invited
to attend an evening with
Governor Christine Richmond.
Date: February 14
Time: 7:00 PM
Place: The Governor's Mansion

"Leave it to Mother to plan a grand party in the Governor's Mansion without mentioning it to us." Christine tilted her head to look up at Ricky. More than anything she wanted the blonde to lean down and kiss her. She saw the indecision in Ricky's eyes as the ranger glanced at Christine's secretary. The woman quickly left the room.

Ricky leaned down and softly brushed the governor's lips. "I thought she would never leave," she smiled as Christine slipped her hands behind the blonde's neck and pulled her into a deeper kiss.

〜〜〜

"So, you and Mother co-hosting a big shindig?" Randall good-naturedly laughed as Christine joined him for lunch.

"Don't even get me started," Christine ordered a glass of wine then returned her attention to her brother. "You will be there?"

"I would never miss the party of the year," he nodded. "Mother is as giddy as a school girl going to her first prom."

"I feel I should warn you," he chuckled, "Mother has told one of the Hogg girls that you are completely enamored of her."

"She is a beautiful woman," Christine nodded, "but nothing to compare to Ricky."

"I agree." Randall held up his drink toast style, and they clinked their wine glasses.

"Randall, I want you to know how much I appreciate the way you take care of Mother and Daddy. You have taken a tremendous load off me. Mother has turned her demand for attention to you, and you are very good with her. I thank you for that."

Randall nodded. "They are my parents too, even if I am a Johnny-come-lately. I am trying to make up for all the heartache I caused them in my younger days."

"You didn't invite me to lunch to discuss Mother's meddling in our lives," Christine smiled. "Is everything okay? Is Daddy okay?"

Randall slowly exhaled as if trying to find a way to jump into the subject he needed to discuss.

"Chris, I can't even begin to tell you how horrified I was watching what went down at your home."

"I..."

He held up a hand to stop Christine's reply. "Please, hear me out. We had no idea what was happening. We thought you were in the house in the middle of all that gunfire." He paused and looked around the room as if trying to get control of his emotions.

"Dad was extremely upset," Randall continued. "I feared he would have another heart attack."

"I...I never thought," Christine stuttered.

"I know you love what you do," Randall smiled. "But what you do is dangerous. How many times have you come close to death in the past two years?"

Christine's eyes opened as the truth of what he was saying dawned on her.

"You know everything Richmond International owns is in your name," Randall said slowly. "You are the sole stockholder in one of the world's largest conglomerates. A lot of people depend on you for their livelihood."

"The legal problems for Mother, Father and I would be insurmountable."

Christine frowned. What her brother was saying made sense. Richmond International and her family would have tremendous exposure and legal problems if something happened to her. All the stock was in her name. She was young and healthy, but she seemed to be the target of every nut in the state.

"I need to share control over the company," she mumbled, thinking out loud. "Someone else needs to have the same powers I have within the company."

She squeezed her brother's hand. "I appreciate all you do for Richmond International and your insight into this matter. I will address it immediately."

She pulled her phone from her purse and made an appointment to see her corporate attorney on Friday.

"We will handle this together," she smiled at her brother. "Have you spoken with Daddy about this?"

"Yes, he agrees with me," Randall smiled brilliantly as the waitress refilled their wine glasses.

~~~

Chapter 38

Christine stood in the receiving line as strangers streamed into the Governor's Mansion gushing their thanks for the invitation. Lady Richmond grandly welcomed her friends and acquaintances, lording it over those to which she felt superior.

"I swear, I don't know how some of these people tolerate my mother. She is so pretentious," Christine groaned as she sat down beside Ricky.

"She isn't pretentious," Ricky smiled. "She is proud of you, and she has every right to be. I am proud of you, too."

"Incoming," Ricky whispered as she nodded toward Katrina Hogg. "Maybe this will help." She slid a gorgeous diamond ring on Christine's ring finger. A mischievous smile spread across the Governor's face.

"Governor Richmond," Katrina beamed, "I have been looking for you."

"And here I am," Christine tilted her head and warmly smiled.

Katrina shot a glance at Ricky then returned her attention to Christine. "Perhaps you could give me a tour of the Governor's Mansion?" Katrina gushed. "I am so impressed with you and all you have accomplished."

"We would be delighted," Christine stood pulling Ricky up with her. "Have you met my fiancée, Major Ricky Strong.?"

"Fiancée!" Katrina raised a quizzical brow as the rest of her face drooped in a frown.

"Christine, dear," Lady charged toward them, "I see you have met Katrina Hogg."

"Yes. Ricky and I are about to give her the tour of the Mansion." Christine looped her arm through Ricky's so her left hand was showcasing the diamond ring.

"You didn't tell me the Governor is engaged," Katrina shot a hateful look at Lady Richmond who stood speechless.

Katrina whirled on her heel and stomped away with Lady Richmond scurrying after her.

Christine held out her hand and admired the ring. "This is exquisite," she smiled the smile that always turned Ricky into jelly. "I hope you don't expect to get it back."

"The only place I ever want to see it is on your finger." Ricky pulled the Governor's arm back through hers. "We should mingle. I see Tex and Martina talking with your brother."

~~~

Troy Hunter looked at his reflection in the men's room mirror. He was dashingly handsome. Wearing a new tuxedo purchased for the occasion—the first he'd ever owned—he had danced with the Governor, but it was like dancing with a group. Ricky Strong and Ranger Crate had danced right beside them. They laughed and teased. He felt at ease. He fit in with the rich and famous.

He had located a door to the Mansion's geoexchange system that provided heat and air for the building. During a tour, earlier today, he hid his hacksaw and drug syringes behind a return pipe. For the first time, he had brought a small caliber gun. Ricky Strong was a force with which to be reckoned. He might be forced to shoot her. Before the night ended, he would slip into the room and hide behind a large recirculating pump. He patted the small caliber pistol he now carried After everyone left he would be alone with the governor and ranger.

The talk of the night was the engagement of the governor to Major Strong. He felt sure the two would be exhausted before the night ended. Then he would strike. First the ranger and then the governor.

At midnight Tex and Martina helped lead stragglers to the door. "Who is up to joining us for a nightcap at Skelly's?" Tex rounded up a crowd and headed for the door.

"It was a beautiful party," Martina hugged Christine.

"You aren't going for a drink, are you?" Christine placed a hand gently on Martina's stomach.

"No, Cara," Martina whispered. "We will get into our vehicle and drive home. Tex is just trying to help you get rid of the people who don't know when it is time to leave."

After everyone had left, Christine closed the door to the coat closet. The arm of a man's overcoat kept the door from closing. "Honey," she called to Ricky who was making her rounds through the mansion, "I think Tex left his overcoat."

~~~

"Tex looked extremely handsome tonight," Christine laced her hand with Ricky's as they climbed the stairs to their private part of the mansion.

"He said he purchased the new tuxedo just for the occasion," Ricky laughed. "It is his first tuxedo."

"I love my ring," Christine leaned her head against Ricky's shoulder. "What made you buy it?"

"It was the least I could do after the gesture you made," Ricky smiled. "Besides, it marks you as being my woman. Maybe your mother will stop trying to hook you up with other women."

"You know I expect you to wear a ring I give you," Christine said coyly.

"You know I want to," the ranger pulled the brunette into her arms.

"Want to, what?" Christine's voice was thick with desire.

"Why don't I show you," Ricky grinned.

~~~

Around three in the morning, something jerked Ricky awake. She lay still trying to pinpoint the sound that had pierced her dreams.

Christine's soft, rhythmic breathing told Ricky she was in a deep sleep. The ranger silently slid from their bed and pulled her Sig from the nightstand drawer. She kept the gun racked and ready. She eased toward the bedroom door.

Ricky held her breath as she slowly opened the door. She thanked God that the maintenance on the mansion was excellent. The hinges made no sound as she pulled the door back far enough to slip out of the room.

Ricky stayed low as she moved down the stairs thankful no creaking boards gave her away. On the first floor, she pressed her back against the wall and listened. Then she heard what she was listening for; breathing.

Troy Hunter soundlessly inched closer to the stairway leading to the women's bedroom. He reached out a hand to steady himself on the stair railing.

"Hello Troy," the voice of death was softer than he had expected, almost hollow. He didn't move. There was no racking of a pistol, no cocking of a hammer, just the cold, hard barrel against his back.

In the darkness, Ricky patted him down. She found no needles and no hacksaw. She also didn't find his gun. "Move into the foyer," she directed.

Ricky opened the front door. "Outside," she hissed.

Troy wondered if Strong would shoot him in the back. Only one way to find out. He grabbed one of the mansion's columns for leverage and kicked the ranger in the chest. Her gun went off as she staggered backward. Troy ran for his life.

Ricky's head landed hard against the wall of the mansion. As she stood, she shook her head to clear her vision. "Stop, or I will shoot," she yelled.

Troy ran faster. A loud explosion—like a large firecracker—filled the night. Fire knifed through Troy's left arm. He stumbled then fell.

"No! No! Don't shoot," a man screamed. Two more shots—fired rapidly—silenced him.

Ricky raced to the body, but it was gone. *Who fired the second shots?* Ricky thought. She looked around and cursed herself for not having a flashlight.

A groan pulled her attention to a spot, twenty feet away.

"He is getting away," the man croaked as he struggled to stand. "He ran through those trees. I tried to stop him, but he shot me."

Congressional security guards ran toward her with flashlights.

"Call an ambulance," Ricky barked. "This man has been shot."

A flashlight illuminated a familiar face, "Randall?" Ricky stared in horror as Randall Richmond passed out.

~~~

"What happened?" Christine demanded as Ricky entered their bedroom.

"I shot your brother," Ricky grimaced. "I mistook him for the Hacker. They are taking him to the hospital."

Ricky related the events as she sped toward the hospital. The women reached the emergency room as attendants wheeled Randall into surgery.

"Can you tell us anything?" Ricky flashed her badge at the nurse.

"He's lost a lot of blood," the nurse said. "That is all I know right now."

"What was he doing on the mansion grounds at three in the morning?" Christine frowned as she looked around the deserted waiting room.

"I have no idea," Ricky shook her head. "Christine, I am so sorry. I…"

"Shush," Christine brushed the blonde's lips with her own. "This is not your fault. You don't know if you shot him or if the Hacker shot him."

"You should call your parents," Ricky suggested.
"Let's wait until he is out of surgery. It is almost daylight," Christine scowled. "Let them sleep."

Two hours later Dr. Cassie Warren joined them in the waiting room. "He will be fine," she smiled. "He lost a lot of blood but we gave him a transfusion, and he is responding well.

"He is lucky. The bullet went through his arm without hitting a bone."

"So, no slug to match to a gun?" Ricky frowned.

"Afraid not," Cassie shrugged.

"May we see him?" Christine pleaded.

"They will move him to a private room in a couple of hours," the doctor nodded. "You can see him then. He is still heavily sedated right now."

Cassie eyed Christine's clothes. "You might want to go home and change, Governor."

In their hurry to get to the hospital, Christine had pulled on her pajama bottoms instead of her jeans. Ricky's sweatshirt hung loosely from the brunette's shoulders.

She is a total wreck, Ricky thought, *but still incredibly beautiful.*

"Come on, honey," Ricky caught Christine's hand. "A fresh cup of coffee and a shower will do us both good."

While Christine showered, Ricky searched the mansion, checking every nook and cranny. She was surprised to find the door to the geoexchange system slightly ajar. She opened it wide and flipped on the bright light. She took photos with her cell phone then called Crate to give him instructions.

~~~

"Your brother is awake," the nurse smiled as the two women approached the nurses' desk. "He is in room 101, two doors down."

"You go ahead, honey," Ricky squeezed Christine's arm. "He will want to see you."

The ranger watched the governor as she disappeared into room 101. "I know it is not kosher," Ricky smiled her brightest smile, "but may I see Randall's chart?"

"I'm not supposed to…"

"Please," Ricky begged. She grinned as the nurse turned the computer monitor so she could see it.

"Thanks, you're a doll," Ricky smiled as she found the information she was seeking.

"How is our patient?" Ricky asked as she entered Randall's room. Christine was holding her brother's free hand.

"Not too bad for a man you used for target practice," Randall flinched as if teasing were too much for him.

"Are you up to telling me what happened?" Ricky asked. "You can leave out the part where I shot you." She grinned sheepishly.

"I was supposed to fly to New York this morning," Randall said. "I discovered I had left my overcoat in your coat closet. I drove to the mansion intending to wake you and be on my way. As I walked toward the door, a man leaped from the porch and barreled over me. I gave chase. He was running toward the woods. He turned and fired at me twice. Honestly, I don't know if you shot me or if he did."

Randall's head bobbed forward as weariness overtook him.

Ricky was certain her bullet had sent him sprawling into the underbrush. She stood as Crate and Barrel entered the room. "May we have a word, Major?"

"I will be right back," Ricky touched Christine's arm and left the room.

"We have the Hacker," Crate nodded. "The DNA matches the skin we pulled from Kay's mouth. The hacksaw still has DNA from the two goons he slaughtered in your home."

"We also received the autopsy you requested. You were right.

"The canines found a gun in the tall grass. It has his fingerprints on it."

"Good work, guys," Ricky beamed. "You just made my day."

"Oh, Major," Crate turned back, "I almost forgot, Governor Richmond's attorney sent this envelope to her office. He said she wanted it as soon as possible."

Randall was awake and admiring Christine's ring. "Bet that cost you a pretty penny," he smiled as he ran his finger over the diamond on the brunette's finger.

"She is worth it," Ricky smiled. "Honey, your office sent this via Crate and Barrel."

"What is it?" Randall asked nonchalantly.

"My grand gesture," Christine laughed. "The final documents transferring fifty percent of my stock to…"

"May I see it?" Randall beamed as he held out his good hand for the documents.

Blood drained from Randall's face as he read the documents. Before he could move, Ricky slapped handcuffs on him and secured him to the bed frame.

"You bitch," Randall raged. "You left half of my company to her?"

"*Your* company?" Christine looked at him incredulously. "It has never been *your* company."

"How could you? I am your brother."

"No, you're not," the brunette shrugged. "I have no idea who you are, but you aren't Randall."

"I'm going to book you under Troy Hunter," Ricky smirked, "unless there is another name you prefer."

Troy went berserk. He tried to stand up on the bed, but Ricky cut his feet from under him. He ripped the IV from his arm and clawed at the handcuffs.

Ricky held down the button on the morphine drip and waited for the drug to take effect. Hunter slowly crumpled forward.

"When did you know, he wasn't Randall?" Christine asked.

"I was certain when his blood type was A negative. Both your parents are type O. As are you. Randall should have type O also.

"When did you know, he wasn't Randall?" Ricky frowned.

"When he talked about playing store with me," Christine grimaced. "My brother never played with me. He had better things to do."

"Will your parents be devastated?" Ricky's blue eyes clouded with concern.

"No, Daddy knew something wasn't right," Christine grimaced. "He thought Randall was someone trying to run a con on us, but he was perfect, neither of us wanted to confront him. He was a perfect big brother. I wanted to forget he wasn't my brother.

He was caring and solicitous of Mother and Daddy, and he shouldered a lot of the workload of Richmond International.

"Daddy had no idea he was the Hacker. Neither did I."

"I am afraid I do have bad news for you," Ricky frowned. "This man is named Vince Edmond. He was in the same cell as your brother. From what I can piece together, he murdered your brother and took his place, so the state released Edmond believing him to be Randall. They cremated Randall thinking he was Edmond.

"I obtained a copy of the autopsy report the prison did on the man they cremated. His blood type was type O."

"What will happen to him?" Christine nodded toward Edmond.

"We will post guards on him until we can move him to jail," Ricky explained. "I have a certain prosecutor lined up to make certain he gets a deep sleep."

~~~

Chapter 39

Three years later

Major Ricky Strong glared at the man sitting across from her. Scott Winslow was waiting for Christine who was in route to the ranger's office.

Christine's four years as governor were a tremendous success. She had passed all the laws that were important to her and completed the construction of the wall, securing the Texas border.

She had insisted that Texans be allowed to vote on the same-sex marriage proposition. It had passed and was now state law.

Texans were a live-and-let-live bunch. They didn't want to dictate what went on in other people's bedrooms. They were more interested in secure borders, law enforcement, the right to carry and good schools than interfering in individuals' rights to the pursuit of happiness.

Christine was like a rock star, not only in Texas but across the U.S. People thronged to her where ever she went. She was in demand for commencement speeches in colleges all over the U.S. Millennials identified with her and embraced her conservatism in things that truly mattered. On social issues, they liked her *live and let live* attitude.

"She is amazing," Scott gushed. "Four years as a U.S. Senator then President of the United States. "Today is the last day for her to file to run for the U.S. Senate. She will be a shoo-in."

A soft knock on her door told Ricky the brunette was about to enter her office.

"Did you file?" Ricky looked up at the love of her life as Christine Richmond moved into view.

"If I win, I will spend most of my time in Washington," Christine said casually. "I will be away from you more than I will be with you. I will be lucky to see you once a month."

They'd had this discussion more times than Ricky cared to count. The decision was Christine's. *I will support her in whatever she wants to do*, Ricky thought.

Ricky tried not to gaze into the eyes that mirrored her soul. Christine knew how Ricky felt about being away from her. If the brunette didn't feel the same, they had a problem.

"The U.S. Senate, then the Presidency," Scott jumped to his feet.

"Can you give us a few minutes?" Christine asked Scott as she pushed him out the door.

Christine locked the door to Ricky's office. She walked to the ranger and sat on her lap, slipping her arms around Ricky's neck.

"Daddy wants to retire," Christine nuzzled her face in Ricky's long blonde hair. "I think it is time for you and me to take the reins of our company.

"It will mean a lot of traveling. Maybe some moonlight cruises, a few weeks in Italy…"

Soft, gentle lips stopped her diatribe. "Sounds like something I could get used to," Ricky murmured against her ear. The movement sent waves of desire through Christine's body.

"One thing I would never get used to is sleeping alone, again," Ricky kissed her slowly, questioningly.

"We agree then," Christine giggled. "I am getting out of politics. I didn't file to run, and you are hanging up your star."

"I did it this morning," Ricky grinned. "Crockett has my early-retirement request on his desk."

"The first time I saw you I knew I would spend the rest of my life with you," Christine smiled.

"The first time I saw you, I wanted you to spend the rest of your life with me," Ricky kissed her again.

"No doubt about it," Christine nibbled at the blonde's lips, "our love is too strong to die!"

The End

Follow Erin Wade at www.erinwade.us

Other books you might enjoy

Three Times as Deadly
(a lesbian action/adventure/romance)
By Erin Wade

Death was Too Easy
(a lesbian action/adventure/romance)
By Erin Wade

The Destiny Factor
(a lesbian action/adventure/romance)
by D. J. Jouett

Made in the USA
Columbia, SC
14 November 2018